WISCONSIN!

The nineteenth riveting episode in the *WAGONS WEST* series—a journey into the most exciting days of our nation's past, where men and women were driven to carve their destinies from a wild land . . . hungry for the limitless promises of fortune and desire.

★★★★★★★★★★★★★★★★★★★★★★★★★★★★★★★★★★★

WISCONSIN!

Across continents and seas they came seeking a place where men forged their own destiny . . . and women created their own dreams

TOBY HOLT—

Burning with the ambition to found a new dynasty from the timber of Wisconsin, he tries to bury the torment of losing his beloved . . . only to find his future threatened by treachery and desire.

CINDY HOLT—

Now a woman ripe with a lush beauty and vivacious spirit, a cruel betrayal can break her young heart . . . and leave her vulnerable to a dashing soldier's embrace.

LT. HENRY BLAKE—

An officer and a gentleman, his dangerous liaison with a German baroness begins as part of an undercover assignment . . . but may end in a devastating choice between honor and lust.

BARONESS GISELA VON KIRCHBERG—

A sensual temptress, her business affairs had been her driving passion, until she met Henry Blake and made him her obsession . . . but can she make him her love slave?

★★★★★★★★★★★★★★★★★★★★★★★★★★★★★★★★★★★

CAPT. RICHARD KOEHLER—
Dashing dragoon of a Prussian regiment, a journey to America becomes an odyssey of love with an innocent girl . . . fast to ignite, impossible to extinguish, and sure to burn them both.

DIETER SCHUMANN—
Head of a powerful dynasty of timber and finance, making money is an insatiable hunger in his blood . . . and nothing, not even murder, is too great a price to satisfy it.

TED TAYLOR—
A new breed of lawman, he brings justice where others dare not . . . but will his blazing guns save Toby Holt, his rival for a woman's heart?

MARJORIE WHITE—
A famous photographer who refuses to play a woman's role and whose independence shocks a nation, she has courage, beauty, and passion . . . but for the wrong man.

URSULA OBERG—
A statuesque German beauty, she too defies convention to found a business for her eccentric but talented daughter . . . and it can cost her the one man she loves.

WISCONSIN!

DANA FULLER ROSS

BCI Producers of **The Memoirs of H.H. Lomax,**
The First Americans, and **The White Indian.**

Book Creations Inc., Canaan, NY • Lyle Kenyon Engel, Founder

BANTAM BOOKS
NEW YORK • TORONTO • LONDON • SYDNEY • AUCKLAND

WISCONSIN!

*A Bantam Domain Book / published by arrangement with
Book Creations, Inc.*

PUBLISHING HISTORY

*Bantam edition published May 1987
Bantam reissue / June 1994*

*DOMAIN and the portrayal of a boxed "d" are trademarks of
Bantam Books, a division of Bantam Doubleday Dell Publishing
Group, Inc.*

*Produced by Book Creations, Inc.
Lyle Kenyon Engel, Founder*

ISBN 0-553-80019-1

Published simultaneously in the United States and Canada

*Bantam Books are published by Bantam Books, a division of
Bantam Doubleday Dell Publishing Group, Inc. Its trademark,
consisting of the words "Bantam Books" and the portrayal of a
rooster, is Registered in U.S. Patent and Trademark Office and in
other countries. Marca Registrada. Bantam Books, 1540 Broad-
way, New York, New York 10036.*

PRINTED IN THE UNITED STATES OF AMERICA

RAD   14 13 12 11 10 9 8

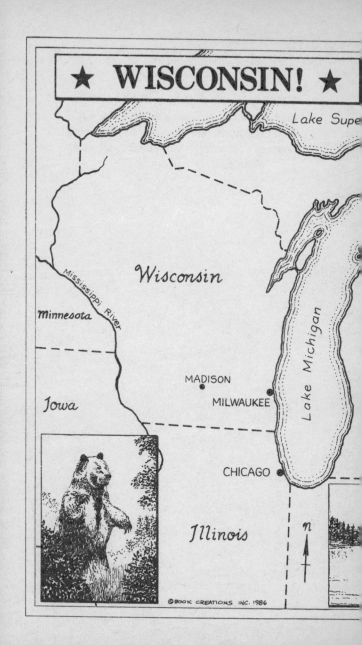

Canada

Michigan

DETROIT

Lake Erie

RON TOELKE '86

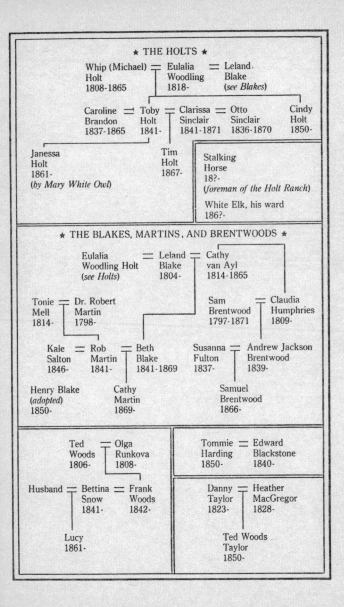

★ THE HOLTS ★

Whip (Michael) = Eulalia = Leland
Holt   Woodling   Blake
1808-1865   1818-   (see Blakes)

Caroline = Toby = Clarissa = Otto   Cindy
Brandon   Holt   Sinclair   Sinclair   Holt
1837-1865 1841- 1841-1871   1836-1870   1850-

Janessa   Tim
Holt   Holt
1861-   1867-
(by Mary White Owl)

Stalking
Horse
18?-
(foreman of the Holt Ranch)

White Elk, his ward
186?-

★ THE BLAKES, MARTINS, AND BRENTWOODS ★

Eulalia   = Leland = Cathy
Woodling Holt   Blake   van Ayl
(see Holts)   1804-   1814-1865

Tonie = Dr. Robert   Sam   = Claudia
Mell   Martin   Brentwood   Humphries
1814-   1798-   1797-1871   1809-

Kale = Rob = Beth   Susanna = Andrew Jackson
Salton Martin Blake   Fulton   Brentwood
1846- 1841- 1841-1869   1837-   1839-

Henry Blake   Cathy   Samuel
(adopted)   Martin   Brentwood
1850-   1869-   1866-

Ted = Olga   Tommie = Edward
Woods Runkova   Harding Blackstone
1806- 1808-   1850-   1840-

Husband = Bettina = Frank   Danny = Heather
          Snow   Woods   Taylor MacGregor
          1841-   1842-   1823-   1828-

Lucy   Ted Woods
1861-   Taylor
                            1850-

WISCONSIN!

I

Ted Taylor held a stubby, sawed-off shotgun ready to fire as he moved slowly through the predawn darkness toward a small, ramshackle house on the outskirts of Harlan, Iowa. Weeds rustled off to his right as the town sheriff and his two deputies advanced with him, pistols in hand.

When the men were twenty yards from the house, Ted motioned for them to stop. As agreed upon, they knelt in the weeds and waited for full daylight. Behind them, smoke rose from chimneys in the town, and windows glowed with lamplight in houses where early risers were moving about. The crowing of a rooster carried through the early morning quiet from a farm a mile away.

The sheriff, a big, heavyset man of fifty named Lambert, leaned toward Ted. "Most of the drifters who pass through here use that house," he said softly. "How do you know that the men in it are the ones you're after?"

"I looked at their horses and saddles in the shed behind the house before I came to get you," Ted replied. "They're the Blount gang, no question about that."

"Well, as long as you're sure they're the same ones who held up the train outside of Council Bluffs two days ago."

"I'm sure."

"There's four men in the Blount gang, ain't there? Are all four of them in that house?"

1

"Yes."

The sheriff was silent for a moment. Then he leaned closer to Ted and spoke softly, to keep his deputies from overhearing. "You've seen my deputies," he whispered. "Cass Whittaker is a good man, but he's getting old, and his eyes ain't too good. Ned Bodie has plenty of guts, but he's young and as green as a spring willow shoot. I'd better go back into the town and round up another dozen or so men."

"No, that would take too long and make too much noise."

"I'd keep them quiet, and I could be back by sunrise."

"That's too long, Sheriff Lambert, and someone might make a noise. I'd rather take them by surprise than have a dozen more men."

"Well, you have the governor's authority," Lambert grumbled, "so it's up to you. But me and my men ain't here to get killed. We'll back you up, but you'll go in first."

"That's what I had intended to do."

The quiet, nonchalant reply seemed to make the sheriff even more annoyed. Sleepy from being abruptly awakened when Ted had arrived at his house a short time before, Lambert resented the newcomer. Ted Taylor was a special law enforcement assistant to the state attorney general, in charge of investigating all train robberies in the state and pursuing those responsible, and he was authorized to conscript whatever help he needed from local law enforcement agencies.

Lambert also envied Ted. One of the heroes of the Great Chicago Fire the previous year, he was a friend of the famed Toby Holt. He was also one of those new breed of lawmen called detectives, and it was rumored the railroads were paying him a bounty of one thousand dollars for every train robber he apprehended, in addition to what the state was paying him.

In his early twenties, Ted Taylor wore a typical western hat and boots. But instead of the casual garb of most lawmen in the area, he had on a neat, brown wool suit, which the sheriff regarded as too citified. Still, Lambert grudgingly admitted to himself, train robberies in the state had become increasingly rare since Ted Taylor had arrived.

The stars overhead dimmed into the light spreading across the sky as Ted double-checked his shotgun and waited for full dawn to arrive. He was outwardly calm, but inwardly he was keenly aware that the next few minutes would bring dire peril. Taken by surprise, the train robbers would fire wildly and blindly—but a wild bullet could kill or seriously wound as easily as one that was carefully aimed.

He was also concerned about the young deputy, Ned Bodie, who might take foolish risks and get himself killed. Lambert and Whittaker were both seasoned, cautious men, but Bodie was young and rash. His bright, youthful face flushed with excitement, he was watching Ted intently and eagerly anticipating the gun battle.

Roosters at the farms all around the small town began crowing as the light flooded across the sky from the east. When the dilapidated, one-room house was clearly visible, Ted rose to a crouch and spoke to the sheriff. "I'll try to get them to surrender," he said. "If they start shooting, you and your men fire into the air so they won't run outside."

The sheriff nodded, his weathered face drawn with tension. Ted cocked the hammers on his shotgun and loosened the Colt in his shoulder holster as he walked toward the house, the other men following. Bodie caught up with him, only to grimace in disappointment as Ted motioned him back.

Ten yards from the house, Ted hesitated and gathered himself. Then he sprinted forward, the long weeds pulling at his boots. Bounding across the tiny porch, he hurled himself at the door. The early morning quiet dissolved into pandemonium as the door splintered around him and he fell into the house.

In the semidarkness of the cluttered, single room he rolled out of the light streaming through the doorway and quickly rose to one knee. He glimpsed movements in the four corners as the men woke and sat up on their pallets. "Put up your hands!" he shouted. "This house is surrounded!"

The man in a corner on Ted's left side reacted more quickly than the others, lifting a pistol that gleamed in the dim light. The enclosed room magnified the roar of Ted's shotgun as it thundered and bucked, red flame darting from a barrel. The hail of buckshot slapped the man off his pallet and ripped into the wall behind him.

The other man on the left fired a pistol, the bullet hissing past Ted's head. Swinging the shotgun toward him, Ted pulled the other trigger. The heavy lead pellets hit the man, lifting him from his pallet and killing him instantly.

Outside the house, Lambert and Whittaker were firing into the air and shouting at Bodie in warning. The younger deputy was silhouetted in the doorway behind Ted, firing his pistol at the men on the other side of the room. As Ted dropped his shotgun and drew out his Colt, Bodie reeled and stumbled backward, clutching a shoulder.

Both remaining outlaws turned their pistols toward Ted and fired rapidly. Ted's instincts clamored for him to respond in kind, panic screaming in the back of his mind. But he possessed the self-control of the professional gunfighter, accepting the risk of being hit by the wild shooting of an opponent in order to shoot accurately instead of quickly.

Dust knocked from the rafters by the concussion of the gunfire was thick in the air as bullets whizzed past Ted, the loud reports of the pistols battering his ears. He aimed his Colt at the dark shadow over the red flashes of one of the pistols and squeezed the trigger.

The bullet ripped into the man, its crushing impact knocking him backward against the wall. Loose boards tumbled down behind him, letting more light into the dim maelstrom of roaring guns and death. For an instant the gunfire subsided, as Ted aimed his pistol toward the last man.

He appeared to be surrendering. His pistol was turning aside and his left hand starting to lift in a gesture of capitulation, his face twisted in terror. But it was too late. Reactions had taken control within Ted, and his finger was pulling the trigger back.

The Colt roared and the man jerked backward, a spreading spot of crimson on his forehead. As the echoes of the last shot faded, Ted holstered his pistol and picked up his shotgun, then rose to his feet. Motes of dust glinted in the sunlight now streaming through the broken boards in the walls.

The gunfire had awakened the town, and people were shouting and hurrying along the street toward the abandoned house. The sheriff and the two deputies crossed the porch and peered inside as Ted stepped toward the door. "Are they the right ones?" the sheriff asked, still resentful. "Are they the Blount gang?"

The mail that the men had stolen from a train two days before was piled inside the door, an untidy heap of envelopes and torn canvas bags. Ted nodded and pointed to it as he went out. "There's the mail from their last robbery," he said. He turned to the young deputy, who had a dirty handkerchief tied around one shoulder. "Does it look serious, Ned?"

"No, sir," Bodie replied, grinning. "It's just a crease. It looks like one got pretty close to you, Mr. Taylor."

The young deputy pointed to a long tear in the sleeve of Ted's coat, where a bullet had ripped it. Ted nodded ruefully, reflecting that the bullet had ruined a good suit. By now the townspeople had gathered in front of the house in a noisy crowd, many of them rumpled and half-dressed. They began asking what had happened. One man's stentorian voice drowned the rest as he shouted, "Say, ain't you Ted Taylor, the one who's after the train robbers? Who'd you catch here, Mr. Taylor?"

Accustomed to dealing with local lawmen, and aware

of the need to make a special effort in this instance, Ted pointed to the sheriff. "I'm here working with Sheriff Lambert," he said. "He's responsible for law and order in Harlan, and any questions you have should be directed to him."

Immediately the people began to crowd around the surprised sheriff, to ask him what had happened. Mrs. Lambert, whom Ted had met when he had gone to the sheriff's house earlier, pushed through to her husband's side and asked him if he was all right. The big man looked embarrassed and annoyed by her concern.

"Yes, they were the ones who robbed the train up by Council Bluffs two days ago," Lambert said, replying to a question. "The Blount gang. There were four of them, but there were four of us, wasn't there?" He shook his head, waving off other questions. "That's enough for now. I have a lot to do here. You two there, go and bring a wagon for the bodies. Ned, go get those horses out of the shed behind the house and lead them down to our stable. Cass, pick out some men here to help you, and get that mail in there gathered up."

When his wife began to question him again, he snapped at her, irritated. "Yes, I'm fine, Marcia. Now, will you go home and leave me alone?" He glanced at Ted, and his frown faded. "And take Mr. Taylor with you and fix him some breakfast. You've been up all night, and I expect you'd like some breakfast, wouldn't you, Mr. Taylor?"

Tired and hungry, and wanting to get away from the noisy crowd, Ted replied quickly, "Yes, I'd appreciate that very much."

"You go ahead, then, and I'll join you directly," the sheriff said genially. "I'll see to everything here."

Ted followed the sheriff's wife off the porch. A path opened for them through the crowd, children gazing up at Ted in awe and men and women expressing their appreciation as he passed.

Marcia Lambert, as cheerful and friendly as her husband was unpleasant, took a motherly attitude toward Ted as they walked toward town. She commented on the tear in his coat sleeve and offered to mend it for him.

"I'd be very grateful if you would," he said.

"I can't make it like new," Marcia went on, "but I can repair it good enough for it to hold together until you can get it to a tailor. I'm sure there are lots of good tailors in Chicago—isn't that where you come from? We read in the newspapers what you and Mr. Toby Holt did there during the fire."

"Actually, I'm from California," Ted replied. "I was visiting with Mr. Holt in Chicago."

"And now you're in Iowa," Marcia sighed. "You detectives certainly do get around a lot. How did you know that the Blount gang was hiding out here? Did you track them all the way from where they robbed the train at Council Bluffs?"

Ted shook his head. He explained how, while examining the scene of the robbery, he had found the half-buried crowbars and sledgehammers the robbers had used to spread the rails so the train would have to stop. The name of the hardware dealer who had sold the tools was on the sledgehammer handles, and he had given Ted a description of the four strangers. A blacksmith in the same town had shod the same men's horses, and he had overheard them discussing Harlan.

"Times certainly are changing," Marcia said when Ted finished. "And everything else along with them. Detectivating isn't my man's way of keeping law and order. He either catches crooks in the act, or else he follows their trail and has it out with them."

"What I do isn't all that different," Ted said. "People leave other kinds of trails besides footprints or hoof tracks."

"Yes, that's certainly true," Marcia agreed. "Here's my place. I have a fresh pot of coffee on the stove."

It was a neat, modest house surrounded by a picket fence. They went inside and through a parlor to a large, spotlessly clean kitchen. Marcia seated Ted at the table and poured him a cup of coffee, put thick slices of home-

made bread and a crock of strawberry preserves in front of
him, then took a flitch of bacon from the food safe and cut
slabs from it.

When the bacon was frying slowly in a pan, filling the
kitchen with an appetizing scent, Marcia went into another room and returned with her sewing basket. She took
Ted's coat and sat down at the table. After expertly threading a needle, she began sewing up the tear.

"So you're from California," she commented, tugging
on the needle and pulling a stitch tight. "Some of my
relatives moved there a few years ago, and from what I
hear they like it. And you're not married? A young, nice-
looking fellow like you must have a sweetheart."

Ted smiled wryly as he slathered the strawberry jam
on a piece of bread. "I do, but I'm not sure she would call
herself that," he said. "She would probably say we're just
friends. Her name is Marjorie White, and she's a traveling
photographist. Right now she's in Boston."

"Boston!" Marcia clucked, shaking her head. "No wonder she wouldn't call herself your sweetheart. You'll never
win her over as long as she's in Boston and you're in
Iowa."

"No, I reckon I won't," Ted agreed. "But we may be
together before long. She's mentioned going to Wisconsin
to photograph the scenery and Mr. Holt's logging operations there. I'm almost finished here, so maybe I'll join
her. The train robberies have just about stopped."

Marcia had put down his coat and got up to break
some eggs into the pan and turn the bacon. "Yes, the train
robberies here are nothing compared to what they were a
few months ago," she said, the bacon hissing and popping
as she flipped it over. "We used to have one every week,
it seemed." She sat back down, picked up the coat, and
resumed sewing. "So Toby Holt has a logging camp in
Wisconsin? Is that where he went after the fire in Chicago?"

"He has a logging camp in Wisconsin and a lumber
mill in Chicago, and he divides his time between them.
Right after the fire, though, he had to go to his home in

Portland, because his five-year-old son, Timmy, was seriously injured. The boy made a large kite and jumped out of a tree with it, trying to fly."

"Trying to fly?" Marcia exclaimed. "My word, what will kids think of next? Is he all right?"

"Yes, but it was a near-miss thing for a while. The boy fell on rocks and seriously hurt himself. He's a strong, healthy child, fortunately."

"Boys will be boys," Marcia sighed. "I raised two, and I wouldn't want to go through that again. It's a wonder any of us survived."

Ted smiled and took a drink of coffee. "He's got a scar across his forehead that he'll have all of his life, though. I sympathize with Toby's sister, who looks after the lad. She sure will have her hands full when he gets a little older."

Pausing in front of a general store on the main street of Portland, Oregon, Cindy Holt straightened her nephew Timmy's hair and coat before going inside. The livid, four-inch scar on the boy's forehead served as a constant reminder of the chilling terror that had gripped her on the day when the boy had been injured. She forced the memory out of her mind.

Satisfied with his appearance, Cindy turned to her niece, Janessa. "Dear, you've already been a great help," she said, "but you don't have to spend all morning with me. I know you'd like to go to Dr. Martin's house."

Slender and tall for her eleven years, Janessa had the same blue eyes and determined features as her young aunt, and the two were often mistaken for sisters. Indeed, Janessa closely resembled her father's side of the family, even though her mother—who had died the previous year after bringing the girl to Portland—had been a full-blooded Cherokee. "I can't let you do all of the shopping and other things all by yourself," Janessa replied firmly. "And I can go to Dr. Martin's house later."

"Well, I certainly do appreciate it," Cindy said, glancing down the quiet street. The wagon from the ranch was still parked by the hardware store, the driver, an old man named Josh Sellars, chatting with the boy who was loading Cindy's purchases there. Cindy took Timmy's hand and started up the steps to the general store. "This store usually has a good selection of cloth remnants, Janessa. If you would, see if you can find material for a new shirt for Timmy."

The girl nodded as they went inside. The store was cluttered, kitchenware hanging from the ceiling, the narrow aisles hemmed in by shelves crowded with goods ranging from clothing to foodstuffs. While Janessa went to a table piled high with bolt ends of fabric, Cindy led Timmy down an aisle to the counter at the side of the store.

Before she got there, however, Timmy suddenly froze in his tracks, his eyes wide and staring at a bin of fireworks decorated with an advertising poster for the upcoming Multnomah County Fair.

On the poster was a large, colorful picture of a hot-air balloon, which was scheduled to be a featured attraction at the fair. The boy pointed to it. "Look, Aunt Cindy!" he exclaimed. "A balloon! What does the writing say?"

"That there will be a balloon at the fair this summer," Cindy explained patiently. "You'll enjoy that, won't you, Timmy?"

The boy grinned and nodded, almost speechless with delight. "And look at all the firecrackers! Can we buy some?"

"Of course not," Cindy replied, pulling him away from the display. "You know better than to even ask, Timmy. We can't have fireworks at the ranch."

Observing them from behind the counter, Horace Biddle, the portly proprietor, chuckled. He opened a candy jar and leaned forward to offer Timmy a piece. "You'd have every horse on the ranch jumping like a nervous flea, son," he commented. He smiled and nodded as the boy put his hand in the jar. "You want a green one this time, do you? Well, I sort of prefer those myself, and that's a fact."

The boy, starting to put the candy into his mouth, hesitated and glanced up at Cindy as she looked down at him narrowly. "Thank you, sir," he said, then popped the piece into his mouth.

"You're quite welcome, young fellow," the storekeeper said, replacing the candy jar. "He's got good manners, Miss Holt, I must say. Your brother is mighty lucky to have you looking after his children. And how can I serve you today?"

"Let's begin with the bagged goods," Cindy said, unfolding her list. "Twenty pounds of flour, please, five of sugar, and a pound of salt. Then ten pounds each of dried beans and peas."

Smiling in satisfaction, the storekeeper began moving back and forth, filling bags from barrels and putting them on the counter. Janessa came down the aisle with pieces of cloth she had chosen from the table. Cindy inspected them and nodded in approval.

The girl put the cloth on the counter, then coughed discreetly. Cindy glanced at Janessa's large, pleading eyes, then looked back at her list, smothering a sigh. All that remained on it was a question mark that had meaning only to her. That same symbol had been on her list several times, but she had never done anything about it. She disliked encouraging something of which she strongly disapproved, but Janessa's pleading gaze disconcerted her.

"What else do you need today, Miss Holt?" Biddle asked.

Folding the list, Cindy weighed all the factors in her mind once again; then she decided. "You have boxes of ready-made cigarettes, don't you?" she asked.

Biddle blinked, the inquiry an unusual one from a woman. He reached under the counter. "Yes, we have Philip Morris, Liggett and Brother, and several other kinds. Some of them come in boxes and others in packages, and ten of those go into these bigger boxes that we call cartons." Placing cartons on the counter one by one, he smiled politely. "Are you buying these to send to your brother?"

His smile faded as he glanced at Janessa, then back at Cindy in sudden understanding. The fact that the girl smoked was known throughout the city, with reactions ranging from outrage to amusement. A stiff silence fell as Biddle finished putting cigarettes on the counter.

Cindy looked at Janessa and nodded toward the cigarettes. The girl moved closer to the counter and examined each carton. After taking packages out to look at them and smell them, she pointed to the Philip Morris.

"Two of the large boxes of those, please," Cindy said.

"Yes, miss," Biddle responded, taking out another carton of Philip Morris and hurriedly putting the others away. "I'll put them in a paper poke for you so nobody will see you with them and think—" He broke off, cleared his throat, and began talking more rapidly. "I'll just throw those pieces of cloth into the bargain, Miss Holt, because we do appreciate your trade. And here—I'll put a few pieces of candy into a poke for the boy."

As the storekeeper bustled back and forth, Janessa took Cindy's hand and squeezed it in gratitude, smiling up at her. Cindy looked down at the girl, and the awkwardness of the moment was quickly forgotten. She tucked a stray wisp of Janessa's hair into place and touched her face affectionately, then looked back at Biddle as he continued talking.

As unobtrusively as she could, Janessa slipped a package of cigarettes out of one of the cartons on the counter and put it into her pocket. She wandered toward the front of the store, waiting for Cindy to finish. As she looked out the window, an unusual scene caught her eye.

Four horses were tethered at the hitching rail in front of the bank diagonally across the street. A grimy, unshaven man was standing on the boardwalk in front of the horses. He looked more likely to be a customer at a saloon than at the bank, and it was still an hour before the bank would open.

Moving to a side window to get a better view, Janessa saw the other three men, all of them similar to the first in appearance. With them was the bank manager, a thin, dour man named Peabody, who always arrived at work early. The three were pushing him toward the side entrance of the bank.

Realizing that she was watching the beginning of a bank robbery, Janessa almost called out in alarm. Although panic swelled within her, she controlled herself and looked around, and her gaze fell on the bin of fireworks, where Timmy was standing. Thinking rapidly, she decided what to do.

The storekeeper and Cindy were still talking, and neither of them noticed as Janessa stepped in front of Timmy and slipped a string of firecrackers into her pocket. The boy, his eyes wide in astonishment, saw what she did. Taking his arm, Janessa called to Cindy that she would wait outside with Timmy. Cindy nodded absently, her lips pursed as she studied her list.

Pulling Timmy toward the door, Janessa whispered instructions. Puzzled, the boy began asking questions. Janessa gripped his arm tightly, cutting him off with a glare as they stepped outside onto the boardwalk. "If you say another word," she hissed, "or if you do anything except exactly what I tell you, I'll slap you so hard that your eyeballs will jump out and knock together. Do you understand?"

Nodding rapidly, the boy stared up at her, not daring to speak. "Most important of all," Janessa said softly, "don't look across the street. Now walk—and I mean *walk*—to the end of this block, then run as hard as you can to the sheriff's office. Tell Sheriff Loomis or one of his deputies that some men are robbing the bank. If they're not there, run across the street to the café. They might be having coffee. Go on, Timmy."

As Timmy walked dutifully away, Janessa glanced

across the street from the corner of her eye. The man on the boardwalk in front of the horses was watching the street in both directions and paying no attention to her. Timmy reached the end of the block and began running along the boardwalk. Down the street in the other direction, Josh Sellars and the boy from the hardware store were standing beside the wagon from the ranch, still talking.

As she waited, time passed very slowly for Janessa. She was keenly aware that at any moment the robbers could run out to their horses with bags of money. No one would be able to stop them.

Josh Sellars was still talking, but he had finally gotten into the wagon, and in a moment he would be driving down the street. Blocks away in the opposite direction, Timmy came into view again, darting across the street toward the café. The café was on the same side of the street as the bank, and Janessa knew she would have to distract the man waiting with the horses to keep him from seeing the sheriff and the deputies approaching.

Her hands clammy and shaking, Janessa opened the package of cigarettes and lit one as she stepped off the boardwalk and started across the street. It was a violation of her agreement with Cindy not to smoke in public, but she had no other choice. Puffing on the cigarette, she stepped onto the boardwalk on the other side of the street and walked toward the man.

The man looked at her, surprised by the cigarette. An instant later his thick, ugly features reflected another thought, one that Janessa could read in his eyes and that turned her apprehension into icy fear: If he had a girl on the saddle in front of him during the escape, no one would shoot at him for fear of hitting her. "How long have you been smoking?" he asked, attempting a friendly smile.

Janessa passed him, careful to stay far enough away to avoid being seized. He turned, keeping his eyes on her, and when his back was to the café, she stopped. "It's none of your business," she replied.

His weak smile started to turn to a scowl, but he

checked himself and smiled again. "Now, don't get sassy with me, girlie," he said. "That's a ready-made cigarette, ain't it? Give me one."

Janessa shook her head, refusing. The man attempted to keep his smile in place, and he took a step forward as he asked her where she had got the cigarettes.

Backing away, Janessa struggled to control her fear, for the crucial moment had arrived. Behind the man, tall, burly Sheriff Loomis and his two deputies, all of them hatless and in their shirtsleeves, were racing along the boardwalk, their pistols drawn. As the man started to turn his head and glance over his shoulder, Janessa snatched out the package of cigarettes. "They're Philip Morris," she said. "What will you give me for one?"

"A dollar," the man replied, reaching into his pocket and stepping toward her. "I'll give you a dollar for one of them."

Janessa waited until the man was very near, then quickly stepped away. "Why would you do that?" she asked. "You can buy several packages for a dollar."

"Because I want one of them!" the man barked, losing his temper. "Now, if you want a dollar for one of them, come here and get it!"

Glancing down the boardwalk, Janessa saw the sheriff motion to a wagon moving along the street. He and the deputies ran out and got behind it, using it for concealment as it approached the bank. Shaking her head, Janessa put the cigarettes into her pocket. "I don't want to sell any of my cigarettes."

"Then get out of here and stop pestering me!" the man bellowed, furious. "If you don't, I'll make you sorry you ever saw me!"

As soon as he turned away, Janessa stepped off the boardwalk beside the horses, took the string of firecrackers from her pocket, and touched the tip of her cigarette to the fuse. Just then the front door of the bank flew open, the other three men running out with bags. The fuse flared, and Janessa flung the firecrackers under the horses and broke into a run, fleeing across the street.

Only seconds later the firecrackers began exploding with a staccato roar, and the horses immediately turned into a rearing, plunging mass. Shrill, frightened neighs sounded over the explosions as the animals jerked the hitching rail clear off its support posts and broke their reins free. Bucking, rearing, and kicking, they began scattering in a cloud of dust.

The four men had whipped out their pistols in reaction to the firecrackers, but then they froze, looking in shock at the horses. The sheriff shouted from behind the wagon as it, too, took off down the street, the driver leaping from the seat. The lawmen spread out, and there was a thunderous roar of gunfire. Janessa, hearing a horse immediately behind her, darted a glance over her shoulder.

Its eyes wide and glaring, the huge animal was headed straight toward her. Too late, she tried to dodge it. The horse's powerful shoulder struck her with a solid, heavy impact that lifted her off her feet and sent her flying through the air. She slammed down onto the street on her back, the breath knocked from her. The street seemed to spin around her, the gunfire sounding as though it came from far away.

Meanwhile, Cindy had hurried to the front window of the store as soon as she heard the firecrackers. Seeing Janessa running from the plunging horses, she dashed out the door, only to be met by the roar of gunfire.

Cindy took in the pandemonium at a glance. Horses were storming about, the street was filled with dust and gun smoke from the blistering exchange of fire between the lawmen and the men in front of the bank, and Janessa lay sprawled on the street, old Josh Sellars running toward her as fast as he could, dodging horses along the way.

Terror raced through Cindy. To her left, she saw Timmy running along the boardwalk toward her. Wasting no time, she darted into the street, shouting to Joshua. "Josh, get Timmy into the store! I'll get Janessa!"

The old man hesitated, then shouted a needless warning for her to be careful as he made for Timmy in a shambling run. A panic-stricken horse charged out of the dust straight at Cindy, but she dodged it. A stray bullet whizzed within inches of her head, while another raised a spout of dirt at her feet. She reached Janessa, scooped up the girl in her arms, and hurried back toward the store.

Joshua ran into the store with Timmy in his arms, Biddle waving him on. A pane in the door exploded into a shower of glass splinters as a stray bullet struck it. Biddle ducked, holding the door open for Cindy as she ran inside with Janessa.

Cindy gently placed the girl on the floor and bent over her. Relief flooded through her when she saw that Janessa was only stunned. The gunfire outside died away, and Cindy helped Janessa into a chair as Biddle brought a small glass of brandy. The girl took a sip of the strong spirit as they listened to Timmy breathlessly relate what had happened.

A minute later the sheriff came in to inquire about Janessa, and he smiled broadly when he saw that she was not injured. "Everybody is mighty indebted to you, young lady," he said. "If it hadn't been for you and this boy here, those men would have cleaned out the bank."

"Did you get all of them, Sheriff?" Biddle asked.

"Yes, every one of them," the sheriff replied. "One is dead, and the other three are wounded." He turned to Cindy and courteously took off his hat. "If these children were anyone else's, Miss Cindy, I guess I'd have plenty to say about what they did. But they're Holts, and no more needs to be said."

He nodded to Timmy and Janessa as he turned to the door and went back out. The color had returned to the girl's face, but she still looked weak and shaken.

"Josh, take the things out to the wagon, if you would," Cindy said. "I want to get Janessa home so she can rest."

"I'll give you a hand," Biddle volunteered. He followed Josh to the counter, but a moment later he was

back, holding out an open package of Philip Morris cigarettes. "Every dime I've worked for for the past twenty years
is in that bank, Miss Janessa, so I can't tell you how
grateful I am for what you did. I have six more cartons of
these, and I'll put them with your aunt's things. When
you run out, just let me know, and I'll fix you up with
another supply."

The girl smiled weakly and took the offered cigarettes. She pulled one out, put it in her mouth, and fished
a match from her pockets, then suddenly looked up at
Cindy, as it occurred to her that she was about to smoke
in a public place. Cindy smiled, taking the match from the
girl. She struck it on the floor and held it up for Janessa to
light her cigarette.

In the wooded hills of eastern Wisconsin, the pristine
beauty of a burbling creek held Ursula Oberg's attention
as she stood waiting for her grown daughter, Maida, to
taste the water.

Giant evergreens along the creek were mixed with
tall oaks, birches, and aspens in an endless variety of
shades of green. The bright sunshine beaming down through
the trees dappled the sparkling water, and the morning
breeze had a cool, fresh feel.

The scene was not unlike some places in Ursula's
native Germany, but the atmosphere was different. There,
the ownership of every inch of land was documented on
records that dated back through generations, and property
rights were jealously guarded. But in this country there
were vast stretches of virgin land that were scarcely ex-
plored. The attitude toward proprietorship was casual,
giving Ursula a sense of freedom to enjoy the beauty of
the creek completely, to walk along it if she wished.

Ursula and Maida were newly arrived immigrants,
having left Germany because of a government policy called
Kulturkampf, a return to supposedly traditional Teutonic
culture. Ursula's family was Catholic, a religion being
suppressed in Germany. Yet in the United States, she had

found, in addition to enjoying freedom of religion, the people had a broad range of personal freedoms unknown in the old country. Already there was a large German community in Milwaukee, and for that reason Ursula had chosen to come to Wisconsin.

Maida dipped up water from the creek and tasted it, then spat it out with a grimace of disgust. "Swamp water," she said, speaking in German. Her mother could speak English, but Maida could not. "It is full of decaying vegetation and other filth."

Ursula had already quenched her thirst with water from the creek and had found it delicious and refreshing. But she made no comment as she and Maida walked back to their rented horse and buggy parked at the side of the road. They climbed in, and Ursula took the reins, while Maida slumped on the seat dejectedly.

The buggy moved along the narrow road, following the stream, swaying as the wheels bumped over ruts. Glancing at her daughter, Ursula reflected that while she had been unable to give her deceased husband a son, she had given him a daughter who was his image in every respect, except that she was a woman. Small and dark-haired, Maida had large, melancholy brown eyes that saw a rainstorm in every bright, fleecy cloud.

Maida also followed her father's profession. A master brewer without sons, he had passed along his skills to his daughter. He had done well, guiding the natural gift that Maida had possessed as a small child, and she had taken his place when he died.

The owners of the brewery back in Saarbrücken had been eager to hire her. Even in Germany, where beer had been a national beverage for centuries, her skill was legend. The rich premium beer that she brewed had been in demand in nearly every capital in Europe.

Sighing despondently, Maida sat up on the seat. "There are breweries in Milwaukee," she said. "I could work there."

Hesitating, Ursula searched for a reply. She knew

that the owners of the breweries in Milwaukee would refuse to hire a woman as a master brewer, but Maida would have difficulty understanding that. Like her father, she was unable to comprehend many of the complexities of life. Ursula decided to discourage the idea.

"Maida, you tasted the beer in Milwaukee," she said. "Would you buy such beer?"

"Of course not!" Maida snapped impatiently. "Do you think I would make such swill? I would make good beer."

"How could you?" Ursula countered. "They use lake water to make beer. How could anyone make good beer with lake water?"

The point was well taken, as Ursula knew it would be. Maida had no reply.

"We have been searching for a good stream for weeks," Maida commented morosely, after a long silence. "We have searched and searched, and we have found nothing but swamp water. Perhaps there is no good water here."

"Be patient, Maida," Ursula advised. "The money we have will last for a few months if we are thrifty, so we have plenty of time. We will find good water."

"Maybe we should return to Germany," Maida grumbled.

"Then we would only have to leave again," Ursula replied. "The government's policy will not change."

Maida was silent for a moment, thinking. "You could tell everyone that you have decided to become a Protestant," she said.

Ursula controlled her urge to smile. Like her father before her, Maida was naive and childishly impractical. Her extremely narrow focus on a single aspect of life, her profession, often made her act and even look like a young girl, though she was twenty-five years old. "That would be a lie," Ursula replied, "which would be immoral and sinful."

Unimpressed by her mother's scruples, Maida sighed gloomily and fell silent. Ursula reflected that, strangely, her relationship with her daughter was in many respects identical to that she had had with Maida's father. Her role in life was also substantially the same as it had been when her husband was alive. She prepared meals that were completely bland to avoid injuring the master brewer's sensitive taste buds; she maintained a comfortable household for the master brewer; and, most important of all, she provided moral support and cheerful companionship to uplift the spirits of the pessimistic, temperamental master brewer.

And now she was also lifting the master brewer to a well-deserved status of independence. *Kulturkampf* had been only an excuse; Ursula could have found a way to remain in Germany. The need to emigrate had been a handy pretext—accepted as fact by the naive master brewer—to break out of the rigid Old World strictures that had kept generations of Oberg brewers in anonymous bondage. In the future, the delicious, full-bodied premium beer brewed by the master brewer would be called Oberg beer.

As the buggy rounded a curve, Ursula stood up and looked at a log bridge ahead. "There is another creek, Maida," she said.

"Another among hundreds," Maida replied glumly. "And all of them nothing but swamp water."

Ursula was more optimistic, because this creek appeared to come from higher ground. It flowed down a hill on the left and under the bridge to join the wide stream they had been following. A dim road near the bridge led up the hill. Knowing that the best water always came from high ground, Ursula turned the horse onto the side road.

The way was overgrown, little more than two wheel tracks hemmed in by brush and trees. It passed through a glade of ferns, and then the trees closed in again. In some places saplings were sprouting in the ashes of underbrush that had burned the preceding autumn. Ursula had heard frequent mention of the fires here last year; they had been started by hot embers borne on the wind from Chicago and later had been extinguished by rain.

The horse puffed and strained as the road curved on

up the hill. Over the noisy scraping of the brush against the buggy, Ursula could hear the creek babbling nearby. For the first time she began to sense that their weeks of prowling the forest roads of Wisconsin would soon be at an end. She was about to comment encouragingly to her daughter when she saw that there was no need for her to say anything. Maida was sitting bolt upright, craning her neck and trying to see through the trees ahead.

The road came to an end, the trees opening into a wide clearing that not long ago had been a farm. Lush grass was growing up from the ashes of a cornfield that had burned the previous autumn. The house itself was a heap of charred timbers, but a large, well-built barn still stood, protected from the fire by the wide, bare expanse around it.

When the buggy stopped, Maida leaped from it and began running up the hill in the direction of the creek. Shouting a warning about dangerous snakes, Ursula ran after her, pausing to snatch up a stick with which to beat the brush and drive away any creatures that might be lurking. She tried to catch up with Maida, but the younger woman could run like a deer. With the brush tugging at her long, heavy dress, Ursula slowed to a trot, panting heavily. Then abruptly the foliage opened out and she found Maida standing at the head of the creek.

The trees and brush were set back around an expanse of rock that a geological cataclysm of eons before had thrust upward from the bowels of the earth. It was ancient granite, split with fissures that reached downward to some deep reservoir and provided egress for the water, which burbled up in a dozen or more large springs that together were the fountainhead of the creek.

It appeared to Ursula that she and Maida had found one of those rare, most precious sources of pure, untainted water—a large, free-flowing artesian spring. "Have you tasted it, Maida?" she asked.

Gazing at the water as though unable to believe what

she was seeing, Maida slowly shook her head. "No," she replied.

"Then taste it. Why are you waiting?"

Maida hesitated a moment longer, in either reverence or fear of abject disappointment—Ursula was unsure which. Finally she knelt at the edge of the water and washed her hands in it, to remove any traces of sweat and grime. She dipped up a handful of water and filled her mouth.

After a moment, she spat it out. She drew in a deep, quick breath through her mouth and nose to exercise the full sensitivity of taste buds that would never sample spices, citrus, vinegar, onions, or any other strong flavor. Then she turned to Ursula with an ecstatic smile. "It is good water," she said softly, in awe. "Pure, clean artesian water."

"Then we have finally found what you need, little one," Ursula said triumphantly. "And it is on land that is not being used. Come, we must find out who owns this property and see if we can buy it."

"You go and find out," Maida replied, dipping a hand in the water and watching it trickle from her palm. "I will wait here."

"No, no," Ursula said, stepping to her daughter and putting an arm around her small waist. "I cannot leave you here alone in the wilderness, Maida. Come, we will return soon enough."

Maida remained reluctant to leave, but Ursula was four inches taller and sixty pounds heavier than her daughter. She gently turned Maida away from the stream and led her back down the hill toward the clearing.

By the time they reached the barn, Maida's pleasure over finding the artesian spring had been replaced by her usual defeatism. With eager pessimism, she was searching for insurmountable problems. "I have no cooperage," she said despondently. "You refused to allow me to bring casks and my tuns. How can I make beer without casks and tuns made of good German oak?"

"The oak here is as good as in Germany," Ursula

replied, pulling open one of the large doors at the front of the barn. "And we will hire the most skilled cooper we can find." Looking into the vast, dim interior, she nodded in satisfaction. "Maida, this barn was built with more care than most houses, and it has a metal roof."

"And so?" Maida said, puzzled. "We have no horses or cattle."

"No, but we need a place to live, and a place for you to make beer," Ursula said. "For the present, this barn could serve both purposes. We could live on one side and use the other side as your brewery. There is more than enough room."

"I am to make beer in this shed?" Maida exclaimed in despair. "I must have a brewery to make beer, not a shed!"

"Maida, this is not a shed. It is a barn, and it is built—"

"It is a shed, with drafts that will blow across my tuns and make the fermentation uneven! How can I brew beer in such a place?"

"We can have partitions built and cover all of the cracks in the walls, so there will be no drafts," Ursula said patiently. She lifted a hand to cut off further protest. "Listen to me, Maida. The owner of the land apparently has no use for it, so we can probably buy it. But at this very moment someone else could be bartering with him for it."

Maida hesitated, her brown eyes wide with alarm. The next moment she was walking rapidly toward the buggy. Ursula smiled at her daughter fondly, then closed the barn door and followed.

The nearest house was at a small, isolated farmstead several miles back down the road. Ursula stopped to talk to a man hoeing in a field, and he told her that the deserted barn and the surrounding land belonged to a man named Fred Guthrie, the proprietor of a tavern in Colmer.

Colmer was ten miles from the farmstead, and the shadows of midafternoon were stretching across the road when Ursula and Maida reached the town. It was small, with a main street little more than a hundred yards long, but it bustled with activity. Serving as a supply depot for logging camps in the area, the town had more warehouses than homes.

Ursula stopped in front of the only tavern in town. Having heard stories concerning the bad reputation of such establishments, she told Maida to remain in the buggy while she went inside.

The door of the tavern was standing open, and three men were seated at a table just inside. Ursula stepped onto the small porch and peered in, trying to decide whether or not to enter. One of the men at the table noticed and grinned lewdly.

"Come on in, sweetie," he called, pointing to his crotch. "I have something I'll give you."

The other men at the table laughed raucously, and Ursula stepped back off the porch, deciding to find another way to talk with the man named Guthrie. The laughter suddenly broke off, however, as the large, aproned figure of the proprietor swiftly crossed the tavern. The three at the table were hefty lumberjacks, but the man approaching was even bigger. He had a peg leg, and it slammed against the floor as he planted himself and grabbed the worst offender by the front of the shirt, dragging him up from his chair. "I won't have ladies insulted on my premises!" he bellowed furiously. "Now you and you other two swine get out of here fast, and don't come back!"

He released the collared lumberjack, who glanced in disbelief at his friends. "What's a gimp like you doing calling me a swine?" he snarled at the proprietor. "At least I'm a whole man, and I'll give you plenty of reason to remember it!"

As he lunged toward the one-legged man, he seemed to run into an invisible wall. In a movement so quick Ursula barely saw it, the tavern owner lashed out with a hamlike fist. It struck the other man full in the face with a meaty thud, reeling him backward over a chair.

The other two at the table rushed the tavern owner. One of them, a swarthy, beefy man, pulled out a knife. Ursula started to shout in warning, but the tavern owner had already reacted. Balancing himself lightly on his good leg, he lashed out with his peg leg. The blunt, hardwood tip rammed deep into the lumberjack's corpulent belly, then flicked sideways, knocking the knife harmlessly to the floor. The man's face twisted in agony as he doubled over, clutching his stomach and retching.

The third man skidded to a stop and wheeled toward the door, but the tavern owner took a quick step toward him and slapped at his ankles with the peg leg. Stumbling, the man fell heavily against a table. The burly tavern owner immediately pounced on him, spinning him around and slamming a hard fist into his face.

The brawl, as it was, had ended before the others in the tavern could come to the owner's assistance. They sat back down, chuckling and commenting in satisfaction as the big man seized the three and heaved them out the door. Dazed and staggering, the troublemakers stumbled off down the street.

The tavern owner stepped outside onto the porch. "I'm Fred Guthrie, ma'am," he said to Ursula, politely touching his forehead. "This is my tavern, and I apologize for what was said to you. If you and your friend would like to come inside for a glass of beer or something to eat, you have my word that you'll be treated with due respect."

"Thank you, Mr. Guthrie, but we do not wish to come inside, and there is no need for you to apologize. I would like to talk with you, though. I am Ursula Oberg, and my companion is my daughter, Maida."

A momentary silence fell. Fred Guthrie was surprised that the two women—obviously recent immigrants—were mother and daughter. Ursula was tall, regal, and buxom, with a touch of gray in her light brown hair, and she had the most beautiful blue eyes he had ever seen. Even her

German accent was pleasing to his ears. The younger woman was small, with dark hair and eyes, and she looked ill-tempered.

Liking the tall, attractive woman immensely, Fred sought for words, his self-assurance suddenly evaporating. He had never found it easy to deal with women who appealed to him. "I'm very pleased to meet both of you," he said, looking away. "Uh . . . your daughter doesn't look like you very much, does she?"

Ursula smiled, shaking her head. "No. Like her late father, she is an Oberg in every respect."

The man silently nodded, gazing down the street. He seemed to be purposely ignoring her.

Puzzled by his sudden reticence, Ursula stared at him. His features were strong and handsome. Gray peppered his beard and his short, neat hair. She wondered why his attitude toward her had changed so abruptly.

Maida, unable to understand English, called out in German, "Mother, is he the man who owns the land?"

"Yes, he is," Ursula replied. She turned back to Fred, to explain the exchange. "Maida was asking about some land we looked at today," she said. "I believe it belongs to you. It has a barn on it, and there is a creek on the hill behind the barn. We would like to buy it."

Fred glanced at her, nodded, then looked away again. "Yes, it's mine," he mumbled. "You can have it for a hundred dollars."

The price was absurdly low. Ursula smiled and shook her head. "Please name a reasonable price, Mr. Guthrie."

"The land is of no use to me, ma'am," he said. "My brother left it to me when he died, but I'm not a farmer." He pointed to his wooden leg. "I was a lumberjack until that happened. Now I have my tavern, and I find lumberjacks for camps that need men. Anyway, the land is worth less because there's no house. I suppose you noticed that."

"Yes, I did. Eventually I would like to have a house, but the barn will do for now. It is built as well as most houses."

"It certainly is," he agreed. "My brother liked a good barn." He was still looking down the street as he spoke. "Like I said, you can have it and the land for a hundred dollars—unless you think that's too much."

"Of course it is not too much," Ursula said, reluctant to agree on such a low price; it would almost be like cheating him. She decided to try another approach, in order to make him realize that she was not poor. "If you know the lumberjacks and other workers around here, perhaps you know of a cooper. I would like to hire one, but he must be highly skilled."

Stroking his beard, Fred tried to shrug aside the confusion that the woman created in him and think of someone who could help her. Maida, becoming impatient, called out again in German. "Mother, will he sell the land to us, and do we have enough money to buy it?"

"Yes, we will buy the land from him," Ursula replied.

Fred shrugged when Ursula explained what Maida had asked. "The bargain's been made, as far as I'm concerned," he said. "And I know a man who can make barrels. His name is Rafferty, and he lived in Chicago until his house burned in the fire. He's a cabinetmaker, but I'm sure he can make barrels and other things. I'll talk to him."

"I would appreciate that very much, Mr. Guthrie. And I would also appreciate it if you would name a reasonable price for your land."

Someone inside the tavern knocked a glass impatiently against the bar for another drink. Fred looked around with a steely glare that stopped the knocking. But when he turned back to Ursula, his eyes still avoided hers. "If you want the land, you'll have it," he said. "Bring your things, and I'll help you get settled in the barn."

Ursula stared at him, musing. All at once she realized what was so plain to see—that the tall, brawny man was attracted to her but was shy about it. She chided herself for being so dense. Knowing now what had to be done, she decided to defer talk about price until later. When she knew him better, she reflected, she could make him see sense. And she was determined to know this man better.

"Very well, Mr. Guthrie," she said, turning toward the buggy. "I will be back tomorrow, and I will bring my things with me."

Fred nodded and smiled happily. He followed her to the buggy. "When you get here, I'll close my tavern and go with you to help. In talking with you, ma'am, it's hard to believe that you've been here only a short time. You speak English better than many who have been here for years."

"I have been studying the language for years, Mr. Guthrie, because I have been planning for years to come here."

"Even so, you still speak English better than most. It'll take your daughter a good while to catch up with you, if she ever does."

"There is no need for her to try," Ursula said firmly. "I can always translate for her."

Noting Ursula's quick protectiveness toward Maida, Fred realized that the one way to alienate the woman was to make the slightest criticism about her daughter. "Of course you can," he said, helping Ursula into the buggy. "As long as you understand each other, nothing else matters, does it?" He stepped back from the buggy as Ursula gathered up the reins and released the brake. "I'll see you tomorrow, ma'am."

"Good-bye, Mr. Guthrie. I am very grateful for all of your help."

"It was my pleasure, ma'am."

As the buggy moved off down the busy street, Ursula thought about Fred Guthrie and her unexpected feelings toward him. His reaction to her, his painful shyness, was both amusing and pleasing. As she thought about the tall, handsome, and charming man, a warm glow was kindled within her. All of a sudden, a new and different phase of life seemed to be opening up before her.

Then she put the subject out of her mind, thinking

about what she had to do. Wagons would have to be hired
to haul her belongings and Maida's equipment stored in
Milwaukee, and she needed to buy food and other supplies to take to the barn. Selecting food was always a
problem; Maida could eat only the blandest things, and
she never had a good appetite.

As the bustle of the town faded behind, Ursula began
talking about all the arrangements that had to be made.
Then, glancing at her daughter, she fell silent and smiled.
Maida was dozing off to sleep. Ursula put an arm around
her and pulled her closer.

When Maida's purpose in life was at hand, Ursula
reflected, she was always in a frenzy of anxiety. During
the last, crucial hours of fermentation, the master brewer's
judgment as to when to start drawing the beer down made
the difference between good beer and premium beer. And
during those long, tense hours, Maida was always harried,
sleepless, and unapproachable.

Supremely skilled in making beer, she was interested
in little else. Talk of food, furniture, a house, and other
trifles merely bored the master brewer. Ursula smiled
affectionately as her small, slender daughter nestled closer
to her and went to sleep.

II

As she looked out the window of the hired carriage at a busy street in the new Back Bay district of Boston, Marjorie White noted with dread that she was near her destination. Within minutes, she would arrive at a photographic assignment of a nature that she viewed with extreme dislike.

To take her mind off the assignment, she opened the large leather-and-brass cases on the floor of the carriage and checked her equipment. The cameras in the cases were the ones she had owned for years, but the cases themselves and other items of equipment were new, the best and most expensive available. Fate had placed her at the scene when the Great Chicago Fire had occurred, and the plates for stereopticon slides that she had made of the fire had brought in a large amount of money.

The demand for the slides had been so great that her business partner, Clayton Hemmings, had been unable to print them rapidly enough. During the months since the fire, instead of venturing off across the country to make plates for slides of other scenes, she had worked with Clayton and helped him print a large supply of slides of the fire.

Along with money had come a degree of fame—and that had led to the lucrative assignment to which the carriage was taking her. She didn't actually need the extra

31

work, but she remembered the lean years of sleeping on benches in railroad stations and skipping meals so she would have enough money to buy photographic supplies.

Her partner, with a family to support, remembered the lean years even more keenly. When the offer of the assignment had arrived in the mail, he had urged her to accept it, and she had reluctantly agreed, despite her strong misgivings.

Marjorie closed the cases as the carriage turned onto a side street. It stopped, and the driver climbed down from his seat. Marjorie straightened her hat, flicked a bit of lint off the shoulder of her short, dark cape, and adjusted the waist of her dark dress.

The driver opened the door and lifted out the cases, then helped Marjorie out. She paid him, giving him an extra twenty-five cents. "Could you wait for me?" she asked. "I'll be here about a half hour."

The man nodded, doffing his tall hat in thanks for the tip. Marjorie picked up her cases and climbed the steps in front of the building. Two men were waiting on the landing at the entrance, both of them dressed in black.

The heavier man, whose impeccably tailored suit testified to his wealth, stared at Marjorie in perplexity, but bowed when she reached the top of the steps. "I'm Milton Farnsworth," he said. "I'm in charge of the arrangements, and I presume you're the photographist. I was expecting M. White, the famous photographist who made the slides of the Great Chicago Fire."

"I'm M. White," Marjorie replied, putting down the cases.

Farnsworth blinked in surprise. "But you're a woman," he blurted.

"Yes, I am a woman," Marjorie admitted gravely. She pointed to her name on the side of the cases. "But I am also M. White."

The man hesitated, then smiled apologetically and bowed again. "Please forgive me if I've offended you," he said. "I was taken aback for a moment, and I meant no offense."

Marjorie was unfazed. "I'm not offended in the least. Is all the family here?"

"Yes," Farnsworth replied. "We can begin immediately, if you wish. I'll be glad to assist you, if I may."

"I would appreciate that very much."

He picked up Marjorie's cases. The other man, the director of the funeral home, opened the door and held it. Farnsworth carried the cases inside, Marjorie following him.

A soft drone of somber organ music drifted into the dimly lighted entrance foyer, which was thickly carpeted and heavily draped in deep blue and purple. The air was thick with the sweet, cloying scent of embalming fluid and an almost overpowering smell of flowers. Marjorie suppressed a shiver as she followed Farnsworth across the foyer.

Glancing around, she concluded that the assignment would be more profitable than she and Clayton had thought. The establishment itself was a very expensive one, and Farnsworth was leading her toward the largest and most opulent of the viewing rooms.

Two attendants were at the door of the viewing room. One held a box of folding silk fans imprinted with the name of the funeral home, plus smelling salts to deal with the inevitable fainting spells. The other, a young man, presented Marjorie with the visitors' book to sign.

As she signed the book, the attendant surreptitiously took out a small box and placed it on the open page. It was one of the boxes in which her slides of the fire were sold. With the young man looking at her in a silent plea, Marjorie dipped the pen again and wrote her signature on the box. The attendant flashed her a quick smile, whisking the box back out of sight.

Marjorie followed Farnsworth into the viewing room and down the side aisle, her estimate of the potential profits of the assignment increasing even more. Not carats but pounds of diamonds were on display, and expensive black brocade dresses were trimmed with costly silk and lace. This was a very large, extremely wealthy family bidding their patriarch farewell.

Several senior members of the gathering shifted in their chairs to stare at Marjorie in puzzled dissatisfaction. After putting down one of the cases, Farnsworth stepped to them and whispered, pointing to her name on the side of the other case. The frowns faded, and he returned to Marjorie, attentively eager to assist her.

While everything had to be done in an appropriate atmosphere of respect and decorum, it was understood by all present that grief now had to take second place to the necessity of recording the event for posterity. The funeral director silently moved along the side aisles and opened the thick, tasseled drapes to let light in, as Marjorie set up her tripod and put her view camera in place.

Looking at the ground glass surface at the rear of the camera, Marjorie framed a view of the mourners and focused the camera. She took a plate holder from her case and quietly slipped it into place in front of the glass, then pulled out the dark slide that protected the plate, exposing it to the rear of the lens. When she held up the dark slide—the signal that she was ready to take a photograph— the fans stopped moving. Everyone froze, gazing toward the coffin.

Marjorie removed the cover from the lens and counted off the seconds for the exposure. When she replaced the cover on the lens and lowered the dark slide, the mourners relaxed with an audible sigh, fans working busily again. With Farnsworth assisting her, Marjorie moved the camera to another position as quietly as possible.

From any angle, some of the forty or so members of the clan were hidden behind others. Moving the camera several times, Marjorie made certain that every family group in the room was prominent in at least one photograph. At the fifty dollars or more that Clayton would charge for each album of prints, it would be a substantial loss if one of the families were piqued and refused to buy an album.

Her mind occupied by what she was doing, Marjorie momentarily forgot her dislike for the assignment. After completing the photographs of the mourners, she took several views of the flower displays and the coffin on its dais. Next came the scene of the principal mourners at the coffin, a conventional pose, and Marjorie whispered instructions to Farnsworth. He sent the funeral director for a velvet-covered kneeling stool, then gathered the widow and her grown children by the coffin. With the aged widow kneeling in place, Marjorie arranged the family members behind the woman.

Marjorie posed the men with their right hands tucked inside their coats and their left feet a half-pace forward. Then she posed the daughter and the widow with their handkerchiefs near but not concealing their faces. As a reward for Farnsworth's efforts—and whether or not the others wished it—she placed him in the immediate background.

When she was done and the principal mourners had returned to their seats, it was time for the final photograph, the centerpiece of the album. Marjorie's dislike of the assignment returned with renewed intensity. She moved the camera close to the coffin and extended the tripod to its full height.

Standing on the stool beside the camera, Marjorie carefully avoided looking into the coffin as she loosened the thumbscrews on the tripod pan and tilted the camera downward. She peered at the ground glass to focus the camera and frame the photograph, all the while trying to maintain a sense of detachment. The light was poor, she noted, and the exposure would have to be a long one—but this was one subject who would not fidget.

Using the judgment she had developed over the years, Marjorie decided to give the plate a three-minute exposure. She removed the cover from the lens and looked at her watch, avoiding the coffin with her eyes. With growing nervousness she waited, the rows of mourners all looking at her and the only sound in the room the soft rustle of fans working busily.

At last it was finished. Marjorie replaced the cover on the lens and stepped down from the stool. Farnsworth helped her disassemble her tripod and pack it away; then he picked up the cases to carry them out. Marjorie followed him along the side aisle, the mourners nodding to her solemnly in farewell.

Farnsworth carried the cases down the steps to the street. As he was putting them into the carriage, he mentioned a close friend of his who had an aged, seriously ill aunt. "If worst comes to worst," he said, "I would be glad to refer him to you for—"

"I'll be leaving the city very shortly," Marjorie interrupted him quickly. "I rarely do anything other than stereopticon slides, and I'm away most of the time. But I do appreciate your offer."

"Not at all. And I'm more than grateful that you accepted us as clients. Your name will be on the albums, won't it?"

"Yes, it will. My partner will develop the plates and send you a sample album within the next few days. You can show it to the rest of the family, and they can place their orders with him."

Farnsworth smiled, helping her into the carriage. "I'll look forward to receiving it. Meeting you has certainly made this a day that I'll long remember."

"I will as well. Good-bye."

Farnsworth bowed as the carriage moved away. Marjorie waited until he was out of sight, then leaned over and opened the windows. The sweet odor of embalming fluid seemed to have permeated her clothes. As fresh air wafted into the carriage, she heaved a sigh of relief and sat back on the seat.

When the carriage drew up in front of her partner's house, Marjorie waved to Clayton's three children, who were playing in the front yard. Since the slides of the

Great Chicago Fire had gone on sale, the children had been wearing new clothes, the house had been repainted and completely refurnished, and a new carriage stood in the drive.

Clara Hemmings met Marjorie at the door and took one of the cases as they walked along the hall to the office and studio at the rear of the house. Clayton and his wife were some fifteen years older than Marjorie, but they were close friends of hers. Clayton had helped Marjorie perfect her skills in photography, and in the past months he and Clara had come to view the younger woman as a family benefactor.

Several years before, while Clayton had been mixing chemicals to prepare wet collodion plates, a spark from some unknown source had ignited the volatile solution. He had almost died from his burns, which had left him disfigured and crippled. During the years after his accident and before his partnership with Marjorie, the Hemmings family had been very poor.

Clayton had once been an extremely handsome man, but now the left side of his face was a mass of red, wrinkled scar tissue, and his left arm and leg were almost useless. A recluse who left his house rarely and only after dark, he was sensitive about his appearance, even with those who were close to him. He was at the desk when Clara and Marjorie came into the office, and he turned the left side of his face away from them.

"I'll make coffee," Clara said, putting down the case she was carrying. "You would probably like some, wouldn't you, Marjorie?"

"I certainly would," Marjorie replied with a warm smile. "You always think of the right things, Clara." She put down her other case and sat in the chair beside the desk as Clara went out. "Clay, no more jobs at funeral parlors," she said firmly.

Clayton smiled, looking straight ahead and keeping his right profile to her; only when they were working together in the dim red light of a darkroom would he face her. "Was it all that bad, Marjorie?" he chuckled.

"Worse," she replied. "When we were first getting started, and before the mail order company began selling our stereo slides, we had to take anything we could get. We don't have to now."

"Yes, that's true," he agreed, looking through the papers on the desk. "Very well, Marjorie—no more funerals. By the way, the mail arrived about an hour ago, and we received some good news and bad news. Here's the good news."

He handed her a letter with a check attached to it, and Marjorie sat back in her chair and glanced over them. The letter, from the mail order company that sold their stereopticon slides, was a request for more slides of the Great Chicago Fire. The check was their share of the revenues from the slides that had been sold during the past weeks.

"This *is* good news," Marjorie commented. "It appears that those slides will continue selling for years."

"It does, and I wish you'd reconsider what you're doing with your share of the money," Clayton said. "Money is like seed that will multiply, but you lose that benefit when you keep it in a bank safety deposit box. I've almost doubled my money on some of my investments."

"No, you haven't," Marjorie replied bluntly. "The papers for which you paid good money are simply selling for twice as much as they were when you bought them. But if you try to buy a loaf of bread with them, you'll find out how much they're worth. I'll keep my money where it is."

"But you could at least place it on deposit at the bank," Clayton said patiently. "Then you'd get interest on it, which is little enough."

Marjorie shook her head, putting the letter and check on the desk. "No, I don't trust banks, Clay. I've read that some people are predicting a financial crisis that could result in bank failures."

"There are always doomsday prophets," Clayton scoffed. "All of the progressive financiers are predicting continued growth well into the future. That's advice worth heeding, Marjorie."

"Or wishful thinking. What's the bad news, Clay?"

He handed her another letter. "It's a reply to the request I made last week concerning your taking a voyage on a whaler. Another polite refusal."

Marjorie glanced over the letter. It was from a company in New Bedford that owned several whaling ships, and it stated that accommodations for a female photographist would not be available on any company ships in the foreseeable future. It was the latest in a series of similar refusals.

As they were discussing what to do next, Clara came in with a coffeepot and cups on a tray. As she set a cup on the desk in front of Clayton, he turned away. Marjorie noted the fleeting expression of hurt on the older woman's face. Clara's deep love for her husband was unaffected by his appearance, yet Clayton's behavior indicated a complete lack of trust and faith in her.

The state of affairs had existed for as long as Marjorie had known Clayton and Clara. It gave her a sense of helpless frustration, because she was extremely fond of both of them, yet she knew that the subject was too sensitive for her to broach with either one. Smiling in thanks as Clara handed her a cup of coffee, Marjorie reflected on the needless complexities of human relationships.

As Clara left the room, Marjorie continued the conversation. "All the large whaling companies have turned us down. I don't believe we'll have any better luck with the small ones."

"I don't either," Clayton agreed, opening a desk drawer. He took out a well-thumbed copy of the catalog published by the company that sold their slides and began leafing through it. "The important thing is to get a new set or two of slides listed in the catalog as soon as possible.

The company intends to feature you as the photographist of the Great Chicago Fire, so everything you do will sell well."

Marjorie took a sip of her coffee. "We've talked about a set of slides on the plantations in Arkansas, and this might be a good time for me to go there. It won't be insufferably hot yet."

"Yes, or you could go to Wisconsin and do a set on the logging there," Clayton said. "That would probably be better, because there aren't any slides on Wisconsin listed in the catalog. They would sell well."

Marjorie hesitated. Her great fear was that something would come between her and her profession. Toby Holt, who owned the logging operation in Wisconsin, had no feelings for her except friendship. But that could change, and she was drawn to him with an intensity that reached the depths of her being, an intensity that could threaten her commitment to her profession.

Then she thought about Ted Taylor. He was working as a law enforcement officer in Iowa, but if there was any possible way for him to do it, he would come to Wisconsin when he heard that she was there. His feelings for her were deeper than hers for him, but she was very fond of him nonetheless. When she had been in Chicago the previous year, Ted's friendship had helped her to put Toby Holt out of her mind.

"I'll go to Wisconsin," Marjorie decided. "I'll send a telegram to Toby Holt and ask if I may visit his logging camp. I'm sure he'll be cooperative."

Clayton nodded in satisfaction. "While you're in that area, you could make a few plates of the rebuilding in Chicago."

"Yes, I'll do that," Marjorie replied. "From what I've read, it's progressing quite rapidly."

Rather than rapidly, the rebuilding of Chicago was proceeding at a frenzied pace. The booming of steam-driven pile drivers pounding foundation supports into the earth could be heard from all parts of the city as Toby Holt left the boardinghouse where he roomed and rode his horse along the streets toward his lumber company.

It was a bright, cheerful early summer day, with a refreshing breeze blowing off the lake. And as always, the sights and sounds of construction gave him a deep sense of satisfaction. The noise of the pile drivers, working twenty-four hours a day and seven days a week, was the sound of Chicago rising from its ashes.

Where the rubble of five-story buildings had been cleared away, ten-story buildings were going up, all conforming to a strict fire code. And occupying its niche in the rebuilding was the North Chicago Lumber Company. Through the money he had invested, plus the value of the land presented to him in appreciation for what he did during the fire, Toby owned fifty-one percent of the company. His friends Rob Martin and Edward Blackstone shared thirty-nine percent, and Frank Woods, another friend, owned ten percent.

A tall wooden fence surrounded the large waterfront property, and the wide gate was standing open for the day's business when Toby arrived. Although it was still early in the morning, the steam engine that powered the saws had already been stoked, and the circular steel blades were whining through wood. The saw house was in the center of the enclosure, with immense stacks of finished lumber off to the left, awaiting shipment. The company offices were in a spacious building against the fence on the right.

A pier jutted out into the water on the lake side of the property. North of it was a breakwater, with a log basin formed by barrels chained together. Huge logs that had been towed from the camp in Wisconsin floated inside the basin, and a steam winch was dragging one out of the water and up an incline to the saw house. The log, some eight feet in diameter and well over forty feet long, would be turned into thousands of board feet of lumber.

In one corner of the property were a pen and stable

for the horses and oxen used with the delivery wagons. Toby left his horse with the stable boy and crossed the yard toward the offices. He stopped as the yard foreman, James Henshaw, waved and called out. Henshaw was a burly Irishman of fifty, with decades of experience in the lumber business. A well-dressed man, apparently a customer, was with him.

"Good morning, Toby," Henshaw said. "This is Carl Roberts, who owns a furniture factory in the city. He wants to buy some hardwood, but he wants to pick through it for boards with a good grain pattern. That hasn't come up before, so I thought I'd better check with you on it."

Toby shook hands with Roberts, a small, wiry man of about forty. "I'm Toby Holt, and I'm pleased to meet you," he said. "If you want to select boards, how does an additional thirty percent of the set price sound?"

Roberts hesitated; then he smiled. "Maybe I shouldn't say this, Mr. Holt, but that's about seventy percent below what the mills in Wisconsin ask. I'm always happy to get materials at the best price I can, but I also like to have a fair bargain all the way around."

"You're not saying anything I don't already know," Toby chuckled. "I know what the mills in Wisconsin charge. I also like a fair bargain all around, and I'm making a profit at the price I quoted."

"Then you've just got yourself a steady customer," Roberts said. "From now on, I won't buy a stick of wood from the mills in Wisconsin. I'll go get busy and pick out my lumber."

"I hope you find what you want," Toby said. "If you ever receive less than full satisfaction, just let me know."

The foreman smiled as Roberts walked away. "There's another happy customer, and I must say that we rarely have any other kind," he commented. "We're down to our last three pine logs in the breakwater, but the launch is supposed to bring pine on its next two or three trips from the logging camp. It should be here about noon, shouldn't it?"

Toby thought for a moment, recalling the schedule that he had discussed with Albert Crowell, the captain and owner of the steam launch. "Yes—or before then if the lake is fairly calm. By the way, Jim, I intend to go to the camp on the launch day after tomorrow, and I'll stay there for a week or so. I'll get together with you either this afternoon or tomorrow to talk about the yard schedule and the work that we have on hand."

The foreman nodded and walked away toward the saw house as Toby went into the office building. It was still a short time before the beginning of the workday, but the office manager was at his desk early, as usual. A tall, thin man of forty named Harold Phinney, he had a pedantic, formal manner and always wore a dark suit and a high, stiff collar. He looked up from his desk and murmured a greeting as Toby went through the outer office and into his own office.

On his desk was a cumulative listing of the month's receipts and expenses, which he looked at each morning and compared with those of the previous months. Ever since the company had begun operating, the monthly receipts had grown rapidly, and the reason for the instant success was reflected in what Carl Roberts had said. The company was putting lumber on the market at prices that were substantially lower than those charged by the mills in Wisconsin.

At the same time, Toby reflected, the profits had hardly begun to earn back the large initial outlay for livestock, equipment, and supplies at the lumberyard and the logging camp in Wisconsin. However, all of the start-up problems had been resolved, and the company was operating smoothly. If the profits continued growing, the initial investment would be paid off within a year or less.

While Toby was studying the listing, the rest of the staff arrived in the outer office and the workday began. A rhythmic clacking sound from the outer office also began, one to which Toby had become accustomed. It was from a machine called a typewriter, and it sounded the death knell of difficulties in communication caused by poor handwriting.

The office errand boy was the last to arrive, since he had to stop by the post office to pick up the daily mail. This morning he was accompanied by a Western Union delivery boy. Harold Phinney signed for the telegram and quickly sorted through the mail, then stepped into Toby's office.

"We have several orders and inquiries about prices this morning, Mr. Holt," he said. "I'll bring them in as soon as they're entered in the log. This personal letter for you was also in the mail, and this telegram just arrived."

The letter was from Toby's daughter, Janessa. He put it down and ripped open the telegram. It was from Marjorie White, stating that she would like to visit the logging camp in Wisconsin the following week, if it would be convenient.

"Send a reply to this, Harold, and tell her that she will be more than welcome," Toby directed. "Also, send a telegram to Ted Taylor, in care of the attorney general's office in Des Moines. Tell him that Marjorie White intends to come here for a visit next week."

Phinney took the telegram and left, and Toby sat back in his chair and opened the letter from Janessa. In his desk drawer was a large stack of letters he had received from her.

In the past, when he had exchanged letters, even with loved ones, the principal purpose had been to communicate information. And although Janessa's letters contained bits of information that his ranch foreman in Oregon, Stalking Horse, had asked her to pass on, for the most part they were simply a reaching out of a girl who had found a father.

The letters had started arriving in the wake of a time of wrenching anxiety for him, after he had rushed home to Oregon because of Timmy's injuries. When it had become apparent that the boy would fully recover, and Toby had returned to Chicago, Janessa had begun writing almost daily. The letters had hardly let up since.

Long and chatty, they related what his sister, Cindy, was doing from day to day, and reported with watchful thoroughness on Timmy's latest activities. There were occasional references to his mother, Eulalia, and to his stepfather, Major General Leland Blake, who commanded the Army of the West from his headquarters at Fort Vancouver, across the river from Portland. But in sum total, the letters were an expression of affection. Toby answered them whenever he could.

Toby smiled reflectively as he read, prouder of his daughter than words could express. Just the other day he had received a letter from Cindy, telling him in glowing terms of Janessa's bravery in foiling a bank robbery in Portland. Janessa's own version of the incident was much more restrained. Toby's smile faded, however, as he turned a page and read a paragraph about his sister.

Cindy apparently was concerned that the letters from the young man to whom she was engaged, First Lieutenant Henry Blake, were becoming infrequent and seemed more impersonal. In his last letter, he had mentioned that he would be going to England in the near future. Cindy had remarked—and Janessa had expressed emphatic agreement in an underlined sentence punctuated by exclamation points—that if Henry had leisure time to visit England, he could come to the United States and visit her.

Henry Blake, the adopted son of Toby's mother and stepfather, had been engaged to Cindy for more than two years. Their marriage had been deferred after his graduation from West Point, because he had been sent to Europe as a military observer with the German Army encircling Paris. There he had somehow learned in advance when Paris would surrender, an achievement that had resulted in his immediate promotion to first lieutenant.

After Paris surrendered, it had appeared that he would return to the United States to marry Cindy. Instead, however, he had been stationed in Germany, and their wedding had been postponed again. At present, Henry was at an armaments factory, reportedly studying the procurement methods of the German Army.

Rereading the paragraph, Toby shook his head, disagreeing with what it implied. His sister and Henry Blake had known each other for years, and he had never seen a couple more in love. Henry, he reflected, was undoubtedly going to England for some official purpose.

The young lieutenant's letters to Cindy might have become infrequent, but that could only be because of the pressures of his work. Nothing, Toby believed, could ever change the fact that Cindy was the only woman in Henry Blake's life.

Both of Toby Holt's conclusions were wrong. When First Lieutenant Henry Blake arrived at Victoria Station in London on a late night train from Dover, he was on a leave of absence—not on duty—and his traveling companion was the Baroness Gisela von Kirchberg, with whom he had been living during the past year.

The vast platform, illuminated by ornate gaslight fixtures, was almost deserted at the late hour. Henry glanced around as he helped Gisela down the step, her senior business manager and a clerk following. As Henry had expected, he saw Commander Stephen Wyndham walking toward them with long, quick strides.

The two officers had become friends when they had met in France the year before, and they exchanged salutes and greeted each other warmly. Stephen, tall and debonair in his Royal Navy uniform, smiled happily as they shook hands. "I'm delighted that you're visiting England at last, Henry," he said, "even though it apparently won't be a very long stay."

"Regrettably, it won't," Henry replied. "But I'm pleased I had the opportunity to come at all. It was very good of you to meet us at this late hour."

The commander shrugged off the comment. He was the military attaché at the British embassy in Berlin, and he had met Gisela several times when she and Henry had visited the capital. Turning to her and bowing as she offered her hand, he said in German, "It is a pleasure to see you again, Gisela. I trust the journey was not too tiring?"

Gisela, strikingly beautiful in a blue traveling cape and a matching hat, was drawing glances from the handful of other passengers who had stepped off the train. Sedately poised, always in control of the situation around her, she smiled serenely. "No, it was a pleasant journey, Stefan. I trust your wife is well?"

"Yes, she is," Stephen replied. "Unfortunately, I came to London on very short notice, so she remained behind in Berlin. I took the liberty of stopping at Dandridge House earlier this evening to make certain that your apartments are ready. Your business agents are waiting there now."

"That was very thoughtful of you," Gisela said. She turned and introduced the men who had accompanied her and Henry from Germany, and Stephen exchanged greetings with them, then beckoned to two porters who were waiting nearby.

"I have a friend who has expressed interest in meeting you, Henry," Stephen said as they walked to the immense, lofty waiting room. "He's Lord Randolph Churchill, one of the Duke of Marlborough's sons. I saw him at lunch the day I received your telegram, and when I told him about you, he asked me to invite you and Gisela to a reception he's hosting at his town house Saturday."

Stephen was speaking in German for Gisela's benefit, and as Henry glanced at her, she squeezed his arm and nodded. "We should not think only of work while we're here, and I'm sure we would enjoy it, Heinrich."

Henry hesitated. Although he was not on duty, he did have some unofficial business he had been asked to look into. But it was unlikely that the reception would interfere with it.

"Very well," he said. "We appreciate the invitation, and we're pleased to accept, Stephen. But what could you possibly tell Lord Randolph that would make him want to meet me?"

"That you're an American, for one," Stephen replied. "He's fond of Americans. He's much enamored of a young lady in New York named Jennie Jerome, and I believe he intends to ask her to marry him."

Outside, carriages for hire were parked in a row along the street, and one moved forward when Stephen beckoned. Henry helped Gisela into the carriage, and then he and Stephen stood at the curb and talked as they waited for the porters to load the baggage.

"I was summoned here to discuss the work that the Germans are doing with submersible craft," Stephen said quietly. "There have been reports that they've developed a very effective torpedo that can be fired underwater—a subject that is of great interest to the Admiralty."

"Yes, I've heard about it," Henry replied. "I talked with Admiral Lutchens at a reception in Berlin, and he mentioned it. He said that an ironclad hulk was sunk off Bremerhaven with two of the torpedoes, and he believed that it might have taken as many as twenty rounds from twelve-inch guns to sink that hulk."

Stephen smiled wryly. "Henry, I do envy the access you have to social events in Berlin. If I had half your opportunities, I would be of twice the value to my government. What sort of business affairs bring Gisela to England?"

"Her agents here have been working on establishing a holding company through which she plans to invest in shipbuilding, woolen mills, and other factories. They've had difficulty getting the company licensed, and she decided to come here and discuss it with them. The agents have also been gathering information on country homes that are for sale here."

"Indeed? Is she considering moving here?"

Henry laughed and shook his head. "No, and I have no idea why she's suddenly become interested in investing in factories here."

"Whatever her reasons, we can be sure they're good

ones," Stephen commented. "Gisela certainly didn't become one of the wealthiest women in Europe by accident."

The baggage was loaded, and they set off. Wisps of fog drifting off the Thames made halos around passing streetlamps as Henry peered out the window, awed by the magnificence of London's buildings. As the carriage approached Dandridge House, only a short distance away, the street brightened. The apartment hotel catered to visiting diplomats, peers attending sessions of Parliament, and other well-off clients, and its portico was as bright as day under the gaslights.

As the carriage stopped in front of the building, the doorman summoned porters. Henry and the others went in and were quickly escorted across the wide lobby and along a corridor to the apartments that Gisela's London agents had reserved. The agents, three members of a prominent law firm in the city, were waiting in the spacious, luxuriously furnished sitting room. James Hollingsworth, a dapper, white-haired man of fifty, was a senior partner in the firm, and the other two were law clerks. Hollingsworth spoke fluent German, and he greeted Henry, Gisela, and her employees.

"You're undoubtedly weary after your long journey, Madam Baroness," Hollingsworth continued, "so we will await your convenience to discuss the affairs you've entrusted to us. However, I would like to mention that the country home in which you expressed particular interest is available at what we consider a reasonable price. Also, we are still having difficulties in licensing a holding company, but we are hopeful about resolving them."

Gisela nodded, and when she indicated that she was ready to discuss business immediately and began asking questions, Henry slipped out with Stephen, to accompany him to the front door.

"It's too bad she's having trouble with the holding company," Stephen said. "The Gladstone government might simply be reluctant to have British industries under foreign control, but I'd hazard a guess that it's somewhat more complicated . . . bureaucratic infighting and all that."

Henry nodded absently, his thoughts again turning to what he had been asked to do in secret while on leave in England. Although he and Stephen were friends, and although they often shared information on matters of interest to their respective governments, Henry had been ordered to talk with no one about what he was to do. Still, he needed some information that Stephen could probably supply him with.

Outside, while a carriage moved up to the curb, Henry decided to depend on his friend's discretion. "The military college at Sandhurst is your equivalent to West Point, isn't it?" he asked.

"More or less," Stephen replied. "Why do you ask? Are you thinking of visiting there?"

"I'd like to," Henry said. "I might not have the opportunity again, and Friday afternoon is probably a good time to do it. If I take an early train, do you think I could get there and back in time to attend Lord Randolph's reception?"

"Yes, I'm sure you could," Stephen replied. "I just happen to know that the commandant there is a Brigadier Halloway. He's a friendly chap, and I'm sure he'd make you welcome."

"I'll go on Friday, then," Henry said. He hesitated a moment, his next question more revealing. "Do any foreign officers attend the training at Sandhurst?"

Stephen shrugged. "I'm a Royal Navy College man myself, of course, and I don't know all that much about Sandhurst. But you'll find out for yourself on Friday, won't you?"

Henry smiled and made his farewells with Stephen. The naval officer stepped into the carriage, and Henry went back inside. Crossing the wide, quiet lobby, he reflected that he knew very little himself about what he was supposed to be doing, and he knew nothing at all about the reasons behind it.

Shortly before he and Gisela had left Germany, the military attaché from the American embassy in Berlin had visited him. That in itself had been unusual, but the attaché's request had been even more unusual: Henry had simply been asked to visit Sandhurst and find out if a Spanish officer was in attendance there. If one happened to be, Henry was to find out all he could about the man without drawing attention to himself.

Above all, the attaché had emphasized, Henry was to exercise the utmost discretion. Thinking about that, Henry smiled to himself. It was just like the army to tell him next to nothing, then ask him to be discreet about it.

III

The nationality of the officer he was supposed to find out about was what first drew Henry's attention to the three men sitting a few seats in front of him in the railroad car.

In contrast to the other passengers, the three men had dark hair and olive skin, and all were wearing suits of a Continental rather than a British cut. His curiosity piqued, Henry studied them more closely. One was a man of about forty, with a scar on his left cheek, and the other two were somewhat younger. While it was clear they were traveling together, the three men sat in utter silence, simply waiting for the journey to end.

At Aldershot, the station nearest to the village of Sandhurst, the three men filed off the train. They disappeared among the other passengers on the platform, and Henry dismissed them from his mind as he went to the line of carriages for hire.

A few miles along the road from Aldershot, the carriage passed through the village of Sandhurst and stopped at the entrance to the military college. A cadet was on guard duty at the entrance, and he pointed out the headquarters building to Henry.

At the headquarters, Henry was immediately shown into the commandant's office. Brigadier Halloway, as Stephen had said, was an amiable man. Portly and immaculately neat in his uniform, he was about fifty-five years old, with a ruddy complexion and snow-white hair and mustache. "So you thought you'd come and have a look around, did you?" he commented affably. "Well, I'm delighted that you did, Lieutenant Blake. And you're on furlough, you say? Did you come all the way from America to England on furlough?"

"No, sir. I'm stationed in Germany."

The brigadier sat back in his chair behind his desk, his blue eyes reflecting interest. "Indeed? At the American embassy?"

"No, sir. I'm a military observer posted to the Mauser factory in Frankfurt to study the procurement methods of the German Army."

"My word!" the brigadier exclaimed in amusement. "Now, there's choice duty that I would certainly enjoy. Or at least I would have when I was your age—I don't know if this old body could endure the rigors of such duty now." He chuckled. "Well, as I said, I'm most pleased that you came to have a look around. But you won't be able to see much on Friday afternoon, because we close down for the student officers to prepare for parade on Saturday."

"The same practice is followed at West Point, sir. But I thought I might look around at the facilities, if it wouldn't be any trouble."

"No, it'll be no trouble at all," the brigadier said quickly, standing up and walking toward the office door. "No trouble whatsoever, Lieutenant Blake. I'll assign a cadet to show you around."

Following the man to the door, Henry dismissed any thought of questioning him about foreign officers at the college. While Brigadier Halloway was heartily friendly, his blue eyes gleamed with keen intelligence. It would be safer, Henry decided, to question his escort.

The escort turned out to be a youth of seventeen, a cadet named Harrison. Rigidly military, he saluted smartly and led Henry outside.

They passed through a quadrangle, the cadet pointing

out the various buildings and telling Henry about them. After touring several classrooms, they went into a large building where huge tables were used to conduct war games, then crossed a yard to a barnlike structure where dismantled cannons were on display for instruction in artillery.

Although he was only going through the motions of looking around, Henry enjoyed the tour. In atmosphere and appearance, the college was much like West Point, and it reminded him of his cadet days. As Harrison took him from one building to another, they occasionally passed other cadets, who looked at Henry curiously as they saluted.

That gave Henry the conversational opening he needed. "You must not have any foreign officers here," he commented.

"No, sir," Harrison replied. "We have an occasional visitor who is a foreign officer, and foreign officers sometimes come here for war games. But we don't have any among the students." He hesitated, then shrugged. "I should say with the exception of Captain Ferdinand, I suppose."

"Captain Ferdinand?"

"Yes, sir. He wears a line army uniform, but he isn't an ordinary sort of officer, and he's Spanish. He attends classes with us, but he's excused from all duties and drills. He's undoubtedly at the firing range now."

"Does he spend a lot of time there?"

"Yes, sir. He has a great fondness for small arms, and he's constantly at the range when it isn't in use. He's always there on Fridays."

"A man after my own heart," Henry said. "I just happen to like small arms, too. Do you think I can have a look at the firing range?"

"Certainly, sir." The cadet led the way toward the drill field, which was set back from the buildings. At the far end of the field, the rifle range came into view. A section of a long hill had been cut away into sheer bluff to make a safety backstop for a line of twenty firing positions. The captain was at a position in the center of the line.

As he and Harrison drew nearer, Henry saw that the captain was firing an Enfield rifle, the standard British infantry weapon. After discharging several rounds, the captain put the gun on a table and walked down the firing range to change the targets on the wooden frame. Walking back, he studied the patterns of holes on the targets he had removed from the frame.

He seemed to be a very small, slender man. As he drew closer, Henry realized with some surprise that Captain Ferdinand was a mere boy—certainly no more than sixteen years old. He was handsome, though, with dark hair and eyes, and he carried himself with an air of authority that belied his youth. Henry thought that the captain insignia on his British uniform did not look entirely out of place on him.

Henry waited by the firing table, where the Enfield lay beside a stack of targets, Webley and Colt pistols, binoculars, and an ammunition box. The young captain, suddenly realizing he was being observed, looked at Henry's uniform with boyish curiosity. As he approached and they exchanged salutes, he smiled. "You're an American, aren't you?" he said with a cultured Spanish accent.

"Yes, that's right. I'm Lieutenant Blake."

"I'm Captain Ferdinand. Why are you here?"

Henry smiled at the unabashedly blunt question. "I'm on furlough and had an opportunity to see Sandhurst, so I decided to visit. How is your marksmanship?"

Smiling, Ferdinand handed Henry the targets. "What do you think?"

Henry shuffled the targets and glanced at them. The youth was a far better marksman than the average soldier, but it was easy to distinguish between the targets that he had fired at from a prone, kneeling, and standing position. "You're very good, Captain Ferdinand," he said.

"Are you better?" Ferdinand asked.

Henry smiled and shrugged. "You asked me to judge

your marksmanship, so it's only fair that you should judge
mine, isn't it?"

"Indeed it is," Ferdinand agreed. "There is the rifle,
and there is the ammunition, Lieutenant Blake."

Henry took off his cap and tunic and put them on the
table, then picked up the Enfield. After making certain
that the weapon was unloaded, he tested the trigger pull.
It was crisp and clean, with no slack. He took bullets out
of the ammunition box and loaded the rifle.

Watching with interest, Harrison sat down beside the
adjacent firing position. Ferdinand picked up the binoculars and focused on the targets. Shouldering the weapon,
Henry sighted down the range. Relaxing, he let the bead
at the end of the barrel swing back and forth across the
bull's-eye from the natural movement of his body.

Then he began firing rapidly. Squeezing his entire
hand together to pull the trigger back, he fired as the bead
crossed the bull's-eye. As the rifle recoiled, he worked the
bolt quickly to reload. When he had finished, he had no
need to use the binoculars. He knew that the holes were
grouped tightly in the center of the bull's-eye.

Ferdinand lowered the binoculars and gaped at Henry
in astonishment. "A perfect round!" he exclaimed. "They're
all bull's-eyes!"

"All bull's-eyes?" Harrison said in surprise.

"Yes, all of them," Ferdinand replied. "How did you
learn to fire a rifle like that?"

"Through practice," Henry replied. "During my lifetime I've probably put a ton of lead into the air. You're an
excellent shot yourself, and you'll eventually be able to
shoot like that. But we may be able to improve your
marksmanship a bit now. Let's see how you hold the
rifle."

The youth took the rifle, shouldered it, and sighted
on a target. As Henry had anticipated, he was using the
standard infantry stance; yet his muscles were more those
of a boy than of a man. "In an army, everyone is taught to
shoot the same way," Henry said. "There are good reasons

for that, but everyone isn't the same. Bring your left elbow in closer to your chest so you can support the weight of the rifle easier."

The end of the barrel immediately stopped weaving as the youth slid his hand back along the stock of the rifle, his elbow near his chest. Nodding in satisfaction, Henry took bullets out of the ammunition box and handed them to Ferdinand. As the youth began firing, Henry observed that he had already mastered most of the essentials, with good breath control and a gentle, steady pressure on the trigger. A quick look through the binoculars determined that the holes in the target were grouped better than before.

Exuberant, Ferdinand reloaded the rifle and began firing again. Harrison, as pleased and excited as the young Spaniard, took the binoculars and called out where the bullets were striking the target. Henry began helping Ferdinand adjust his posture in the kneeling position so he could hold the heavy rifle with less effort.

After the better part of an hour, Henry had finished coaching Ferdinand in the standing, kneeling, and prone positions with the rifle, and the youth's marksmanship had improved substantially in each position. As Harrison went down the range to exchange the rifle targets on the wooden frame for the larger pistol targets, Henry inspected the Colt and Webley pistols on the table.

At the same time, he pursued a chance comment Ferdinand had made about a large collection of weapons he had at his house. "So you don't live in the barracks?" Henry asked.

"No, I have a house in the village," the youth replied. "When we're finished here, could you go there with me? I would like to show you my . . ." His voice fading, he hesitated a moment; then he shrugged. "I have a houseguest, but an American visitor shouldn't put him out. I would like to show you my collection of weapons."

The offer was more than Henry could hope for. The reference to a houseguest puzzled him, but so did every-

thing about the youth. He could only assume that Ferdinand was some scion of the nobility in Spain, which was in
an upheaval of civil war over the succession to the crown.
Queen Victoria was noted for giving refuge to European
nobility in difficulties.

Glancing at his watch, Henry nodded. "Yes, I have a
few hours," he said.

"Good, I'm sure you'll enjoy seeing my collection,"
Ferdinand replied happily. "Shall we practice with the
pistols now?"

Ferdinand was also accustomed to firing a pistol from
the standard military position, standing sideways to the
target and holding the weapon at arm's length in his right
hand. Henry had him use the Webley, which was lighter
than the Colt, and hold it in both hands as he faced the
target squarely.

The youth took aim in the new stance, and Henry
picked up the binoculars to see where the bullets struck.
As he focused down the range, however, a movement
behind the target frames to the left caught his eye. At first
he thought it might be an animal, but when he turned the
binoculars, he stiffened in shock and disbelief.

A man was lying behind the target frames, aiming a
rifle at Henry and the two youths.

Reacting immediately, Henry lunged, shoving Ferdinand with his shoulder, and reached out to push Harrison
aside, shouting at them to get down. Ferdinand staggered
sideways, pulling the trigger on the revolver. Its loud
crack blended with the distant report of a rifle. An impact
like a heavy hammer blow struck the point of Henry's
shoulder, which was where Ferdinand's heart had been an
instant before Henry shoved the youth.

As the three of them fell to the ground, the table
tumbled over, targets, ammunition, and weapons spilling
off it, along with Henry's cap and coat. The numb feeling
in Henry's left shoulder began fading into a sharp, stinging
pain, blood soaking his shirt sleeve. The two youths, frightened but not panic-stricken, lay flat on each side of Henry

as rifle shots rang out rapidly and bullets struck the ground around them. Clearly there was more than one person shooting at them.

Ferdinand looked at Henry. "You're wounded, Lieutenant Blake!" he said in alarm.

"It's only a flesh wound," Henry said, taking out his handkerchief. "Tie this around it, if you would. But stay down."

As the young Spaniard took the handkerchief and tied it over the wound, Henry glanced around and analyzed the situation. The firing range was completely level, so he and the two youths were in an exposed position, unable to move. The holes that the rifle bullets had made through the overturned table dramatically illustrated that it was useless as protection. Henry detected two clouds of gun smoke at the far end of the range, which meant at least two men armed with rifles.

Keeping low to the ground, Henry reached out for the weapons that had fallen off the table. He pushed the Colt and a box of ammunition toward Harrison, then began loading the Enfield. Ferdinand finished tying the handkerchief around Henry's shoulder and reached for the Webley.

"Who could that be?" Harrison exclaimed, loading the Colt. "Why would someone try to shoot us?"

"For the moment," Henry said, "that isn't important. I think there are two of them, and they're behind the target frames to our left. Captain Ferdinand, I want you and Cadet Harrison to give me covering fire while I return the fire."

Ferdinand nodded, cocking the Webley. As Harrison finished loading the Colt, Henry lifted his head to take a quick look at the gun smoke and make certain the man he had seen had not moved. He had not, and as both rifles immediately fired, Henry ducked back down, the bullets hissing past only inches above his head. The two men were expert marksmen, with fast reactions. Henry worked the bolt on the Enfield to load the chamber.

"Both of those men know how to shoot," he said to Ferdinand and Harrison, "so keep your heads down. Just give me covering fire, and don't lift your heads to aim. Are you ready? Commence firing."

The two youths began firing rapidly and blindly toward the end of the range. The two riflemen stopped firing, the hail of bullets flying in their direction taking them by surprise. Henry lifted his head and shouldered the Enfield in one smooth motion.

As his sights lined up on the man who was partially exposed, he squeezed the trigger. Through the haze of gunpowder smoke, he saw the man lurch up to a sitting position and fall back.

The other man, completely concealed behind a target frame, fired his rifle. The bullet clipped hairs from Henry's head as he ducked back down. The two pistols empty, Ferdinand and Harrison began reloading.

The rifle fired again, knocking splinters from the overturned table. Ferdinand grinned as he pushed bullets into the Webley. "There's only one rifle firing now," he said in satisfaction. "You must have hit one of them, Lieutenant Blake."

"Yes, I did," Henry replied. "But we're not out of the woods yet. That other fellow's an expert rifleman, and he picked a better place to hide. I can't see him at all."

The rifle fired again, the bullet striking directly in front of Harrison and knocking dirt into his face. The youth brushed the dirt from his eyes and continued reloading the Colt. Henry waited for a lull in the rifle fire, but there was none. The man was replacing each spent bullet as he worked the bolt on his rifle, a tactic used by the most expert riflemen to keep a full magazine.

Reloading the Enfield, Henry reflected that the bullet holes in the overturned table illustrated a way to shoot at the man, whether or not he could be seen. When the youths had their pistols reloaded, Henry told them to begin firing. As they did so, gunpowder smoke boiling up, Henry lifted his head and aimed his rifle toward the lower part of the target frame where the man was lying in concealment.

The paper target rippled slightly as the Enfield fired, and Henry worked the bolt quickly. The bullet missed the man, but his head and shoulders came into view as he scrambled for a safer position. Henry squeezed the trigger again.

The bullet knocked the man onto his back, and he dropped his rifle. As Henry swiftly worked the bolt to reload, the man rolled onto his stomach and picked up his rifle again. Then, across a distance of some one hundred yards, Henry and the man aimed at each other.

Henry pulled his trigger an instant sooner than the other man. The Enfield recoiled, and the bullet slammed through the man's chest. His rifle fired harmlessly into the air as he rolled onto his back.

After a few seconds, Henry stood up and told Harrison to go get the brigadier. The cadet raced away while Henry and Ferdinand crossed the rifle range to the two bodies. They were two of the three men Henry had noticed on the train, and the rifles beside them were new Mausers. When he asked Ferdinand if he knew who they were, the youth shrugged.

"I couldn't say, Lieutenant Blake," he replied quietly.

The reply was an evasion to avoid an outright lie, Henry realized, because he could see that Ferdinand knew far more than he was saying. Leaning over, Henry began to search the bodies and found that the pockets were empty, as he had expected. Obviously the men had been sent on a risky mission where identification could be embarrassing to their employers.

The incident deepened Henry's perplexity about the youth, but it was obvious that Captain Ferdinand, whoever he was, had some very determined enemies. Two expert riflemen, equipped with the best weapons available, had been sent to kill him. Knowing that he was always on the rifle range on Friday, a place where their gunfire would pass unnoticed, they had expected to find him alone.

A few minutes later, Harrison returned with the brigadier and another, slightly younger man, who was in civilian clothes. Distinctly Spanish in appearance, the younger man was dark-haired, heavyset, and walked with an unmistakable military bearing. As the three approached, Ferdinand told Henry that the other man was the houseguest he had mentioned, a Mr. Moncaldo.

The name seemed remotely familiar to Henry, but he was unable to place it. In any case, he had no time to think about it as he saluted Brigadier Halloway, whose former hearty friendliness was now replaced by a brisk, businesslike manner. The man touched his quarterstaff to his cap to return Henry's and Ferdinand's salutes, his keen eyes taking in the scene. Then he dismissed Cadet Harrison and introduced Moncaldo to Henry. The brigadier nodded toward the blood-soaked handkerchief tied around Henry's upper arm. "I see that you were wounded, Lieutenant," he said.

"It's only a flesh wound, sir," Henry said.

"Even so, our doctor had better have a look at it. Harrison told us what happened, and my gratitude for what you did exceeds my ability to properly express it. I will have to place myself further in your debt, however, by asking for your total discretion in this matter."

"I'm obliged to report the incident to the military attaché at the American embassy upon my return to Germany, sir. But other than that, I can give you my assurance I will mention it to no one."

The brigadier pursed his lips and stroked his mustache. It was not the answer he wanted, but he nodded. "Very well, Lieutenant," he said. "If you will do that, I'll be grateful. That will amount to considerable restraint on your part, considering that your life was placed in peril and you had to kill two men here."

"I'm more than willing to cooperate in any way I can, sir. It may be of benefit for you to know that these two men were on the train that brought me from London. They were accompanied by a third man who was a few years older and somewhat taller than either of them. He had a scar on the left side of his face."

The brigadier looked at Moncaldo, who spoke in a quiet, assured voice: "That was Emilio Garcia," he said. "He is a Carlist agent."

Immediately after he spoke, the Spaniard looked regretful that he had made the comment in Henry's presence, as did the brigadier. Halloway nodded briskly. "Thank you for the information, Lieutenant," he said. "You'd best have the doctor look at that wound now. Captain Ferdinand, perhaps you'd like to show Lieutenant Blake to the hospital. I'll summon some of the staff and attend to things here."

After exchanging salutes with Halloway, Henry and Ferdinand walked away. They retrieved Henry's cap and tunic, then followed the path toward the headquarters quadrangle, discussing the incident as they went. Henry's thoughts, however, were no longer on the shooting, but on another matter entirely.

Moncaldo's remark had been vastly revealing: The Carlists were one of the factions involved in the civil war in Spain. Suddenly everything was becoming clear to Henry, including the identity of Moncaldo and of Ferdinand himself.

For obvious reasons, all European nations took a keen interest in who ascended to the throne when a European monarch died or was deposed. One of the main causes of the recent war between Germany and France had been a dispute over who would rule Spain, ever since the former monarch, Queen Isabella II, had lost control over the country a few years before.

All the European governments would have continued to support Isabella, but through petty intrigues she had alienated even her own army. If a direct successor to the queen could be found and the support of the army secured, the matter might be resolved to the satisfaction of all European governments.

Apparently Great Britain was quietly attempting to do just that. Queen Isabella had a teenage son named Alphonse Ferdinand. Rafael Vincente Moncaldo was a senior general in the Spanish Army. Other European governments might be aware of what was being done, but only at the very highest levels. No doubt the entire matter was being kept secret until the moment arrived to act swiftly and decisively.

Through some means, however, Washington had heard rumors and had taken action to try to confirm them. Henry saw no point in beating around the bush. "Isn't Queen Isabella your mother?" he asked Ferdinand.

The youth, who had been smiling, looked at him in abject disappointment. "I didn't think you would know," he said sadly. "I hoped we could be friends."

"Of course we can be friends," Henry said. "Why can't we? I have nothing to do with the affairs of Spain."

Ferdinand thought for a moment, then nodded. "Yes, that's true. But how did you know who I was?"

"Through Mr. Moncaldo's slip of the tongue about the Carlists. And I've heard of General Moncaldo. The rest followed from that."

"The general is usually more careful about what he says," Ferdinand commented. He looked at Henry wistfully. "I do hope you will be my friend. I don't have very many friends here. Will you be able to visit me?"

Henry shook his head regretfully. "My duties keep me in Germany. Could you come there?"

"No, I can't leave England," Ferdinand replied dejectedly. "At least not at present." He sighed, shrugging. "But we can write to each other for now, can't we? And perhaps we can visit at a later time."

"That's true," Henry agreed. "I'll look forward to that." He smiled. "Maybe we can have some target practice again. I'll have to get used to addressing you more respectfully, though."

"No, absolutely not," Ferdinand replied firmly. "Whatever happens, I want always to be Captain Ferdinand to you. That must never change. Americans are republicans, so that shouldn't make you feel ill at ease."

The already regal bearing that the youth displayed was evident to Henry, with Ferdinand's handsome, almost delicately featured face and large brown eyes reflecting warm regard. Henry liked the youth, but he also felt a twinge of pity for him. The boy had been born into opulence beyond what most people could even imagine, but his life was more rigidly restricted than that of someone raised in poverty.

"Very well, Captain Ferdinand," Henry said, smiling.

As they resumed talking, Henry reflected that his visit to Sandhurst had been infinitely more eventful than he had expected. In addition to being involved in a gun battle, he had befriended a youth who was destined to become a European monarch. And he had obtained a wealth of information that would more than fulfill the most optimistic expectations in Washington.

Upon his return to London, Henry explained his wound to Gisela as the result of an accident on the firing range at Sandhurst. More alarmed over the fact that he was hurt than over how it had happened, Gisela wanted to send for other doctors to examine his shoulder. Henry insisted that was not necessary.

He barely had time to prepare for the reception at Lord Randolph Churchill's town house, and he regretted having accepted the invitation. His shoulder had begun to throb painfully since he had left Sandhurst, and he would have preferred to remain in his room and rest. However, he knew Gisela wanted to go to the reception, and she would not go if he stayed at the hotel.

Some thirty people were already there when Henry and Gisela arrived with Stephen Wyndham. It was a small group for the large drawing room, which was furnished expensively but with emphasis on utility and durability rather than the current style.

A dozen musicians in an alcove provided soft back-

ground music to the laughter and conversation of the
guests, most of whom were gathered around a buffet at
one side of the room. A few uniforms were scattered
among the bright gowns worn by the women, but most of
the men were businessmen or politicians.

Lord Randolph Henry Spencer Churchill, a well-built
man of medium stature, was about Henry's age. His blue
eyes and strong, handsome face revealed keen intelligence
and a forceful personality, as well as a ready sense of
humor. Henry liked him from the moment they were
introduced.

One of the guests, an elderly insurance factor by the
name of Sir Joseph Lowry, immediately claimed Gisela's
attention, and Henry began talking to a group of military
officers and their wives. After a while Churchill rejoined
him and offered him a drink as they stepped over to the
buffet. "The punch is quite good," he said. "We also have
hock and liquors."

"I'd like a glass of hock, please."

"I'll have the same, then," Churchill said, glancing at
the waiter on the other side of the buffet and pointing to
the hock, a white German wine. "I'm not fond of strong
drink, particularly when I have interesting company."

The waiter poured glasses of wine and handed them
to Churchill and Henry as they continued talking. At the
other end of the buffet, Lowry had momentarily lost Gisela to other guests who were introducing themselves and
talking to her.

In a green silk gown that was distinctly Continental in
style, and with her long, gleaming black hair arranged on
top of her head, she was captivatingly lovely. The high
collar of her dress matched the modest Victorian styles
worn by the other women, but a diamond-shaped opening
in the bodice revealed her cleavage.

Charming and witty, she chatted with the other guests
in French, as completely at ease in the London drawing
room as she was at the Reichstag receptions in Berlin. In

both places, her exceptional beauty and the magnetic quality of her personality set her apart from others.

Churchill sipped his wine, looking at Gisela and those around her. "Sir Edward arrived here early," he said. "He told me he had heard that the baroness was coming this evening and that he's long wanted to meet her—in order to discuss business, I presume. I hope I haven't offended her by allowing someone to infringe upon her leisure time."

"No, I'm sure not," Henry replied, laughing. "Her business affairs occupy her constantly, and she wouldn't enjoy leisure time away from them."

Returning his gaze to Henry, Churchill said, "I must admit I was intrigued by what Stephen told me about you and the baroness. If I may be blunt, you're not at all what one would expect of a young man and a wealthy older woman."

Henry took a sip of his wine. "I presume you mean I'm a soldier, not a gigolo."

"That's plain to see," Churchill said good-humoredly. "It's also plain to see that the baroness would have no use for gigolos or flatterers. Stephen tells me that you met her through her nephew."

Henry nodded, then told Churchill about his friend and Gisela's nephew, Captain Richard Koehler, whom he had met the previous year while stationed as a military observer with the German armies surrounding Paris. Encouraged by his host's questions, Henry told the story of how he had met Gisela, which delighted Churchill, who was similarly candid as he talked about the young woman in New York whom he loved deeply, Jennie Jerome. He added that his parents viewed the match with disapproval—a fact that was known only within the family and to close friends.

"That makes it very difficult," Henry commented.

"Indeed it does," Churchill said with a deep sigh. "What does your family think of the baroness?"

"They don't know about her," Henry replied. "I'm

adopted, and I'm engaged to be married to my stepmother's daughter."

"My word!" Churchill exclaimed. "The problems I have are absolutely dwarfed by yours, old chap. I do hope things work out for you. Let's have another glass of hock and sit on a couch to talk. I'm pleased that you accepted my invitation to come here tonight."

Gisela had finished chatting with the other guests, and she and Lowry were sitting on a couch, talking quietly. Churchill and Henry sat down on a couch facing theirs and resumed their conversation. They moved from one subject to another, and time passed swiftly for Henry. Churchill was an observant, well-traveled man, with a seemingly inexhaustible store of amusing anecdotes; he was also extremely intelligent, and Henry found the conversation fascinating.

Eventually Churchill was drawn away by some other guests, and Stephen Wyndham joined Henry and Gisela. Lowry had left for a few minutes to send a message summoning one of his clerks, and by the time the man arrived with a folder of papers, the remainder of the other guests and the musicians had left, and the gathering had turned into a private party.

Gisela scrutinized the papers through her pince-nez and talked quietly with Lowry, while Henry, Stephen, and Churchill continued their conversation. At one point, Henry asked Gisela how she felt. During the past few months, she had suffered occasional attacks of stomach pain and nausea, and he was concerned that she might become too tired. But she looked at him over her pince-nez and smiled as she reassured him.

The conversation among the men turned to country homes, Churchill talking about the one his family owned. Henry mentioned that Gisela was contemplating buying a place called Fenton Hall, and Churchill frowned in concern. "I know it well, Henry, and she should think twice about that. It hasn't been occupied for a generation or more, and it must be in an awful state—" He stopped in midsentence as he saw his butler leading a man across the wide drawing room. "Good evening, Sir Charles," he said, standing up, a note of surprise in his voice.

Of medium height and thin, the newcomer had a pale, sharp face and eyes that were light, icy blue. He was unsmiling and perfunctory as he apologized for intruding. "I'm sorry for interrupting you and your guests at such a late hour, Lord Randolph," he said.

"You're welcome here at any time," Churchill replied courteously. "You've met Commander Wyndham and Sir Edward Lowry, haven't you? This is Lieutenant Henry Blake, and this is the Baroness Gisela von Kirchberg. Henry, Gisela, this is Sir Charles Willoughby of the Foreign Office."

Willoughby bowed as Henry and Gisela greeted him. "I had intended to meet with you at your apartment, Lieutenant Blake," he said. "When the hour grew late, I decided to come here. If I could have a moment of your time, I should like to speak with you in the entrance hall."

Silence fell as Henry nodded and stepped around the couch to accompany Willoughby. Churchill and Wyndham looked puzzled. Gisela frowned in concern, insecure about her relationship with Henry and always worried that something would come between them. He smiled back at her reassuringly.

As he followed the man across the room, Henry wondered if Willoughby was an official of the Foreign Office in name only. It seemed likely that he was a member of the British secret intelligence service, a shadowy organization about which there was little public knowledge.

In the entrance hall, Willoughby glanced around to make certain they were alone, then turned to Henry. "I have talked to Brigadier Halloway and General Moncaldo," he said, "who informed me of the substance of your conversations with Captain Ferdinand. When you make your report to the military attaché in Berlin, you may inform him that complete details of the matter are being communicated to Washington by the Foreign Office."

Before Henry could reply, Willoughby went on: "With regard to your arrangement to correspond with Captain Ferdinand, however, I regret to say that it is out of the question. Security requirements simply won't permit it."

"I regret it as well," Henry said. "The boy seems very lonely."

"He is, but his personal safety is involved, and perhaps such a correspondence will be possible in the future. Needless to say, my colleagues and I are very grateful for what you did at Sandhurst, and we would be more than pleased to render any service to you that we can."

"I did only what I thought best under the circumstances," Henry replied. "I'm glad I could help the young man, and I don't expect a reward."

"All the same," Willoughby insisted, "we would like to demonstrate our gratitude in some small way. I believe your friend, the Baroness Kirchberg, is having difficulty securing a license for a holding company. You may inform her that the license will be granted by Monday."

Henry hesitated, surprised. Then he grinned. "I appreciate that very much, and so will the baroness. You are well informed, aren't you?"

"Having met you," Willoughby said dryly, "I believe I am far more well informed than before. When my colleagues and I were told that a visitor at Sandhurst had come into possession of the full details concerning Captain Ferdinand, it appeared to us that we had a loose cannon aboard. Now I believe that cannon was very firmly fixed, but we were simply unaware of the direction in which it pointed."

"I'm not sure I understand your meaning."

"Last year," Willoughby said, "Washington took actions prior to the surrender of Paris that indicated a very lucky guess as to when it would happen. Now I believe that it wasn't a guess at all, because I recall there was a certain Lieutenant Blake among the American military observers with the German armies. You have a talent for being in the right place at the right time, it seems, and

perhaps your presence at Sandhurst today wasn't as fortu-
itous as it appeared. I see that I shall have to keep my eye
on you, young Henry Blake. Perhaps we shall meet again."

"I'll look forward to it," Henry said. "And I hope it
will be as amicable as this time."

"I do as well," Willoughby replied, revealing a hint of
a smile as he turned and walked toward the door.

IV

Able to read only a little English, Gisela for some reason still enjoyed looking through the sheaf of papers that was the company charter. The pages rustled as she turned them, the carriage bumping along the rutted road. Glancing at her, Henry smiled. His smile faded, however, as he thought about the unanswered questions surrounding the purpose of their trip to England.

During the weeks before they had left Germany, she had been evasive each time he had broached the subject. She had always been more than willing to discuss her business affairs with him—even though some of them were so complex that he had difficulty understanding her explanations—but her reluctance to talk about the apparent urgency of this trip aroused his suspicions that it might be a part of some maneuver to make him stay with her.

The previous year, he had said that he would remain with her for one year. The months were passing, the time drawing to a close. His assignment at the Mauser Arms Works in Frankfurt was not finished, but that would not prevent him from returning on leave to the United States and marrying Cindy Holt, the woman he loved. That would fulfill a dream he had cherished for years, and it would end the confusion of having two women in his life.

It would also end his feeling of duplicity, but it would not be easy. The previous year, he had known he was deferring a break that seemed impossible at the time. Even if Gisela did nothing to make him stay, he wondered how he could ever pull himself away from her. The strange, indefinable bond that held him was not love, but it was as powerful and enduring as the most ardent love.

Gisela folded the papers and put them into the bulging briefcase on the seat beside her. "I'm pleased that you allowed me to use your name for the company, Heinrich," she said. "Yours is better than mine for the name of an English company. Also, it is appropriate for the company to be called Blake Enterprises, because you persuaded that man Willoughby to assist me."

"If you're pleased, then I am," Henry said. "How did your conversations with Sir Edward Lowry turn out?"

"They were promising," Gisela replied. "He is an underwriter at Lloyd's, you know, and I will probably form a financial partnership with him. But the company charter was the most important thing."

"No, your health is most important. How do you feel?"

Her large blue eyes sparkling suggestively, Gisela put her warm, soft hand on his. "When we get there, I'll show you how I feel, loved one. We're almost there, aren't we?"

"Yes. Perhaps, when we have time this week, you could see an English doctor. The doctors here are very good, and they might—"

"The doctors in Germany are equally good," Gisela interrupted, dismissing the subject of her illness, as she always did. She took his hand and held it on her lap as she pointed to the window. "There is the village. We must be very close now."

Henry looked out the window. It was a dark, windy day, and the carriage windows were flecked with rain. The landscape, near the western coast of England at the Bristol Channel, was rugged and austere. Solitary trees were twisted and gnarled by the force of the offshore winds that had scoured the earth away from expanses of black, rocky ridges.

Sheep pastures lay on the windward sides of the hills, crop fields on the leeward. The village, clustered in a shallow valley, consisted of a score of wattle-and-daub cottages with thatched roofs. As the carriage rumbled along the narrow main street, people looked out of doorways and windows in curiosity.

On the other side of the village, the road passed through a dark, thick woods. As the trees opened out, the road curved left and led up a rise overlooking the woods and the village. At the crest of the rise was Fenton Hall. It was an enormous stone structure, its outbuildings like foothills around the mountainous main building, from which a square tower rose at one side.

The caretaker's cottage, where they would be staying, was adjacent to the lower courtyard, and Henry could see smoke rising from its chimney. A youth who was sitting under a tree and watching the road leaped up and ran toward the cottage, shouting. A tall, thin man came out of the cottage as two more youths stepped out of a shed. Standing in a row, the four of them took off their caps as the carriage drew up.

The thin man opened the door for Henry, who stepped out and helped Gisela down. "I'm Silas Wilkerson, sir," he said. "I was hired to prepare the cottage for you."

"I'm Lieutenant Blake, and this is the Baroness von Kirchberg." As Henry exchanged a few pleasantries with Wilkerson, the youths scrambled for the baggage, which the driver handed down to them. Gisela walked a few paces toward the house. It loomed over the cottage like a stone cliff, the dark, scudding clouds almost brushing the spires and angles of its slate roof. Narrowing her eyes against the wind, she stared up at it with something approaching awe.

Wilkerson, who looked to be about forty, smiled, clearly pleased. "She likes it, doesn't she, sir?" he commented.

"It would appear so," Henry agreed.

"I hope she likes it," Wilkerson said, "as does everyone in the village. We would all like to see Fenton open again, because the village would be a much happier place."

"If the baroness buys it, her visits here will be infrequent."

"Yes, of course, sir," Wilkerson replied. "It's often that way with country homes. But simply to have it open again is the important thing, with the windows lighted up and all. It's the village manor, sir. Its being closed makes the village very dreary now, particularly at Christmas and such."

He turned to shout directions to the youths, telling them to be careful with the bags. The driver resumed his seat, then called down to Henry, "I'm to come back Friday morning, sir?"

"Yes, as early as possible," Henry replied. "We would like to reach Bristol in time to take the evening train back to London."

The driver tipped his hat and gathered up the reins. The horses turned, and the carriage rumbled back along the road. Scattered drops of rain began falling.

"Let's go inside," Henry said to Gisela. "It's late, and we've had a long journey. We can see the house tomorrow."

She smiled at him and took his arm. "I'm looking forward to seeing every part of it."

The youths, who had already carried the baggage inside, listened to the exchange in German with intense curiosity, grinning at each other. Wilkerson glared at them, then turned and led Henry and Gisela inside.

The cottage was small but spotlessly clean and cozy. Fires blazed in the bedroom, front room, and kitchen fireplaces. The bathroom had a coal-fired water heater that was fed by a spring on the hill. The cupboards were stocked with food, and a small pork roast was sizzling on a spit in the kitchen fireplace.

Gisela began opening the bags as Henry went back outside with Wilkerson. The man looked up at the huge house, again commenting wistfully that he hoped Gisela liked it.

"I had one of my daughters put on the dinner to cook," he said. "If you wish, I'll have her come up and cook all the meals."

"No, thank you. The baroness planned to cook."

"As you wish, sir. A storm is on the way, and it'll make landfall tonight. But this cottage and Fenton have weathered storms for generations, so there's no cause for worry. If you need anything, I live in the third cottage on the left as you enter the village."

"Very well. Thank you for all your help."

"It was my pleasure, sir, a pleasure and an honor."

The man tipped his cap, then walked away. The rain was pattering down more heavily, and the dark woods were a mass of movement as the trees tossed in the wind. Henry looked up at the house, wondering what had attracted Gisela to it. Then he went back into the cottage.

The bathroom was fragrant with the cologne that Gisela had put in the bath she had drawn. After they had both bathed and changed, they sat sipping coffee in the kitchen, where a delicious scent rose from the pork roasting on the spit. Potatoes were baking in the fire, and Gisela had put up a pot of peas seasoned with drippings from the pork.

Darkness fell and the rain became heavy while they were eating, the stormy night outside making the cottage even cozier. After lingering over glasses of sweet, heady port, they went to bed, Gisela as always eager for variety in lovemaking. As the storm raged outside, the bed that had provided country folk with rest from their labors was the stage for her uninhibited quest to fulfill the range of urges that her inventive mind created. Perfumed and alluring in the glow from the fireplace, she plunged them into a frenzy that left both of them emotionally and physically spent.

The next morning, the last of the storm had passed. A few fleecy clouds floated in the sky, the sun beaming down on the landscape that had been washed to a verdant green by the rain. The chattering of birds came through the kitchen windows with the fresh breeze as Gisela toasted muffins over the fire and fried eggs and slices of the pork.

After breakfast, they crossed the wide, sloped courtyard to the huge house. From the upper yard, the village came into view. Villagers who were watching the house called to each other and pointed at Henry and Gisela.

The lock was rusty, and it took Henry several minutes to work it open with the long iron key. Finally unlatched, the tall, heavy door groaned ponderously as he pushed against it. As he and Gisela stepped inside, she gasped in delight, putting her hands to her face. The entry hall was immense, its vast stone walls braced with towering piers that soared upward four stories to support a side-lighted dome. Sunshine spilled down through the dome onto the broad staircase that rose to the mezzanine floor. To Henry, the entire effect was one of grace and solidity.

The owner and the architect of generations before who had collaborated on this building had reached back to Anglo-Saxon roots for its design. Instead of being used as a surface for decoration, the masonry walls had been left simple and plain. Everything had been built to look and be ageless, enduring.

As they began looking through the ground-floor rooms, Gisela commented on the surprisingly good condition of the house. Birds that had gained access through a broken window chattered in a side stairwell, but otherwise it was evident that the villagers had jealously guarded the manor. The thick dust of decades lay on the canvas covers over the solid, heavy furniture. Everything had remained untouched.

Long, heavy drapes for the towering windows were stored in wooden boxes, and thick carpets were rolled and wrapped in old sail canvas. The tall bookshelves in the library were filled with thick tomes bound in leather. In the vast kitchen, the pans on the walls and the pewter placed in neat rows on shelves had tarnished through the years.

Their footsteps stirred echoes as Henry and Gisela

returned to the entry hall and climbed the wide staircase to the second floor. The master bedchamber was at the end of one of the hallways. The huge bed had a headboard that reached up toward the lofty ceiling, and the long dressers, chests, and couches were bulky forms under their canvas covers. French doors opened onto a small balcony.

Gisela dragged the canvas cover off the bed and sat down on the edge of it, bouncing. "The mattress is comfortable," she said, smiling.

"Then that makes the house complete, doesn't it?" Henry laughed.

Gisela was serious as she glanced around the room. "I intend to buy the house, Heinrich," she said quietly.

Henry nodded, then unlatched the french doors and opened them. Their rusty hinges squeaked, and the fresh breeze rushed into the room. He stepped out onto the balcony. There was a panoramic view of the countryside and the village, with an inlet of Bristol Channel in the distance.

Gazing out over the rolling hills, he thought about Gisela's decision. While he could understand her attraction to this particular house, why she wanted a residence in England remained an unanswered question. It seemed at least possible that she intended to use the prospect of vacations in England as an inducement to keep him from leaving.

She spoke his name, and he turned. She was standing just inside the doorway, naked. With her long, black hair tumbling over her shoulders, contrasting with the alabaster whiteness of her perfect body, she was a vision of beauty. His need for her, part of the indefinable, compelling force that held him to her, was never fully satisfied. As he looked at her, desire exploded to life within him.

She went to the bed and lay on it as he followed her back to the room. He undressed, tossing his clothes onto the couch where she had put hers, then lay down beside her and took her in his arms. Impatiently eager for him, she pulled him over her and, her lips against his, gasped softly as she guided him to her. Then, instead of the leisurely lovemaking of other times, it was a swift rush. Their bodies moved urgently, hungrily seeking fulfillment, until Gisela's soft cries echoed through the bedchamber.

Minutes later, she was asleep. Breathing the scent of her perfume and holding her, Henry looked out the french doors at the clouds in the sky. He should have been content, but contentment had become rare for him as the time drew closer for him to leave Gisela and return to the United States to marry Cindy Holt. That time was now four months away.

Sitting on the deck of the steam launch as it moved through the low waves toward the Wisconsin shoreline, Toby Holt leafed through a letter from Cindy that had arrived in the morning mail at the lumberyard. Most of the news in it concerned the affairs of the horse ranch, but there was a paragraph at the end about Henry Blake.

Toby had read the paragraph several times because it troubled him. Although Cindy expressed anticipation for when Henry would return—in about four months—there was no mention of letters from him, which was unusual. Janessa's last letter to Toby had observed that Henry had not been writing as often as he should. But there was no hint in Cindy's letter of any cloud over the relationship.

Dismissing the subject from his mind, Toby folded the letter and put it in his pocket. Captain Albert Crowell, a portly man of about fifty and the owner of the launch, was sitting in his chair at the helm in the small wheelhouse. The deckhand, a gangling youth named Turner, lounged beside the wheelhouse door and whittled on a piece of wood. The engineer, Jimson, sat near the stern of the wide, stubby craft. An unshaven, wiry man of sixty, he was chewing tobacco and spitting over the rail.

Toby stood up and stepped to the wheelhouse. "We're almost there, aren't we, Albert?" he asked.

"Yes, the camp should be in sight in a few minutes,"

the captain agreed. "We may as well get ready." He turned and called through the doorway. "Jimson, get on down to the engine room. Turner, check the winch and secure the cable clevises on the tow cleats."

Jimson, a skilled engineer who had worked on the launch for years, was outspoken in questioning the captain's orders. He paused as he lifted the hatch cover to the engine room. "Why are you putting them clevises on now, Captain?" he called back. "It'll be sunset directly. Are we going to tow at night again?"

"Yes, we are, Jimson," the captain replied patiently. "I hope that doesn't interfere with any plans you have."

"It might, because I was counting on eating breakfast tomorrow," Jimson said. "But if you run into a log or something in the dark and sink us all, I'll drown. Then I won't eat no breakfast, will I?"

The captain drew in a deep breath and released it in a sigh. "Jimson, I've been towing at night on this lake with this launch for years, and I haven't sunk it yet. You know that as well as I do."

"Yes, I do, Captain. I also know that every boat sitting on the bottom of this lake wasn't sunk until it did sink."

The captain reached for the engine-room telegraph and pulled the lever back from standard speed to slow ahead, the signal clanging. Jimson scrambled down the ladder into the engine room to change the engine setting, the hatch slamming closed behind him. Toby chuckled, turning his attention to the shoreline ahead.

Each time he approached the logging camp, Toby was reminded of the first time he had come to this spot in the launch. The powerful updrafts of the fire in Chicago had carried burning embers far north and ignited the forest around here for miles. Toby had arrived just in time to save his friends and partners in the logging business, along with a number of other people.

Even from a distance, the scars from the fires were still visible. But the forest was beginning to heal itself, and

Wisconsin remained a place of breathtaking beauty and promise. Its cities were small; Milwaukee, the largest, was less than a third the size of Chicago. In the southwest of the state were vast prairies that were being turned into wheat fields, and lush grass that fed huge dairy herds. The northern two-thirds of the state, as well as wide belts along the lake, were covered with forest. A place of wondrous natural beauty, Wisconsin had immense potential.

As the launch drew closer to shore, Toby could make out buildings at the logging camp, which was located in a clearing at the top of a steep bluff. A chute for logs reached down to a new timber breakwater and a catch basin like the one at the lumberyard in Chicago. At one side of the breakwater was a pier. As the launch slowed, turning toward the pier, a huge log slid down the chute. It knifed into the water, caroming into other logs floating in the basin.

The waves stirred by the log made the launch bob as it edged up to the pier. Captain Crowell pulled the engine lever back to stop, and Turner jumped onto the pier with a rope to secure the launch. As the captain stood up from his chair, Toby stepped into the wheelhouse to get his traveling bag.

"Thanks for the ride up, Albert," he said.

"It was my pleasure," the captain replied. "When do you think you'll be returning to Chicago?"

"In about a week or so," Toby said. "I'll be here at the camp at least part of the time, so I'll see you before then and let you know when I'll need a ride back."

Toby jumped onto the pier, exchanged a farewell nod with Turner, then quickly strode to the foot of the pier and started up the steep path to the logging camp. Two lumberjacks were coming down the path to help the crew of the launch hook up a tow of logs, and they touched their caps and smiled as Toby passed them.

At the top of the bluff, virtually all traces of the fire were gone, the burned trees having been cleared away and the buildings replaced. Set back at one side of the large, open yard were the dormitory and dining hall for the lumberjacks. At a distance from them were the stables and corrals for the oxen used to drag the massive logs through the forest to the camp.

Across the clearing from the dormitory was the tidy, spacious log house where Frank Woods lived with his wife, Bettina, and her daughter, Lucy. Four small cabins for visitors stood to one side of the house, and on the other side was the assembly shed and office where the men gathered to receive their work assignments.

A cool breeze off the lake was keeping the sunny day from becoming too warm, and the air was sweet with the scent of the nearby forest. Flowers that Bettina had planted around her house added bright splashes of color. It was a pleasant, rustic scene, and it always gave Toby a deep sense of contentment, especially after the bustle of Chicago.

Frank Woods emerged from the open doorway of the office, and he smiled and waved to Toby. Huge and muscular, with a guarded friendliness, he was the perfect man to superintend a logging camp and control rowdy lumberjacks. "Bettina!" he shouted toward the house in his booming voice. "Toby's here!"

Bettina, a tall, shapely woman in her early thirties, looked out the back door of the house. Wiping her hands on her apron, she smiled and came outside to greet Toby. Lucy, a small, quiet girl of eleven, followed her out.

Toby's friendship with the Woods family dated back many years. But the previous October the bonds between them had been cemented more firmly than ever when Toby had arrived with the steam launch moments before they would have suffered a fiery death. The memory of that day was always in their eyes when they greeted him, even after a separation of only a few days.

His hand still tingling from Frank's crushing grip, Toby shook hands with Bettina and smiled as Lucy curtsied shyly and insisted on taking his bag. "Are you hungry, Toby?" Bettina asked. "If you are, I have stew in the warming oven."

"No, I had a big breakfast at my boardinghouse, then a sandwich on the launch, Bettina," he replied. "I'll be fine until dinner."

"Very well, if you're certain," Bettina said. "Lucy will put your bag in your cabin, and I'll make something special for dinner."

The women left, and Toby and Frank walked toward the assembly shed. "I'm always glad to see you for the sake of seeing you, Toby," Frank commented dryly, "but I also get better meals when you're here." He held the door open as they went into the small, spartan office at one end of the shed. "Did you have a good trip up the lake?"

"Yes, it was very smooth today," Toby said, "and we made good time."

"I think Captain Crowell will be able to make his trips somewhat faster now, because he won't have any delay on this end. We've learned how many of what size logs he can tow, so we're connecting a dozen or so together with a cable and having them ready when he gets here."

"Yes, he mentioned that and said it would save him a lot of time. Incidentally," Toby added as he seated himself on a rough wooden chair beside Frank's desk, "you'll have one and possibly two visitors here within the next few days. Marjorie White, that photographist who was in Chicago during the fire, will be coming for a week or two. And Ted Taylor may be with her."

"I'll make them welcome," Frank said. He sat down at his desk and turned to the map on the wall behind him. It showed all the property—tens of thousands of acres—on which the company owned logging rights for the next ten years. The areas that had been damaged by fire were drawn in on the map. For the most part, the trees in those areas had been killed but not destroyed, so they were being logged first, before the timber began rotting. Ironically, the fires had actually increased the value of the timber, because seasoned wood was being brought out.

Other lines on the map indicated where logging roads

had been cut through the forest to connect the camp with the burned areas, and Frank pointed to where recent progress had been made. "We're working in this area right now," he said. "Would you like to look at it tomorrow?"

"No, I can't tomorrow," Toby replied. "I've been putting off going to see the governor because things kept cropping up, but I intend to go to Madison tomorrow. We're in business in Wisconsin, which gives us a civic responsibility to the state, and I want to make certain the governor knows I'm aware of that. Besides, I'd just like to meet the man. When I get back, though, I'll go take a look."

"Very well. Anyway, right now I'm concentrating mostly on clearing roads to the burned areas. I'm not making progress as rapidly as I'd like, because I need a few more men."

"Yes, that's a problem that won't go away," Toby mused. "Lumberjacks are just as independent here as they are out in Washington. If one of them gets wind of a friend who's working at another camp, he'll quit and go there. And two or three more might follow him. Are we keeping the ones we have?"

Frank nodded. "I know how to deal with them, Toby. We're spending more for food than most camps, and I'm giving them rations of tobacco. Also, I'm hiring through Fred Guthrie."

"He's the fellow who owns the tavern in Colmer, isn't he?"

"Yes, that's right. He's been in this area for years, and he knows most of the lumberjacks. By hiring through him, I avoid getting slackers and troublemakers. I rode over to Colmer a few days ago and told him that I needed another five or six men."

"When does he think he'll find them for you?"

"It won't be long," Frank replied, then broke into a grin. "It might be a few days, though. When I last talked to him, he was having trouble keeping his thoughts organized. He had something more important on his mind."

"What was that?"

"A woman," Frank said. "What else?"

Fred Guthrie held out his hand as the woman he loved, Ursula Oberg, passed a large bowl of carrots down the table to him. "This certainly is good food," he said. "Much better than you can get anywhere in town."

"Sure and that's the truth and all," Paddy Rafferty put in. He was sitting across the table from Fred. "Mrs. Oberg is a fine cook, as is my Colleen here. When you put the two of them together, they can't be beat."

Smiling in agreement, Fred spooned carrots onto his plate. He liked Paddy, as well as the Irishman's pretty wife and their three redheaded children sitting along the other side of the table. But then he liked almost everything having to do with the tall, buxom Ursula, who was sitting at the end of the table. He was uncertain how she felt about him, but her attitude seemed promising.

The setting for the noon meal was also exceptionally pleasant. A large man, Fred felt confined in most houses. But Paddy had put up partitions inside the barn that his family and the Obergs were using as a home, dividing it into huge rooms. The ten-foot-high walls, together with the substantial furnishings Ursula had brought with her from Germany, gave the impression of an enormous dining hall. Fred had to glance up at the rafters overhead to remind himself that he was in a barn.

The only subdued person in the gathering was Maida Oberg. To Fred's mind, she was an attractive young woman but exceedingly strange, totally unlike her mother. Ursula was tall, sturdy, and fair-haired, but Maida was small and dark. In disposition the young woman was also completely different from Ursula, as well as from anyone else Fred had ever met.

While the others were talking and enjoying the delicious food, Maida sat silent and preoccupied, eating her own specially prepared meal. It looked unappetizing to Fred—a salad with no dressing, stewed vegetables, and meat without gravy. Her eyes blank, she was completely detached from her surroundings. She was either that way, or she was in a tumult. She was rarely in a mood between the two.

After helping himself to more carrots, Fred made another attempt to show goodwill, by holding out the bowl to Maida. She stopped chewing, her eyes focusing on him in a fixed stare of disbelief, as though he was doing the most senseless thing she had ever seen.

"The carrots are seasoned, Fred," Ursula said. "Maida doesn't eat seasonings. They would dull her sense of taste, and she must have a very precise sense of taste in order to make beer."

Paddy chuckled. "She doesn't eat seasonings, but I do. I'll have another spoonful of carrots, Fred."

Fred passed the bowl across to Paddy, concluding that Ursula was trying to be courteous and excuse Maida's rude behavior. The idea that seasonings could damage anyone's sense of taste seemed absurd to him. Even if they could, he failed to see what a sense of taste had to do with making beer. Brewing was a mechanical process, nothing more.

Then another thought occurred to him. Bottles. When Ursula had first mentioned that Maida intended to make beer, he had naturally assumed that it was going to be some kind of home brew. Even then it had been obvious that Ursula was completely devoted to her daughter, so to be accommodating he had told her that he would sell it in his tavern.

His trip to the barn today had been to deliver bottles that Ursula had ordered in Milwaukee and which had arrived at a warehouse in Colmer. They were a special type, with a ceramic stopper held in place by a wire frame, and there were several cases of them. In his preoccupation with Ursula, he had failed to connect the bottles with Maida's beer-making. Wondering just how much home brew Maida intended to mix up, Fred began feeling uncomfortable.

Paddy finished spooning carrots onto his plate and

passed the bowl to his wife. "Fred," he said, gesturing with his fork, "you've made a friend for life by telling me to see Mrs. Oberg about this job here. Sure and it's like a dream come true for me."

"I thought it would be a job that would suit you," Fred said. "I also thought it would be a good place for your family."

"Aye, that it is," Paddy agreed. "The place we had in Chicago before the fire wasn't good for the children, and the one in Milwaukee wasn't much better. But this is like paradise for them. Mrs. Oberg has bought a cow and chickens, so they have ample milk and eggs. The pigs are fattening, we have a good garden, and on the whole we're living like kings."

"I am very grateful that you accepted the job, Paddy," Ursula said. "You can do any sort of work, and you work very hard."

"Sure and I believe in earning my wages," Paddy replied. "And I'll have a go at whatever needs to be done. But if I get very far from working with wood, I'm never certain of what the results will be."

"You did an excellent job in bricking up bases for Maida's coppers," Ursula said.

"Aye, well, setting some bricks together isn't so much," Paddy offered modestly. "I'm always pleased to do what I can, Mrs. Oberg."

Taking a bite of food, Fred thought with growing edginess about the huge copper kettles the drivers had carried into the barn on the day he had come to help unload the drays. "What does Maida do with those coppers?" he asked.

"They are for cooking mash to make beer," Ursula replied.

It was the answer he had been afraid he would hear. Now he remembered how Maida had hovered around the coppers anxiously while they had been carried into the barn. Taking another bite of food, he wondered how he

was going to fulfill his promise to sell the beer that Maida
made.

He glanced at Maida. She was eating a piece of to-
mato, wincing and blinking her eyes over the taste of it.
The canned tomatoes tasted delicious to Fred. He smoth-
ered a sigh, reflecting on how odd it was that Ursula, who
seemed perfect in every respect, could have a daughter
like Maida.

On the day that the drays had been unloaded, Maida
had been in a frenzy instead of half asleep, as she was
now. In addition to being worried over the coppers, Fred
now recalled, she had guarded several leather cases as if
her life depended on their safety. They had apparently
contained something breakable.

Wanting no one else even to touch them, Maida had
carried them into the barn herself, one by one. When
Ursula had moved one of them so that a barrel of china
could be carried out of the dray, Maida had become
furious. Ursula had remained serenely good-natured, hardly
seeming to notice her daughter's temper tantrum.

The relationship between Maida and Ursula was as
puzzling to Fred as the young woman herself. At first he
had thought that Ursula was in complete control, as she
should be. But now he was beginning to suspect that it
was far more complicated. In some odd way, it seemed
that Maida was actually in control, while Ursula only
decided how to go about what her daughter wanted to do.
It was a strange, complex situation.

Paddy continued talking about his work. Then, when
coffee was served, he sat back and moved on to a subject
that made Fred feel even more uneasy. He told about a
trip his family and the Obergs had made to Milwaukee the
week before. They had done some shopping, but the real
purpose of the trip had been to bring back a large wagonload of ingredients for Maida to make beer with.

Fred listened morosely. When he had promised to
sell Maida's beer, he had been thinking in terms of a keg
of home brew fermenting behind the kitchen stove. And

he had resolved to sell whatever she made and called beer, as long as it poisoned no one. If anyone complained about it, they would find his knuckles a hard meal to digest.

However, he sold mostly whiskey and brandy. The beer he bought from Milwaukee was usually weak and flat, so few of his customers asked for it. And it appeared he had vastly underestimated the quantity of beer that Maida intended to make. All during the meal, what he had heard had forced his estimate higher and higher.

"Sure and I thought we were going to be there for another day," Paddy went on. "We took Maida to most of the suppliers in the city, but she wasn't happy with what they had. Then we finally found this small place where they had what she wanted. The owner there certainly was pleased to meet Maida. What was his name, Mrs. Oberg?"

"John Kirchner," Ursula replied. "His grandfather had met Maida's grandfather and talked about it constantly when John was a boy."

"Aye, that was it," Paddy said. He finished his coffee and stood up. "Sure and I hate to leave good food, but I've eaten all I can. And I hate to leave good company, but I've work awaiting me. I'm putting together a pair of tuns, so I'd best get back to it. It was a pleasure talking with you, Fred."

Fred hesitated, thinking for a moment about what Paddy had just said. Then he nodded as he pushed his chair back and stood up. "It was a pleasure for me as well, Paddy, and it's time I was getting on back to town."

"I'll walk out with you, Fred," Ursula said. "Colleen, I will be back in a moment to help with the dishes."

Colleen and the children had already begun clearing the table. Maida was still in her chair, paying no attention to the conversation. She was still eating, taking small bites and chewing slowly, her mind elsewhere. The others were apparently perfectly accustomed to her, letting her follow the cadence that only she could hear.

Limping on his wooden leg, Fred followed Ursula out

into the wide center aisle of the barn. He wondered about
Paddy's precise meaning when he had referred to "tuns."
A tun was a good-sized cask; but the term was also used in
referring to huge, stationary brewing vats. He earnestly
hoped that Paddy had been using it in the former sense.

As he and Ursula started down the center aisle, Fred
peeked into the doorway through which Paddy had disappeared. Then he stopped and took in the scene. His heart
sank.

With the former stall partitions removed, it was now
a single, immense room. The leather cases had apparently
contained flasks, pipettes, and other glass instruments of
various sorts, which were now in racks on benches at the
rear of the room. The four large coppers were on brick
bases along the side wall, the bases vented to the outside
and ready for fires. Paddy was moving about, assembling
two large containers out of seasoned oak boards that he
had notched so they would dovetail together.

The two wooden containers would be open vats—
brewer's tuns. Maida Oberg would be equipped to make
hundreds of gallons of beer at a time.

Walking on out of the barn with Ursula, Fred reflected that the complication of Maida and her beer was
the last thing he needed. Under perfect conditions, trying
to court Ursula would be difficult for him. No lumberjack
could match his pace with an ax, and when customers in
his tavern became too rowdy, he could throw them out
bodily two at a time. He could even seize a stubborn ox by
its horns and stop it in its tracks. But when it came to
dealing with women, any puny weakling could best him.

Outside, the early afternoon sunshine was bright, but
the day seemed gloomy to Fred as he tried to think of
some way to broach to Ursula the subject of the beer. Off
to one side of the barn, a wooden chute that Paddy had
assembled to channel water from the spring at the top of
the hill emptied into a pond. As he walked with Ursula
toward his wagon, Fred noticed bundles of staves in the

pond, the wood soaking so that it could be warped into a slight curve to make casks.

"It looks like Paddy is soaking a lot of cask staves there, Ursula," he commented. "How many casks does he intend to make?"

"About twelve, to start with," Ursula replied.

Fred sighed heavily and shook his head. "Ursula, I know that I said I would sell the beer that Maida makes, but I spoke before I knew how much she intended to make. At the most, I use a cask of beer every week or two, and sometimes I go a month on a single cask."

Ursula smiled, seemingly unconcerned. "If you can sell a cask a month, Fred, we will appreciate it."

Fred frowned, perplexed. "Ursula, those tuns in there will hold at least five hundred gallons of beer. That's as much as some of the breweries in Milwaukee can make at a time. What are you going to do with it?"

"Maida does not intend to start both tuns fermenting at the same time," Ursula replied, "so we will be drawing down two hundred and fifty gallons at a time." She lifted a hand as he started to interject a comment. "Yes, I know, Fred. That is still a large quantity of beer. But we will find markets. It may take time, but we will find markets."

As they stopped beside the wagon, Fred was relieved that he had at least cleared up any misunderstanding about his being able to sell all of the beer. But he was still worried, because it appeared that Maida had talked her mother into a scheme that was doomed to failure. "Ursula, I just don't know what you're going to do with all that beer," he said sadly. "You're out here in the woods, miles from any city. If you try to send it anywhere, it'll be flat and sour by the time it gets there."

"No, beer that is brewed properly will last in casks," Ursula replied firmly. Then she smiled and changed the subject before he could debate the point. "We have not seen you since you came to help us move in, Fred. Why have you not come to visit us?"

All thoughts of the beer suddenly disappeared from

his mind. Looking away, he cleared his throat uncomfortably and tried to think of something to say. Each day had been a torment, for he had wanted to come to see Ursula. But it had required a kind of courage he had been unable to summon, until the need to deliver the bottles had presented itself.

Ursula looked up at him, waiting for a response. Then she spoke again. "If you are not too busy, why do you not come to have dinner with us tomorrow night?"

Fred looked down at her, able to respond now that the subject had been opened. He grinned widely. "Yes, I'd like to do that, Ursula. And I certainly enjoyed lunch today."

"I am very pleased that you did, Fred, and I will look forward to seeing you tomorrow evening. Good-bye for now."

"Good-bye, Ursula," he replied.

An instant passed before she turned away. Her smile had a touch of amusement, but it was warmly affectionate, and Fred's hopes soared as he climbed into his wagon and gathered up the reins.

As the wagon moved down the lane, the day was the brightest and most cheerful he had ever seen. The colors were more vivid, the singing of the birds more melodious. An exhilarating feeling he had never before known glowed within him.

Then he thought again about the beer. It appeared likely to him that Maida had talked her mother into making home brew on an immense scale, which was certain to result in disappointment and financial ruin. He wished that he had said nothing to Ursula about how much he could sell. Then at least he could have tried to scrape together enough money to buy all of the home brew himself and pour it out somewhere.

However, he concluded, sooner or later he would have run out of money. And if he poured it out, whatever Maida Oberg cooked up in the barn would probably kill the grass, the trees, and the fish in any streams that happened to be nearby.

V

Governor Cyrus C. Washburn, a dapper, white-haired man in his early fifties, picked up a cigar box from his desk and held it out to Toby. When Toby shook his head, the governor himself took a cigar, leaned back in his chair, and struck a match. "I read all about the fire, of course, Mr. Holt," he said between puffs. "But Governor Palmer down there has a much better perspective on it. He said quite simply that Chicago owes its continued existence to the fact that you were on the scene."

"No, that's giving me too much credit," Toby objected. "There were many people involved, and I was only one."

The governor shrugged. "Jack Palmer's not one to exaggerate, and he also said that you're inclined to be modest, Mr. Holt."

Toby changed the subject. "The fires here in Wisconsin that were started by hot ashes from Chicago were certainly disastrous."

The governor frowned behind his cigar, then began talking about the loss of life and the property damage that had resulted from the fires in his state. Most of the fires had occurred in the deep forest, where there had been no means of escape for the isolated settlers and those in tiny communities.

A momentary silence fell after the governor stopped

talking. Both men were deeply affected by the recent tragedy. The governor asked Toby a few questions about his term as territorial governor of Idaho, and then they moved on to the subject of Toby's logging operation in Wisconsin.

"I'm very pleased that you've gone into business here," the governor said. "Every new venture does its part to improve the economy of the state, of course, but you're the type of individual who will be a credit to the business community. I wish you every success."

"Why, thank you, Governor," Toby replied. "We seem to be off to a good start. Of course, in return for doing business here, I'm always ready to fulfill whatever civic duty I can."

The governor's eyebrows rose as he puffed on his cigar. "I'm gratified by your attitude, Mr. Holt. I'm also pleased that your business is doing well thus far. Quite frankly, I'm a bit surprised. This doesn't seem to me to be the best of times to start a business."

"It doesn't to me, either," Toby replied. "I would have preferred a more settled time. With the stock speculation that's going on these days, and the railroads capitalized beyond what they can ever earn, the outlook isn't exactly cheery."

"Indeed," the governor agreed. "There comes a point at which the paper profits and losses in the world of finance lose track with the real world out there. It's all a house of cards that can come tumbling down at any time." He flicked an ash from his cigar. "Looking at the bright side, though, some people think the economic situation will moderate gradually."

Toby nodded, reflecting that after other times of overheated activity, the national economy had slowed at a reasonable rate. But on other occasions it had not; in 1837 and 1857 financial panics had occurred, bankrupting thousands of businesses and throwing millions of people out of work. The outcome was impossible to predict, and Toby dismissed the thought for now, bringing up the subject of lumber prices in Wisconsin.

The previous year, while he had been planning the logging operation in Wisconsin, he had learned that the price of lumber in Madison and Milwaukee was unusually high, evidently because of the hefty charges levied by all the Wisconsin lumber mills. Ordinarily, competition would lead one of the mills to lower its prices and claim more of the business, but that had never happened.

"The charges at the mills here were what led me to set up my own mill in Chicago," Toby said. "Otherwise my investment might have been limited to a logging operation. With what's being asked for lumber shipped out of Wisconsin, the farmers on the plains would be living in sod houses for years to come. They can afford my lumber, though, and I intend to keep it that way."

The governor was silent for a long moment. "You're right, of course," he said at last. "The charges at the mills are excessive, but I don't know the reason for it."

"Do you think there is collusion between the mill owners?"

"No, I don't," the governor replied. "Not actual collusion. But I do think pressure is being exerted from some source." He puffed on his cigar. "Of course the pressure might not be all that intense. It's hardly necessary to crush people in order to persuade them to charge more for what they sell."

Toby frowned. "Yes, that's true. But fair is fair. The pressure being exerted, or whatever it is, has kept those farmers on the plains in sod houses."

"And has hurt business in general," the governor added. "In addition to working a hardship on individuals, the high price of lumber has been harmful to the commercial interests of Wisconsin. However, maybe all that will change now that you're on the scene."

Toby nodded. "Once I reach full production, I'll be serving the same markets as the Wisconsin mills. And once I start taking their business, they'll have to lower their charges in order to compete with me."

"Or you may find out what is keeping their charges high," the governor suggested quietly. "You can't entirely discount the possibility that it may be some kind of threat, Toby. Such things have happened before."

"I've dealt with threats before," Toby replied calmly, taking out his watch. "That's part of life." He stood up. "It was very kind of you to see me, Governor Washburn, and I've taken up enough of your time. But I did want to meet you and to let you know that I stand ready to perform any civic duty that I'm called upon to do."

"I'm delighted that you came to see me, Mr. Holt," the governor said, standing up and walking toward the door with him. "And as far as civic duty goes, if you can bring the price of lumber from the Wisconsin mills down to a reasonable level, you will have performed a great civic service."

"Well, we'll see what happens soon enough," Toby said as they shook hands.

Outside, Toby paused on the marble steps of the capitol building and looked at his watch again. His meeting with the governor had ended at a convenient time, less than thirty minutes before the train left for Wedowee, the stop nearest the logging camp. He put his watch away and continued down the steps.

A man standing on a corner across the street was conspicuously unmoving in the bustle along the sidewalks. It occurred to Toby that it was the same man who had been on the corner before, when he had gone in for his meeting with the governor.

Then the man began walking along the street, blending into the crowd. He was too far away for Toby to see his face clearly, but he seemed an average man in every respect; there was nothing about him that set him apart. Concluding that the governor's warning about possible trouble could be making him overly suspicious, Toby dismissed the man from his mind and walked along the street toward the train station.

Clarence Quigley knew he had made a mistake as soon as Toby Holt looked in his direction. He immediately began walking along the street, mingling with the other people.

He was upset that he had allowed himself to be noticed. After all, he had vowed never to be careless again. Carelessness had caused him to be fired from the New York and the Philadelphia police departments, as well as from several small private detective agencies—fired because he had been careless enough to get caught for overzealous use of a nightstick, extorting bribes, pocketing valuable items at the scene of a crime, and various other misdemeanors. He had never been fired for incompetence, though, because he was good at what he did.

Of average size and build, he wore a suit and hat that were neither conservative nor loud, cheap nor expensive. His face had no distinctive characteristics, and he neither hurried nor loitered as he walked along the street.

At the train station, the sun was shining at an angle on the windows of the waiting room restaurant, making them opaque with glare from the tracks outside. Clarence Quigley stood at the window and looked out at Toby Holt on the platform. Accustomed to assessing the difficulties that opponents could present, he felt uneasy as he stared at the tall, lean man with the strong, chiseled features and vigilant gaze.

An incident that occurred as he watched made Clarence feel even more uneasy. Two traveling salesmen in loud checked suits were laughing and talking on the platform. Two women accompanied by several children were sitting on a nearby bench. They appeared to be embarrassed, the salesmen evidently using coarse language.

Toby Holt stepped to the salesmen and spoke quietly. One of them started to move away, but the other made a blustering reply. Then he broke off, his face turning pale as Holt spoke again, his features stony. The two salesmen then walked rapidly toward the other end of the platform, silent and mortified.

The women called to Holt and thanked him. He lifted his hat and nodded to them in reply. His bearing had no hint of bravado, no suggestion of self-satisfaction. Clarence decided that Toby Holt was a dangerous opponent.

After the train to Wedowee left, with Holt on it, Clarence bought a ticket and boarded the next train to Milwaukee. It was late afternoon when the train arrived at the main depot, near the Lake Michigan waterfront. Clarence left the depot and walked to the central business district.

He reached a block of large buildings that were occupied by a newspaper, a bank, law offices, and other businesses. After buying a newspaper from a paperboy, he walked across the street to a tall, stone office building owned by Schumann Enterprises. He passed the entrance and stopped a few yards down the sidewalk. Then he unfolded his newspaper and waited.

At five o'clock an exodus began from the buildings as the workday drew to a close. Carriages moved along the street and stopped at the curbs for businessmen, while clerks and others filed past, walking home. Clarence did not meet their eyes.

A conspicuously large and expensive carriage, drawn by spirited bays, approached and stopped in front of the main entrance. A few minutes later, Dieter Schumann, a red-haired, heavyset man in his late forties, came out. As the driver scrambled down from his box to open the carriage door, Clarence folded his newspaper and tucked it under his arm.

He walked back past the entrance of the Schumann Building, not looking at Dieter. Glancing at Clarence, Dieter Schumann told his driver that he intended to walk in the park before going home, and to come for him there in an hour. As the driver closed the door and climbed back up to his seat, Dieter followed Clarence along the street.

One of the wealthiest men in Milwaukee, Dieter Schumann retained the approach to business and to life that he had learned as a boy peddling produce out of a cart on the streets of Chicago: He always seized the best location, pushing others out of the way. And if another vendor sold for less, Dieter wrecked his cart and broke his melons.

A thick and solid man, he walked with his shoulders and chin thrust forward, his footsteps heavy and deliberate and punctuated by the tapping of his gold-tipped cane. His normal expression was a belligerent scowl. Accustomed to dominating others, he glared at those walking toward him, making them step out of his path. He had no friends, but his social life was active; few dared to omit inviting Dieter Schumann and his pretty young wife to social events.

Several blocks down the street, across a square from the courthouse, was a shady park where nurses brought the young of the wealthy to play, and where a band gave concerts on Sunday afternoons. At this hour it was mostly deserted, only a few young couples wandering through the trees in lingering farewells until they met at work the next day.

Clarence stopped at a bench facing the courthouse and sat down. A moment later, without looking at the other man, Dieter sat on the same bench, at a distance appropriate for strangers. Glancing around and making certain that no one was in hearing distance, Clarence spoke quietly. "I've just come back from Madison," he said. "He went there today and had a meeting with the governor."

Dieter shrugged impatiently, uninterested in Toby Holt's visit to the governor. "What about his logging camp?" he growled.

"It's on the lakeshore, to the southeast of Wedowee and near Colmer," Clarence replied. "A steam launch owned by a man named Crowell tows the logs to the mill in Chicago, a dozen to fifteen at a time. He makes about one trip a day."

"Did you see the mill?" Dieter asked. "More important, did you see the mill without making anyone suspicious?"

"I know my job, Mr. Schumann," Clarence said in an offended tone. "I've worked for you a good many years now, and I've done every job you sent me on, without making any mistakes. And I haven't asked any questions."

"You've also been paid well. And you're paid to follow orders. Now answer my question."

"I saw the mill. I went there as a carpenter looking into their prices. About twenty men work there, and they stay busy. They're putting out as much lumber as any two mills in Wisconsin. All of it is selling fast, because they charge well below the going price elsewhere. It's only a matter of time until they take over the whole market."

Frowning in dissatisfaction, Dieter pondered. Among his other holdings, he owned two large mills that yielded a significant portion of his income. During the past years, in dealing with competition from other mills, he had used the same tactics that he had used when he sold produce in Chicago. When another mill underpriced his mills, an anonymous warning was sent to the owner. If it was not heeded, Clarence Quigley caused accidents to happen, thus crippling the mill.

None of the other mill owners knew the source of these threats. Four years before, one mill owner had called a meeting of all owners to discuss means of acting in concert and requesting assistance from state law enforcement officials to counter the unknown force in their midst that was keeping the prices high. That night, the mill belonging to the one who had called the meeting had burned to the ground, ruining him financially. No one had called another meeting since.

The Madison and Milwaukee mills exercised a choke hold on the timber in the state, because it was not economical to ship raw timber out of the state to have it milled. Heretofore, Dieter's mills had wrung as much profit as they could from their customers. Now, however, the situation was changing; someone had found an economical way to transport timber to a mill outside the state.

The situation was changing, Dieter reflected, yet it was the same. The North Chicago Lumber Company was selling to the same customers as the mills in Wisconsin. A large, well-financed company, it would soon take over the market, as Clarence had said. In order to stay in business, the mills in Wisconsin would have to lower their prices.

Or, alternatively, the prices charged by the North Chicago Lumber Company would have to be increased. It would be more difficult and dangerous than with the other mills, Dieter mused, because the owner was Toby Holt. Thinking about what he had heard and read concerning the man, Dieter felt uneasy; Toby Holt was not an ordinary businessman. But a threat had arisen, and it had to be dealt with in the way that he had always dealt with threats.

"Meet me here at this same time tomorrow," he said quietly. "I'll give you some extra money for expenses this time."

A man was approaching along the sidewalk. Clarence waited until he passed; then he spoke. "Do you want me to send a warning?"

"Yes, but mail it from Chicago. Wait a few days to see if he heeds it. If he doesn't, take the same action as before."

"He won't," Clarence said firmly. "I got a good look at him in Madison, and I believe all they say about him is true. But I'll wait for a few days, like you say. Would you rather I concentrate on the mill, or do you think it would be better for me to go to the logging camp?"

"That's up to you; but it would probably be better to go to both. But whatever you do, you must be very cautious."

"I know that, Mr. Schumann. Like I said, I got a

good look at him in Madison. I may have to hire a couple of men this time."

"Then hire good ones, not drunks from some tavern. You'll have enough expense money to pay good men."

"All right, Mr. Schumann," Clarence said, standing up. "I'll see you tomorrow at this same time, then."

As the man walked away, Dieter Schumann remained sitting on the bench, staring into space and thinking. All of his life, he reflected, had been a battle. From his earliest memories as the son of a penniless German immigrant, his boyhood had been a battle, as had been his youth. Nothing had changed during his manhood. Now, when he was approaching his mature years, life still remained a constant battle, with obstacles and threats always rising in his path. To his mind, success seemed to come very easily to Toby Holt and men like him. For them, life was simple and pleasant, rather than the constant struggle it was for him.

His carriage stopped on the street in front of the bench where he was sitting. The driver climbed down from his box, then patiently waited for Dieter to decide to go home. Dieter still sat on the bench, the thought of home unappealing to him.

His young and beautiful wife—a tribute to his wealth in her elegant clothes and expensive jewelry—was there. His two strong, healthy sons—evidence of his virility— were there. But tonight there would be only a quiet evening at home, with no occasion to display his success in life.

Yet there was nowhere else for him to go. The next day would present more threats and obstacles for him to battle, and he had to rest and gather his strength. Feeling weary and strangely despondent, he stood up and walked to his carriage.

The North Chicago Lumber Company had changed out of recognition since the last time Ted Taylor had seen it. He asked the driver of the hired carriage to wait for him, then he walked through the wide gate and across the yard toward the office building.

When he had last been here, it had been a scene of confusion—the fence and offices being built, the steam engine being assembled, and men moving about among a jumble of equipment and materials. Now it was obviously organized and thriving, a bustle of orderly activity. The company's rapid progress gave Ted a deep sense of satisfaction, because he knew how much money and effort Toby had put into the venture.

The company office was just as organized and industrious as the lumberyard, if considerably less noisy. Clerks at desks leaned over ledgers and papers. A young woman in a bright blouse with leg-of-mutton sleeves and a starchy cotton skirt was working at a typing machine similar to one Ted had seen in the state capitol building in Des Moines.

He closed the door behind him, then nodded to the tall, thin man sitting at a desk in the center of the office. "I'm Ted Taylor," he said. "Is Toby Holt here?"

The man, meticulously neat and formal in a black suit and high, stiff collar, stood up and bowed gravely. "I'm Harold Phinney, and I'm pleased to meet you, Mr. Taylor," he said. "Mr. Holt is at the logging camp, and he will be there for three to four more days. He asked me to present his apologies if you arrived in his absence."

"Have you had any further word from Marjorie White?"

"Yes, sir," Phinney replied, picking up a telegram from his desk. "Yesterday we received this telegram, in which she states that she will arrive by train this evening. I've reserved rooms for both of you at the Palace Hotel, and I had planned to meet her train."

Ted took the telegram and read it, then handed it back to Phinney. "I'll meet the train, so there's no need for you to bother," he said.

"As you wish, sir. If you and Miss White would like to go to the logging camp tomorrow, I can arrange to have Captain Crowell notified that he will have passengers."

Ted hesitated, thinking, then shook his head. "Marjorie may want to stay here in Chicago for a day or two to photograph the rebuilding. We'd better wait and see what she wants to do."

"Very well, sir. The launch makes daily trips, so you and she will be able to go to the logging camp in Wisconsin on any day you wish."

"I'll bear that in mind," Ted said, turning back to the door. "Thank you very much for your help."

"It was my pleasure, sir."

Ted went out and returned to the hired carriage, telling the driver to take him to the hotel. They proceeded at a trot past docks and warehouses and then through Lincoln Park, until they reached the part of the city that had burned. With construction on all sides, the carriage was forced to a halt several times and moved along at a slow pace.

Some streets were being resurfaced, while others were torn up for the sewer and water pipes to be replaced. Piles of bricks, stone, and lumber for the buildings going up encroached on the streets, while huge drays were everywhere. The traffic was heavier than Ted had ever seen it, but everyone seemed to be taking the inconvenience in stride. Instead of arguing and cursing, the drivers chatted and waited patiently in place when the traffic came to a standstill.

In front of the Palace Hotel, underground pipes were being installed, with heavy boards laid across the deep ditch. Ted paid the driver and went inside, a bellboy carrying in his baggage.

His room, adjacent to Marjorie's, was on the second floor. After unpacking his bag and washing up, he shaved for the second time that day. He polished his boots and brushed his hat, then put on a clean shirt and a new suit and tie he had bought in Des Moines. At last he felt ready to meet Marjorie, but it was barely dusk, still hours before her train would arrive.

Anticipation making him uncharacteristically edgy, he left the hotel and walked along the streets as darkness fell.

Construction work continued unabated, with bonfires blazing and workers with miners' lamps on their caps. The scent of food wafted out of restaurants that had opened for business in buildings still being erected. Ted felt a gnawing emptiness in his stomach from not having eaten for hours, but he decided to wait in the event that Marjorie wanted to have dinner when she arrived.

Thinking of how long it might take him to reach the depot through the confusion on the streets, he hailed a carriage and set out early. His estimate of the travel time proved much too long, and he arrived at the station two hours before Marjorie's train was due. Only the platforms had as yet been completed, the enormous building still being constructed around them. Ted walked about, looking at the work in progress.

Finally it was nearly time for her train to arrive. He was the only one on the platform for a while; then others who were meeting the train gathered in small groups. Gazing along the tracks through the blur of lights in the rail yard, he finally saw the train approaching.

A minute later, as the engine moved slowly past him, it occurred to Ted that Marjorie's plans could have changed, or that she might have missed a connection somewhere. Then he spotted her among other people at the end of a car. It was almost like seeing her for the first time, her beauty still having a numbing impact on him.

The conductor reached up and took her equipment cases as she came down the steps. Looking around, she saw Ted. Her smile was tentative as she seemed to glance past him to see if anyone was with him. Then her smile became radiant. For an instant Ted wondered why she would be pleased that he was alone. He waved and hurried toward her.

Tall and slender, Marjorie was dressed in her usual style: a simple, durable dress made of dark, heavy fabric, with a short cape and a wide, dark hat. To Ted, it was the most becoming outfit she could have chosen.

Smiling happily, she offered him her hand, and they

almost embraced. She held back, however. As always, she smelled of chemicals, a scent that was more pleasing to Ted than the most expensive perfume. Each time he passed a photography studio, he thought of her.

She released his hand and glanced around to make sure her equipment cases were still there. Her face was so beautiful that Ted felt a bittersweet pang.

"You look like you've been out in the sun a lot, Ted," she said. "As you always do."

"And you look like you've been taking a prettiness tonic, as you always do. How are you, Marjorie?"

"I'm well," she replied, blushing slightly. "Are you on vacation from your work with the attorney general in Iowa?"

"No, I'm finished there. Toby sent me a telegram and informed me that you were on your way, and I was doing more sitting around than anything. So I came here."

There was an awkward silence for a moment, which was broken when a porter came up and loaded Marjorie's cases onto a handcart. He followed Ted and Marjorie as they walked down the platform toward the station. "Have you seen Toby?" Marjorie asked. "And has his son completely recovered?"

"I haven't seen him, because he's at the logging camp. But Timmy is fine now and has been for some time. He has a scar on his forehead, but no other ill effects."

"I'm pleased to hear that. When will Toby return?"

"Within three or four days, I understand."

Marjorie's attention seemed to wander as she gazed up at the station under construction. "I'd heard that the rebuilding was progressing rapidly, and now I can see why. How late into the night will they continue working?"

"Until it turns into dawn," Ted replied. "I've heard the work continues twenty-four hours a day, seven days a week, and it's this way all over the part of the city that burned. Do you intend to photograph it?"

"Yes, I think I'll stay here for at least a few days before I go to the logging camp."

"I can help you lug around your cases and things, then," Ted volunteered. "Toby's office manager made reservations for us at the Palace, and the restaurant there stays open late. We can have dinner."

At the lines of carriages outside, the porter gave Marjorie's bags to the driver, and Ted put her equipment cases on the floor. She started to pay the porter, but Ted had his money out first. After they got into the carriage and it was moving along the street, Marjorie thanked Ted for paying the porter; then she told him that she wanted to pay her own expenses.

"It was only a quarter," he protested.

"That isn't the point," she replied, her tone pleasant but firm. "I look forward to our spending time together, but we must have a clear understanding that I will pay my own way."

"If you insist, then," he agreed. "I'm sure you can afford it now, seeing that you are the famous M. White."

Marjorie laughed. "Yes, I'm pleased to say I can. I'm sure you're not in a state of poverty yourself, though. You're wearing a new suit that looks quite expensive."

Ted smiled in the darkness of the carriage, pleased that she had noticed. "The railroads paid a bounty on the train robbers I put out of business, in addition to what the state was paying me. I did all right, but I'm not ready to retire just yet."

When they reached the hotel, Ted waited in his room while Marjorie put her things away. After she finished, she tapped on his door, and they went back downstairs to the dining room. Only a few patrons were in the large, softly lighted room at this late hour.

While they were eating, they discussed plans for the next day. Ted described the construction sites he had seen that afternoon, suggesting several that she might want to photograph. They finished eating and remained at the table, talking.

"The way the streets are torn up now," Marjorie said,

"it's going to be difficult to get around. I certainly am grateful that you can help me, Ted."

"I'm grateful that you're allowing me to help you, Marjorie. You know how I feel about you."

Marjorie sighed wistfully. "Yes, but I'm married to my profession, Ted. We both know that, don't we?"

Ted hesitated, then shook his head. "No, I don't think you can dismiss everything that easily. Your profession is your life, and I realize it's something you wouldn't ever give up. But I wouldn't want to change that, even if I could, because it makes you who you are."

The subject had never been broached so openly between them, and Marjorie looked at him in silence, thinking. After a moment, she nodded and stood up from the table, her expression revealing no reaction to what he had said. She remained silent as they left the dining room and went back upstairs. When they said their good-nights and went into their rooms, however, Ted noted that her smile and voice were warmly affectionate.

With much to think about, Ted was unable to sleep for a time after he went to bed. When he and Marjorie had been in Chicago the previous year, circumstances had severely limited his opportunities to be with her. They had talked and eaten a few meals together, with others present, but that was all. Now he would be able to spend days alone with her.

In her room, Marjorie was weary from traveling, but she was also wakeful for a time after she went to bed. She felt deeply relieved that Toby Holt was at the logging camp, his absence having helped her to decide to remain in Chicago and photograph the rebuilding before going to the camp. But her relief was mixed with a vague sense of disappointment.

Toby's feelings toward her, she knew, were only those of a friend; he had summed it up when he had once commented that she reminded him of his daughter. But for her, he was the one man who could possibly be a force in her life equal to her profession. The intensity of her feelings made her fear them.

However, something had changed since the previous year. While she had expected her friendship toward Ted Taylor to be simply a diversion, an escape from her feelings for Toby Holt, it was something more. Away from the overshadowing presence of Toby Holt, Ted Taylor was more interesting and appealing. And, as he had said, he would never interfere with her work.

VI

The grimy, sweaty workmen and their foreman relaxed from their frozen positions as Marjorie put the cover back on the camera lens. Looking at one another, they laughed and heaved sighs of relief. Ted strolled forward. "Thanks very much for your cooperation," he said.

"We're always glad to help a lady," one of the workmen replied. "Besides that, it got us a minute's rest."

The foreman grunted. "It did, but now it's over," he said. "We're running behind schedule, so get back to work."

The men grumbled jokingly as they moved about and resumed working on what would be the front wall of a large bank building. Ted helped Marjorie as she closed the front of the camera and took the box off the tripod. He disassembled the tripod and put the sections into one of the equipment cases while Marjorie slid the camera into its padded slot in the other case.

"There's a large mercantile building under construction just down the street," he said, closing and latching the cases.

Marjorie was jotting down notes on the photograph she had just taken. "Yes, I noticed it, but I believe I have enough photographs of buildings under construction. Unless we see one that's very unusual, I'd like to forget about them for the time being and concentrate on the new grain elevators and bridges."

Ted glanced up at the sun, then took out his watch and looked at it. "It'll take us quite a while to get to those grain elevators, and it's almost time for lunch. What do you say we eat?"

"Very well, Ted," Marjorie said, looking along the street. "I haven't seen any places to eat near here. But here comes a carriage for hire, and we could ask the driver to take us to a restaurant."

Ted started to flag the carriage, then stepped back. "I think he already has a fare. I noticed one parked at the end of the street, so we could—" Suddenly he started waving. "Look who's in that carriage, Marjorie."

Marjorie turned, then exclaimed and starting waving, too. Sticking his head out the carriage window was Claude Leggett, the owner of a photography store where Marjorie had developed sets of her photographic plates the previous year, before the fire. A middle-aged man with graying hair parted in the middle, Claude had a round, ruddy face that radiated his cheerful good nature. He shouted for the driver to pull over.

The carriage stopped, and the chubby man scrambled out and greeted Ted and Marjorie exuberantly. "I've heard about what both of you have been doing," he said, shaking Marjorie's hand. "I guess everybody in the world has bought sets of your slides of the fire, Marjorie. And I read about you in the newspapers, Ted, and about the train robbers."

Ted shook the offered hand. As usual, he tried to shift the subject from himself. "And what have you been doing, Claude?"

Claude shrugged. "So much that it would take hours to tell, but all of it put together hasn't amounted to anything. But we can't stand here and talk. Have you had lunch?"

"No, we haven't," Marjorie replied. "Ted and I were just discussing where we could go."

"Your discussion is over," Claude said, urging them toward the carriage. "Come on, I know a good place not far from here."

As the carriage moved off, Claude talked about what he had been doing since the fire. Like many others in Chicago, he had lost everything, his photographic studio and all of the equipment in it destroyed. He had gone to Springfield and borrowed the money to open another studio there, then had decided to return to Chicago. He had just leased space in a new building and would be open for business in a week or so.

The carriage stopped at a restaurant, and they went in, Claude and Ted carrying the equipment cases. As the waiter took their orders, Claude finished his story. "I've been losing money every day since I've been here, of course," he said wryly. "But I've been no worse off than I was in Springfield. I was on the same street as another photographist, and we were both trying to underprice each other. But what about you two? Will you be in Chicago long?"

"I'm afraid not," Marjorie said. "Ted has been helping me photograph the rebuilding for the past two days, and we're going to a logging camp in Wisconsin within the next day or two. You'll probably have your studio set up by the time we return. If you do, I'd like to rent your darkroom to develop my plates."

"Rent?" Claude exclaimed, then shook his head firmly. "You'd better not leave Chicago without developing your plates in my darkroom, but you won't pay a dime in rent. What kind of plates are you using?"

"Those new Hill Norris gelatines. They're cured with heat, which makes them much more sensitive."

Claude nodded knowingly. "Yes, I've heard they don't need near as long an exposure, but you have to make certain you don't have even the smallest crack in your holders that will let in light, don't you?"

The conversation between the two of them became technical and meaningless to Ted, and he listened in silence as the meal was served and Marjorie ate without seeming to notice her food. An hour or so later, the three of them went back outside to the busy street.

Passengers were getting out of a hired carriage, and Claude shouted and waved his hat to attract the attention of the driver, then turned back to Ted and Marjorie. "I was on my way to see how my new studio is coming along," he said. "It's just two blocks down the street, so I'll walk and you two can have this carriage. Marjorie, the darkroom will be ready for you to use within the next few days."

Marjorie shook his hand again. "I'll be there when I return from Wisconsin. And if you have any developing to do, I'll help out. Do you remember those extra cartons of plates you gave me when I did your developing last year? I'll never forget that, Claude, because if I hadn't had them, I wouldn't have been able to do my slides of the fire."

Claude's smile faded as he released her hand, and he glanced guiltily at Ted. "I'm sorry, Ted, but I can't keep the agreement we made last year. Marjorie, Ted paid for those extra plates."

Puzzled, Marjorie glanced at Ted, then at Claude. "What do you mean?"

"Just what I said," Claude replied. "Ted paid me for the extra plates while you were in the back room, and he told me not to tell you. I'm sorry, Ted, but I couldn't keep on taking credit for that."

Ted colored slightly and glanced at Marjorie, afraid she would be offended. He knew only too well that she took pride in obtaining everything she had through her own efforts. There was no hint of resentment in her expression, however. "No harm done, Claude," he said.

"Why did you do that, Ted?" Marjorie asked.

Her tone was not accusing, and Ted put the equipment cases into the carriage before he answered. "Do you really have to ask that, Marjorie?"

She shook her head. "Well, no, but—" The sentence

remained unfinished, and she turned to Claude. "I'm certainly glad that you told me about it, Claude."

He shrugged. "I just hope there's no hard feelings."

"Of course not." Ted offered his hand, and they said good-bye.

As the carriage headed toward the new grain elevators rising on the lakeshore, Marjorie was silent for several minutes. Finally she looked at Ted and spoke. "The fact that it was through you I was able to make my slides of the fire really isn't the point," she murmured. "The point is that you did something for me without telling me about it and with no expectation that I would ever know. No one else has ever done anything like that for me, Ted."

Ted didn't know what to say, but Marjorie didn't seem to expect a reply. During the rest of the afternoon, the change in her attitude toward him was marked. Her smile was much warmer, and she appeared to enjoy his companionship more. Ted had thought that nothing could increase his pleasure over being with her, but he found that he had been wrong.

That evening, following dinner, the change in her feelings toward him was demonstrated in an even more forthright way. In the upstairs hall, after Marjorie had unlocked her door, she turned back to him and looked up expectantly. Ted was barely conscious of having moved, but suddenly they were in each other's arms and kissing.

It was a gentle, almost tentative kiss, Marjorie's arms around his neck as he held her. She stepped back, gazing at him with a unforgettable smile, then went into her room. Ted stepped on down the hall and went into his own room. After he went to bed, hours passed before he fell asleep.

Early the following evening, when Ted returned with Marjorie to the hotel, he saw Toby Holt sitting in one of the chairs at the far side of the lobby, reading a newspaper. Spotting them, Toby put down the newspaper and walked across the room with long strides.

Toby had not seen Ted for many months, and their greeting was boisterous, other people in the lobby turning to look. Then Toby turned to greet Marjorie. In the past, Ted had observed that Marjorie seemed vaguely distant toward Toby, and his impression was no different this time. Only moments before, in the carriage, she had been laughing and talking gaily. Now her smile seemed forced as Toby took her hand.

If he noticed her reserve, Toby concealed his reaction, his smile remaining relaxed and friendly. "I returned to Chicago this afternoon," he said, "but I knew it would be a waste of time looking for you two in the city. So I came here about an hour ago to wait for you. Do you intend to take more photographs tomorrow?"

"No, I'm through here," Marjorie said as Ted started to speak. "If possible, I'd like to go to the logging camp tomorrow."

"That'll be easy to arrange," Toby replied. "The launch will leave for the camp early in the morning, and it will get you there by late afternoon. I'd go with you, but I have a number of things here that I must see to first. I do want to spend some time with both of you, and I'll see if I can come to the camp within the next few days. In any event, we can have dinner together now, can't we?"

Marjorie hesitated, and for a moment Ted thought that she would refuse. But she didn't. "Yes, of course, Toby. I'll go freshen up."

"I'll carry the cases upstairs," Ted said, picking them up. "I'll be back in a moment, Toby." As he followed Marjorie upstairs, Ted puzzled over why she was so reserved with Toby, and he wondered if she had become moody toward himself as well, because suddenly she was strangely silent. But when he put her cases into her room, if anything her smile was even warmer than before as she thanked him. Feeling somewhat relieved, Ted went back downstairs to the lobby.

Fifteen minutes later, when Marjorie rejoined them and they went into the hotel dining room, Ted observed that she seemed less reserved toward Toby, but he wondered if it was only less obvious. Sensitive to her moods and her nuances of behavior, he knew that she was not acting the way she felt. He concluded that she was tired.

Over dinner, Marjorie contributed to the conversation only occasionally. Toby and Ted, however, had much to talk about, with Toby wanting to know all about Ted's work in Iowa and Ted asking about the lumber business and the camp in Wisconsin.

The conversation moved to the subject of Toby's ranch in Portland, and Ted smiled, commenting on Toby's amazingly thorough knowledge of what went on there in his absence. "You must spend a lot of money on postage, because it sounds like you exchange letters with your relatives very frequently."

"No, not all of them," Toby replied. "I exchange a few letters with Cindy and my mother, but Janessa is the one who keeps me in touch with everything that happens. She began writing almost daily to let me know how Timmy was getting along, and she didn't stop when he got well. And now I hope she never does, because I would miss her letters."

"I noticed that you and Janessa are very close," Ted said. "Is she still studying with Dr. Martin?"

"Yes, she is," Toby replied. "And I must say he is genuinely determined that she become a full-fledged doctor."

"Toby," Marjorie said, "you once remarked that I reminded you of your daughter. In what respect did you mean that?"

Toby smiled broadly. "Yes, I said that the day of the fire, didn't I? You remind me of her in that you both decide what you want to do, then you don't let anything stop you."

"That's a quality to be admired," Ted commented.

"It certainly is," Toby agreed. "I'm depending upon that quality in Janessa to get her through medical college. Another thing that you and Janessa have in common,

Marjorie, is that you are both fully absorbed in something. Your passion is photography, and hers is medicine."

"One thing about them that's different," Ted said, chuckling, "is that Marjorie doesn't smoke."

"Your daughter smokes?" Marjorie exclaimed. "How old is she?"

"Eleven," Toby replied, startled by Marjorie's reaction. "My sister Cindy, who takes care of the children, tried for a long time to get her to stop but was unsuccessful. Janessa has a mind of her own, you see."

"You don't mind if she smokes?" Marjorie asked.

"I'd rather she didn't," Toby said. "But then again, I'm not sure I'd want children who always did exactly what I thought best for them. Who would tell them what to do when I get old and die?"

Marjorie puzzled over that, falling silent again as Ted and Toby continued talking. After they had finished eating, they lingered for a long time over coffee, recalling the events of the great fire the previous October. The three of them were still talking when everyone else had left the dining room.

At last Toby took out his watch and looked at it. "I certainly hate to bring this to an end," he said, "but it's getting late, and you'll need to be at the lumberyard early tomorrow morning to go on the steam launch."

Nodding regretfully, Ted stood up and moved Marjorie's chair back as she stood up. They went back into the lobby, Ted and Toby discussing the time that the steam launch would leave.

As soon as Toby had gone, Marjorie seemed to become more relaxed. She put her arm through Ted's and talked about the logging camp in happy anticipation. They walked upstairs to her room, and Marjorie unlocked the door. As she had done the night before, she turned back to Ted and smiled up at him. He bent over her and kissed her. It started as a gentle kiss, but then it grew more passionate.

Fiery desire for her began flaring within Ted. Marjo-

rie reached behind her back and pushed the door open.
Still kissing, they stepped into the darkness of her room,
and he closed the door.

Their embrace and kisses grew abandoned. As Ted
caressed her, she sighed and moved against him, her
breasts surging with her rapid breathing. Ted began groping with the buttons at the back of her dress. She reached
back, placing a hand over his and holding it.

After a long, breathless hesitation, she released his
hand. Cupping his face between her palms, she kissed
him. Then she began unfastening the buttons herself.

Soon they were both undressed. Her slender, nude
body was outlined in the dim light as she stepped to the
bed. Ted's desire for her was a force he could no longer
control. As he came to her and lay down beside her,
taking her into his arms, he could hardly believe that what
was happening was real. Marjorie White, the woman he
loved with all his heart, was his at last.

During the trip up the lake the next day, Ted asked
Marjorie to marry him. She was noncommittal, replying
that there was ample time for them to discuss marriage
plans. Yet she was warmly affectionate toward him, and
her sparkling blue eyes shone with an unspoken comment
about their secret knowledge of each other. To Ted she
was more bewitchingly beautiful than ever as they sat on
the deck of the launch and talked.

The sun was dipping toward the western horizon
when the logging camp came into sight. As the launch
approached the breakwater and log basin at the foot of the
bluff, two men on the pier exchanged comments as they
noticed Ted and Marjorie on the deck. One of them ran
up the path to the camp. A moment later, Frank, Bettina,
and Lucy came down the slope to the pier.

Ted's father had named him after Frank's father, and
the friendship between the two older men had been passed
down to their sons. Ted helped Marjorie off the launch,
then greeted the tall, burly Frank. Marjorie was intro-

duced to Bettina and Lucy, and the five of them headed
up to the camp, the lumberjacks following with the luggage. Ted, however, insisted on carrying Marjorie's equipment cases.

By the time Ted and Marjorie had settled themselves
in their cabins, the sun was setting. They joined the
Woods family for dinner, which consisted of a juicy beef
roast with mashed potatoes and all the trimmings.

The rustic simplicity of the setting was as enjoyable as
the delicious food. The windows were open to let in the
cool evening breeze, and the calls of the night birds and
the chirping of crickets in the nearby forest carried into
the kitchen. An oil lamp hanging above the large pine
table cast a warm glow as Bettina urged second and third
helpings on Ted and Marjorie.

Dessert was thick slices of apple pie topped with
sweet clotted cream. Afterward, they remained at the
table and talked, Frank describing for Marjorie's benefit
just what was being done at the camp. "The work we're
doing right now isn't typical logging," he explained. "We're
clearing roads to the areas where the trees were killed by
fires, because we want to get the timber out before it
starts rotting. Clearing the roads is producing all of the
timber that we're sending to Chicago."

"When will you start logging one of the areas?" Marjorie asked.

"Within three or four days, depending on how the
work goes," Frank replied. "In the meantime, if you want
to do some photographing elsewhere, you and Ted are
welcome to use the horses in the corral."

Marjorie gratefully accepted the offer, and as Frank
began describing for her the surrounding area, Ted listened with satisfaction. Marjorie had never mentioned
how long she would be staying at the logging camp, but
now it appeared it might be for two weeks or more.

When Ted and Marjorie left the house and returned
to their cabins, the night was alive with the sounds of the
forest. The clearing around the camp was illuminated with

a soft light as the moon turned passing clouds into radiant silver. Ted waited in his cabin for a few minutes, then went to Marjorie's cabin and tapped on the door. She opened it, in her nightgown, and lifted her lips to his as he stepped inside.

The next morning, Ted went to the corral and saddled two horses and put a pack saddle on a third for Marjorie's cases. With the equipment tied firmly in place, he and Marjorie left the camp. Riding along the rugged shoreline, they stopped occasionally for Marjorie to photograph scenic views. The day passed swiftly for Ted, as it always did when he was enjoying Marjorie's company, and that night he again visited her cabin.

The following day they rode inland, along the road leading to Colmer. Side roads branched off every mile or so, and there was an isolated homestead here and there, but they saw no other traffic until they neared the town, which was several miles from the logging camp. Here they passed other riders and wagons, and then the road was deserted again. About ten miles farther along, they came to a small bridge and another side road that apparently led to another isolated farm. The sun was near its zenith, and it was almost time for them to turn back toward the logging camp, so they decided to look at the farm and then ride back. They turned their horses onto the side road, which led up a slope through open woods.

As they approached a clearing, they saw a young woman who was obviously in distress. Wringing her hands and talking to herself, she was pacing back and forth across the road. Ted and Marjorie exchanged a glance of concern and urged their horses forward. Ted called out to the woman.

The woman looked at them, then turned and ran. Following her, Ted and Marjorie rode out of the trees into a wide clearing around a large barn. A garden was off to one side, and a pigpen was set back at the edge of the trees beyond. On the other side of the barn, water was running down a wooden chute into a pond.

The young woman ran into the barn, past a tall, buxom woman of about forty-five who stood near the door. A man was seated nearby, shaving barrel staves. The barn was apparently being used as a house, because yet another woman and three children came out of it as the two visitors rode up.

Ted tipped his hat as he and Marjorie halted their horses. "Good day," he said. "I'm Ted Taylor, and this is Marjorie White."

"A very good day to you," the tall woman replied, smiling amiably and speaking with a German accent. "I am Ursula Oberg. This is Paddy Rafferty, and this is his wife, Colleen."

Ted tipped his hat again as the Irish couple, both with thick brogues, greeted him and Marjorie. "We saw the young lady who went inside," Ted said, "and we were concerned about her. She seemed to be very upset about something."

The Raffertys and the German woman smiled, and the children giggled. "That is my daughter, Maida," Ursula said. "She is making beer, and she is worried about how it will turn out."

Ted had noticed a strong, yeasty odor and now realized what it was. "She must be making a lot of it," he commented.

"Yes, we intend to sell it," Ursula replied. "Would you like to dismount and rest? We have an urn of cold buttermilk in the pond."

Ted exchanged a glance with Marjorie, then shook his head regretfully. "We appreciate the invitation, but we'd better ride on," he said. "It will be late in the day by the time we get back to the logging camp where we're staying. Perhaps another time."

"You'd be more than welcome," Ursula said. "We don't have many visitors, and we enjoy company."

After making their farewells, Ted and Marjorie started

back toward the main road. When they were out of ear-
shot, Marjorie commented that the young woman had
seemed to be worried about something far more serious
than beer.

"Yes, she did," Ted agreed. "But then again, she
might just be concerned about selling it once it's made.
For the life of me, I can't understand why anyone would
set up a brewery out here in the woods, miles from any
city."

In fact, selling beer was of no concern whatsoever to
Maida Oberg. She was involved only in brewing. And that
involved her totally, consuming her every waking moment.

It was her world—a vast, complex world of beers and
ales. Most of it was second nature to her: the musty odor
of rice and hops from a warehouse; the distinct differences
in grains harvested at different times of the year; the smell
of a good batch of malt; the successive stages of heating
the mash. But beyond such basic matters were closely
guarded secrets of technique that had been handed down
through generations of Oberg master brewers.

Standing beside the tun and leaning her head against
it, she could feel the faint vibrations of life stirring within
the vast oak vat. The fermentation was supposed to be
culminating in that most princely of beers—lager. But the
brew inside the tun did not seem to be forming into a
young, healthy beer. Instead, it appeared to be turning
into a deformed monster.

Her hands damp and trembling with anxiety, Maida
stepped onto the short ladder beside the tun and took
another reading with a hydrometer. Squeezing the rubber
bulb on the end of the instrument, she carefully avoided
disturbing the foam on the surface as she slid the glass
tube into the liquid. When she released the bulb, liquid
flowed into the instrument and filled it.

Stepping down from the ladder, Maida watched the
float in the hydrometer become stationary. It was lower
than it had been an hour before. The readings had been

dropping all day, indicating that the fermentation cycle was drawing to an end. Maida put the mouth of the tube into a testing bottle and squeezed the rubber bulb to empty the hydrometer.

A good, rich head of foam built on the liquid as it gushed into the clear glass container. Maida picked up the bottle and held it to the light. The color was also good, a golden yellow with effervescence swimming in it. Then she tasted the brew, first filling her mouth, then spitting out into a bucket and drawing in a deep breath through her mouth and nose.

There was the reason for her gnawing uncertainty, for the knot of fear in the pit of her stomach.

The raw, bitter taste of hops was so powerful that it brought tears to her eyes, but that was normal. Green beer was always strong with hops. Later, when it was drawn down and its gases contained in sealed casks or bottles, it would change and mature, the taste of the hops subsiding to a tart, lively overtone.

Disregarding the astringent bite of the hops, Maida searched behind it for the other tastes. They were muddled, strange and unusual. No two brews were ever the same to taste buds that had been protected since infancy and trained to detect the most subtle variations, but this was completely different from any lager she had ever made.

Anxiety churning within her, Maida washed the hydrometer and the testing bottle. Then she paced back and forth between the tuns. The other one was just beginning to ferment, and she feared a repetition of what appeared to be a disaster with the first one. Thinking back over the steps of cooking the coppers of mash, boiling, filtering, and cooling the wort, and blending in the yeast, she searched for some mistake she could have made.

While the process was so familiar to her that it was like a part of her being, in this place her things were not arranged as she was accustomed to having them. One small mistake somewhere along the way was all it took to ruin a tun of beer. Through working in unfamiliar surroundings, she could have made some small error that was enormous in effect.

The door squeaked, and her mother came in. "Try to calm yourself, little one," Ursula said gently, smiling reassuringly. "You have been through this many times before, and it will happen many more times."

"It is different this time."

"It is different every time, Maida," her mother said soothingly. "You yourself have said that no two brews are identical, and your father said the same thing many times. I am sure that it will turn out well. If we do not have a premium beer, then we will have a good beer."

Exasperated by her mother's lack of understanding, Maida brushed past her and stamped out the door. The casks in the shade beside the barn seemed to mock her as she passed them. Walking to the pond fed by the spring on the hill, she mournfully recalled the promise that the water had seemed to offer when she first saw it. Feeling miserable, she sat down on a rock.

Hours passed as she sat beside the pond. She knew that the process in the tun would gradually slow as the temperature dropped, but for now there was nothing to do but wait. At sunset, Ursula came out to tell her that dinner was ready. Maida silently glared at her until she left.

Finally, an hour after nightfall, Maida went back inside. The others were in bed, and her mother had hung lighted lanterns in the brewery side of the barn for her. Apprehension making her hands clammy, Maida began testing the brew in the tun again. The float in the hydrometer settled precisely on the dark, heavy line on the glass. According to the instrument, the tun now contained beer.

It was what Maida had anticipated. But anyone could read a hydrometer, which was useful only as a general guide. It was up to the master brewer's judgment as to precisely when to start drawing down the tun, making the difference between a good and a premium beer.

Fearfully, she tasted it. Then, for the first time since the hydrometer readings had begun falling, she experienced a faint hope. The flavor behind the acrid taste of hops had changed. It remained completely unlike any lager beer that she had ever made, but at least it tasted like beer.

Going back outside, she paced to and fro in the darkness as she waited for time to pass. Then she went back inside and tasted the brew again. The heat of the day yet lingered in the depths of the tun, and the brew was still evolving. It was not yet complete, but the tastes were starting to combine into the character of at least a good beer.

The hours passed as she paced outside the barn and went back in at intervals to taste the brew. It continued changing, with subtle transformations that she had not expected.

Then, in the thick darkness and quiet an hour before dawn, Maida went into the barn one more time. The chill of the night had settled into the mass of liquid in the tun. The change in it since the last time she had tasted it was only slight.

Yet, to Maida, the change was enormous.

Even as she was spitting the brew into the bucket, the taste was distinct. It was that of a premium lager with a lusty, brawny character. Her strength drained by the hours of tension, she staggered to a stool beside the wall and sat down heavily.

Understanding of what had happened and the reasons behind it suddenly came to her. As it did, triumphant, exultant joy exploded within her. It made her voice shrill as she drew in a deep breath and shouted the traditional cry of the master brewer. "We have beer! We have beer!"

As her cry shattered the quiet in the barn, her mother hurriedly got out of bed on the other side of the partition. "We have beer, Paddy," Ursula called. "We must begin drawing it down immediately."

"Right you are, Mrs. Oberg," he replied, scrambling out of bed. "I'll bring in the casks."

As they moved about on the other side of the barn and dressed rapidly, Maida sat on the stool and wearily leaned against the wall, still holding the last testing bottle she had filled. Ursula came in, still fastening her gown. She smiled at Maida affectionately, touching her face, then reached up to take down the siphon hoses.

Colleen Rafferty came in and began opening the bottles that had been washed and scalded, ready to fill. Paddy carried in casks, and they began drawing down the beer. A sense of excitement and victorious achievement gripped them as they worked; soon, for no explainable reason, they were laughing and talking elatedly.

The golden brew gushed into the casks, foam spurting out as they filled. Paddy slammed in the bungs with a mallet and hefted the heavy containers to a rack against the wall. Colleen moved a smaller hose from bottle to bottle, filling them and closing the tops. It was full dawn when they finished, nine casks and eight dozen bottles filled.

Paddy lifted the last cask and put it on the rack. Then Ursula stepped to Maida and leaned over her, patting her shoulder. "When will it be ready to drink, little one?" she asked.

"It will be potable within five days," she replied tiredly. "It will be premium lager within a month."

"Good, good," Ursula said, taking Maida's arm. "Come, little one. Now you must lie down and rest."

Maida shook her head and stood up, pulling away from her mother. Carrying the testing bottle, she stepped past the others and went outside. The sun was rising, dew sparkling on the grass. Birds were chattering and flying about the trees. Maida walked to the edge of the pond and sat down on her stone.

In the sunlight, the beer had a beautiful golden color. Maida looked at it a long time, then tasted it again. It was a fine, premium lager, but in every respect it was different from any beer she had ever made. The understanding of why it was different had come slowly to her, evading her through the night, but it was logical.

The ingredients of this beer had grown here, not in Germany, taking their nutrients from this soil. The wood in the tun had also grown here, and the beer had a hint of its nature. The water, as clear and as pure as it was, yet had the nature of the rocks through which it rose.

Her inborn talents had come from generations of master brewers in Germany. She had been born in Germany, and there she had developed her skills and experience. But her talents, skills, and experience had been applied to making beer that took its essence from this land.

The beer that had just been drawn down was possibly the finest premium beer that she had ever made. And it was American beer.

VII

As Toby Holt stood in the saw house and listened to the yard foreman over the loud whine of the saws, he noticed water dripping from a steam pipe on the boiler. It annoyed him, for the pipe had apparently been improperly joined and was leaking.

The yard foreman, James Henshaw, was telling him about a special order of hardwood for a furniture manufacturer in the city. Toby waited for him to finish, intending to tell him to send for someone from the company that had installed the steam engine. He wanted to talk to the individual himself and make it clear that all of the pipes were to be fitted correctly.

The saws screamed through the wood, Henshaw talking over the noise. Toby glanced over the other pipes on the boiler a few feet away, his annoyance growing as he saw two more that were leaking. One of them was near the pressure stopcocks. The stopcocks were turned all the way in.

That was wrong, because the boiler would build up too much pressure and blow its safety release valve. That would make it lose its head of steam, and then the saws would stop until enough steam was built up again to turn the drive shaft that spun the belts leading to the saws.

As he started to interrupt Henshaw and tell him about the stopcocks, Toby glanced at the pressure gauge on the boiler. Its needle was all the way to the right, across the red zone and against the peg. The safety release valve should have long since blown. He darted his gaze to it.

It was wired closed. The boiler was a giant bomb about to explode.

Time seemed to become warped, everything taking place at a slow, dragging rate. The emergency lever for use if someone was caught in a saw was a few yards away. Beside it was a workbench, and Toby spotted a hatchet among the scattered tools.

Leaping toward the lever, Toby bumped heavily into Henshaw. The man staggered back, looking at Toby in surprise. To Toby it seemed to take a long time to reach the lever, but he was finally there, scooping up the hatchet as he jerked the lever back.

Saws squealed, jamming in wood, then silence fell. Men called out and looked around. In the relative quiet, Toby heard the rumble of the awesome pressure that had built up in the boiler. "The boiler is about to explode!" he bellowed at the top of his voice. "Run! Run!"

Time was still stretching out, everything moving slowly. The men stood and gaped at him for an instant that seemed an eternity. "I said, run!" he shouted. "The boiler is about to explode! Move! Move!"

The men finally began scattering, hurrying out the open sides of the saw house. Henshaw stumbled, regained his footing, and ran out. As Toby drew back the hatchet to throw it, he too began running. No human could be near that steam when it released. The scalding heat would kill instantly, and the intense pressure would tear living flesh from bones.

He threw the hatchet as he passed the boiler. Seeing the keen blade bite into the wire, he put his head down and threw every ounce of strength into his legs. As he ran out of the building, the blast of the steam erupting from the safety valve was deafening.

Steam instantly filled the building and billowed out

its open sides in a thick, hot mist that enveloped Toby as he ran across the yard. When he was a safe distance away, he stopped and turned back to look. The roar of the steam was joined by a ripping sound. As Toby watched, boards and shingles on the roof over the boiler exploded into the air.

Henshaw, his grizzled face pale, looked at Toby in shock; then both of them were dodging shingles spilling down out of the sky. As the last of the shingles and boards fell to the ground, the steam from the valve was a giant plume spouting up through the hole it had ripped in the roof of the saw house. The cloud of steam in the yard slowly dissipated.

"What happened, Toby?" Henshaw shouted over the noise of the steam.

"I noticed that the pressure stopcocks were all the way in," Toby replied. "Then I saw that the needle on the pressure gauge was against the peg, and the safety valve was wired closed. I threw the hatchet at the wire on the safety valve and cut it so the valve could blow."

The foreman listened, his eyes wide and his mouth open. He was silent with astonishment for a moment, then found his voice. "So it was deliberate!" he exclaimed. "Somebody tried to blow up the boiler!"

"Yes, that's what it was," Toby agreed grimly. The foreman started to say something else, then stopped himself, suddenly chagrined; checking the steam engine was one of his responsibilities. It was early afternoon, and the boiler had obviously been building pressure since that morning, because the wiring down of the safety valve must have been done the night before.

"I should have checked that engine this morning," Henshaw admitted, embarrassed. "But we got busy on—"

"It doesn't make any difference," Toby interrupted, his voice calm. "We have ripsaws on hand for use when the engine is out of operation. After a few hours of using them, all of the men will start keeping their eye on that engine."

"They certainly will," Henshaw agreed. "Still, it's my job to check it, and I didn't. I'm mighty sorry, Toby."

"What's done is done, Jim. Have the men put out the fire in the firebox as soon as it's safe, and send for someone from the company that installed the engine. I want that boiler and all of the pipes checked to make sure they're safe before we pressurize it again."

"All right, Toby," the foreman said. "And I'll have them get out the ripsaws and start using them." He started to walk away, then stopped and turned back. "Who would want to sabotage the boiler?"

Toby shrugged and shook his head. He wished he knew, but he had no idea. He had a strong suspicion, however, as to *why* it was done.

The office staff had come outside to see what had happened. As Toby approached, Harold Phinney beckoned to the others, and they went back inside. Toby followed them, walking through the outer office and going into his office.

Sorting through the papers on his desk, he picked up an envelope. He opened it and took a sheet of paper out of it. In block letters on the paper were two sentences. The first stated that his low prices were unfair competition. The second stated that he had been warned.

When it had arrived a few days before, he had put it aside, thinking it was foolishness from a disgruntled competitor. But the stopcocks on a steam engine turned in for maximum pressure and the safety valve wired down were not foolishness. He sat back, thinking about what to do.

He could investigate the matter himself, but his name and face were too well known in Chicago, and it would be impossible to make discreet inquiries. The guilty party would be warned off, in all likelihood, only to strike again later.

No, his best course of action was clear. At his disposal was one of the most capable men alive for dealing with the situation—Ted Taylor. The steam launch would arrive and leave again for the logging camp the next morning, and he would have to go talk with Ted about what had happened. Toby tossed the envelope onto his desk as he stood up and went out.

The shrill whistling of the escaping steam had faded, and the spout of steam was much lower. Men were moving about, morose and silent as they prepared to begin using the handsaws. Toby crossed the yard and beckoned to the foreman.

Henshaw spoke first. "I've sent a man for someone from the steam engine company," he said as Toby approached. "He'll be here within an hour or two. Then we'll know if anything was damaged."

"Good, Jim. I'm going to the logging camp tomorrow to talk to Ted Taylor about what happened, and I'll be back as soon as I can. In the meantime, post an armed night watchman in the yard."

"All right, Toby," Henshaw replied, then chuckled dryly. "After the men use those ripsaws for a while, I'll probably have plenty of volunteers."

Toby walked back to the office building. In the outer room, he paused beside Harold Phinney's desk. "I'll be going to the logging camp tomorrow morning," he said. "If you have anything for me to sign or that I should see, please bring it in this afternoon."

Toby went into his office and sat down at his desk. Looking at the envelope again, he thought about his conversation with Governor Washburn. It appeared the governor had been correct in his belief that pressure was being exerted to keep the charges high at the lumber mills in Wisconsin. Toby put the envelope into his pocket, then turned back to his day's work.

When he left on the steam launch late the next morning, the saw house engine was still out of operation, but a repairman was working on it. After the launch was clear of the port, Toby talked with Captain Crowell about what had happened and showed him the note that had arrived in the mail.

The captain read the two short sentences and handed the paper back. "It seems to me there's no question as to why it was done," he commented. "The problem now is to find out who's behind this. It was pure luck that no one was killed."

"Yes, it was," Toby agreed, replacing the paper in the envelope and putting it in his pocket. "Several men were in the shed at the time. This is just the sort of problem that Ted Taylor can solve, and I'm fortunate he's here now."

The captain gave a wry smile. "If you can get him to show as much interest in this as he does in that lady photographist, he'll nab the guilty party in no time. Marjorie White is a pretty one, no doubt about that, and Ted is doing his best to put a ring on her finger."

"He has been since the first day he saw her," Toby said.

"From what I hear, he's been using his time with her to good advantage," the captain went on. "A couple of the lumberjacks told me he's with her every minute, riding around the countryside and seeing the sights. Sounds like a lot more fun than hunting train robbers."

Toby smiled. Looking out at the vast expanse of Lake Michigan, he thought about Marjorie's attitude toward him. He was puzzled, as always, that she remained so distant, as if he had offended her. But he was pleased by the fact that she seemed to be growing fonder of Ted Taylor.

The day passed, the launch making steady progress up the lake, and the sun had set behind the Wisconsin mainland when the vessel approached the pier at the logging camp. As soon as the mooring lines were secure, the captain told Jimson to bank the firebox for the night, then accompanied Toby up the path to the camp.

The lighted windows in the lumberjacks' dormitory glowed in the dusk, and inside one of the men was playing a harmonica while others sang. At the Woods cabin, moths fluttered around a lantern on the porch where Ted and

Marjorie were sitting and talking with Frank and Bettina. Toby called to them, and they stepped off the porch to greet him, surprised that he had returned already.

"We weren't expecting you so soon, Toby," Frank said. "But of course we're always happy to—" His words cut off as he glanced between Toby and the captain as they walked into the light of the lantern. "Has there been some trouble?"

Toby nodded, then went on to briefly describe what had happened at the lumberyard. "So I decided to come here and talk with Ted about it," he said as he finished. "This is the sort of thing you've handled before, isn't it, Ted?"

"Yes, many times," Ted replied. "And I'll be more than glad to do anything I can to clear this up, Toby."

"Let's go inside," Bettina suggested, stepping to the door. "I have a pot of coffee on the stove."

They all followed Bettina into the kitchen, where the men sat down around the large table. While Marjorie helped Bettina with the coffee, Toby took out the letter he had received and handed it across the table to Ted.

Ted read it, then examined the postmark on the envelope. "It was mailed in Chicago," he said, handing it back to Toby, "but I believe it originated in Wisconsin. Specifically, at one of the lumber mills. They're the ones whose business you're cutting into."

"Yes, I think you're right," Toby agreed. "When I talked with Governor Washburn, he said that he thought pressure was being exerted on the mills to keep their charges high. This has evidently been going on for some time in Wisconsin."

"Well, we'll put an end to it as soon as we find who's behind it," Ted said. "First, though, we have to set up defenses. We must try to prevent any further incidents. The outcome might be much worse the next time."

Toby nodded. "I told my foreman to post an armed night watchman. That's the first step, I suppose."

"It is—and you should also have guard dogs," Ted

said. "A good guard dog is worth ten night watchmen. That won't protect your property at all times, though, because your wagons leave the lumberyard. When they do, your men should keep an eye on them and the animals. Also, the lumberyard is only one part of the operation. The camp here is part of it. The steam launch is also a part of it."

"Yes, that's true," Toby agreed, turning to Captain Crowell. "Albert, dealing with dangers like this wasn't part of our agreement. If you want out of the contract, there'll be no hard feelings on my part."

The captain's only reply was an unwavering scowl.

Toby laughed and shrugged. "In all fairness, Albert," he said, "I felt I had to make the offer."

"You made it," the captain replied sourly. "Now let's get on with business and discuss what we need to do."

"Either you or one of your crew should be on the launch at all times," Ted said. "Particularly if you're at the docks in Chicago."

"I'll do that," Albert said, then took a drink of his coffee. "And whoever is on watch will have a gun at hand."

"The launch and the lumberyard can be guarded, but this camp can't," Frank pointed out. "Everything is too spread out. We've got equipment and animals at the logging sites, as well as here at the camp. It would take a dozen men doing nothing else to guard even the camp. We're surrounded by forest, where anyone could watch us without being seen."

"Yes, but they can't get to the forest without being seen," Ted replied. "They would have to come through Wedowee or Colmer. The ones we're after are hirelings, not lumberjacks. Maybe they could hide in a city, but here they would be noticed immediately. If we can stay informed about strangers in the area, we'll know when to expect trouble."

Frank pursed his lips. "Yes, then we could at least be alert. The best one to keep us informed is Fred Guthrie, who runs the tavern in Colmer. He knows all about everything that goes on around here."

"We should talk to him as soon as possible," Ted said. "Let's you and I ride over to Colmer tomorrow morning. Do you want to come along, Toby?"

Toby nodded, and Ted and Frank continued talking, discussing what the lumberjacks should do to protect the livestock and other property in the event that suspicious strangers were reported in the area.

Listening to them, Marjorie was seeing a new Ted Taylor. It was the first time she had seen him in control of a situation while Toby Holt was present. Younger and more reserved than Toby, Ted had always been overshadowed by the tall, lean man. Now, however, the problem at hand was one that required Ted's expertise, and suddenly his normal reserve was gone. Instead he was forceful and decisive.

No one else could dominate a gathering when Toby Holt was present. The man had a personality that made him the focus of any group, even when he was only listening. However, Ted was now a force himself, a fact that was reinforced by the absolute confidence in him that Toby was displaying.

A fundamental shift in Marjorie's attitudes toward the two men had occurred during the conversation. When Toby had first arrived, she had summoned her defenses to conceal the compelling attraction he still exerted upon her. But now her fondness for Ted had suddenly become a richer, deeper feeling, and for the first time she felt that she could relax her defenses. Something of her former guardedness still remained, but Toby's presence was no longer a threat.

Ted was talking to Toby. "After we've spoken with Fred Guthrie, I'll take the train down to Milwaukee. I'll spend a few days there and quietly investigate the owners of the mills. Unless I'm badly mistaken, one of them is behind this. But getting enough evidence to take him to court may be a problem."

"All I need is a name," Toby replied. "I can settle this without lining some lawyer's pockets." He glanced around the table. "It's late, and I think we've covered everything. Does anyone have any questions?"

The others shook their heads as they got up from the table. Toby walked outside with Albert and told him there was an extra cabin if he wanted to use it.

"No, I'll sleep on my launch," the captain replied. "I sleep better on my chair in the wheelhouse than I can in the softest bed made. I'll set up a tow of logs tomorrow and be ready to leave when you get back from seeing Fred Guthrie."

Toby said his good-nights and went into his cabin. As was his habit, he opened the windows to let in fresh air. He undressed and got into bed, but sleep evaded him as he thought about the conversation around the table in the kitchen.

As he started to fall off to sleep, a sound outside his cabin brought him wide awake again, the threat of sabotage central in his mind. Listening, he heard a cabin door open. Marjorie laughed softly, then said something. Ted laughed as he replied quietly. Then the cabin door closed.

Toby smiled to himself as he turned over in bed and relaxed to go to sleep. While marriage plans had yet to be announced, it was obvious that Ted had been highly successful indeed in courting Marjorie.

It was midmorning when Toby, Ted, and Frank reined up in front of the tavern in Colmer. Going inside, they found the place empty of customers, the chairs stacked on the tables, and a wizened old man mopping the floor. He told them that Fred had gone to see the woman he was courting and wouldn't be back until late afternoon.

"Does she live far from here?" Toby asked.

"Ten, twelve miles," the old man replied. "She and some other people live in a barn that used to belong to Fred's brother. If you're in such a hurry to see Fred, though, you might be able to catch up with him on the road, because he ain't been gone all that long."

"I know where the place is," Ted said. "Marjorie and I saw it and met the people there while we were riding around one day."

Toby thanked the old man, and he and the others went back to their horses. They rode on through the town and along the road leading north.

Less than an hour later they spotted Fred Guthrie in a wagon ahead of them. He stopped when Frank called out his name, and waited for the horsemen to catch up, his wooden leg propped on the splashboard in front of the seat.

Fred knew Toby and Frank and greeted them warmly, and Frank introduced him to Ted. The big man's smile faded, however, when Toby told him their purpose in coming to see him.

"I haven't heard of any strangers around here," Fred said, "but you can be certain I'll let you know if I do. And if they turn out to be troublemakers, I'll provide the rope."

"We appreciate your help," Toby said, "but I don't think that will be necessary. We're only taking precautions. Nothing may happen here."

"Well, I hope it doesn't," Fred said. He gestured to the sacks in his wagon. "Ursula Oberg invited me to lunch today and asked me to bring this feed and salt for her cow. We're almost there, so why don't you come along and join us for lunch?"

Toby and the other two men shook their heads. "No, we don't want to intrude," Toby replied. "People getting started don't need strangers dropping in on them and eating their food."

"You won't be strangers there more than a minute," Fred said. "Ursula is as sweet-natured as a woman can be, and Paddy Rafferty is the friendliest man on earth. And as far as food goes, there'll be more than enough. Ursula and

Paddy's wife, Colleen, always prepare plenty, because those Rafferty children can eat."

"Paddy Rafferty?" Toby mused, thinking about the name. "I believe I met him and his family in Memphis last year, not long after they first arrived in the country."

"That's right—I almost forgot!" Fred exclaimed. "I mentioned you to him one day, and he told me about it. He's been wanting to get over to the logging camp to see you. But I told him that you're not there all the time, and his work here has kept him busy. I know he'll be pleased to see you, and you can be certain Ursula will make all of you welcome. What do you say?"

Toby had fond memories of the amiable, talkative Paddy Rafferty and his charming family, and he wanted to see them again. He turned to Ted and Frank, and when they nodded in agreement, the three of them fell in behind the wagon. A short while later, they crossed a bridge and turned off onto a side road to the farm.

Fred grinned widely when Frank called to him to ask him how his courtship was proceeding. "I know that she likes me," he replied, looking back. "She's made that clear, I guess. I think I'll be able to win her over, Frank."

"How are you getting on with her daughter?" Ted asked. "The day Marjorie and I were here, she was acting strangely."

Fred sighed glumly. "You didn't see anything out of the ordinary, I can tell you that. Maida is a strange one, all right. Part of the time she acts like she's asleep, and the rest of the time she acts like the world is coming to an end. And nobody else could even think of some of the ideas she gets. Somehow she got it into her mind that she wouldn't be able to taste anything if she has pepper on her food. Ursula loves her so much that she coddles her, and she fixes Maida her own food without any pepper on it."

"I understand that Maida is making some beer," Ted said, pulling alongside the wagon as the road widened.

"Yes, she is," Fred replied morosely. "When Ursula

first mentioned it to me, I told her that I would sell it in my tavern. But I didn't know what I was getting into."

"You do sell beer in your tavern, don't you?" Frank asked.

"Not hundreds of gallons," Fred said, "and that's how much Maida is making. Her mother humors her and listens to her too much, and they're going to spend every penny they have in making beer that no one will buy out here in the middle of the woods. I have an idea that Ursula wanted me to come here today because some of it is ready to drink."

Disliking beer himself, Toby chuckled as he listened to Fred grumble. "Love has its price, Fred," he said. "More often than not, it's far more expensive than gold."

"That's true," Fred agreed resignedly. "Maida is an odd fish, but there are always drawbacks of one sort or another to everything. And nothing is too much trouble for me if it has to do with Ursula. There's no other woman like her in the world."

They had reached the farm, the road emerging into the clearing in front of the barn. To Toby it looked like a comfortable, thriving place, the barn in good repair and the garden flourishing. Fat pigs were in a pen at the far side of the clearing, and a cow lounged in the shade under a tree.

Paddy Rafferty, with his bright red hair and a constant smile on his round, ruddy face, was unchanged since Toby had first seen him. He was also as outgoing and exuberant as before, whooping with delight and shouting for his wife as he ran to greet Toby. Toby dismounted and exchanged greetings with the couple, and then Fred introduced him to Ursula Oberg.

"I don't like to be unexpected company," Toby said to Ursula, "but Fred told me that Paddy and his family were here, and I wanted to see them again and find out how they're getting on."

Ursula's smile was genuine, and Toby could see why Fred was attracted to her. "I am pleased that you and your friends came, Mr. Holt," she said in her slow, deliberate English. "We do not have as much company as we would like. There is more than enough food for everyone, and you are all more than welcome here."

"That's very kind of you," Toby said. He glanced around, curious about the Oberg daughter after having heard so much about her. "I understand you have a daughter."

"Yes, she is inside," Ursula replied. "A tun of beer has almost finished fermenting. Maida is worried about it, and she is staying near it. Paddy, if you show our guests to the table, Colleen and I will finish preparing lunch."

Toby noticed that when Ursula mentioned even more beer was being made, Fred had tried unsuccessfully to hide a wince. The two women went back inside as Paddy led Toby and the others around to the shady side of the barn, explaining that his family and the Obergs usually ate outside on warm days. A long table and benches sat in the shade, the table covered with a snowy white cloth.

As they sat down, Fred asked Paddy if he had tried the beer. "No, all I've done is smell it," Paddy sighed. "It smells like proper good beer. Maida won't let anyone near it until a certain time passes, and the first lot she made is supposed to be ready now. Ursula said it would be very good."

"Ursula has tasted it?" Fred asked.

"No, Maida told Ursula it would be good," Paddy replied.

Fred looked increasingly ill at ease as Paddy continued talking about the beer, describing the growing number of casks that were racked inside the barn. Evidently Maida was finishing a tun of beer every week or so. Listening to him, Toby recalled something he had heard about beer. "I never cared for beer very much," he said when Paddy had finished, "and I don't know much about it. But I've heard that storing it in wooden casks for very long will give it a bad taste and eventually spoil it."

"That could be, because Maida's casks are lined with

pitch," Paddy replied. "Sure and you've never seen an army sergeant looking at a private's boots for dirt the way Maida inspects those casks to see if I've left a splinter uncovered. She even has me cover the bungs with pitch." He laughed, shaking his head. "Next she'll want me to put pitch on the mallet I use to drive home the bungs."

Fred forced a weak, worried smile as Toby and the others laughed heartily. Paddy continued talking about his work, while Ursula, Colleen, and the children began bringing out tableware and covered trays of food.

The warm breeze and its forest smells made the delicious scents of roast pork, vegetables, and fresh bread even more appetizing. When the table was set, Colleen poured buttermilk for the children as Ursula went to the pond at the edge of the trees. She brought back two buckets, one containing large bottles of beer and the other chilled glasses.

After she poured the beer, everyone began eating. Toby, hungry after a long ride, found the food superbly delicious. The thick slices of juicy, tasty pork loin were tender and succulent on the inside, crisp outside. The fried potatoes had bits of onion in them, and the fresh peas and beans from the garden were seasoned with pork drippings. The bread was hot from the oven, light and chewy with a thin crust.

Paddy, the first to try the beer, exclaimed with delight. Frank's eyes opened wide and he murmured in pleasure over his. Ted, characteristically showing little reaction, nodded as he took a second deep drink. Fred sipped his cautiously. Then he sat up with a surprised smile on his face as he took a deep drink.

Curious, Toby tasted his. On a warm day, it was just the thing. Beads of moisture slid down the chilled glass, and the cold beer was very refreshing. Taking another drink, Toby reflected that the thin, sour brews he had drunk before scarcely deserved the same name as this beverage. Its hearty flavor was bracing, substantial, yet the cold, golden liquid was light and smooth, alive with effervescence. Toby emptied his glass.

"Now, this is beer!" Fred exclaimed happily, looking around the table with a triumphant smile as he wiped foam off his upper lip. "This is by far the best beer I've ever tasted, but it doesn't surprise me one bit, no sir. The minute Ursula told me that Maida was making some beer, I knew we'd have something worth drinking. Not many of my customers drink beer, Ursula, but those who do will certainly like this."

All of the glasses were empty, and Ursula took another bottle from the bucket. "We will be grateful for whatever you can sell, Fred," she said. "It will be even better within a few more days." She thumbed back the wire frame on the neck of the bottle, and the ceramic top jumped off with a pop. "Maida told me that it has not completely lagered and matured."

"I'm sure she knows what she's talking about," Fred said confidently. "I don't see how this could be any better, but I knew from the beginning that Maida knows what she's talking about when it comes to beer. Where did she get the recipe to make this, Ursula?"

"Her father trained her," Ursula replied, refilling the glasses. "The Obergs have been master brewers for several generations. Everyone, drink all you want, because we certainly have plenty of beer."

As he listened to the conversation, Toby thought of a way in which some of the beer could be useful to him. "When we finish lunch, Mrs. Oberg," he said, "I'd like to talk with your daughter for a few minutes about buying some of her beer."

Ursula laughed, clearly amused at the idea. "It probably never occurred to Maida to wonder what happens to the beer she makes, Mr. Holt. But I will sell it to you in casks at fifty cents a gallon. The casks must be returned, because Paddy has worked very hard to make them, and I would not want them destroyed."

Figuring in his mind for a moment, Toby concluded

that the lumberjacks at the logging camp could have a glass or two of beer with their dinner each night at a cost that was less than that of the coffee they drank. He mentioned it to Frank, who reacted enthusiastically. "That's a good idea, Toby! Keeping lumberjacks in camp is always a problem, but this beer with their dinner would take care of that. In fact, it would draw lumberjacks to us."

"It certainly would," Fred agreed. "And if the owners of two or three of the camps started buying this beer, the others would have to follow suit to keep their lumberjacks from leaving."

"Let's hope they do," Toby said. "Spread the word around from your tavern, Fred, and perhaps they will. In the meantime, Mrs. Oberg, I'll take two casks of beer every month."

"Thank you very much, Mr. Holt," she replied. "And thank you for your idea. If we could start selling beer to all of the logging camps, that would take care of part of the beer that Maida is making."

Ursula refilled the glasses as the meal continued. Before long, they were all as cheerful as a group of old friends, and by the time lunch was over, a half dozen of the large bottles had been emptied. Paddy's ruddy face was flushed, Fred was jolly, and a tingling in Toby's limbs warned him that he had drunk enough. Along with its delicious flavor, the beer had a hefty impact of alcohol.

Toby drained his glass, then shook his head as Ursula started to refill it again. "No, thank you," he said. "It's delicious, like the food, but I've had enough of both. If I may, Ursula, I'd like to speak with your daughter and compliment her on the beer."

Ursula looked doubtful. "Maida understands little English, Toby, and she does not like to talk with anyone when she is worried about her beer. But you are welcome to try. The tuns are inside the door on the right after you go into the barn."

Toby excused himself and stood up, confident that he would be able to make Maida understand that he had enjoyed the beer. Frank and Ted also got up, and they followed Toby as he went inside the barn and knocked on the half-open door.

Getting no answer, he peered inside and saw the huge beer tuns. Maida was sitting on a stool beside one of them. Small and slender, she looked nothing like her mother; and her behavior was certainly unlike that of the serenely composed Ursula. Her elbows on her knees, the young woman was holding her head between her hands and muttering to herself despairingly in German.

Toby coughed to reveal his presence and began to tell Maida how much he enjoyed the beer, but his voice faded as she stood up, glared at him, then picked up her stool and stepped around to the other side of the tun, out of their line of view. Toby heard her put the stool down and sit on it again. He looked at Frank and Ted, who both shrugged. They went back outside.

"You were right, Ursula," Toby admitted. "She doesn't want to talk with anyone."

"I did not think she would," Ursula replied, her tone resigned. "I hope you are not offended."

"No, no, of course not," Toby said, smiling. "Perhaps I can talk to her another time. We must get back to the camp, so we'd better be on our way. A wagon will come within the next day or two for the beer, and you can depend on us to take two casks each month."

After farewells were said all around, Toby, Ted, and Frank mounted their horses and rode back down the hill to the road.

Toby was silent for a few minutes, still bemused by the way Maida Oberg had acted. Then he chuckled. "I suppose anyone who is as much of an expert at something as Maida Oberg is has a right to act a bit strangely," he said. "What do you think?"

Ted and Frank laughed, clearly in agreement.

The lift to Toby's spirits from the delicious food, heady beer, and cheerful companionship faded when he reached the logging camp and boarded the launch to return to Chicago. The afternoon passed and dusk thickened into darkness as the launch steamed south, towing a load of logs at the end of a thick cable. Toby sat on the deck, thinking about the uneasy future his company faced. The economic uncertainties in the nation always remained as a dark cloud in the back of his mind. But what had happened to the steam engine at the lumberyard was a dire warning of a much more immediate threat.

Chicago was a sprawling blanket of winking lights, brightening as the launch approached. The captain, as familiar with the shoreline here as he was with the inside of his wheelhouse, maintained the same speed as they passed the first piers along the north end of the waterfront. Not until the lumberyard itself was in sight did he begin slowing to allow the tons of logs in tow to lose their forward momentum.

The yard, Toby noticed, was lighted more brightly than before so that the night watchman would be able to see any intruders. In addition to the lanterns that had always been left on the pier to guide the launch in at night, other lanterns were hanging at intervals around the fence, inside the saw house, and in front of the office building.

There was also more late-night activity than ever before. In addition to the night watchman, who was pacing just inside the fence with a shotgun under his arm, the foreman and a half dozen workmen were in the saw house. Looking at them, Toby was reminded that the lumberyard was just as important to his workers as it was to him. It was their livelihood, and they were protective of it.

"I see that several of your men are staying around at night," Captain Crowell commented. "You have some good workers, Toby."

"Yes, I do," Toby agreed.

As the launch edged up to the pier, the men came out of the saw house to help disconnect the towing cable so that the logs could be winched into the log basin. Toby said good night to the captain, confident that he did not have to remind him of Ted's warning about having someone on the launch at all times.

On shore, James Henshaw informed Toby that the steam engine had been repaired. Toby then told the foreman about his conversation with Ted and the decisions that had been made.

"Getting guard dogs is certainly a good idea," Henshaw commented. "I'll see about that tomorrow." He pointed to the men on the pier. "But this lumberyard is being guarded like an army fort. Several of the men are taking turns, going home for supper and then coming back. They're worried that something will happen to shut us down."

"I certainly appreciate what they're doing," Toby said. "It's very gratifying to have men like them and like you, Jim. At the same time, though, working in the saw house is too dangerous for men who haven't had plenty of rest. The night watchman can take care of this place tonight, and we'll see about getting some guard dogs tomorrow."

Henshaw reluctantly agreed. "I guess you're right, Toby. As soon as they've winched those logs in, I'll send them home and go home myself. Do you think Ted Taylor will be able to find out who's behind the trouble?"

"If he can't, no one would be able to," Toby said, turning toward the office building. "I'm going to see if I have any important paperwork waiting on my desk before I leave. Good night, Jim." He walked across the yard, unlocked the office door, and stepped into the quiet, dark building. The light of the lanterns outside shone through the windows and cast shadows on the floor as Toby went into his office. He lit the lamp on his desk and sat down.

On his desk were bills, as well as checks to sign in payment for them, including one for the repairs that had been done to the steam engine. There was an updated listing of expenses and receipts, still showing a substantial profit, and correspondence to and from customers. And there was a letter with a Portland postmark. It was from Janessa.

Smiling, Toby opened it and began reading. There were several pages of information about events at the ranch and in Portland. On the last page, she had added a postscript concerning, of all things, the visit of a German military officer.

The officer, a Captain Richard Koehler, had apparently met and befriended Henry Blake in France the previous year. As part of the exchange of military observers between the United States and Germany, the captain was touring several posts in the West and was scheduled to arrive soon at Fort Vancouver, across the river from Portland. Janessa and Cindy had heard of the visit from General Lee Blake, Toby's stepfather.

As Toby refolded the letter and put it away, he wondered how the German officer would react to the American West. Certainly, he thought with a smile, the fellow would enjoy meeting Cindy and Janessa.

VIII

As the steam packet from San Francisco came into view, nosing around the large, wooded islands in the Columbia River, Second Lieutenant Reed Kerr took out his watch and looked at it. The lean, sandy-haired young officer was only a year out of West Point. "It appears that the packet will dock right on time, sir," he commented.

Colonel John Forbes, the new post commander of Fort Vancouver, took out his own watch and glanced at it, then put it back into his pocket. "Yes, it does, Reed," he replied.

Noting the use of his first name, Reed reflected that his previous impression of the officer had been correct. The colonel was a relatively informal man and not overly conscious of his rank. He could have sent one of the captains on his staff to meet the visitor arriving on the packet, but he had chosen to meet the German officer himself.

The appearance of the packet in midstream created a stir of activity among the ferry terminal workers as they prepared for the vessel to dock. The men bustling about disturbed roosting gulls, which took wing in a clamor of shrill cries.

"Incidentally," the colonel said, "General Blake tells me that you and our visitor both are friends of Henry Blake. That gives you something in common, and I thought

149

that you might like to be his escort while he's visiting here."

Reed hesitated in surprise, then replied quickly, "Yes, I'd like that very much, sir."

"Good." The colonel brushed his mustache with a finger. "We'll see how things work out, then. If the man seems to be a stickler for protocol, I'll have to assign a captain to be his escort. Otherwise, I'll have your troop commander relieve you of other duties while our visitor is here."

"Thank you very much, sir."

"It'll be good experience for you, Reed. However, you must bear in mind that while the visitor is an officer from a friendly foreign nation, he *is* from a foreign nation. You can take him anywhere on the post that he wants to go, but you shouldn't discuss the overall strength of the Army of the West with him, or our defense plans."

"I understand, sir."

The colonel continued talking, giving Reed advice on what to do if he was the visitor's escort. He mentioned the Multnomah County Fair, which was due to open in Portland two days later, and other things that the German officer might find interesting. Reed listened, but his mind was racing ahead to an opportunity that the assignment opened to him.

Being the visitor's escort would certainly be a welcome respite from his routine duties, but more important, General Blake, the commander of the Army of the West, would have the visitor at his home for dinner at least once. And it was likely that the general's stepdaughter, Cindy Holt, would also be there.

Reed's friendship with Henry Blake, who was engaged to Cindy, was important to him, and he placed a high value on it. Indeed, his sense of honor had restrained him from making any overtures to Cindy in Henry's absence. At the same time, simply being in the presence of the tall, blond, breathtakingly beautiful woman was sheer bliss to him. It also appeared to him that Henry was taking his engagement to Cindy too much for granted, having already postponed their wedding twice.

Reed watched intently as the packet, an oceangoing vessel that dwarfed the ferries that plied back and forth between Portland and Fort Vancouver, eased up to its pier in a rumble of reversed engines and a blare from its horn. The colonel stepped closer to the exit gate from the pier as passengers from the packet began disembarking. Reed hung back for just a moment, having caught a glimpse of the German officer on the deck. What he saw gave him strong doubts that he would even be the visitor's escort.

The man was wearing an immaculate pale-blue tunic, with brilliant white facings and elaborate braid that matched his tight white trousers. A saber hung from a white baldric across his chest, and his shining black boots curved up above the knee in front. The fringes on his epaulets and a tall plume surmounting the spike on his gleaming helmet stirred in the breeze.

Between the low visor on his helmet and the wide metallic strap on the point of his chin, only the lower half of his face was visible. But his mouth was set in a firm, straight line, and he had the bearing of a rigidly disciplined officer who would expect every consideration due his rank. As he tramped down the gangplank, his spurs jingled and his saber clanked, causing people on the pier to crane their necks to look at this display of martial splendor.

The captain came out of the gate and halted in front of Colonel Forbes, snapping his heels together and lifting his right hand to the visor of his helmet in a stiff salute. "Sir, I am Captain Richard Koehler," he said in fluent English, "presently detached from the Twelfth Dragoon Brigade."

"It's a pleasure to meet you, Captain Koehler," the colonel replied, returning the salute and introducing himself and Reed. "I bid you welcome, and I trust you will enjoy your visit here."

The captain took off a glove to shake hands. "I'm

certain that I will enjoy my visit, and I'm honored by your coming in person to greet me, Colonel Forbes." He offered his hand to Reed. "Lieutenant Kerr."

"We're honored by your visit, Captain," the colonel said urbanely. "I've been told that Lieutenant Henry Blake is a friend of yours. Reed here also happens to be a friend of Lieutenant Blake's, as well as one of his classmates at West Point."

For the first time, Reed saw that he had been mistaken in his impression of the man. In the shadow of the visor on the gleaming helmet, a waggish sense of humor shone in the man's blue eyes. "So you are a friend and a classmate of Heinrich's," he said. "Did you attend the same classes that Heinrich did, Lieutenant Reed?"

The German form of Henry's name made Reed hesitate; then he nodded. "Yes, sir," he replied, puzzled. "All of the cadets at West Point attend the same classes."

"Then you must have slept during a class in which Heinrich was listening carefully," the captain commented, his tone of voice droll. "Obviously he learned something at West Point that you did not. Otherwise, how is it that he is enjoying the pleasures of Frankfurt, while you are stationed here at an army post?"

A wide, friendly smile spread over the captain's face as he asked the joking question, and both he and Reed laughed. "That's a good point to consider, Reed," the colonel interjected. "Captain Koehler, let's walk down the street to the dock for the ferry over to Fort Vancouver. I have a man assigned to collect your baggage."

As the three of them walked along the line of docks, the captain gazed across the river and commented on its scenic beauty. He said that of all the wonders he had seen in the United States, the endless variety and the grandeur of the landscape impressed him most. By the time they boarded the ferry to cross the river, Reed Kerr readily understood why Henry Blake had become good friends with the German officer. He was a well-built, handsome man, obviously intelligent, and had the bearing of one who was accustomed to a position of leadership. At the same time, he had an amiable personality and a quick sense of humor.

On the other side of the river, soldiers were waiting with horses for them. During the short ride up the slope to the fort, the colonel broached the subject of Reed's acting as escort. "It wouldn't be strictly according to protocol," the colonel observed. "However, your mutual friendship with Lieutenant Blake gs you something in common."

"It does," the captain agreed. "And as for protocol, I have yet to see it win a battle. I would be pleased to have Lieutenant Reed act as my escort."

As they rode through the main gate of the fort, Reed reflected that the main barrier to a blissful few hours in the presence of Cindy Holt had been removed. It seemed certain that the general would invite the captain to dinner, but whether Cindy would be present remained to be seen.

In addition to being the commander of the Army of the West, Major General Leland Blake was one of the original settlers in the area. In his late sixties, with snowy hair and a tanned face that was deeply creased with age, the general remained a healthy, active man. Tall and lean, he was impeccably neat in his uniform.

In Reed's experience, the general was a difficult man to impress, but he appeared to be very favorably impressed by Richard Koehler. As Colonel Forbes and Reed sat on a couch in the general's office, mostly listening, the captain told the general that he had seen his adopted son a few weeks before leaving Germany, and that Henry was in good health and spirits.

"The specific places where I would visit hadn't been determined when I last saw Heinrich," the captain added. "However, he asked me to present his best regards to you if I came to Fort Vancouver."

Lee Blake smiled warmly. "When you see Hank again,

please convey my best regards in return," he said. "On the other hand, I may see him before you do, because he should be returning within a few months. I'm very gratified by this wider exchange of military observers between your nation and mine, Captain Koehler. It will be of mutual benefit."

"It will indeed, sir," the captain agreed. "Of course my view is affected by the fact that it gave me an opportunity to travel abroad, but as a soldier I can see its advantages to our armies. An understanding of how others do things is very valuable."

"It is, and we'll do our best to make your visit here as informative as possible. You say you'll be here only three days?"

"Yes, sir. I would like to stay longer, but my schedule unfortunately leaves me with little latitude."

"That is unfortunate, but we'll help you use your time here to best advantage. John, who will escort Captain Koehler?"

"Lieutenant Kerr, sir," the colonel replied. "I discussed it with the captain, and that meets with his wishes."

Lee Blake nodded and turned to Reed. "Show the captain around the fort, our training areas, and anywhere else he would like to go, Lieutenant Kerr," he said. He looked at Richard. "I'm sure you'd rather not limit yourself to military affairs, Captain Koehler. A county fair is due to open in Portland two days from now, and you may find that interesting. Also, I would like to invite you to have dinner at my home this evening."

"That would be an honor and a pleasure, General Blake," the captain replied. "I accept with thanks."

"We'll be very pleased to have you, and my wife will enjoy your company. She'll want to hear all about Hank. My stepdaughter, Cindy Holt, will also want to hear about him, so I'll invite her over." He turned to Reed. "You're invited as well, of course, Lieutenant."

"Thank you, sir," Reed replied.

Glowing with satisfaction, Reed listened as Lee Blake

and Richard talked for a few minutes longer. Then Reed and the other two officers exchanged salutes with the general and left his office. The colonel went to his own office as Reed and Richard crossed the courtyard to the officers' quarters.

After the captain was settled in a room that had been prepared for him, Reed took him on a brief tour of the fort. The military post had spread outside the actual stockade originally built by the British decades before. There were warehouses and barracks situated adjacent to the old log walls, and down by the riverbank a small town was developing. After looking around, Reed and Richard returned to their quarters to get ready to go to the general's home for dinner.

The quarters for married officers were located on a rise that offered a view of the Columbia River. It was a beautiful scene, with the last light of sunset gleaming on the river and tinting the fleecy clouds with warm tones. Anticipation of seeing Cindy made it even more beautiful to Reed as he and the captain walked along the road to the row of houses.

The general's large, comfortable house was the last one in the row. Eulalia Blake, an attractive, gracious woman in her fifties, greeted Reed and Richard at the door, then led them to the living room. It had not escaped Richard's attention that Reed was looking forward to the evening with keen anticipation, and when they went into the living room he saw why.

Cindy Holt, who was wearing a dark blue muslin dress that seemed to enhance her large blue eyes, rose to greet them. While Richard had expected her to be attractive, it was her forthright manner that immediately struck him. Combined with her beauty, it made her one of the most intriguing women he had ever met. As he shook her hand, he understood why Henry was so unwilling to give her up.

With her were two children. Cindy introduced them as her niece and nephew and explained that she lived at her brother's horse ranch outside Portland and looked after his household and children. Richard commented on the unusually close resemblance between Cindy and the two children.

Everyone laughed except Janessa, who smiled politely. "All Holts look alike, Captain Koehler," Eulalia said. "If you met my son, Toby, you would know him immediately from having seen his sister and children."

"I see," Richard said. "In that case he must be a remarkably handsome man." His gallantry brought a smile from Cindy but no acknowledgment from Janessa. Richard bent down and looked at the scar on the boy's forehead. "If Timmy were a few years older, I would say that he had overmatched himself in saber practice."

"He got the idea that he was a bird," Cindy explained. "He made a large kite and jumped out of a tree with it, and cut his head on a rock. He also broke his left leg and two ribs."

"And caused us no end of worry," Eulalia added, shaking a finger at the boy. "It appeared so serious at the time that we summoned his father, who was in Chicago."

"From the look of the scar, it must have been a severe wound," Richard commented, then smiled at the boy. "You won't do that again, will you, Timmy?"

"No, sir," the boy replied. "Josh was looking after me when I did it, and my father told me that Josh and Aunt Cindy blamed themselves for what I did. He told me that it isn't right to do something that others will blame themselves for, so I won't do that again."

Richard nodded in approval, then turned to greet General Blake, who had just come into the room.

Having already eaten, Janessa and Timmy went upstairs, leaving the adults alone, and a few minutes later an orderly appeared with a tray of drinks. Richard sat down and chatted with the others, observing that each time Reed Kerr looked at Cindy, it was with an adoring gaze.

Much of the conversation was about Henry Blake, which made Richard uneasy. He had never specifically asked Henry if his family was aware of the circumstances of his life in Germany, and Henry had never commented about it. But during his brief interview at the fort just after he had arrived, Richard had detected a broad lack of knowledge on the general's part about Henry's personal life in Germany.

That lack of knowledge, which extended to all of those present, became more apparent by the minute. Richard knew that Henry was engaged to be married to Cindy Holt—Henry had told him as much—yet for some reason he had assumed that the match was more one of convenience than of genuine love. But the way Cindy talked about Henry did not support that view.

Avoiding any references to Henry's personal life, Richard replied to questions as best he could and related how he and Henry had met the previous year. Mercifully, the conversation ended as an orderly came to the doorway and announced that dinner was served.

They went down the hall to the dining room, where the soft light from the candelabra gleamed on the silver and china. Richard stood behind his chair, as did the others, while an orderly moved around the long table, filling the wineglasses.

The glasses filled, the general picked up his. "Ladies and gentlemen," he said, "let us drink a toast to Ulysses S. Grant, President of the United States." The glasses were lifted, and everyone took a drink. Then Lee Blake turned to Richard. "Captain Koehler, do you wish to propose a toast?"

"Yes, thank you, sir," Richard replied, lifting his glass. "Ladies and gentlemen, please drink with me to Prince Otto Eduard Leopold von Bismarck, Chancellor of Germany."

The others lifted their glasses and drank, then everyone sat down as an orderly began serving the soup course. Cindy looked across the table at Richard. "You do know that Henry and I are engaged, don't you?"

"Heinrich has mentioned his engagement to me numerous times," Richard replied, smiling. "Now that I've met you, I can easily understand why his marriage plans are constantly on his mind."

Cindy fell silent for a moment as she began eating her soup. Then she mentioned a trip that Henry had made to England. "His letters weren't clear about the purpose of the trip," she said.

Lee Blake interjected a comment. "You shouldn't expect Hank to detail everything he does in his letters to you, my dear. After all, there are sensitive aspects to his assignment."

Richard nodded, relieved that the general had turned Cindy's question aside. "There are," he agreed. "And Heinrich has a friend who is a British military observer, Commander Stephen Wyndham. He may have gone there to see him."

Cindy repeated the name thoughtfully. "Yes, I've heard about him," she said. "Last year I talked with Colonel Brentwood, who was with Henry in France, and he mentioned Commander Wyndham. He also told me that Henry is acquainted with an aunt of yours, Captain Koehler. A Baroness von Kirchberg."

Richard hesitated, formulating a reply. He often jokingly referred to Henry as his common-law uncle-in-law, in German a sonorous compound word that they both found amusing. It was not as amusing in English, and in the present company it was unamusing to him. "Yes, the baroness visited me briefly at the lines around Paris last year," he said. "Heinrich happened to be there at the time, for which I was thankful."

"Why is that, Captain Koehler?" Cindy asked.

"The baroness and I have never been on the best of terms," Richard replied. "We have little in common, of course, because she is a widow and older than I am. Also, she is very wealthy, and her social and business circles are far removed from my own."

The answer apparently satisfied Cindy's curiosity and any suspicions that she had, for she changed the subject to the county fair that would open in Portland in two days. She explained that Timmy was looking forward to it with great excitement, because one of the events would be a hot-air balloon ascent. The boy had an intense interest in mechanical devices, especially those having to do with flying, and his enthusiasm had been unaffected by his accident with the kite.

The meal continued, a fish course of fresh salmon following the rich turtle soup. The main course was a juicy, tender sirloin roast with fresh vegetables, accompanied by a delicious wine from California. The conversation was lively, and Richard exchanged comments with everyone at the table. But mostly he talked to Cindy.

A bit guiltily, he acknowledged to himself that he was being derelict in his duty. He had a rare opportunity to elicit opinions from a major general on a range of matters, which would make a valuable addition to his report when he returned to Germany. Instead, he was chatting with a young woman.

She was, however, one of the most irresistibly charming young women he had ever met. He enjoyed their conversation, and he could see that she enjoyed it as well. It was not flirtation, because she was too practical and straightforward for that. In any case, Richard had to keep reminding himself, she was engaged to Henry. Yet at the same time, he sensed a subtle interaction between himself and Cindy. Perhaps she found him as intriguing as he found her.

After dinner, everyone returned to the living room and talked for a time before Richard and Reed had to depart. General Blake invited Richard to come to his office and discuss military matters whenever he liked. Richard viewed it as a chance to make up for his neglect of the opportunity to talk with the general during dinner, and he privately resolved to make good on the offer the next afternoon, as soon as he had finished touring the fort and the training areas.

But fulfilling his responsibilities again took second

place to his interest in Cindy Holt. As he and Reed were preparing to leave, she invited him to the Holt ranch the next day. "After seeing nothing but military bases, you'll probably find it relaxing," she said. "And I'll prepare lunch. It won't be as elaborate as dinner this evening, but it should be satisfactory."

As he quickly accepted the invitation, Richard noted that something more than courtesy was in her blue eyes and tone of voice. "I'm certain it will be far more than satisfactory," he said. "You know where the ranch is, don't you, Lieutenant Kerr?"

"Yes, sir," the lieutenant replied eagerly. "We're touring the fort tomorrow morning, Cindy, so we'll be there about midday."

Richard and Reed made their farewells, then walked back to the fort. Richard was not surprised that the lieutenant was buoyantly cheerful over the invitation to the Holt ranch.

When he was in his room, Richard sat at the desk with his journal to make notes on what he had observed during the day. But he could not concentrate. He was thinking about his aunt and Henry Blake. The affair between them had always been a complete puzzle to him.

His aunt had never before shown interest in anything except money and power. But for some reason she had fallen in love with Henry, becoming devoted to him with all of the single-minded intensity of which she was capable. And while she was an often ill-tempered, ruthless woman, something about her had drawn Henry to her.

Until today, Richard had simply accepted the affair and had not searched for reasons. Now, however, his curiosity was aroused. He was unable to understand why Henry had delayed his marriage to Cindy Holt for the sake of Gisela von Kirchberg.

For a moment, he wondered if the stir of interest between Cindy and himself could ever become anything more. He could, he reflected, send a telegram to the embassy in Washington, notifying the military attaché that he had an opportunity for extended talks with a major general. That might lengthen his stay at Fort Vancouver for at least a week or two.

Then he dismissed the idea. His plans for himself were as firmly established as they were sensible. Ulrica Fremmel, the strong and healthy if somewhat plain daughter of Colonel General Hans Fremmel, would provide children and advance his career. And if he ever decided to keep a mistress in a nearby town, both the general and his daughter would understand.

An even more compelling reason for him to dismiss any notion of a romantic liaison with Cindy Holt was the fact that she was engaged to his friend Henry Blake. Richard picked up his pen and began writing notes in his journal.

His plans for his future, tinged with regret, came forcefully to Richard's mind again the next day when he saw Cindy Holt again. As he and Reed rode up to the house at the Holt ranch, she was standing on the porch. Her long, blond hair was pinned up, and she was wearing a summery yellow dress with a high, lacy collar and a fitted bodice that outlined her full breasts. If any woman could tempt him away from his plans for himself, Richard reflected, it would be Cindy Holt.

"We're not late, are we, Cindy?" Reed asked anxiously as the two of them reined up and dismounted. "We were at the cavalry training fields longer than we had expected, and then we just missed the ferry and had to wait for the next one."

Cindy smiled, shaking her head. "No, you're not late, Reed. I decided to wait out here for you to arrive, since it's such a warm day. It's good to see you again, and you, Captain Koehler."

The lieutenant beamed and replied to her greeting as he and Richard tied their horses to the hitching rail. Richard unfastened his chin strap and lifted off his plumed helmet, then climbed the steps to the porch. "It is a pleasure to see you again," he said. "It would be an additional pleasure if we could be less formal with each other."

Her blue eyes lingering on his for a moment, she seemed almost reluctant to permit familiarity between them, but she nodded as she looked away. "Very well, Richard. What do you think of the ranch?"

Tucking his helmet under his arm, Richard gazed around. It was far different from the western ranches he had seen on his journey cross country. Most of them had been desolate places with primitive shacks for houses. This house was a large brick-and-clapboard structure with a rustic atmosphere, nestled in a cluster of tall shade trees surrounded by grassy fields. The setting was beautiful, with the snow-capped peak of Mount Hood towering into the sky to the east.

"It is magnificent," Richard replied. "Not far from the city, yet it is completely private, very peaceful and comfortable. You must enjoy it very much, Cindy."

"I love this place," she said, turning to the door. "Toby is happy that I came here to keep house for him and to look after the children, but I'm even more happy to be here. Henry Blake is the only one who could ever take me away from here. Come on in, and we'll have lunch."

As he went inside with her and Reed, Richard reflected that her comment about Henry had been somewhat too emphatic and pointed, almost defensive. It matched the hint of reserve in her manner toward him, a reserve that had not been there the previous evening.

He wondered if she had thought about him the night before, the same way he had thought about her. It seemed likely, and it also seemed likely that she had reproached herself for feeling even the slightest interest in another man. Richard was more intrigued with her than ever.

The inside of the house matched its rustic exterior. The walls were paneled with wood, and the furniture was solid and heavy, built to last for generations. Unlike the Victorian decor of the Blake home, it was uncluttered and airy. In the dining room the windows were open, and the curtains swayed in the breeze, which smelled of the trees and the fields.

The atmosphere was not as genteel as it had been the previous evening, either, with Timmy helping Cindy carry in the food from the kitchen. Janessa, Cindy explained, was with friends of the family in Portland. The relaxed, simple hospitality was a welcome relief to Richard, and the food was delicious. A large platter of fried chicken was flanked by bowls of spicy potato salad and vegetables, and there were fresh rolls and tall glasses of tart, icy-cold buttermilk.

As they ate, Reed told Cindy what he and Richard had done during the morning. After touring the fort and talking with several of the staff officers, they had gone to the cavalry training fields. "The instructor, Sergeant Carstairs, got a surprise," he said, laughing. "Are you familiar with the saber course, Cindy?"

"Yes, I believe so," she replied. "Isn't that the one with straw targets on each side that the rider must cut with a saber?"

Reed smiled. "Yes, that's it. Captain Koehler rode through it and scored as many points as Sergeant Carstairs ever does."

"No, no," Richard chuckled, shaking his head. "I saw what the sergeant can do, and Reed is overly generous in his remarks. Even when the man rode at full speed, he struck all of the targets like a blacksmith striking an anvil. I barely hit some of them. But I console myself with the fact that I'm a dragoon, not a light cavalryman."

"Still, the sergeant was impressed with your skill," Reed said. "While we were talking with the officers this morning, I found it interesting that you think artillery can sometimes be more effective than cavalry. I'm sure the other officers did as well, because that's an unusual attitude for a cavalry officer, whether heavy or light cavalry."

Richard smiled and shrugged. "I hope to be a general someday, in command of the full range of arms. Accordingly, I study artillery tactics as much as I do infantry or cavalry."

Timmy, biting into a piece of chicken, was suddenly interested. "What kind of rockets do you have, sir?" he asked.

Cindy frowned. "Now, Timmy, remember what I told you about interrupting when adults are having a conversation. And please don't speak when your mouth is full of food."

Richard smiled across the table at the boy. "The rockets we have in Germany are very similar to the Hale rockets at the fort, Timmy. Have you ever seen them fired?"

The boy, chewing a large mouthful of chicken, grinned and nodded gleefully. Cindy sighed, explaining. "Papa lets me know a day ahead of time when the rocket companies will be going out to the artillery range to practice," she said. "Then he sends a soldier over to take Timmy to watch them. Papa thinks he's making an artilleryman out of Timmy, but Timmy simply likes anything that goes up into the air."

"And mechanical devices," Richard added. "Your mother said last night that he's very interested in steam engines."

"Yes, that's right," Cindy agreed. "Janessa and I both will be pleased and relieved when he starts school and begins learning how to read. He can already pick out a few words, and he's forever pestering us to read things to him that he finds in the newspaper about new steam engines and such."

"He'll certainly enjoy the county fair tomorrow," Reed commented. "In addition to the hot-air balloon ascent, I understand they'll have an exhibit of road locomotives, those wagons that run on steam."

"I know," Cindy replied. "He's been talking about them incessantly, and I'll probably end up spending most if not all of the day at the fair with him tomorrow. Please have some more chicken, Richard."

They fell silent for a moment; then Reed brought up the subject of the fair again. "You haven't said whether or not you'd like to go, Captain Koehler," he said. "I believe you would enjoy it."

Richard reflected that the next day would be his last opportunity to talk at length with Leland Blake. But then he noticed that Cindy was plucking restlessly at the edge of her napkin. She was, he realized, listening intently and waiting for his reply. He nodded. "Yes, let's go there tomorrow, Reed," he said. "I haven't had an opportunity to see a fair during my visit here, and I am certain I will find it interesting."

"I'm sure you will," Reed agreed happily. "If you wish, we'll take an early ferry across the river so you'll have plenty of time to see everything. You'll be at the fair early, won't you, Cindy?"

Cindy nodded, folding her napkin and putting it beside her plate. "Yes, Timmy won't give me any peace until we get there," she said. "I hope you've had an opportunity to see many things to tell your family about when you return to Germany, Richard."

The remark was uncharacteristically awkward, the implicit question so transparently obvious that Richard saw a faint blush rise to her face. "I don't have a family," he said. "I've been concentrating on my career thus far. However, I am certain that I will be a popular dinner companion among the other officers for at least a time, because they will want to hear all about what I've seen here."

"Yes, without a doubt," Cindy said as she stood up. "Shall we go out and look around the ranch? I can see to the dishes later. Come along, Timmy."

The boy climbed down from his chair, and Richard and Reed followed him and Cindy out. The midafternoon sunshine was bright and warm, a few white clouds drifting across the sky and casting shadows on the rolling pastures that reached back to the horizon. Corrals, barns, a bunkhouse, and other buildings were set back from the house, and men were working around them. A few horses and colts were in the corrals, and scores of horses were grazing and frolicking in the pastures.

A tall, lean man crossed the grassy expanse to meet Richard and the others as they walked toward the corrals. He was wearing a wide western hat, boots, and denims, and Richard was surprised to see that he was an Indian. He looked fairly old, his hair white and his brown, good-natured face creased with age, but he walked with the firm, lithe stride of a much younger man. Cindy introduced him as Stalking Horse, the ranch foreman.

As they all continued toward the corrals, Stalking Horse explained that the ranch specialized in quarter horses, a breed developed for working with cattle and other livestock. Descended from the wiry, hardy wild horses of the West whose ancestors had escaped from the Spanish explorers, they were compact, muscular animals.

"We have ranchers from hundreds of miles away coming here to buy them," Stalking Horse said, "because this is some of the best stock in the West. The food and care that colts receive during their first six months has a big effect on their strength and health all during their lives, and we give them the best of both."

They had stopped beside a corral, and Richard admired the sleek, glossy horses inside the fence. "I've never seen horses in better condition than these."

"They are cow ponies rather than the cavalry mounts you are accustomed to," Stalking Horse said, "but in many ways we treat them like cavalry horses. For example, to keep them high-spirited, we gentle them rather than break them to saddle. Come over here and I will show you how we go about it."

They walked to the corral, where several young horses were tethered inside the fence, some with only bridles on them, others with saddle blankets strapped to their backs, and yet others with full riding equipment on them. Two men were leading first one horse and then another around inside the corral.

Stalking Horse explained that only bridles were put on the horses at first, then saddle blankets, and finally saddles. When a rider at last mounted them, few of the horses bucked. The animals were then trained to turn quickly in response to knee pressure from the rider, to stand as though tethered when the reins were dropped to the ground, and in general to behave in ways that made them useful while working with livestock.

As Stalking Horse led Richard and the others around to a blacksmith shop at the rear of one of the barns, he explained that the horses were shod as soon as their training was completed. Horses were tethered outside the smithy, and a forge glowed in the dim interior. Stalking Horse called an Indian youth out of the shop and introduced him to Richard.

The slim, muscular boy, who looked to be about twelve or thirteen, was named White Elk. Sweaty from the heat of the forge and wearing a blacksmith's leather apron over his denims, he was as friendly as Stalking Horse. The foreman's voice rang with pride as he told Richard that he was training White Elk to take his place eventually as foreman of the ranch.

"My work will be easier when I have only one job," White Elk said jokingly. "Now Stalking Horse has me working from dawn until dark, doing everything from training horses to cleaning the stables."

Stalking Horse laughed at the youth's comment. "You may not think so now, White Elk, but you will find that the foreman always works harder than anyone else. And he must know all of the work."

"There is not much to know about pumping a bellows," the youth joked as he went back into the smithy, where he and the two men inside resumed work. When the tour of the outbuildings was finished, Richard shook hands with Stalking Horse again and made his farewells, then returned to the house with Cindy and Reed.

The remainder of the afternoon passed swiftly for Richard as he sat at a lawn table on the shady side of the house with Reed and Cindy, talking and drinking lemonade. When the shadows were growing long, with sunset near, Janessa returned home from Portland. Richard observed with considerable surprise that she was puffing on a cigarette as she rode past the house to take her horse to the corrals. Cindy, however, seemed not to notice, so he said nothing.

During lunch and throughout the afternoon, Richard had seen a guarded reserve as well as pleasure in Cindy's eyes, his presence creating warring impulses within her. As she walked around the house with him and Reed to their horses, her large blue eyes mirrored regret mixed with relief.

"This has been an afternoon I shall never forget," Richard said. "I am most grateful for your hospitality."

"It was a very pleasant afternoon for me as well, Richard," she replied, her smile polite and her eyes avoiding his. She exchanged a few words with Reed about the next day's fair, and then the two men mounted their horses. As they rode away, Timmy and Janessa came out on the porch and stood beside Cindy. Richard waved farewell, reflecting that they were the most intriguing family he had ever met. But most fascinating of all was the bewitchingly lovely Cindy.

To Fred Guthrie, the most fascinating woman in the world was Ursula Oberg, and there were few things he enjoyed more than sitting outside with her on a warm summer's evening, drinking beer.

Darkness had fallen and the moon had risen high in the sky while Fred and Ursula sat together, talking. While Fred enjoyed Maida's beer, he had also been fortifying himself to broach a subject that he found intimidating. By now several of the bottles were empty and the hour was late, but Fred still felt as uneasy as ever about bringing up the subject.

As he listened to Ursula talk on about Maida's activities in the barn, something she said caught his attention.

"You say that you're starting to make a profit?" he exclaimed. "How can you make a profit when dozens of casks of beer are still stacking up in there?"

"Ever since the Holt logging camp began buying beer, others began buying it, too," Ursula replied. "We are making a substantial profit, because our expenses are relatively small. Most of our food is grown here, so buying malt for Maida and wood for Paddy's cooperage are our main expenses."

"But what will you do with all the beer that's stacking up?"

"People will eventually learn about it, and then it will sell. In the meantime, we will be accumulating a stock of premium beer. Would you like another bottle?"

"No, I've had plenty, thank you," he replied. Picking up his glass, he drained the last drops of foam, again thinking about the subject he had intended to bring up. Deciding to let it wait until another time, he put down his glass and stood up. "Well, I'd better be on my way."

Ursula walked with him to the wagon. Just as he started to climb in, she said, "Do you want to ask me something, Fred?"

"Yes, I do," he replied, turning back to her and squaring his muscular shoulders with determination. In the soft moonlight, she was more alluringly beautiful than ever. His courage again deserting him as quickly as he had summoned it, he looked away and scratched his beard. "When you order more bottles, do you want me to bring them here?"

"Yes, I would appreciate that very much, Fred."

Again he put a hand on his wagon. "All right, I'll bring them as soon as they get to Colmer. Good night, Ursula."

"Just a moment, Fred." She took his arm and turned him back. "Is there something else you want to ask me?"

Fred sighed mightily, shifting his weight from his wooden leg to his good leg. "Yes, actually there is. What would Maida think about it if you got married again, Ursula?"

"I doubt if she would notice, Fred."

"That's what I thought," he said, turning to his wagon again. "She doesn't notice much, does she? Well, good night, Ursula."

Ursula took his arm once again, turning him back around to face her. "Is there something else you want to ask me, Fred?"

After a long pause and an agony of confusion, Fred made a choked sound, trying to speak. Then he finally got the words out. "Will you marry me, Ursula?" he blurted in a loud voice.

"Yes."

Numb with shock, he looked down at her. Suddenly she was in his arms, her body warm, soft, and fragrant. He kissed her, her lips far more intoxicating than the rich, hearty beer her daughter made.

IX

"It appears that almost everyone is at the fair," Richard commented as he and Reed rode along a street leading from the ferry docks to the fairgrounds on the edge of Portland. "The city is very quiet today."

"Yes, sir," Reed agreed, glancing around. The businesses lining the street were closed, and the few people in sight were all heading toward the fairgrounds. "There isn't a lot of entertainment hereabouts, and the fair is the biggest event of the year. Fortunately it's a sunny day, but it appears to be too windy for a balloon ascent."

Richard looked at the swaying branches of the trees. "Yes, and the wind is gusty instead of steady, which is extremely unsafe for a balloon. An observation balloon wouldn't be put up in wind like this unless it was an absolute necessity."

"Timmy has certainly been looking forward to seeing that balloon," Reed said. "It would be a great disappointment for him if the event were canceled. But it's scheduled for later in the day, so perhaps the wind will die down by then."

"Yes, perhaps so."

Something more personal than the possibility of Timmy Holt's being disappointed was also on Reed's mind as he looked at the trees swaying in the wind. If the balloon ascent were canceled, Cindy would probably leave the fair early. And his opportunity for more than an occasional glimpse of her at the fort was drawing to an end, since Richard would be leaving the next day.

At the edge of the city, the quiet of the streets dissolved into the noisy bustle of the fairgrounds. Lines of brightly colored pennants fluttered over the expanse of tents and awnings, and people crowded the walkways beyond the entrance gate. A brass band at one side of the fairgrounds competed with the cheerful braying of a steam calliope on the other side, and the shouting of barkers rang out over the hubbub from the crowd.

Leaving their horses in a rope enclosure, Reed and Richard mingled with the crowd milling among the sideshows. Stalking Horse, White Elk, and other employees from the Holt ranch were at a booth, trying their skill in tossing rings over pegs to win a prize. Reed and Richard stopped to watch and to talk with them for a few minutes, then walked on along the line of booths and tents.

The judging among entries in the prize livestock, home products, and handicrafts competitions was being conducted in tents and enclosures situated past the sideshows and amusement booths. Farther back in the fairgrounds were exhibits set up by farm equipment manufacturers. Here the crowd thinned out and the noise faded, with scattered men and women looking at the exhibits and talking quietly with the salesmen.

Cindy Holt's green dress was a bright spot of color among the sober clothing worn by the farmers. She was holding Timmy's hand in resigned patience as the boy gazed in fascination at a road locomotive pulling a large sled loaded with rocks. As Reed and Richard approached, Cindy smiled in relief to see them. "I can't tell you how pleased I am to have company," she said. "We've been here no more than an hour, but it seems forever to me."

Reed pointed to the leaflets that the boy had collected from various exhibits and stuffed into his pockets. "It appears that you'll have to set aside a few days to read those to him, Cindy," he commented, laughing.

"Indeed I will," she sighed. "Fortunately I won't have to do all of it, because Janessa will take a share. But he has enough for both of us."

Her tone was affectionate as she looked down at the boy and pushed his hair back from his brow. He scarcely noticed her touch, his eyes fixed on the road locomotive. It was a large vehicle with three steel wheels and cleats on the two rear wheels to give it traction on soft ground. Smoke billowed from its stack as it dragged the sled and rumbled around in circles, the operator leaning against the steering lever.

"He could stand and watch it for hours," Cindy said fondly. "It's been doing nothing but dragging that sled back and forth, but that's enough for him."

After watching the road locomotive for another few minutes, the three adults took Timmy to see a steam-engine exhibit in a nearby tent, then another road locomotive. By the time he had seen enough, it was nearing noon. They all agreed to have lunch, and as they were walking toward the refreshment tents, they passed a middle-aged couple who greeted Cindy warmly. The man and woman, wearing the plain, sturdy clothes of farmers, had been looking at a dairy equipment exhibit. Cindy introduced them to Reed and Richard as Horace and Wilma Givens, who owned a dairy farm adjacent to the Holt ranch.

"Just call me Horace," the man said as he shook hands with the two young officers. Grinning proudly, he turned back to Cindy and took out a large blue ribbon with the seal of the fair attached to it. "Look at this, Miss Cindy," he said.

"One of your cows was awarded first prize?" Cindy exclaimed. "Congratulations, Mr. Givens. Was it for the best dairy cow?"

"No, the prize heifer," Givens replied happily. "And I owe it all to Miss Janessa. It was that calf she delivered for me last year."

Cindy did not seem to want to discuss the subject.

She started to edge away. "Yes, well, I'm very pleased you won the blue ribbon, Mr. Givens."

"I owe it all to Miss Janessa," Givens repeated, waving the ribbon. "If it hadn't been for her, my best cow and that calf would have died. Tell Miss Janessa that I'll always be indebted to her."

"Yes, yes, I will," Cindy said, pulling Timmy along as she walked away. "Good-bye. Good-bye, Mrs. Givens."

The man and woman waved, then turned back to the dairy equipment. Reed was curious about how Janessa had been involved with the man's livestock, but the subject was obviously one that Cindy preferred not to discuss. He said nothing about it, and Cindy resumed talking with Timmy about the road locomotives as they walked toward the refreshment tent.

Inside the tent, they bought drinks and plates of sandwiches, then sat down on a bench at one of the long tables. The wind was still gusty, the tent tugging at its ropes as the canvas rippled. Reed spoke quietly to Cindy, explaining that the balloon ascent would undoubtedly be canceled. Nevertheless, when they had finished eating, they walked toward the edge of the fairgrounds, to the field that had been reserved for the balloon. As they approached, they saw men sorting out ropes and unrolling the large expanse of balloon fabric. Reed exchanged a concerned glance with Richard.

The area around the balloon had been roped off to keep spectators at a distance. A few people had already gathered and were watching the preparations, as fairground workers moved about following the balloonist's directions.

A man of medium height and about thirty years old, Calvin Rogers looked as though his vocation had taken a heavy toll on him. He was thin and pale, his face scarred from injuries, and he walked with a heavy limp. Reed observed that the man's suit was cheap and threadbare. The balloon also looked shabby, the fabric patched and many of the ropes frayed and spliced.

One of the fairground stewards arrived in a wagon,

and a worker untied the rope so he could drive through. Other workers climbed into the wagon and unloaded bundles of advertisement leaflets, stacking them beside the wicker gondola as Rogers and the steward talked. From their gestures, they were discussing the wind.

Rogers smiled and shook his head, pointing upward. Shrugging, the steward turned away, then climbed into the wagon and drove off. As Rogers straightened up from inspecting the cable winch beside the gondola, he caught sight of Richard in his Prussian uniform. He limped toward the rope.

"Excuse me, sir," he said. "Are you a German officer?"

"Yes, I am," Richard replied. "I am Captain Richard Koehler. This is Miss Cindy Holt, and this is Lieutenant Reed Kerr. The boy is Miss Holt's nephew, Timmy."

Rogers lifted his cap and bowed, acknowledging the introductions, then turned back to Richard. "Captain Koehler, I've read about many recent advances in hot-air balloons that have been made in Germany. Do you happen to be at all familiar with them?"

Richard shook his head. "No, you undoubtedly know much more about it than I do. Observation balloons are assigned to artillery batteries, and I am in a dragoon brigade. However, to my untrained eyes it appears much too windy today for a balloon ascent."

"Yes, it is windy today," Rogers mused, looking around. "But I've been up in wind before, and I believe I'll be all right. The fact is I need the money. I had an accident at a circus in Ohio last autumn that tore up my balloon pretty bad. I've been in the hospital since then, and now I'm trying to get started again."

"What happened?" Richard asked.

"My cable broke," Rogers replied. "It was a good flight for a time, but then I ran out of straw and the balloon came down in a stand of trees. Anyway, I managed to patch that one together, and I'll be able to make a better one after a few more fairs and circuses."

Cindy frowned in perplexity. "But why do you do something that is so dangerous?" she asked.

"I can't explain it," Rogers replied, smiling wistfully. "The reason I can't is that you've never been up in a balloon, Miss Holt. If you had, you wouldn't need to ask that. Would you like to bring the boy over to the balloon so he can look at it? Here, I'll untie the rope."

He limped to the nearest post and unfastened the rope, and Reed stepped across it with Cindy and Richard, as Timmy excitedly ran toward the balloon. The workers had finished attaching the ropes to the gondola and were opening a bale of straw.

The wide mouth at the base of the balloon had a wire frame inside it to keep it rigid. The workers held up the frame and fabric as Rogers piled straw into a wire basket suspended under it. He struck a match and lit the straw, then added more as it blazed up. The hot air flowed into the huge envelope of fabric, and after a few minutes it gradually began swelling, the wrinkles in it smoothing out.

A worker handed Rogers a water bottle when he pointed to it. He sprinkled water on the burning straw to make it smoke, then looked at Timmy. "Do you want to run around the balloon and see if I have any bad leaks, Timmy?" He laughed as the boy eagerly nodded. "Go ahead, then. Look it over good."

The boy raced away, his gaze fixed on the swelling mass of fabric. A moment later, he slid to a stop and called out, pointing to a wisp of smoke that was coming from a tiny hole. Pushing straw into the basket, Rogers craned his neck and looked at it. "That isn't too bad," he shouted. "See if you can find any more."

Reed looked at the thin stream of smoke, then turned back to Rogers. "Are there always leaks in hot-air balloons?" he asked.

"Yes, always," the man replied. "Even the most expensive muslin isn't airtight, and there are always leaks in the seams. But a good balloon won't have as many leaks as this one. With fewer leaks, it doesn't take as long to get a balloon aloft or as much straw to keep it there."

He turned to look as Timmy called out again, pointing; then he waved for the boy to continue looking. Timmy ran back and forth around the balloon, finding several more small leaks and pointing them out to Rogers. When the boy returned to the gondola, the fabric bag was bulging seven or eight feet high.

A half hour later, the balloon was upright, and a crowd had gathered outside the rope. Rogers clambered into the gondola, and Cindy took Timmy's hand firmly and led him back toward the rope, Reed and Richard following. The workers put the bales of leaflets into the gondola as Rogers pushed more handfuls of straw into the blazing fire in the basket. A few minutes later, the gondola rose slowly off the ground, halting a foot or two in the air as it strained at its safety ropes.

A mountainous globe of fabric that towered high into the sky, it was like a living thing as it swayed in the wind. Timmy was in a rapture of excitement. As Rogers directed the workers to cast off the safety ropes, Reed thought he saw in the man's flushed face the same excitement that was gripping the boy.

Once the ropes were released, the gondola strained at the cable on the winch. Rogers glanced up at the balloon bobbing in the gusts of wind, but his momentary apprehension seemed lost in his eagerness to be aloft. He motioned to the men to begin unwinding the winch, then waved to the crowd. An approving roar rose from the people as the balloon began ascending.

The lively melody of the calliope from across the fairgrounds was drowned in the shouts and whistles. Then a harder gust of wind caught the balloon, making it lean far forward of the gondola. As the gondola swept back down toward the ground, a bedlam of screams and shouts of fright rose from the crowd.

The gondola brushed the tall grass, then soared upward again. Rogers pushed straw into the basket as he

laughed and waved to the crowd. The outcry of fear changed
to a roar of cheers. The workers turned the winch, and the
balloon rose higher.

Cindy held her wide hat with one hand as she looked
up at the balloon. "The man is insane," she said quietly.
"He is totally insane."

"No," Richard said, shaking his head as he looked up.
"He has found his dream, and it means more to him than
life."

"But it is purposeless," Cindy objected. "If he's killed
at this, his death will be futile, an utter waste."

"Some would say the same of soldiers," Richard replied. "Duty, honor, and country are a purpose you understand, Cindy, because you share that purpose. Some,
however, do not share it. I do not understand Rogers's
purpose, but I accept it."

Cindy looked at Richard closely for a moment, then
gazed back up at the balloon. Swaying in the wind, it was
fifty feet off the ground and edging higher as the workers
slowly turned the crank on the winch. In the distance the
road locomotives had stopped moving about, and other
activities had ceased. All across the fairground, people
were pointing and watching the balloon.

The cable was paying out at a sharp angle because of
the wind, and part of the crowd was looking straight up at
the balloon as it rose higher. Rogers tossed out handfuls of
leaflets, the wind catching them and scattering them. Some
drifted down onto the fairground, people leaping to catch
them, and others were carried toward the city.

The balloon was more than a hundred feet off the
ground when suddenly a powerful gust of wind surged
against it. It tilted violently, the gondola sinking rapidly.
As the fabric bag leaned over at a sharp angle, its base
brushed against the basket containing the fire, spilling
burning straw into the wicker gondola.

In an instant, the side of the gondola and the leaflets
were blazing. As the balloon staggered, starting to right
itself, flames raced up one side of the flammable fabric.

Losing its heated air and starting to collapse, it began falling. The crowd scattered from under it in screaming confusion.

Reed ran toward the impact point, with Richard close behind. As the balloon plummeted straight down, Rogers tried to climb over the side of the gondola to jump clear, but he fell back. Richard called out to Reed in warning, shouting in German in his haste. Reed had seen the danger, though, and he dodged as the heavy cable lashed through the air and fell beside him.

The gondola slammed down in the tall grass. Reed and Richard ran into the shadow of the balloon, the expanse of fabric settling over them and covering them in a blinding nightmare of heat, smoke, and suffocating cloth. Reed pushed at it and fought his way toward the gondola, feeling more than seeing Richard at his side.

Flames lightened the darkness ahead as Reed ran into the side of the gondola. Groping in it, he gripped one of Rogers's arms. Then Richard was there taking the other, and they dragged the man out of the gondola. They pushed at the fabric and started back, choking and coughing in the thick smoke.

The wind was cool and fresh against Reed's face as he and Richard dragged Rogers out from under the fabric, the balloon an inferno of flames behind them. People in the scattered crowd shouted, pointing to Reed and Richard. Cindy ran toward them, carrying Richard's helmet and Reed's cap.

Cindy knelt beside Rogers, who was unconscious, blood trickling from his mouth and nose. She turned to the fairground workers. "Please fetch a wagon!" she shouted. "This man is seriously injured, and he must be taken to the doctor immediately!"

Two of the workers began running toward the tents. Cindy handed Reed and Richard their headgear. "That was the most courageous act I've ever seen," she said. "God bless both of you." She turned to comfort Timmy, who was weeping in despair.

Still coughing from the smoke, Reed looked down at Rogers. The man's thin, scarred face was deathly pale, the blood from his nose and mouth a bright crimson against the pallor of his skin. Reed glanced at Richard, who shook his head grimly.

People began gathering around, and Cindy motioned them back. "Please give him air," she said. "Here comes the wagon to take him to the doctor. Please make way for it. Let the wagon through, please."

The people moved back and made a path for the wagon, and as the fairground steward reined it to a halt, Cindy called out to him. "Do you know where Dr. Martin lives?" she asked.

"Yes, miss," the man replied. "I know the fastest way, don't you worry." He helped her up to the seat as Reed and Richard carefully lifted Rogers into the back. Reed boosted Timmy up, and then he and Richard climbed in. The steward whistled to the horses and snapped the reins, and the wagon lurched forward.

A mass of people flowed across the fairgrounds toward the smoking remains of the balloon as the wagon took the back road out. Timmy was staring at Rogers and struggling to control his tears. Cindy called to him and lifted him onto the seat beside her.

The city streets were quiet after the bustle of the fairgrounds. As the wagon came to a halt before a modest, white-clapboard house, Cindy jumped down from the seat and called to Janessa. A moment later the front door of the house opened and the girl looked out.

"Janessa, we have a seriously injured man," Cindy said as she hurried up the walk. "Is the doctor at home?"

The girl nodded, shouted at the men to wait a moment, then ran down the drive to the carriage house. An instant later she reappeared carrying a stretcher, and Reed helped her open it. He and Richard put Rogers on the stretcher and followed the girl toward the door.

Dr. Robert Martin, white-haired and thin with age, was waiting inside the door. He led Reed and Richard to the surgery room, where they put Rogers on the examination table. Janessa followed them in.

The doctor took rimless spectacles from his waistcoat pocket and put them on. After Reed quickly explained what had happened, Dr. Martin turned to Janessa. "Please show these gentlemen into the other room, Dr. Janessa," he said. "Then come back in and assist me with the examination, if you would."

In the hall outside, the doctor's wife, Tonie Martin, was talking with Cindy. After being introduced to Reed and Richard, she led them into the parlor, then excused herself and went into the kitchen, returning a little while later with a coffee service and a glass of juice for Timmy. They talked quietly about what had happened, until the doctor's footsteps came along the hall.

Dr. Martin's manner was grave as he stepped into the room. "The patient is conscious now," he said tersely. "He has some burns and bruises, but the worst injury is to his left leg. It's been broken several times before, and this time it may not heal. He may be on crutches for the rest of his life."

"But he doesn't have any internal injuries?" Cindy asked.

"No, no internal injuries," the doctor replied. "But I'm not very hopeful about this man's recovery. He's just spent months in a charity hospital, and he's in very poor physical condition. He needs good food and care, but he doesn't have any money. He'll have to go to a charity hospital again. Considering the condition he's in, I'm not at all sure he will leave there alive."

"I'll take him to the ranch," Cindy said. "Janessa can look after him until he improves sufficiently for the hands to be able to take care of him. There are extra rooms in the bunkhouse, and he can eat with the hands when he's well enough to get about."

The doctor pursed his lips, frowning. "Well, it's up to you, Cindy, and it would be very good of you to do that. However, I want to make certain that you know what's

involved. Your family might end up supporting a handi-
capped man for the rest of his life, and he's far from being
an old man. As I said, he might be on crutches the rest of
his life."

"I realize that," Cindy replied. "But we've never
turned our back on someone in need, and we won't now.
If he gets well enough to do chores, he can work around
the barns, hoe the kitchen garden, and milk the cow. If he
doesn't, then he needn't do anything. In any event, one
more man among the hands will be very little additional
expense."

The doctor smiled. "I believe he'll be able to get
around some, but I'll know more when I see how that left
leg does within the next few days. He shouldn't need
more than a day or two of constant care, and it would
probably be better for him to stay here tonight. We can
move him out to the ranch tomorrow afternoon."

"Very well," Cindy said, standing up. "I'll talk to him
now and explain what his situation will be at the ranch."

The doctor nodded and turned back to the door.
Timmy, who had been listening to the conversation with
growing excitement, scrambled down from his chair. He
smiled up at his aunt and took her hand, and together
they went into the examination room.

Reed and Richard finished their coffee, thanked Tonie
Martin, then went out to the porch to wait until Cindy
was ready to leave.

"From what I've seen of the Holt family," Richard
said, "Cindy's offer does not surprise me. And I would
hazard a guess that her brother will be pleased by what
she has done, and would have been displeased if she had
done otherwise. Am I correct?"

"Yes, sir," Reed replied. "The Holts are very generous. They're always ready to help anyone in need."

Richard gazed out at the street. "That is commenda-
ble, and the world would be a much pleasanter place if
there were more people like them. In this instance,
though, I believe that Cindy's generosity will have a

result she hasn't foreseen, and one that she certainly will not like."

"What's that, sir?"

"The influence that Calvin Rogers will have on her young nephew," Richard replied. "Timmy shares that man's dream, but there was nothing in the boy's surroundings to develop it beyond a childish interest. He would probably have become a rancher who would occasionally gaze up at the sky with longing. But now Calvin Rogers will be there. I believe Cindy will not like the effect that will have on the boy."

The next morning, Richard and Reed discussed the accident involving the hot-air balloon as they waited for the ferry to cross the river to Portland. Neither of them was in a mood to talk, and the events of the previous day served as a handy topic of conversation to fill the silence. The San Francisco packet was at its pier across the river, where it had docked the previous afternoon, and Richard would board it shortly to leave.

During his tour of the United States, Richard had visited a large number of army posts, some for longer periods than he had spent at Fort Vancouver. But he knew that his visit to this place would remain in his memory long after he had forgotten all the others.

A friendship had formed between him and the lieutenant at his side, a man with whom he had shared a moment of danger when they rescued Calvin Rogers. Other events had occurred that would remain a part of him. Most of all, he knew he would never view life again as he had before meeting Cindy Holt. As the moment to depart approached, he had a sad sense of leavetaking, of leaving a part of himself behind.

"The fair organizers will probably pay Calvin Rogers at least part of the money they agreed to pay him for making the balloon ascents," Reed was saying.

"They certainly should," Richard replied. "They wanted

an unusual attraction, and no one can question that Calvin Rogers gave them that."

They fell silent for a moment, watching as the ferry approached the dock. "We'll get to the other side well before the packet leaves," Reed said.

Richard was staring at the approaching ferry. "I will be happy to get home," he said, "but I regret leaving here. I have enjoyed my visit very much, and I have enjoyed meeting you and making friends with you. Have you ever thought of applying for military observer duty? I would be pleased to host you in Germany."

Reed smiled and shook his head. "I'm sure it would be a very pleasant as well as valuable experience, but I'm content here."

Richard eyed his friend, strongly suspecting that Reed's reason for wanting to stay at Fort Vancouver was identical to his own reason for not wanting to leave—Cindy Holt. That was certainly understandable.

As the ferry eased up to the pier, one of the soldiers with the baggage spoke to Reed. "Sir," he said, "here comes the general."

Sitting straight but with the relaxed ease of an expert horseman, Lee Blake was riding toward the pier at a canter. Richard, Reed, and the soldiers stood at attention and saluted. The general returned their salute as he reined up and dismounted. "It appears that I arrived just in time, Captain Koehler," he said, nodding toward the ferry. "I meant to see you off on the packet, and I almost delayed too long."

"I'm very honored, sir," Richard said.

"It was our honor to have you visit us," Lee replied, handing his reins to one of the soldiers. "My only regret is that your visit was so brief."

People from the town of Vancouver were filing onto the ferry, going to the fair in Portland. The three officers followed them aboard, the soldiers taking Richard's baggage to the lower deck. As the ferry moved away from the pier and started back across the river, the general mentioned the near tragedy involving the hot-air balloon.

"You and Lieutenant Kerr acted commendably in rescuing that man," he said, "and I want to congratulate both of you." He questioned the two men about the incident and was amused when each of them insisted on giving the other most of the credit.

After the ferry docked at the Portland piers a short time later, the three men walked along the waterfront to the pier where the San Francisco packet was tied up.

Smoke trickled from the stacks on the large steamer, crewmen bustling about in preparation to leave. Other passengers were making their farewells with friends and relatives and filing aboard. The soldiers unloaded Richard's baggage from the wagon and gave it to the porters as he stood at the gate and talked with Reed and the general.

The clatter of a horse's hooves and a flash of bright color caught Richard's eye, and he looked down the street to see Cindy Holt approaching. No one he knew could match the composed, graceful ease with which she sat her horse and brought it to a halt.

Conflicting emotions vied within Richard as he stared at her. He had yearned to see her once more before leaving, yet seeing her made leaving that much more difficult.

Lee Blake helped her down from her sidesaddle, and she handed her reins to one of the soldiers. "Thank you, and good morning, Papa," she said. "Good morning, Richard, Reed. I came to town to see how Calvin Rogers is this morning, and I decided to come and see Richard off."

As he and the other two officers replied to her greeting, Richard could see in her blue eyes that what she said was true only in a literal sense. He knew that the real purpose of her trip had been to come to the docks to see him once more.

"Your mother is very pleased that you're taking that man to the ranch, Cindy," Lee said. Cindy dismissed the subject with a few words, as if she had done only what anyone else would have; then the conversation turned back to Richard. As the general asked him about the remainder of his tour of the United States and his plans for returning to Germany, Richard noticed that Cindy had become pensive and was silently staring out at the river, as though she were experiencing feelings similar to his own.

The horn on the steam packet droned in a final call for passengers to get aboard. Richard exchanged salutes and shook hands with the general and Reed. As he turned to Cindy, she stepped closer to him and offered her hand. Lee and Reed, as near as they were, failed to see that it was more than a farewell between friends.

Her handkerchief was clutched in her hand. As Richard took her fingers in his, he bowed, then straightened and met her gaze. She hesitated for a bare instant, then pushed the cloth into his hand. With the small handkerchief folded tightly in his fist, Richard went through the gate and up the gangplank.

He stood at the rail and waved to them as the steam packet moved away from the dock and out into the river. They remained standing on the pier and waved until the vessel passed between the islands in the river. Cindy's dress was a bright, distant spot of color; then the piers disappeared from view.

Richard took the handkerchief from his pocket and looked at it. Fragrant with her perfume, it was a small square of linen that she had embroidered with her name and trimmed with lace. Taking it, he reflected, had been absurd, but he had wanted some physical reminder of her. Their lives had touched briefly, and his, for one, would never be the same again. Marriage with Colonel General Hans Fremmel's strong and healthy if somewhat plain daughter seemed a very unrewarding prospect.

X

As was his habit on Friday afternoons, Henry Blake left the Mauser Arms Works early. It was only a few minutes' walk from the vast, multistoried brick factory near the center of Frankfurt-am-Main to the *Bahnhof*, the main train station.

On the platform for the local to Mainz were a few wealthy businessmen who were also leaving the city early. Acquainted with most of them from his daily commuting on the train, Henry touched his cap as they lifted their hats and bowed in greeting.

The local arrived punctually at three o'clock, and Henry took his accustomed seat. The conductor merely nodded as he came by to collect tickets, knowing Henry had a daily pass. The train pulled out of the station, soon leaving the city and its smoking factories behind.

Henry stared out of the window at the vineyards and farms that dotted the wooded hills reaching back from the valley of the Main. Every few minutes the train stopped at a small station to let off passengers.

At the last station before Mainz, the town of Grevenburg, Henry was the only one who got off the train. On a siding was a luxuriously appointed private car with the Kirchberg arms on its sides; it was the car Gisela used when she traveled to Berlin and elsewhere. A porter had already brought Henry's horse from the stable behind the

station, and the man lifted his cap as he handed Henry the
reins.

Grevenburg was ancient, its plaster-and-beam buildings curved to fit turns in the narrow, cobblestone streets.
Henry skirted the town and took the road leading up the
hill, passing through vineyards that were a brilliant green
in the afternoon sunshine.

As the road wound higher, the city of Mainz at the
junction of the Main and the Rhine came into view. Then,
cutting back suddenly onto a broad plateau, the road
turned into a wide, tree-flanked avenue with fountains in
the center. The avenue led back in a long, straight vista to
a palatial mansion of some one hundred rooms. Dominating the landscape, it was called Grevenhof.

The acres of plateau surrounding the mansion were
covered with formal gardens. Rigidly straight and carefully
pruned rows of trees and shrubbery bordered well-tended
flower gardens and gleaming statuary on marble terraces.
Off to the left, overlooking the mansion and the town from
the top of the hill, rose the ruined walls of Castle Greven,
in past centuries the refuge for those from the manor and
the town in times of war.

Gardeners trimming the hedges greeted Henry cheerfully, and the stable boy waiting at the front steps grinned
as he took Henry's horse. The butler bowed and smiled as
he opened the door. Henry was liked and respected both
among the mansion staff and in the town, where he was
known as *nicht zu kaufen sein*—he who cannot be bought.
It was obvious he was not interested in the baroness's
immense fortune, and he was the only one who could
control her volatile temper.

Henry went straight into the wing that housed the
business offices, which consisted of a series of lofty drawing rooms with mural ceilings and ornate pilasters. The
clerks and accountants looked up from their work and
greeted him warmly.

The office manager, Hans Guenther, stood up and

bowed stiffly. "Good afternoon, Lieutenant Blake," he said. "It is a very bright and pleasant day today, is it not?"

"Good afternoon, Herr Guenther," Henry replied. "Yes, it is a very sunny day today, and I enjoyed my ride from the town."

Guenther glanced around as he sat back down, and the clerks and accountants busied themselves with their work again. The office staff had expanded during the past weeks, with two clerks and an accountant having been added. The new employees were all English, though fluent in German, and their primary responsibility was the affairs of Blake Enterprises, Limited, in England.

In the next office, Helmut Brunner, Gisela's business adviser, was going over some papers with Emil Koehler, Gisela's father as well as her legal adviser. The elderly Koehler was also Richard Koehler's grandfather, and like Richard he was as easygoing as Gisela was aggressive and driven. Henry liked him immensely.

"Good afternoon, Herr Koehler, Herr Brunner," Henry said. "I hope you both have had a pleasant day with which to end the week."

"The day that ends the week is always pleasant, Lieutenant Blake," Koehler replied with a smile. "I received a letter today from Richard. He informed me that he will be visiting the army post near your home during his tour of the United States."

For a moment Henry worried that Richard might inadvertently say too much about Gisela while he was there, but he dismissed the thought, knowing that Richard would be discreet. "I'm very pleased to hear that," he said. "My parents will make him welcome at Fort Vancouver."

"Yes, I'm sure they will, Lieutenant Blake," Koehler said. "I trust you have had an informative day?"

Henry nodded, amused by Koehler's thinly veiled reference to the nature of his assignment in Frankfurt. Working with the procurement officers of the German Army in order to study their methods was Henry's official reason for being at the Mauser Arms Works, but he had other, unstated, objectives, such as finding out how Mauser mass-produced infantry rifles that were as accurate as the best American handmade rifles, and learning what improvements over the Gatling gun Mauser had made on a similar weapon. So far he had made some progress in these areas, but he had not achieved complete success.

Brunner introduced the subject of Fenton Hall. "We received a report from Wilkerson today," he said. "He says that the house is fully staffed now and that all of the necessary cleaning and repairs will be completed within the next few days. If you and the baroness decide to take a vacation later in the year, it will be ready for you."

A tense silence fell, Brunner's expression indicating that he immediately realized his mistake. He well knew that Henry's relationship with Gisela was temporary and that it would soon end.

"Is Gisela well today?" Henry asked, breaking the silence. "She was ill last night, and she didn't have breakfast this morning."

"She has said nothing about feeling ill," Koehler replied, shrugging. "If she is ill, it hasn't prevented her from finding mistakes. And it certainly hasn't interfered with her temper."

Brunner agreed heartily, and Henry laughed, stepping toward the tall door that was the entrance to Gisela's office. He knocked softly and went in.

The room had a vast, spartan aspect that was always intimidating. Its walls were bare except for thick window drapes that reached to the lofty ceiling. The expanse of gleaming floor led back to a plain desk that looked diminutive in the empty space around it. Behind the desk, her pince-nez perched on her nose, Gisela sat reading a folder of papers and frowning.

As Henry closed the door, she looked up. She put down the folder and took off her spectacles, her frown changing to a dazzling smile. The blue eyes that could be cold and indifferent at the prospect of casting widows and orphans into the street became warm with complete, abandoned devotion to him. He crossed the room to her desk.

"And so," she said quietly, taking his hand as he stood beside her, "my loved one has returned to me. Now I am complete once more, because my heart is absent when he is gone. Did you have a pleasant day, loved one?"

"Yes, pleasant enough. Are you still ill?"

Gisela shook her head. "No, I am well, as you can see. It was only a stomach disorder, and it passed quickly."

"But you didn't have breakfast this morning."

"I wasn't hungry, and I don't want to become fat. When I am naked for you, I can feel your eyes caressing me and desiring me. If I were fat, you wouldn't look at me in the same way."

Henry smiled, putting a hand on her forehead. He was concerned that her illness of the night before had been an onset of the fever, nausea, and stomach pains that she occasionally suffered. But her skin was smooth and cool. "You don't feel feverish now," he commented.

Grasping his hands and pressing them to her firm breasts, Gisela stood up. "Tell me how I feel here, loved one," she said softly.

Henry pulled her to him and began kissing her. As always, she searched for a closer intimacy, moving her body against him with tantalizing promise.

"Sit in the chair," she whispered against his lips. "I will lock the door, then I will make you numb with ecstasy."

"While your employees slave over their ledgers?" he chuckled. "Let's go upstairs, Gisela. You haven't forgotten that Stephen and Alicia are visiting this weekend, have you? We must get ready for them."

"Of course I haven't forgotten," Gisela said. She gathered up the folder of papers she had been reading, and they walked toward the door. "The carriage will meet them at the station, and the butler is making preparations to receive them. But they won't arrive until late this evening, so we will have hours to spend together before then."

"Hours during which you should rest, Gisela. You were ill last night, and it could lead to those stomach pains and fever you have at times."

Gisela laughed lightly, refusing as always to dwell on the subject of her illness. As she and Henry went out, the two men in the next office stood up. Gisela handed the folder to her business adviser. "This appears to be a good investment to make through the company in England, Herr Brunner," she said. "But I must question why the owners of a woolen mill would wish to sell it if it is as profitable as this report states."

"The same point occurred to me, Madam Baroness," he replied. "I sent a letter today to our London agent and asked him to investigate the mill discreetly to see if the information is accurate."

"Ask him to investigate the owners also, because they may need money to pay overdue mortgages. If that is the case, we will buy the mortgages from the lenders, foreclose them, and simply take possession of the mill."

Brunner nodded, making a note on a piece of paper.

Gisela and Henry walked quickly through the outer offices and up the curving stairway to their apartments on the second floor. Henry went into his rooms, and Gisela went to hers. A servant had drawn a bath for Henry and put out a set of the comfortable, informal shirt and trousers that he preferred. After bathing and dressing, he went into the sitting room that connected the apartments.

Gisela, in a fur-trimmed robe and slippers, had also finished her bath and was sitting on a couch, studying a folder of papers. Quickly putting the folder and her pince-nez aside, she patted the couch beside her.

Glasses and wine were on the rosewood table in front of the couch. "We will have a late dinner when the Wyndhams arrive," Gisela said, pouring the wine as he sat down. "We'll use the small dining room in the west wing, shall we?"

"Yes, I like it better than the main dining room."

Gisela handed him a glass. "Alicia always enjoys looking at the gardens, so she and I will spend the day tomorrow on the grounds. What will you and Stefan do?"

Henry took a sip of the tart, light Rhine wine. "Pheasant and hares are in season now, so we'll probably go hunting."

"Good. I'll send word to the town gamekeeper to be here tomorrow morning. And we can go to the opera tomorrow evening. . . ."

Henry sipped his wine as Gisela continued discussing plans for the weekend. As she talked, she moved closer to him. Her hand lay on his thigh, and her fingers moved restlessly. She looked into his eyes as she spoke, her smile wide and bright. When she leaned over to refill their glasses, her robe loosened, revealing the cleavage between her large, firm breasts. She left it loose.

After they finished the wine, she asked him if he wanted another bottle. Henry laughed and shook his head as he put his glass on the table. "No, one bottle is enough. I want to be able to talk with Stephen when he gets here."

"We have hours before they will arrive," Gisela said, cupping his face between her hands and kissing him. "More than enough time to do anything we wish, loved one."

The touch of their lips became a passionate kiss, the constant sexual magnetism between them turning into fiery desire. She lay back against the couch with a sigh of contentment as he took her in his arms and caressed her. Then he hesitated, still worried about her illness. He knew that she would eagerly endure pain to please him; the many love games her inventive mind devised had to cause her at least some discomfort.

He put a hand inside her robe to press her stomach gently and see if she flinched. His fingers touched warm, smooth skin.

"Do you wish to feel me, loved one?" she whispered. She unfastened her robe and opened it. "Here, look at me as well. Feel me and look at me however you wish. Shall I lie down, or shall I stand up for you? Tell me what you want me to do, loved one."

"I want you to tell me if that causes any pain," he said, pressing her lower stomach with his hand. "And I want you to be truthful."

"The only pain I feel is a pain of need," she said, taking one of his fingers and guiding it lower. "Your touch can never cause me pain, loved one. Only the lack of your touch causes me pain."

"Please be serious, Gisela," he said. "I don't want to hurt you. You were very ill last night, and I'm afraid that—"

"You cannot hurt me," she interrupted, an edge of impatience in her voice. "Whatever you do, you give me only joy. Your touch is pleasure, and my only pain is one of need." She pressed his hand to her, and his desire for her overcame his hesitancy. As he fondled her, a quick tremor raced through her body and her lips parted in a soft gasp. She wriggled out of her robe, pushing it aside and to the floor.

She was soft, beautiful, and perfumed, her full, high breasts firm against his palms. In a mounting frenzy of desire, he quickly took off his clothes and tossed them aside. Gisela pulled him down to her on the couch. Then, at the last moment, he gathered her up in his arms and carried her into her bedroom.

Her private bedchamber and the canopied bed had the sweet, strong fragrance of her perfume and her body, but even more, they had a feel of her inner being. In these surroundings that were imbued with the essence of her personality, Henry had a closer affinity with her. Through her, he could grope within himself for that powerful, ill-defined need that bound him to her. Reaching it as her soft, warm body arched up to his in a heated climax of passion, he became fulfilled in a flood of ecstasy of such intensity that it crossed a subtle border to the edge of an exquisite agony.

*   *   *

Henry and Gisela sat in the small, richly furnished anteroom off the entrance hall, waiting for their guests to arrive. He was in uniform, and she was dazzlingly beautiful in a green brocade gown.

Her eyes sparkling, she laughed as he told her about an incident that had occurred at the Mauser Arms Works. "So until you went to the testing range," she said, "the new officer from Berlin didn't know how expert you were with a rifle? Didn't the other officers tell him?"

"No, they didn't," Henry replied. "They wanted to take the wind out of his sails by letting him find out for himself."

As Gisela laughed merrily, there was a knock on the door, and the butler opened it and looked in, bowing. "Madam, the carriage is now at the end of the drive."

Gisela stood up and adjusted her gown. "Are the preparations complete to receive the guests?"

"Yes, madam."

Walking out of the anteroom with Gisela, Henry saw that the preparations were indeed complete. The vast entrance hall was as bright as day, all of the chandeliers and wall sconces lighted. Uniformed footmen stood inside the front door. As the butler crossed the entry hall and opened the double doors wide, the footmen filed outside and stood in a line beside the steps. The grounds, too, were ablaze with light, with reflecting lanterns shining up onto the statuary, and the fountains along the wide avenue sparkling in the glow of lanterns under the spraying streams of water.

Gisela linked her arm through Henry's as they stood on the portico outside the front door. The large, ornate carriage with the Kirchberg arms on its sides moved along the drive, drawn by four matched, spirited bays that pranced and tossed their heads. As it drew to a halt, the footmen hurried forward to drop the step into place and open the door.

Tall and distinguished in his Royal Navy uniform,

Stephen Wyndham stepped out of the carriage and assisted Alicia out as Henry and Gisela walked down the steps to greet them.

Gisela was gracious and charming, the perfect hostess as she chatted with Alicia and Stephen. "I've prepared rooms overlooking the garden for you," she said. "Everything is in bloom, and there are new shrubs and flowers that I will show you tomorrow, Alicia. For now, though, I know both of you must be weary after your long journey from Berlin. After you've been shown to your rooms, let's have dinner. Then you can retire early."

Stephen and Alicia agreed to the suggestion, and a little while later they all sat down in a small, candle-lit dining room. The windows were open onto a terrace, letting in the faint evening breeze. A waiter moved silently in and out of the shadows at the sides of the room, serving the meal.

After several appetizers and a soup course, the main course was served, consisting of thin slices of veal stuffed with bits of smoked pork and tangy cheese. Together with side dishes of well-seasoned vegetables, it was a thoroughly satisfying meal. The food was accompanied by a series of delicious, aged wines from Grevenhof's well-stocked cellar.

Over dessert and coffee the conversation turned to Stephen's friend Lord Randolph Churchill, who apparently was encountering stiff opposition to his proposed marriage to the American Jennie Jerome.

"The duke's dim view of the match is more or less an open secret," Stephen said. "And surprisingly enough, the young lady's father is also less than enthusiastic about it. The fact that Spence is a duke's son doesn't impress him in the least."

"I can't disagree with him on that point," Henry said.

Stephen raised an eyebrow. "I do happen to know that Mr. Jerome was a self-made millionaire when he was Spence's age. Perhaps he thinks Spence is an idler."

"Perhaps," Henry replied with a smile. "After all,

he's only been involved in local government, politics, and countless civic affairs."

Laughing, Stephen said that Lord Randolph planned to visit New York in the near future, undoubtedly to convince the Jerome family of his ambitiousness.

During a lull in the conversation, Gisela patted Alicia's hand and suggested that the two of them go to their rooms. "You're tired from your journey," she said. "I'm somewhat weary myself, and we'll have a busy day tomorrow. Heinrich, we'll leave you and Stefan to your brandy and cigars."

When the two men were alone, Henry dismissed the waiter.

"I can't tell you how good it is to have you here," Henry said after they had been talking for a while. "It's the only time I'm able to use my own language."

Stephen laughed. "Yes, that's right, you're around no one but Germans all the time. I must say, though, that your command of the language is perfect, as far as I can tell."

"It should be," Henry said, sipping his brandy. "I've had enough practice, and Gisela doesn't hesitate to correct my pronunciation. Unfortunately, being able to speak German like a German will be of doubtful value when I leave here."

Stephen started to say something, then hesitated and changed his mind. He put his cigar in the ashtray beside his chair. "Yes, I'm sure that's true," he said as he stood up. "Henry, I'll shoot myself in the foot tomorrow if I don't get some sleep tonight."

Henry smiled, rising from his chair to bid his friend good night.

When Stephen had left, Henry thought about their conversation. He knew what Stephen had started to say: that he would be foolish even to contemplate leaving Germany, given his present circumstances. However, Henry reflected, Stephen had only a limited knowledge of the situation. Stephen had never met Cindy Holt.

The following day was cool and sunny, perfect for a hunt. The gamekeeper had recruited three youths from the town for bearers, and they were waiting as Henry and Stephen came outside. A servant handed the gamekeeper two large lunch baskets, which the boys eyed in anticipation.

The deep forest that stretched back from the grounds behind the mansion was crisscrossed with woodcutter's trails. Walking side by side, Henry and Stephen took turns with their shotguns, bringing down the hares that leaped from the underbrush and the snipes that flew across the trails. The youths raced forward and gathered up the game, stuffing the birds and the hares into bags slung over their shoulders.

Farther back in the hills, the dense forest opened into meadows that teemed with grouse and pheasant. Wading through the tall grass, Henry and Stephen brought down the birds that burst from cover. Walking at a distance ahead of the others, they talked quietly as they hunted.

Since the last time he had reported to London, Stephen had been concentrating on the work that the German Navy was doing with submersible craft. But because of the secrecy surrounding the research, he had been unable to obtain much useful information.

"It does appear they have a propulsion system capable of a speed of several knots, but I have no idea what kind of system it is," he said.

"It couldn't be steam," Henry offered. "Not in a submersible."

"No, not unless they have some means of providing oxygen and an exhaust for the combustion in a firebox. That hardly seems possible. I have an idea that it's a mechanism along the lines of the dynamo motors Michael Faraday was experimenting with before he died. But that's only speculation."

"How would they drive a dynamo? That takes a stream of water or some other constant source of energy, doesn't it?"

"Ordinarily. But Faraday and others experimented

with battery cells that stored electrical energy to drive the motors."

"Yes," Henry said, "I've read about that. They were no more than interesting toys, though."

"So were steam engines at one time."

The conversation was interrupted as a covey of grouse exploded into the air a few yards ahead. Henry and Stephen emptied both barrels of their shotguns, and feathers burst from four of the birds and they tumbled to the ground. As the bearers gathered up the birds, Henry and Stephen reloaded their shotguns and walked slowly ahead.

It was Henry's turn to talk about his work, and he explained some of the difficulties he was having. "Military secrecy isn't involved," he said. "It's proprietary information, trade secrets that Mauser wants to keep from other arms manufacturers. There are several parts of the plant that are closed to all but a very few employees, and even the German Army officers can't go there."

"Have you managed to find out anything at all?"

"Enough to keep my project officer in Washington satisfied," Henry replied. "What seemed to interest him the most, however, was a report I wrote on the procurement methods of the German Army. That's what I'm officially supposed to be studying, of course. The report created as much interest in Washington as the excellence of Mauser weapons."

Stephen shook his head. "One can never be certain of how a headquarters will react."

"That's for sure," Henry said. "In fact, the War Department may be thinking of changing our procurement methods, because I've received several requests for further information on the subject."

"You must be doing something right," Stephen commented, glancing around. "It's near enough to midday, and that creek over there looks like a pleasant place to stop for lunch."

The shady glades along the tree-lined creek were inviting, and Henry called to the gamekeeper. He and

Stephen took one of the lunch baskets and sat down under
a tree, while a short distance away the youths exclaimed
with delight over the food in the other basket.

Along with bottles of wine and glasses, the baskets
contained several small loaves of bread, slices of smoked
meats and cheeses, and several kinds of fruit. The setting
was as enjoyable as the food, with the babbling of the
creek blending with the cheerful calls of birds overhead.

As they ate, Stephen smiled and shook his head
wistfully. "Henry, you live in a fashion that is beyond the
wildest dreams of most men. Here we are, enjoying idyllic
countryside, excellent hunting, and a delicious lunch, but
for you it's only an average day."

"Yes, I'm more than comfortable here," Henry agreed.
"However, there is more to life than physical comforts."

"Of course there is," Stephen said. "And the fact that
you're here on a very important mission for your government must give you a great deal of satisfaction. And there's
Gisela. You can't deny that you're extremely fond of her."

Henry looked out at the meadow, his mood thoughtful. "It's impossible for me to explain how I feel about her,
Stephen, even to myself, but I'm more than just fond of
her. These bouts of illness that she has worry me, and
there are other things. I'm even involved to an extent in
her business affairs."

"You've mentioned before that she gets ill from time
to time. She's consulted a doctor, hasn't she?"

"Yes, several doctors from Frankfurt and Berlin have
examined her. They say it's nothing to worry about, but
that's difficult for me to believe. When those stomach
pains start, she seems very ill."

Stephen was silent for a moment. Abruptly he changed
the subject, mentioning their plans to go to the opera in
Frankfurt that evening, which meant they would have to
dine early. He and Henry decided to hunt for another
hour and then start back toward Grevenhof.

While they were crossing the meadow, Stephen again
brought up the subject of Gisela's illness. He commented

that she was the kind of person who might refuse to accept the fact that she was ill. "It's conceivable that she might have browbeaten those doctors into telling her what she wanted to hear. Gisela can be very charming, but she could also intimidate Bismarck himself if she set her mind to it."

The possibility was one that Henry had not considered, and he frowned as he thought about it. It was true that Gisela always turned aside the subject of her illness when he mentioned it.

"When we were in England," Henry said, "I suggested that she see a doctor there. Now I wish I had been more insistent."

"I have a suggestion," Stephen offered. "At the embassy in Berlin, we have a doctor who may be able to deal with her. And I'm sure the ambassador would be more than pleased to send him here to examine Gisela."

"She might simply ignore what he had to say."

"I don't believe so, Henry. This fellow has the disposition of a hedgehog, and he knows how to deal with difficult patients. He's a Scotsman, by the name of MacAlister—"

A brace of pheasants burst from the grass ahead, interrupting the conversation. Stephen downed both birds, and as the youths ran to retrieve them, he continued talking. He told Henry that Dr. MacAlister was an excellent physician, with a degree from the medical university at Edinburgh.

The more Henry listened, the more appealing the suggestion seemed. Then, without realizing the full range of consequences that could result from his decision, he agreed to talk with Gisela and get her to see the doctor.

It was not easy, and he needed the Wyndhams' help, but before Stephen and Alicia boarded the train back to Berlin the following afternoon, Henry had succeeded in persuading Gisela to see Dr. MacAlister. Stephen promised to send a telegram informing them when the doctor would arrive.

Thus, Henry was at the Grevenburg station the following Tuesday when the doctor's train pulled in. Upon seeing the man, Henry was reminded of Stephen's apt description. Small and squat, with a peppering of gray in his long, thick side-whiskers and a scowl on his face, the man did resemble a hedgehog.

The hasty trip from Berlin had done nothing to improve his disposition. Rumpled and haggard, he was carrying a medical bag and a carpetbag that looked almost empty. Without thinking, Henry greeted him in German.

"Have you forgotten how to speak English?" MacAlister growled in a thick Scottish accent. "I was told that you're an American. And unless that uniform is a disguise, I was told the honest truth of the matter."

"I'm so accustomed to speaking German that I didn't think," Henry said, exerting an effort to maintain an even temper. "Come, the carriage is this way. You do speak German, don't you?"

"Aye, well enough," MacAlister replied curtly. "I have a few German patients in Berlin. For the most part, though, the only remedy I use amongst them is to tell them to curb their besotted gluttony. This appears to be an entire nation of people who are digging their graves with their teeth. Have I come all the way here to see another of the same?"

"No, you haven't," Henry said, his temper flaring. "And I suggest that you reserve your judgment until you meet the lady."

The doctor looked up narrowly, then grunted, seemingly undaunted. As they walked in silence toward the waiting carriage, Henry was beginning to think he had made a mistake. He was about to talk to Dr. McAlister and warn him about his attitude, when the man paused, looking first at the ornate carriage with the Kirchberg arms on its door, then at the luxurious private railroad car parked on the siding, with the same coat of arms painted on its side.

"Who is my patient here?" he asked.

"Baroness Gisela von Kirchberg," Henry replied. "Weren't you told?"

"I was told only that it was a woman, and that an American would meet me here," MacAlister said. "So the patient is a baroness, is she? Apparently she isn't proud and titled but penniless."

"No, she isn't," Henry replied.

"Well, let's not keep her waiting," the doctor said briskly, stepping into the carriage as the driver opened the door. "You can tell me about her condition on the way there."

The doctor's mood continued improving as he observed pedestrians lifting their caps or bobbing curtsies as the carriage skirted the town. When it breasted the hill and Grevenhof itself came into view, his expression became almost amiable. But he remained quiet and attentive as Henry described Gisela's symptoms.

When the carriage stopped, Henry led the doctor inside and sent the butler for Gisela. A few minutes later she appeared, smiling in resigned patience. Henry watched them go upstairs, then stepped into Hans Guenther's office to arrange payment for the doctor. A few minutes later he went upstairs.

From the sitting room, he could hear Gisela and the doctor talking quietly in her bedroom. At length, the doctor came out of the room. His expression revealed nothing as he silently folded his stethoscope and put it into his medical bag, then closed the bag. A moment later, Gisela came out.

She smiled at Henry as she sat down on the couch. "As I told you, Heinrich," she said, "I am not ill. At most, I have a minor disorder that occurs occasionally."

The doctor, still standing, shook his head. "No, I did not say that, Madam Baroness," he pronounced firmly in heavily accented German. "You are ill, and it is a serious illness."

Gisela blinked, as if surprised. "But how can that be?" she demanded. "I have been examined by five other doctors, and each of them said that I am completely healthy."

"That is entirely understandable," the doctor said, "especially if you were examined at times when you were feeling well. In any case, most doctors would find nothing. However, I have made a study of your condition, and the symptoms are unmistakable. You have a perityphlitic abscess."

"What is that?" Henry asked.

"An inflammation in the lower abdomen," the doctor replied. "Its precise origin is uncertain, but there is a theory that it originates in the veriform appendix. However, it is only a theory."

"What treatment do you prescribe?" Henry asked.

The doctor pursed his lips. "I regret to say that there is no effective treatment. There are some claims of success for a surgical procedure to excise the inflammation, but I consider the risks too high." He turned to Gisela. "Madam Baroness, the type of abscess you have eventually becomes acute and in most instances is mortal. However, the danger of infection from abdominal surgery is even more grave. I know of no doctor who would recommend it."

Silence fell. Gisela tapped her fingers on the arm of the couch and looked away. Her face was pale, and Henry could see the terror in her eyes. He realized that all along she had suspected she was seriously ill and had been trying to ignore it.

"There is nothing that can be done?" Henry asked.

"There is no cure," the doctor replied. "But there is no reason for despair. It is a serious illness, but many people with serious illnesses live for many years. The baroness is a strong, healthy woman in all other respects, so her outlook is better than for most. When the attacks of pain and fever occur, she should eat light, soft foods and drink mostly boiled water. If she will do that, then she may very well live into her old age."

Gisela, Henry noted, looked serenely composed. "Very well," she said. "I will follow your advice, Doctor, and I am grateful for your coming here to examine me. My staff will see to your needs."

MacAlister bowed and made his farewells, and Henry led him back downstairs. Hans Guenther, waiting in the entry hall, handed Henry a fat envelope of money. The doctor demurred weakly, then took the envelope and pocketed it when Henry insisted.

"You and the baroness are very generous," the doctor said. "If I can ever be of further assistance, I will be more than pleased to make myself available."

Henry nodded and beckoned the butler. "Take the doctor to the kitchen and have the cook prepare a meal for him," he said. "When he has eaten, have the carriage take him back to the train station. And bring me a bottle of Steinhager and glasses. I'll wait here."

The butler bowed and led the doctor away. Pacing back and forth in the entry hall, Henry thought about the look of terror he had seen in Gisela's eyes. Dread, even shock over what the doctor had said would be only human, but Gisela was not a woman who yielded easily to fear. Only to him did she ever reveal her feelings without restraint. Henry knew what awaited him upstairs.

The butler returned with an earthenware bottle of Steinhager and two small crystal glasses on a tray. Henry took the tray and went back upstairs. As he entered the sitting room, Gisela was staring numbly at a wall. She glanced at him, then silently looked away as he poured the liquor.

Her hand trembling, Gisela took the glass from him. She drank the fiery liquor in a single swallow, showing no reaction to it. He refilled the glass, and she downed the second drink in a single gulp. Then she coughed, and a faint tinge of color returned to her face. Henry refilled her glass once more, then drank the liquor in his.

"Gisela, the doctor said that your condition is far from hopeless. And while he knows of no treatment, others may. We will have to consult other doctors and find out."

"No, he is a good doctor," she replied dully. "Far better than I wanted him to be. I believe there is no cure for my illness."

"Even so, he said there is no reason for despair. He said that you may live for many more years."

Sipping her Steinhager, Gisela shrugged and shook her head. "A successful life is better than a long one, and I've done all that I intended to do. When I was a young woman, I wanted wealth and power. Now I have more money than I can count, and even those boasting, swaggering fools at the Reichstag fawn over me. I am satisfied with what I have done."

Henry frowned, perplexed. Her words suggested that she had immediately come to terms with her illness, yet the terror he had seen was still in her eyes. "When you have the pain and fever, you must follow the doctor's instructions," he said.

"Yes, I will," she replied indifferently. "When do you intend to leave me, Heinrich?"

The question was revealing, and suddenly Henry understood. "Gisela, this changes nothing between us," he said.

"Do you think I am a fool?" she demanded bitterly. "It has never been a secret between us that I am fonder of you than you are of me. My money means nothing to you, so why would a young, handsome man like you stay with a woman who is growing old and who has a mortal illness?" Her composure began breaking. Her eyes filled with tears as she pushed at her hair. "Only this morning I found two white hairs. Two!"

Under the circumstances, her concern over white hairs was laughably absurd, but Henry knew that she was keenly sensitive about the difference in their ages. As she lost control over herself and began weeping, he pulled her to him and put his arms around her. He wanted to talk to her, to reassure and comfort her, but in the back of his mind he could not forget that the time when he intended to go to the United States and marry Cindy Holt was drawing near. Yet now, he suddenly realized, it would be brutally cruel of him to leave Gisela. The most basic consideration of humanity demanded that he stay with her. At the same time, he could not ask Cindy for an indefinite postponement of their marriage.

Almost a year before, when he had been forced to choose between similar courses of action, he had suffered through weeks of torment, and in the end he had put off the decision. This time it was worse, because he had no choice. The circumstances of Gisela's illness had trapped him no less inexorably than they had her. He had to stay with her.

Leaning against him, Gisela clutched a handkerchief to her face as she sobbed. "My life was without joy before I met you," she murmured. "I thought it was a good life, but it had no meaning. You are more to me than all the power and wealth in the world. I could meet death bravely if you were holding me like this."

"I will stay with you, Gisela," he said quietly.

His flat, definite tone startled her, and she looked up at him. Studying his eyes, she lifted a hand that was damp with tears and touched his lips. "For how long, loved one?" she whispered.

"Always," he replied. "My duties may call me away at times, but I will always return. I will stay with you always."

Gisela was motionless for a long moment, stunned. Then she burst into tears again, weeping with joy as she clung to him. His sense of loss a searing agony within him, Henry held her. After a few minutes, he gathered her up in his arms and carried her into her bedroom. He put her down on the bed and covered her, telling her to rest, then went back into the other room.

Sitting down at the small desk in the corner, he

began the letter that he had to write to Cindy. But no matter how hard he tried, the words seemed wrong. After crumpling up several sheets of paper and tossing them into the wastebasket, he realized that he could not adequately explain the situation in a letter. He knew that he would have to go to Oregon on leave. He owed Cindy that much.

With that decision made, writing the letter was easier for him. When he finished, he addressed an envelope and sealed the letter in it. On a fresh sheet of paper, he wrote out a telegram to his project officer in Washington, requesting authorization to report in person on his progress and then to have a leave of absence. Then he took the letter and the telegram downstairs and gave them to the office manager to dispatch.

Reed Kerr was overseeing the unloading of a supply barge anchored just upriver from the Fort Vancouver docks, but his heart was not in his work. He was gazing out over the river, absently watching a ferry approaching from the Portland side. The days since Richard Koehler had left had been boring. Not only did Reed miss the German officer's companionship, but he now had no ostensible reason to see Cindy Holt. Of course he could call at the ranch to visit Calvin Rogers, but he had been delaying that until Sunday, when Cindy was most likely to be at home. Even then, though, she might be visiting her mother and stepfather.

The Portland ferry docked at its pier just downstream, Reed still idly watching it. Then he straightened up and looked more closely. Cindy was among the people coming off the ferry. Reed called to the sergeant in charge of the work party and told him that he would return in a few minutes, then mounted his horse and urged it to a run as he rode along the bank toward the ferry pier. Cindy had disappeared from view, but he saw her again as she led her horse off the pier. As he drew nearer, he reined back to a more sedate pace to make the meeting seem less contrived.

To his surprise, Reed saw that Cindy was pale and distraught. Struggling to mount her horse, she showed no sign of even noticing him as he halted and dismounted. "Here, let me help you, Cindy," he said. "Is something wrong?"

She shook her head curtly. Reed cupped his hands for her foot and lifted her to the sidesaddle. "Cindy, you're very upset. Why don't you let me ride with you?"

Still making no reply, and barely holding back her tears, Cindy turned her horse away from the pier, then snapped the end of the reins across its shoulder. The animal bolted into a headlong run. Reed hesitated, watching in consternation, then leaped onto his horse and rode after her.

His cavalry mount was no match over a short distance for her powerful quarter horse gelding, which raced ahead effortlessly, past the town and toward the fort. Near the the top of the hill, Cindy turned onto the road leading to the married officers' quarters. Reed rode after her.

Pulling back on her reins in front of General Blake's quarters, Cindy brought her horse to a sliding stop. She jumped down from the saddle and ran toward the front door. Reed slowed his horse, then stopped it. Whatever had upset Cindy, he reflected, was probably none of his business, and he would be an intruder. He glanced toward her horse, which was standing a few feet from the hitching post.

He knew that the horses at the Holt ranch were trained to stand when their reins were dropped, but it seemed possible to him that something could frighten the animal and make it wander away. He rode forward, then dismounted and led the horse to the hitching post as Cindy jerked the front door open and ran into the house, leaving the door open.

"Mama!" she shouted, her voice a heartbroken wail that was clearly audible outside. "Mama, where are you?"

"Here, Cindy, here!" her mother replied, rushing toward her from another part of the house. "What is it, child? What's wrong?"

"I've just received a letter from Henry," Cindy cried, bursting into sobs. "Mama, he's breaking off our engagement!"

There was a long silence, then an exclamation of disbelief. "What?"

"He's breaking off our engagement," Cindy sobbed. "He didn't give any reason, but he said he's coming home to explain why. Here's the letter from him. . . ."

Suddenly becoming aware that he was eavesdropping, even if it was unintentional, Reed quickly finished tethering Cindy's horse, then remounted and rode away from the house. What he had overheard created a turmoil of emotions within him.

It appeared that he would at last be able to court Cindy Holt. Yet he felt no sense of happiness, no pleasure. The torment that he had seen in her beautiful eyes and the anguish he had heard in her voice only made him feel a deep regret over the pain she was suffering.

Most of all, however, he felt bewildered. The news Cindy had received seemed so inconceivable that he wondered if she had misinterpreted something Henry had written, or if some other grotesque mistake had been made. Whatever the circumstances, Reed was unable to comprehend how Henry could have ever written such a letter to Cindy.

XI

The sultry heat was like an oppressive blanket around Janessa as she returned to Dr. Martin's house after running an errand for him. In the past week, the ocean breezes that normally cooled Portland in the evening had stopped blowing. Each day had become more oppressive, and the stagnant air over the city was thick with dust and smoke.

As she turned up the front walk, Janessa noticed a horse tethered in the shade in the drive. Even before she saw that the horse had a sidesaddle on it, she knew that it was Cindy's. Ever since Henry Blake's letter had arrived a few days before, Cindy's mood had matched the weather. She had been going to Fort Vancouver every afternoon to talk with her mother, often remaining late and taking the last ferry back, and she always asked Janessa to look after Timmy while she was gone.

The windows and doors were open, and as Janessa climbed the front steps she heard Cindy talking with Dr. Martin and Tonie in the parlor. She went inside, and the three grown-ups greeted her. Their clothes were limp with perspiration, and they were sipping lemonade and fanning themselves with cardboard fans.

She crossed the room to Cindy and kissed her. Although Janessa had never met Henry Blake, her blazing resentment toward him would make the sun outside seem

211

pale in comparison. "Are you going to Grandma's today?"
she asked.

"Yes, I'd like to," Cindy replied, smiling wanly. "Do
you mind very much missing another afternoon of studying with Dr. Martin?"

"I think I can skip Greek verbs this afternoon," Janessa
said, straight-faced. "And I'm sure Dr. Martin can."

The doctor, in his shirt sleeves, smiled wearily as he
worked his fan. "We can always catch up, Dr. Janessa," he
said. "You're making good progress, and we have plenty of
time. When you get to college, I have no doubt that you'll
leave everyone else behind."

"There's certainly no question about that," Tonie
agreed, starting to get up from her chair. "I'll make you a
glass of lemonade before you go, my dear."

"No, please don't, Mrs. Martin," Janessa said quickly.
"I'm not thirsty. I'll go saddle my horse, Cindy."

Janessa rode with Cindy most of the way to the ferry
landing, before turning onto the road to the ranch. "I
thought we would have a storm before now," Cindy commented before they parted. "Two or three days of hot
weather like this usually brings one on."

"At least you'll be able to cool off on the boat ride
over," Janessa offered. An idea suddenly occurred to her.
"Why don't you stay at Grandma's tonight? You can talk
with her as late as you like and not worry about catching
the last ferry. You can take the first ferry back tomorrow
morning."

Cindy hesitated, then shook her head. "I'd better
not. It would be too much trouble, and you'd have to
watch Timmy."

"That's no good reason," Janessa said firmly. "You
need the rest. Stay at Grandma's tonight."

It was, Cindy reflected, sometimes difficult to remember that Janessa was only eleven years old. She had a
maturity about her that made her seem like a small,
slender adult. During the past days she had been a god-
send, reaching out with love and sympathy. Cindy had no

hesitation about leaving Timmy in Janessa's care overnight. The girl could control him as well as anyone could.

Cindy leaned over to touch her niece's hand, and the girl's small hand squeezed hers affectionately in return. "All right, I'll stay at Mama's house tonight, and I'll see you tomorrow morning."

They waved and parted, and Janessa turned her horse onto the road to the ranch. As she left the city behind, she thought she heard thunder in the far distance and halted her horse so that she could listen. Thunderstorms frightened her, but the heat was becoming so unbearable that rain would be welcome. Hearing nothing, she continued along the road.

At the ranch, nothing moved around the house and the outbuildings. Horses stood motionless in the shade of the barns, and chickens sat under the bunkhouse porch. The only sound was the shrill chatter of cicadas in the fields. Janessa unsaddled her horse and put it in the corral, then carried the saddle to the tack room.

White Elk was at the workbench in the hot, cluttered room, sweat gleaming on his bare chest as he replaced a strap on a set of harnesses. Janessa put her saddle on a rack.

"Hello, Miss Janessa," he said, smiling cheerfully. "You're home early again today, aren't you?"

Janessa nodded as she glanced around at the empty saddle racks. "Where is everyone?"

The Indian youth was used to her abrupt manner, and he took no offense. "They're moving most of the horses to the north pasture. Stalking Horse left me here to repair this harness because we might have to start hauling hay out there."

"This time of year?"

"Yes, the north pasture is the only place where the horses will have plenty of water and shade if this heat continues, but it'll get grazed down fast."

Janessa noticed that Timmy's pony saddle was also gone from its usual place on the racks. "Where is Timmy?"

"He must be with Stalking Horse and the others," White Elk replied. "Right after Miss Cindy left, he came in here for his saddle. I offered to help him with the pony, but he didn't want any help. He likes to do everything by himself."

"What time will Stalking Horse and the others be back?"

White Elk shrugged. "They have a lot of horses to move, so it may be dark before they're through. I'll be finished with this harness directly, and I'll go get Timmy for you."

"No, thank you," Janessa replied. "He knows better than to stay out late. If he does, I'll go get him myself and deal with him."

White Elk frowned. "I wouldn't like to see Timmy punished, Miss Janessa. I'll go get him."

"No, he isn't supposed to forget the time. He knows that, and dealing with him is my job."

White Elk hesitated, trying to think of another way to phrase the suggestion. Then he realized he had encountered the same stubbornness when he had tried to help Timmy saddle his pony. Arguing with a Holt was a good way to waste time. Remaining silent, he nodded as Janessa left the tack room.

Janessa's next stop was the bunkhouse, to check on Calvin Rogers. Calvin's left leg was still in a splint from his ankle to his hip, but he had been improving every day.

The room was sweltering under the metal roof, and the open door and windows provided little relief. Calvin was sitting up in his bunk, reading. His face was flushed and sweaty from the heat, and he was still in some pain, but he smiled as Janessa came in.

After feeling his pulse, Janessa asked him how many times he had been up on his crutches during the day. Calvin replied that he had been up twice, for a few minutes each time. Janessa nodded, commenting that he was getting stronger. As she began straightening the things on the table beside the bed, she noticed an almanac and several sheets of paper on which circular designs had been drawn. Timmy's latest interest was astronomy, and she assumed that the circles were planetary orbits that Calvin had drawn for the boy. "Timmy isn't making a nuisance of himself and keeping you from resting, is he?"

"No, not at all," Calvin replied quickly. "I enjoy talking with him, and I'm looking forward to when I'll be able to get around and help him with his kites and such. He's the smartest little boy I've ever met, and he has a wide range of interests." He gestured to the papers on the table. "He grasped the concept of the solar system and the stars so quickly that it amazed me. I was telling him that there's a lunar eclipse tonight, but unfortunately the sky is too hazy. We'd have to go to the foothills of Mount Hood in order to get above the haze and see it, and I certainly can't get around that well yet."

"No, not for a time," Janessa said. "Did the cook bring you a good lunch?"

"Yes, and he visited with me for a while. I don't know how I'll ever repay the kindness I've been shown here."

She ignored the comment. "I'll stop in again tomorrow."

"I'll look forward to it. Thank you, Miss Janessa."

Outside, as she walked toward the house, she distinctly heard thunder far off to the west, and she felt herself tremble with fear. If the storm came that night, she would be alone in the house except for Timmy. She quickened her pace and went inside.

Cindy always kept the house meticulously neat, and it was obvious at a glance that Timmy had been inside after Cindy left. A chair was at the sink, and water was splashed all over. Janessa pulled the chair back to the table and began wiping the sink with an old dish towel.

When she bent down to wipe the floor, she noticed a small cork disk lying there. She picked it up and examined it. It was damp and blackened by water, and compressed around the edge by pressure. It looked like the cork insert from a canteen cap. Shrugging, she placed it on the windowsill.

Thinking about what to prepare for dinner, she went to the food safe and opened it. She sighed in annoyance. Timmy had hacked a large, ragged slice from a cake Cindy had baked, and left the knife on the plate. She took the knife to the sink to wash it.

As she pumped some water, she reflected that Timmy had taken an unusually large piece of cake, much more than even he could eat at one sitting. She thought about that, and about the fact that he had filled a canteen. Then she thought about what Calvin Rogers had said.

Anxiety growing within her, Janessa ran through the house toward her father's room. She opened the door and looked at the bureau. The telescope that was normally there in its leather case was gone.

Her anxiety turned into gripping fear. Timmy was on his way to the foothills of Mount Hood to watch the lunar eclipse through the telescope. In her mind flashed tales of hunters who had been killed by wild animals in the deep forest around Mount Hood. Others had become injured or lost. It was a deadly perilous place for a small boy.

"I'll saddle a horse and ride out to the north pasture for Stalking Horse," White Elk said when she had finished explaining. "We'll find Timmy and bring him back."

"No, that would take too long," Janessa protested. "Just come with me and help me find him. You can track his pony. We've got to get to him before that storm starts."

"Stalking Horse can track much better than I can, and it will only take me—"

"No," Janessa interrupted, almost in a panic. "The first thing he would do is send word to Cindy, and I don't want her bothered."

"But she should know about it," White Elk said patiently. "Miss Cindy would want to know about it, and she should know."

"Why?" Janessa demanded. "All she would do is rush back here and worry. Now, if you don't come with me, I'll go for him myself."

Against his better judgment, White Elk reluctantly agreed. "All right, I'll saddle a couple of horses. I don't know if that storm will come this way, but we still have plenty of daylight, and he couldn't have gotten too far away."

"Thank you, White Elk," Janessa replied gratefully. "I'll go close the windows and light a lamp in the kitchen in case we're out past dusk. That way Stalking Horse and the others won't worry when they get back."

The house was hot and silent as Janessa went from room to room, closing the windows. In the quiet, she heard thunder again, far to the west. By the time she had lighted the lamp, she heard the horses outside.

White Elk had his Spencer rifle resting across his saddle horn. In the holster on his belt was a long, heavy pistol that looked to be of Civil War vintage. "There's always a chance of running into a bear or a cougar back in the woods," he explained, handing Janessa the reins of her horse.

The powerful, muscular quarter horse geldings were high-spirited and wanted to run, but White Elk advised that they keep them to a fast canter to conserve their strength. The farms along the road east of the ranch were few and far between, and in less than an hour they had left the last one behind. Mount Hood, always in front of them, seemed deceptively near, its snowcapped peak towering into the sky and filling the horizon.

When they stopped to let the horses drink in a stream beside the road, White Elk expressed doubt that Timmy would stay on the main road. "He could have turned off on one of those side roads, or he could have even started out along an entirely different road."

Janessa shook her head. "No, he would take the easiest and most direct route. This is it."

They began riding at a fast canter again, White Elk frowning doubtfully over the wisdom of what they were doing. Then, about a mile farther on, the Indian youth smiled in relief as he reined up and pointed to some small hoofprints in the soft dirt where a creek crossed the road. They had been made by Timmy's pony. Janessa paused, nodded, then urged her horse on.

The road went up a long, gradual incline through a meadow. When they had reached the top of the rise, overlooking a shallow valley, they saw the pony in the distance. Riderless, it was running toward them, reins flying and stirrups bouncing. Janessa and White Elk moved apart to stop it.

Its eyes glaring in terror, the pony was gasping for breath and streaked with sweat, foam flying from its mouth. As it approached, it veered off the road and through the meadow. Taking his lariat off his saddle, White Elk wheeled his horse and gave chase.

Janessa followed him. She watched with relief as he swung the rope and expertly looped it around the pony's neck, then tightened it and dragged the animal to an abrupt halt by reining back. Quickly White Elk dismounted and calmed the frightened pony. Janessa noticed the canteen and her father's telescope in its leather case on the saddle.

"Maybe the pony shied from a rattlesnake or something and threw Timmy," White Elk said anxiously. "I hope he isn't hurt."

Janessa rode around to the other side of the pony. On the leather saddle skirt were four deep gashes, one reaching as far as the pony's shoulder, where it turned into a thin scratch, beaded with blood. The gashes were clearly claw marks.

As she silently pointed, White Elk stepped around the pony. His bronze face turned a shade paler. "Grizzly!" he gasped.

Glancing over the saddle, Janessa saw no other sign of blood, which could mean nothing or everything. She bit her lip, forcing aside the fear that was welling in her. Now she wished that the men from the ranch were with them, but it was too late to go back for help. She and White Elk would have to continue on by themselves.

"I knew I should have gone to get Stalking Horse!" White Elk exclaimed in self-disgust. "I knew I should have, and I was a fool for not doing it!"

"You were right and I was wrong," Janessa said. "But it's done, and we don't have time to get them now. Let's go, White Elk."

The youth's face flushed with anger. "I was a fool for listening to you instead of doing what I thought best!" he snapped. "That's the last time I'll ever listen to a girl about anything!"

"You watch your tongue, or you'll be listening to something you certainly won't want to hear!" Janessa retorted. "Now let's go!"

His only reply was a silent, smoldering glare, which Janessa returned. The boy fashioned a lead for the pony and remounted. Jerking his reins, he turned his horse to continue along the road, Janessa riding beside him. They adjusted their pace to that of the small, weary pony.

After a few minutes, White Elk turned to face her. "I'm sorry for what I said," he muttered.

"I know you didn't mean it," Janessa replied. "You're worried, like I am. Let's just find Timmy."

The boy looked back at the road ahead. It had become no better than a trail, overgrown with weeds. The tall weeds were crushed down in spots, revealing where the pony had run. White Elk kept alert, and after another mile or so he found a place where the pony had apparently run out of the forest and onto the road.

Turning off the trail, they began following the pony's hoofprints in the mat of fallen leaves. Now they could no longer see Mount Hood in the distance. Along with her gnawing anxiety over Timmy, Janessa felt a clammy fear as the trees closed in all around. It was strangely quiet, and the noises the horses made were loud in the stillness.

The hoofprints led up a slope, the underbrush gradually thinning out and the forest becoming more open again. When she could see fifty to sixty feet away on every

side, Janessa felt less uneasy. Then she detected a strong
stench in the hot air: a putrid odor of decaying meat.

White Elk had smelled it too, and he motioned them
to halt. Quietly, he explained to Janessa that when grizzlies
killed a deer or other large animal, they fed off it for days.
The stench of rotting meat in the forest was a warning,
because grizzlies protected their food against intruders
with savage fury.

A moment later the horses began balking, and when
they started trying to rear up, White Elk waved Janessa
back toward the road. He followed her down the wooded
slope, the pony scurrying along behind them.

Near the road, White Elk and Janessa dismounted
and tethered the horses to trees. The boy began checking
his rifle and pistol. "Stay here, and I'll go take a look
around for Timmy," he said. "It might be best for you to
get up into a tree."

"No, give me your pistol," Janessa replied. "I'm going
with you."

White Elk shook his head firmly. "This time we're
going to do what I say, Miss Janessa. You stay right here."

"I will not! Give me that pistol!"

"You're only ten years old!" the youth exclaimed in
exasperation. "Little girls don't go into the woods after
grizzlies!"

"I'm eleven, and you can't shoot two guns at once!"
she countered. "Now give me that pistol!"

White Elk knew it was no use arguing. Sighing in
resignation, he took the pistol out of his holster and gave it
to her. It was massive in her hands, and her finger could
barely reach the trigger. It was also heavy, and she carried
it by the grip and its long barrel as she followed White Elk
through the trees.

As they walked back up the wooded slope, Janessa
thought about the various things she had heard concerning
grizzlies. They were very large, she knew, yet were re-
puted to have the speed of cats. And they were strong.
Even one that was shot near the heart could remain alive

for two or three minutes and do devastating damage. You had to shoot them in the legs, it was said, in order to cripple them. Janessa had never before been so terrified, yet the thought that Timmy was somewhere out there was even worse, and she forced herself to think of the bear.

Passing the place where they had turned back, White Elk and Janessa followed the pony's tracks farther up the slope. The stench of rotted meat became stronger. The slope leveled off into a clearing, and White Elk paused at a place where the leaves on the forest floor were churned up—apparently where the grizzly had charged the pony. But there was no sign of Timmy.

"Timmy!" Janessa called, not too loudly, for fear of alerting the bear. "Timmy, can you hear me?"

"Janessa!" a frightened voice shrieked back, not more than a hundred feet away. "Janessa, I'm over here in a tree! I'll climb down and come over there!"

"Timmy, you stay in that tree!" Janessa shouted back. "You stay there! Do you understand me?"

"Yes, I understand!" the boy called, his voice breaking with a sob. "But you hurry up and come over here! I'm scared, because there's a bear that's been trying to get me!"

"Do you see the bear now, Timmy?"

"No, but it's still around here somewhere."

"All right. White Elk is here, and we'll be there in a moment. You stay in that tree and wait until we get there."

The boy's reply was a sobbing, terrified wail for them to hurry. White Elk, his face pale and tense, held his rifle ready to fire as he looked from side to side and walked slowly forward. Janessa cocked the pistol and held the grip with both hands, walking just behind him.

With each step, the cracking of twigs under their feet was a loud, unnerving noise in the forest stillness. By now the putrid stench was overpowering, and Janessa saw a mangled deer carcass off to one side.

Finally she glimpsed Timmy, high in a tree ahead.

The bark on the trunk and branches was shredded where the bear had reared up and slashed. Timmy saw the two of them and began shouting again for them to hurry.

They had almost reached the tree when Janessa heard a sound to her right. At almost the same instant she saw White Elk stop and shoulder his rifle. As she turned and looked, her heart missed a beat and she felt half paralyzed from the fear that gripped her.

Some twenty yards away, the bear looked as large as a horse, but much bulkier. Everything about it seemed menacing, from its dirty brown color to its bristling upright stance. Janessa could clearly see its lips peeling back from long, yellow teeth as it growled.

Then it charged. Timmy screamed in terror. White Elk fired his rifle. Janessa raised her pistol.

The bear flinched from White Elk's bullet, then snarled louder and kept charging. White Elk fired again. Janessa aimed the pistol at arm's length, struggling to keep the end of the long barrel from dancing and weaving. With her heart pounding, she pulled the trigger back.

The pistol roared, pain shooting through her wrists and the recoil of the heavy weapon staggering her backward a step. The bear's right foreleg folded and it went down. Snarling furiously, it gathered itself and struggled back up, laboring forward on three legs.

Janessa cocked the pistol and fired again and again. On the edge of her vision, White Elk was firing steadily. Gunpowder smoke obscured her view, but she cocked the pistol and kept firing. The bear grew larger and larger, until finally, only a few yards away, it went down again.

The pistol hammer snapped on an empty chamber. The bear gnashed its teeth as it clawed at the ground with its hind feet and pushed forward, still trying to reach them. White Elk took careful aim and fired. The hair on top of the bear's head stirred, then became damp with blood. Its gleaming eyes turned dull and glazed,· and the animal lay still.

The forest seemed to spin around Janessa, and she

felt faint. Tears burned in her eyes, and sobs welled up within her. She was trembling all over. White Elk, after watching the bear for a long moment, turned to her. "Are you all right?" he asked.

Despite her sorry state, the question stirred her pride and determination. Summoning her will, she controlled her trembling and straightened up, blinking back her tears. "Of course I am," she replied. She handed him back the pistol. "Are you?"

White Elk blinked in surprise, his hand not completely steady as he took the pistol and holstered it. "You might be a girl, Miss Janessa," he said in admiration, "but you're also a good man to have around." He looked up at the tree. "You can come on down now, Timmy. We'll take you home."

The boy sobbed fitfully as he slowly climbed down from limb to limb. When he had stepped to the lowest limb, White Elk reached up for him and lifted him down to the ground. Janessa immediately gathered him up in her arms and held him to her. She took out her handkerchief and wiped his face and nose.

"You can hold on to me as tightly as you want," she said. "But be a little man and don't cry, Timmy."

Timmy nodded, holding back his sobs as his arms clamped around her neck. They began walking toward the horses, White Elk reloading his weapons and Janessa carrying the boy. She stumbled along, barely able to support Timmy's weight, but his solid, clutching presence reassured her, and the toil of carrying him was deeply satisfying after her agonizing ordeal over his safety.

As they rode back to the ranch, the wind picked up and the sky swiftly grew dark. In the distance ahead, bright flashes of lightning arced between storm clouds, and thunder rumbled ominously across the intervening miles, making Janessa uneasy.

The temperature had plummeted, and a few raindrops began falling as the horses approached the ranch.

The lamp that Janessa had left burning in the kitchen made the windows glow, and she could see men with lanterns moving about around the barns. She dismounted with Timmy at the kitchen door, and White Elk led the horses and the pony away.

After directing Timmy to return his father's telescope and wash up, Janessa busied herself preparing dinner, trying to control the twinges of fear that raced through her as the storm closed in.

A few minutes later, Timmy came into the kitchen and climbed onto his chair at the table, his chubby face bright from being scrubbed. Janessa poured him a glass of milk, then dished up the food and put it on the table. The boy was much more subdued than usual, but nothing interfered with his appetite.

The storm made Janessa too nervous to eat, the loud cracks of lightning followed by booming roars of thunder that vibrated things in the kitchen. She picked at her food, then pushed her plate aside and went to the cabinet for her cigarettes. After lighting one, she filled her coffee cup and sat back down at the table.

The boy finished eating, then waited apprehensively for the reckoning that he knew was coming. As he looked at her, Janessa moved in her chair and took a quick puff on her cigarette to conceal her flinch from an especially loud thunderclap. "You waited," she said quickly, "for Aunt Cindy to leave before you sneaked off. You knew she would tell you not to go. Now you know why she would have told you that, don't you?"

The boy looked down.

"Answer me, Timmy."

"Yes, I know," he muttered.

"When people tell you not to do things, it isn't just to keep you from doing things you enjoy. It's because some things aren't good for you, or they're dangerous. Do you understand?"

"Yes, I understand."

"I'm not going to tell Aunt Cindy about this, and I'm

not going to take a switch to you myself, but only because I think you've learned your lesson. Now go get ready for bed."

Vastly relieved, the boy jumped down from his chair and ran out of the room. Janessa cleared the table and began washing the dishes. The storm seemed to be directly over the ranch, the lightning flashes followed immediately by thunder. Janessa almost dropped a dish as a lightning bolt struck nearby, filling the kitchen with its glare and shaking the walls with a boom.

Timmy came back into the kitchen, wearing his nightshirt. The storm was making him nervous, but he was cautious about trying Janessa's patience after his day's escapade. He followed meekly as she led him to his bedroom and tucked him in.

Janessa had returned to the kitchen and just finished cleaning up when the back door suddenly opened and Cindy ducked in out of the rain and wind.

Janessa was surprised, but mainly she was relieved to have company. "Cindy!" she exclaimed in pleasure. "Why did you come back tonight?"

Cindy took off her cape and hung it up. "I thought that the ferries might stop if the storm lasted through tomorrow. So I caught the last boat, and it tossed around like a cork." She glanced up as rain began pelting in a torrent against the roof. "It appears I made it just in time, didn't I?"

"Yes, you did. There's hot coffee on the stove."

Cindy hesitated, sensing the girl's nervousness. "Is Timmy all tucked into bed?"

"Yes, of course. But now that you're back, he'll probably run into your room and get into bed with you."

The girl's superior tone amused Cindy, and she smiled. "He doesn't like thunderstorms, but they also frighten me." She stepped to Janessa and kissed her and patted her shoulder. "And when you're a little older, dear, you won't mind admitting that certain things frighten you as well."

Janessa gulped, suddenly thinking about the charging grizzly bear. Then she decided to have another cigarette.

Henry Blake had received a reply to his telegram to his project officer in Washington. His request for leave had been approved, and he was also instructed to bring to Washington all of his notes and other material on the procurement methods used by the German Army.

From the moment the telegram arrived, Gisela was grief-stricken, in spite of her knowledge that Henry would soon return. Their past year of living together had been like a lifetime to her, so closely had it bound her to the man she loved. Indeed, the immediate prospect of their parting brought her close to despair. Henry also dreaded the separation, and more than ever he knew he had made the only possible choice when he had decided to break his engagement with Cindy.

Gisela buried her grief in activity, taking charge of Henry's travel arrangements. She found that the luxury steamer *Adlergau* was in port at Bremerhaven, scheduled to depart for New York, and after sending an urgent telegram to the managing director of the steamship line to book Henry the best cabin possible, she summoned the stationmaster from Grevenburg to work out a routing for her private car.

On their last night together, they were both sleepless, Gisela clinging fiercely to Henry through the hours before dawn. Their parting the next morning was agonizing for both of them, and Gisela looked pale and distraught as Henry stepped into the carriage to go down to the village, where the private car was waiting. A few hours later, the car was connected to an express freight and speeding northward, and Henry sat in an easy chair and looked out at the passing countryside as a servant prepared a meal in the kitchen at the front of the car.

Early the following morning, the third officer of the *Adlergau* met the private car when it arrived in the Bremerhaven freight yards, and Henry was whisked in a carriage directly to the docks. Only hours later, when the ship was moving through the North Sea swells outside the harbor, there was a knock on Henry's cabin door. It was not the steward, as he had expected.

"I am Captain Schroeder," the bearded man in the passageway said, bowing stiffly. "Are your accommodations satisfactory?"

At first taken aback, Henry quickly stepped into the passageway and introduced himself, speaking in German and bowing in return. "Yes, the accommodations are excellent, and I wish to apologize for whatever inconvenience my last-minute arrangements might have caused, Captain."

The man stroked his beard as he eyed Henry curiously. "I presume that Baron Hohenfels, the director of the Hamburg Lines, is a friend of yours?"

"We have a friend in common," Henry said.

"Yes, I see. You will have a place at my table for meals. If you need anything during the voyage, please contact me or one of the officers."

Henry thanked the captain, then stepped back into his cabin, smiling and shaking his head at the trouble Gisela must have gone through on his account. But by now he was almost used to it.

The ship reached the approaches to Southampton, in the English Channel, the following day. A cargo lighter pulled alongside, and Henry stood on deck with other passengers and watched the loading operations. A bosun's chair was lowered to bring another passenger aboard, and to Henry's astonishment and delight he saw that it was Randolph Churchill.

"My word!" Churchill exclaimed when Henry came up to greet him. "Of all people, it's Henry Blake! What on earth are you doing here?"

"I might ask you the same," Henry replied, laughing as they shook hands. "Have you been exiled from London?"

Laughing, Churchill explained that urgent affairs involved with his campaign for Parliament had caused him to miss an earlier steamer. "I was stranded in Southampton until I heard about this ship."

"Well, I'm pleased that you're here," Henry said. "I need cheerful company, because my journey isn't for entirely pleasant reasons."

"You must tell me all about it over dinner, and I'll tell you about my Jennie," Churchill said, putting an arm around Henry's shoulder.

As the two of them walked down the deck toward the main saloon, the emotional turmoil of the past days was suddenly less burdensome to Henry. He laughed heartily as Churchill began telling him an amusing story, and for a while, at least, he forgot about Cindy Holt.

XII

"I don't see Jennie anywhere," Churchill said worriedly, scanning the mass of people on the pier as he and Henry walked down the gangplank. "I do hope she received the telegram I sent her from Southampton."

"I'm sure she did," Henry replied, looking at the milling, noisy crowd that had gathered to meet passengers from the ship. "But I'm not surprised you don't see her. It would be hard to find anyone in this crowd."

"Not Jennie," Churchill said. "She's a lady that stands out in a crowd. When you meet her, you'll see what I—" He broke off, craning his neck, then waving. "There she is! Jennie! Jennie!" He began pushing past others on the gangplank.

Henry laughed, watching as Churchill rushed ahead and plunged into the crowd, shouting and waving. When Henry reached the foot of the gangplank, he began working his way through the press of bodies in the direction that Churchill had gone. Finally, at the edge of the crowd, he spotted his friend kissing a young woman. Seeing Jennie Jerome, Henry understood why Churchill had begun to court her upon their first meeting.

During the voyage, Churchill had talked at length about her, and Henry had attributed some of his friend's more extravagant comments to the enthusiasm of love. However, what Churchill had said seemed largely true.

Slender and shapely in a blue silk dress trimmed with lace, Jennie Jerome was nineteen years old and bewitchingly lovely. With a pang, Henry thought about Cindy Holt and imagined what his own homecoming might have been like.

Churchill, smiling happily, beckoned him forward. "What held you up, Henry? Come and meet my Jennie. Jennie, my love, you remember Henry Blake from my letters?"

"Yes, of course," she said, smiling warmly. "It's so good to meet you in person, Mr. Blake. Spencer has written so much about you that I feel I know you already."

Henry bowed over her hand. "I share that feeling, after having heard your praises sung all the way across the Atlantic. I'm delighted to meet you."

"Spencer wrote that you're assigned to some sort of military duty in Germany," Jennie said. "Have you come home on vacation? If so, I would appreciate it if you would spend at least a day or two with us. Spencer and I would enjoy it, and so would my father."

Henry knew that her father, Leonard Jerome, was a business partner of Commodore Vanderbilt's, and he was flattered by the invitation, but he had more important business at hand. "Thank you, but I must decline," he replied. "I'm still on duty at the present, and I'm expected in Washington. Then I must travel to Oregon to see my family."

They exchanged a few more words, but when Henry tried to take his leave, Jennie insisted on driving him in her carriage to the train station. Arguing was useless, and a half hour later, after having collected their baggage and gone through customs, they were crossing Manhattan Island in the large Jerome carriage. Jenny asked questions about the voyage, and Henry enjoyed chatting with her, yet something about her—perhaps simply the fact that she was American—reminded him uncomfortably of Cindy. By the time they reached the railroad station, Henry was almost relieved to make his farewells.

*   *   *

It was late evening when he arrived in Washington, and the train station was nearly deserted. Henry took a carriage to a hotel, and early the next morning he walked along the bustling streets to the offices of the War Department, which occupied a large building a few blocks from the White House.

John Simpson, the deputy undersecretary of war for ordnance and Henry's project officer, was an energetic, outgoing man of forty. Henry had met him once before and liked him instantly. After the two men greeted each other, Simpson took Henry down the hall to the office of his superior, the undersecretary of war for materiel.

"He's Mr. Charles Rollins," Simpson said, pausing at the door. "He wants to talk with you about what you've been doing, as well as tell you about a project we have in mind. After you're through with him, you and I will get together with my staff and go into some of the details."

A gray-haired clerk showed Henry and Simpson into the undersecretary's large, well-furnished office. Rollins was a dapper, portly man of fifty, and he greeted Henry with a warm smile and firm handshake. He explained that the information Henry had been sending back from Germany was of profound interest throughout the War Department.

"To give you an idea of the importance with which your reports are regarded," Rollins said, "the secretary of war has asked to see them. So, as a vast understatement, we're absolutely delighted with what you've been doing, Lieutenant Blake."

"Indeed we are," Simpson agreed. "We can still scarcely believe our good fortune in having an officer inside a German armaments factory. Of course we're not unaware that you were the one who managed to develop such a valuable contact."

Rollins smiled in agreement. "It's clear to everyone here that you're quite an exceptional officer, Lieutenant Blake. I see from your report that you're still concentrating

most of your efforts on finding out what you can about how
Mauser manufactures their infantry rifles."

Henry nodded and replied that many questions about
the weapon remained to be answered. Somehow, the Mauser
Arms Works was producing assembly-line rifles that were
as accurate as the best custom-made rifles. He had found
out that the reason for the accuracy was in the rifle barrels, and although he had not determined the secret of
how the barrels were made, he had several promising
leads.

The conversation continued, and as Henry had anticipated, the subject turned to the German Army's method
of testing and buying small arms. It was the consensus in
the War Department, Rollins explained, that Germany's
efficiency in arms procurement had given that country a
decided advantage in the recent Franco-Prussian War.
That was the reason Henry had been asked to bring his
notes and other materials on the subject from Germany.

"We wouldn't want to simply copy what the Germans
are doing, of course," Rollins said, "but for some time we
have been considering new procurement procedures. You
happen to be the only one available, Lieutenant, who has
actually seen different procedures in operation, so we'd
like to take advantage of your experience and advice."

Henry nodded. "I'll certainly be more than pleased to
do everything I can to help, sir," he said.

"Good." Rollins stood up, offering his hand. "Mr.
Simpson will take over from here and tell you just what
we have in mind."

The rest of the day passed quickly, with Henry and
the other men poring over files concerning the United
States Army's recent weapons tests and purchases. To
Henry, it soon became apparent that virtually all of the
existing difficulties could be eliminated by the simple
expedient of placing procurement specialists at the factories to inspect and approve weapons shipments, as was
done in Germany. However, that would require a many-

fold increase in the number of personnel, at a prohibitive cost.

Then a solution occurred to Henry, and the others became excitedly enthusiastic as he talked with them about it. His proposal was to establish a central office where weapons inspectors would be located, and a team would be sent out when a factory was ready to test or dispatch a shipment of weapons.

"Some ninety percent of the small arms and ammunition comes from factories in and around Connecticut," he said. "The office could be set up in that state, in a place convenient to all the factories. In those few instances when a shipment comes from a factory located elsewhere, a team of inspectors could be sent there."

"That would be far more efficient than our present system," Simpson agreed. He looked at Henry. "Before I get back to Undersecretary Rollins, I guess I should ask you the obvious question. If and when this suggestion is approved, would you like to volunteer to organize the office in Connecticut, Lieutenant Blake?"

Henry hesitated only briefly. "Yes, sir," he replied. "I would look forward to it."

It was late by the time Henry returned to his hotel, with his leave papers in hand. He was hungry and tired, but the work he had done gave him a sense of accomplishment. Certainly it was far more agreeable than what lay ahead of him. Aside from his deep regrets and sorrow over breaking his engagement with Cindy, he knew that his reception in Oregon would be cool at best.

Henry enjoyed the journey west. As he observed the growth and the developments since he had last traveled across the United States, he felt a sense of awe. The freedoms and rights possessed by the people of his land released immense energies that enabled them to accomplish prodigious feats. Refusing to acknowledge obstacles, they overcame all obstacles.

Henry thought of Germany. He had made a life for

himself there, and he enjoyed that life. But it was a land that was confined by its past, its people in bondage to roles they had inherited from birth. With a certainty he had never felt before, Henry knew that his own country was the only one he could ever love.

While he was on the steam packet between San Francisco and Portland, the soap in his shaving mug ran low, and he opened a package of toilet soap, cologne, and other articles Gisela had prepared for him before he left. The package had seemed heavy to him in his bags, and when he opened it he found out why.

Inside was a leather purse, along with a note from Gisela. Written in the angular, backward-slanted German script she always used, the note began with an apology that acknowledged his refusal ever to accept anything of value from her. However, it concluded, she wanted to make certain that he had pocket money during his journey.

The purse contained newly minted American double eagle gold coins that she had apparently obtained from the bank in Berlin. What she considered adequate pocket money for his journey amounted to some five times his annual salary and allowances.

It was a bright, warm afternoon when the steam packet arrived in Portland and was made fast to a pier for its layover until the next day. Henry had planned to spend at least a week of his leave at Fort Vancouver and had brought along sufficient clothes for that length of time; however, depending upon how cool his welcome was, his stay could be much shorter. Checking his luggage at the terminal and carrying only an overnight bag, he walked along the piers to take the ferry across the river.

When he arrived at the general's quarters, his reception was exactly what he had feared. Eulalia came to the door, her expression changing when she saw who it was. The lovely face that he always pictured in his mind with a warm, motherly smile became hostile as she looked at him. Despite his disappointment, Henry bent to kiss her, but she stepped back.

"Your room is ready," she said. "Go and put your things away, and I'll send an orderly to tell Lee that you're here."

"Won't you give me an opportunity to explain what happened?" he asked. "This isn't fair, you know."

"Fair?" she echoed bitterly. "You use that word with me? But you'll have an opportunity to explain. I'm more than ready to hear it."

Henry sighed and nodded. "You look well, as you always do."

"Then the way I look is deceiving," Eulalia replied curtly. "These past weeks have been a sore trial for me. I've had to help my daughter accept something that I can't accept myself."

With that, she walked down the hallway and disappeared into the rear of the house. Henry went upstairs to his room. It was just as he had left it, and it reminded him of happier times. But those times now seemed to be in the remote past, almost in another life. Henry put his bag down and sat on the bed until he heard the general come in; then he went back downstairs.

The tall, gray-haired general, who had always been affectionate and fatherly, seemed more troubled than angry. Still, he was distant, and his handshake was perfunctory as he studied Henry. "You've changed a lot," he commented.

"Yes, I've gained some weight, sir," Henry replied.

His expression thoughtful, Lee said, "It's been well over a year, but that didn't seem so long until just now. Come on, let's go out onto the back porch."

Henry followed his adoptive father along the hall and out the back door. Eulalia was sitting at the wrought-iron table on the porch. She glanced at Henry, her eyes frigid, then looked away again as Henry and Leland sat down at the table. The silence was tense as Henry organized his thoughts. Then he began trying to explain what had happened.

To an extent, he was constrained in what he could tell

them, because of the secrecy surrounding his work in Germany. For the most part, however, it was Gisela who was impossible to explain. The conversation was the most awkward and stilted Henry had ever experienced.

If the two people sitting with him had been complete strangers, it would have been easier. But they had once loved him and now felt betrayed, and while they waited for an explanation, their attitudes conveyed that no explanation would be adequate.

In the tension of the moment, Henry had difficulty organizing his thoughts. Even what had once seemed simple and straightforward to him was now difficult to put into words. He was barely more than halfway through when Eulalia had heard enough.

Moving her chair back, she stood up. "It's clear what happened," she said acidly. "You forsook marriage with a good woman, my daughter, in favor of lust for a German harlot. That is your choice to make, of course, but it reflects as poorly on your character as it does on your judgment."

"It wasn't that simple," Henry objected. "I had no control over many things that happened, and if you would let me explain—"

"It's simple enough to me!" Eulalia retorted. "And you did have control over what happened. However you may try to complicate it, you simply chose to abandon yourself to lust. So be it, but don't expect me to soil my ears with the full details of such a sordid affair."

Her words left a ringing silence in their wake as she went inside and closed the door. Looking at the general, Henry saw that there was still no anger in his attitude. His weathered face was set in lines of sorrow and disappointment, not resentment.

Henry sighed, shaking his head. "I'm truly sorry for the pain I've caused, sir," he said. "Most of all, I wish I could have avoided that."

"I believe you've hurt yourself more than you have

anyone here," Lee replied bleakly. "In time, I believe you'll regret this more than anyone else involved."

"I don't know how I could regret it more than I do now, sir. The fact of the matter is, though, I didn't have full control over events, and many considerations were involved. To go directly to the heart of the matter, I was unable to leave her last year. Now the situation is even worse. It's impossible for me to leave her now."

"The way to leave her," Lee said quietly, "is to turn around and walk away. The right choices are not always the easiest ones to act upon. However, they are always the right ones."

Silence fell again, Henry resigning himself to the fact that no explanation, however compelling, would be sufficient. He wished he could simply say that Gisela was dying and that he had to stay with her, but even that was not strictly true. She might live for many more years, and in any case he had to go where the army sent him. Nothing, it seemed, was simple anymore.

He stood up as Lee pushed the chair back. "I'll only be staying the night, sir," he said. "I'll be on the packet when it leaves for San Francisco tomorrow. Considering all that's happened, it would probably be better if I stayed in the quarters at the fort."

"No, stay here tonight," Lee replied tonelessly. "If you stayed at the fort, it would only cause speculation and gossip. We have more than enough of that already."

His lack of insistence that Henry stay longer was a glaring omission, and Henry felt deeply hurt. As the general went inside, Henry sat back down at the table. Drained and depressed after the conversation with his adoptive parents, he knew that the worst still remained. He had to go to see Cindy. Wearily, he stood up and went inside. He walked along the hall and out the front door, then turned toward the fort.

At the fort, he went to the stables and saddled a horse, and then he rode down to the ferry landing. The ferry had just docked, and he boarded it and crossed the river. Portland had changed during his absence, and none of the passersby seemed to recognize him. As he rode through the city and along the road toward the Holt ranch, memories of the countless happy times he had come this way whispered across the years to him.

When the Holt ranch came into view, an even more poignant memory returned to him from years before. The memory was sharp and clear, evoked by a startling and completely unexpected sight.

For several seconds he was at a complete loss as to who the girl might be. Finally, he realized that she had to be Toby Holt's daughter, Janessa, who had suddenly shown up in Portland; Cindy had mentioned her at length in her letters. Henry had expected the girl to show some trace of Indian blood, but in every respect her characteristics were those of a Holt.

In every respect, she was also Cindy Holt as a young girl. Cindy had been a few years older when he had first met her, but still the resemblance between them was extraordinary. The pretty face, sun-streaked straw blond hair, and blue eyes were identical. It was like being lifted back in time and seeing Cindy again.

A timid Holt was a contradiction in terms, and the girl gazed at him with a belligerent, bristling glare, evidently knowing who he was. Toby's son Timmy was playing in the front yard, and the boy started to grin and wave as Henry approached. A command from Janessa, however, sent him scuttling up the steps and inside the house.

Henry reined up, touching his cap. "You must be Janessa," he said. "I'm Henry Blake."

"I know who you are," Janessa replied quietly, her glare unwavering. "You wait out here, and I'll see if Cindy wants to talk to you."

She went into the house, and Henry dismounted and tethered his horse, then climbed the steps to the porch. A moment later, the front door opened and Cindy stood there.

Moments passed in silence as they looked at each

other. To an extent, Henry had forgotten the sheer intensity of her beauty, its forceful impact. Her face was paler than he remembered, and her lips were pressed together in a thin, straight line, yet she was still bewitchingly lovely.

Janessa was behind her, peering at him with the same penetrating glare as before.

Finally Cindy broke the silence. "What do you want, Henry?" she asked quietly.

"I'd like to talk with you," he replied. "I'd like to apologize and try to explain what happened."

"Your letter was explanation enough, because you made it clear what you want to do. And I don't need or want any apologies from you."

Henry hesitated, not knowing how to reply. It seemed that he had innumerable things to tell her, enough to fill volumes; yet somehow he had nothing to say. "Cindy, I'm sorry. I'm sorry that—"

She turned her head away, refusing to listen. "I don't think we have anything further to say to each other, Henry."

"Cindy—"

She shook her head violently. "Please, Henry, just go."

After a long pause, he nodded and touched his cap. "Good-bye, Cindy."

"Good-bye."

He went down the steps and mounted his horse, the door closing quietly behind him.

As he rode back along the road toward the city, the image of Cindy's averted face stayed in his mind. He had an eerie sense of not belonging, of being isolated from even his memories. He had anticipated resentment, but instead there seemed to be an invisible wall between him and others that blocked communication, turning them into strangers. Even the place now seemed unaccountably changed.

Then he recalled a conversation with Gisela. Once,

when he had talked wistfully about wanting to return to the United States to visit the scenes of his childhood, she had told him that he would be disappointed. Those who visited places associated with fond memories, she had explained, were in fact attempting to return not to a place but to a time in the past, which was impossible.

In coming to Portland, he had been fulfilling an obligation to Cindy. But he had also been trying to return to a happy, carefree time, and he had been disappointed. The place and the people had changed, and he had changed even more. What he had wanted was in the past, out of reach.

Gisela had been right, he reflected, as she always was. He thought about how she had never been worried about Cindy. Gisela was constantly worried about other women, and a chance comment from him about a woman he had glimpsed on the street in Frankfurt would immediately arouse her suspicions. But she had never been worried about Cindy.

He wondered if Gisela had known all along what would happen. During their conversations, her brilliant mind often made intuitive leaps that left him plodding along in the wake of her thoughts until she patiently explained. He wondered if she had confidently waited for him to discover for himself what she had known all along—that he had changed irrevocably.

Whatever had happened, he decided, the situation had turned out the best for everyone involved. Despite Cindy's hurt and his sense of loss, he was now convinced that the scenes of his youth in Portland were gone, vanished in a time that was past. What could have been between him and Cindy was also somewhere in that limbo, and it would never return. When he had decided to stay with Gisela, he had broken forever with his past.

As she sat at the kitchen table, similar thoughts were racing through Cindy Holt's mind. After weeks of emotional turmoil, she had finally concluded that the situation had turned out for the best.

When she had looked at Henry on the porch, it had almost seemed that an impostor had taken his place. The man on the porch had not been the Henry Blake she had known. They looked the same, like identical twins, but they were different. And even though her lost love was a torment within her, that pain was preferable to being married to the man she had seen on the porch. He was a stranger.

Janessa poured a cup of coffee and brought it to the table. She stirred sugar and milk into it, then put it in front of Cindy. "There you are, Cindy," she said. "Why don't you forget him, just forget him? He isn't worth thinking about, much less being sad over."

The fierce protectiveness in the girl's voice was amusing, but it was also deeply comforting. Cindy put an arm around Janessa's waist as the girl hugged her and held her close. Janessa had been a constant source of comfort to her during the past weeks, and somehow even the odor of tobacco that always lingered around her now seemed pleasant to Cindy.

Janessa kissed Cindy, then pulled a chair closer and sat down beside her. "Drink your coffee," she said. "I must be honest about it and say that I don't understand what you ever saw in him. He looks sly and mean."

Taking a sip of coffee, Cindy reflected that what Janessa had said was an exaggeration. At the same time, there was a basis for her reaction. Before, it had been easy to interpret Henry's moods and to know what he was thinking. Now there was a guarded secretiveness about him. It was like a mask over his face.

His eyes had changed, too. Instead of the cheerful, smiling eyes of the Hank Blake she had known, they were the eyes of an old man who has seen too much of the world. Despite what had happened, Cindy knew that she would always love Henry. But she feared those eyes.

"He's changed, Janessa," she said. "He's changed so much that he's like someone I've never known before."

Janessa shrugged. "I'm beginning to think that men in general can't be trusted," she said. "That Captain Koehler who was here liked you, and he must have known what Henry Blake had been up to. But he didn't warn you, did he?"

Cindy smiled, thinking about Richard. When he had been in Portland, she had been constrained by her engagement and had fought her reaction to him. "No, you don't understand, Janessa," she said. "Soldiers have a code of honor among themselves. They don't discuss each other's personal affairs or try to take advantage of each other in that respect. Richard had no choice in what he did."

"No, I certainly don't understand," Janessa said. "And I don't think I ever will. Anyway, there's plenty to take Henry Blake's place. You could have pity on Lieutenant Kerr and invite him in for lunch sometime. His excuse about coming to see Calvin Rogers is starting to sound a little silly."

That, Cindy reflected, was a good idea. Reed Kerr was a guileless, uncomplicated man, and she liked him well enough.

"Yes, I'll do that," she said. "The next time he comes here, I'll invite him to have lunch with us."

XIII

Dinner that evening at the general's quarters was a thoroughly unpleasant experience for Henry. Eulalia said nothing at all, and Leland asked Henry only a few terse questions about his assignment in Germany. During the long, stiff silences, Henry longed for a lusty, hearty display of anger such as Gisela could have provided, shouting at the top of her voice and breaking things.

After a sleepless night, Henry made his farewells the next morning. The general's face was lined with fatigue, and Eulalia's eyes were red from weeping, lack of sleep, or both. Their attitudes conveyed the same regret that Henry felt, the same inability to turn back and recapture what had been lost.

The high point of his visit to Portland came unexpectedly when he met his old friend and classmate Reed Kerr at the ferry pier. Reed apparently had been waiting for him, and Henry was relieved for once to be greeted warmly. Even when Reed somewhat guiltily admitted his desire to court Cindy Holt, Henry sensed that the man's friendship was still genuine.

"I'm glad I had a chance to talk to you, sir," Reed said, "because I felt obliged to do so before I make my feelings clear to Cindy. I'm quite fond of her, you know."

For the first time since arriving in Portland, Henry felt at home. While few things were the same as before,

Reed Kerr had not changed. He was still the good friend who had remained loyal to Henry at West Point when everyone else had turned away.

"I'm also pleased to talk with you, Reed," he said, laughing with relief. "And you have my blessings with Cindy, but only if you stop addressing me like a senior officer. And if you've forgotten my name, I'll put you in a brace and order you to button that blouse pocket."

Reed blinked, taken aback, and looked down at his blouse. Then he laughed, fastening the button. "Well, I wasn't certain how to approach you, Hank," he explained. "What I had to say wasn't easy, even between the best of friends. And things seem so different now."

Henry nodded as he looked away. "Yes, there's no question about that, Reed. Things are entirely different."

"This has been a miserable homecoming for you, hasn't it?" Reed commented sympathetically. "When I first heard about what happened, I simply couldn't believe it. I know it's none of my business, Hank, but you must have had a very compelling reason to do what you did. The more I've thought about it, the more I've become absolutely certain about that."

Henry hesitated. He wanted to explain everything to Reed, to confide in the one friend he still had. But the ferry was approaching, and it was all too complicated. "There were reasons," he said. "But what's done is done, and there's no going back."

"Perhaps so, but I know what the people here mean to you, Hank," Reed insisted. "I also know what their regard means to you, and I'd like to be in a position to argue your cause. Once tempers cool and time eases hard feelings, I could talk to them."

"No," Henry said, shaking his head. "I appreciate the offer, but it would be a waste of time, and you would ruin your own cause in the process. If you want to get along with one of the Holts, you must stay on good terms with all of them. I only wish everyone was as understanding as you, Reed. Are you happy here?"

Reed nodded. "Yes, this is a good post. I'm sure it isn't as interesting as your assignment, but I'm better at soldiering without complications. I was Captain Koehler's escort while he was here, by the way. He's a fine man and a fine officer."

"Yes, he certainly is," Henry agreed. "I value his friendship highly."

"When you see him, give him my best regards. You are going back to Europe, aren't you?"

"Yes, after I stop in Chicago to talk with Toby Holt. I have most of my leave remaining, so I'll probably spend it in Europe. And when I see Richard again, I'll give him your regards."

The ferry was easing up alongside the pier, bells ringing and its engine rumbling. The two officers fell silent, watching as the passengers began filing off. "I hope my courting Cindy won't cause hard feelings between us," Reed said at last.

"I would think you foolish if you didn't court her," Henry replied. "No, I wish you well, Reed."

"I appreciate that, Hank." Hesitating, Reed searched for words. "It bothered me a lot to see Cindy hurt, but I know you, Hank, and I know there had to be good reasons behind what you did. I just want to say that you can always depend upon my friendship, and if there's ever a way in which I can help you, you only need let me know." He held out his hand for Henry to shake.

Henry took it. "I'm grateful for that, Reed, truly I am. And I'm grateful for having seen a friendly face before I leave here." He glanced at the ferry, which now was taking on passengers. "Well, I'd best be on my way or I'll miss the packet."

"Sure, Hank. Good luck to you."

"And to you, Reed. Good-bye."

Since his return to the United States, Henry had read numerous accounts in newspapers about the rapid rebuilding after the disastrous fire in Chicago. It was also a topic of conversation among the other passengers as the train drew closer to the city. When he walked out of the station late in the evening, the night outside was alive with lights and the clamor of the rebuilding, and Henry saw that the accounts had not been exaggerated.

As Henry rode in a carriage to the Palace Hotel, where he had wired ahead for a room, he wondered if Gisela had received the telegram he had sent her from San Francisco. Although he had informed her where he would be staying, he knew it was unlikely that a reply would be waiting for him at the hotel. Still, he asked at the desk as soon as he arrived, and when the night clerk shook his head, Henry was deeply disappointed.

The next day, when he went to see Toby, he was not met with the hostility and automatic condemnation that had confronted him in Portland and Fort Vancouver. Toby had been a great influence in Henry's life, and their deep friendship and the camaraderie that had come from their shared experiences prevented that. Toby was also more understanding when it came to difficulties with women.

However, he was understanding only to a point. Over lunch at a downtown restaurant, he listened to Henry quietly, obviously wanting an explanation he could accept. But all during the conversation, Henry was acutely aware that the tall, lean man facing him was a Holt. Toby was trying to avoid a dispute and a permanent rift with his friend, but his eyes were uncomfortably like those that had looked at Henry when Cindy and Janessa had stood in the doorway of the ranch house.

"So you met this woman in France," Toby said, summing up what Henry had told him. "You got transferred to Germany, and now she's with you there. Is she French or German?"

"German."

"I see. And now she's ill," Toby continued. "You feel that you can't leave her, and I agree with you absolutely on that. The woman needs you, so you should stay with her. However, it was at the beginning of the whole business that you made your mistake, Henry."

"What do you mean?"

"I mean you should have let Cindy know about it when you met this woman and became involved with her. These things happen, and I can accept that. However, you should have let Cindy know."

"But it was only a passing thing at the time, Toby. I had no idea that it would continue until now."

"Then you should have let Cindy know that you were involved in a passing thing, Henry."

"I didn't want to hurt her."

"But you have, and you've hurt her worse than you would have last year. By letting it drag on, you also hurt her pride."

Henry hesitated, reflecting on the fact that he was unable to tell Toby everything. His duty had been one of the major factors involved, but that was a subject he was unable to broach. Indeed, Henry's commanding officer back in France had encouraged him to spend as much time as possible with Gisela, because of the privileged military information to which she had access. "It wasn't that simple, Toby," he said. "There were other things involved."

Toby nodded, though clearly he was unconvinced. After admitting that he himself had learned only from his own mistakes, Toby changed the subject, asking Henry about his future plans. Henry said that he would be returning directly to Germany but that he did not know for how long. Thinking of the proposal that he had helped write in Washington, he mentioned that he might be returning to the States within a few months. Then Toby brought up a completely unexpected subject.

"When you get back to Germany, I suppose you'll be getting married, won't you?"

The question took Henry aback, because he had never contemplated marriage with Gisela. It was a matter about which she was supremely indifferent. "I hadn't thought about it, Toby," he replied.

Toby stopped eating and looked at Henry in surprise. Then he continued eating. "Perhaps you should think about it," he said. "Even aside from the right and the wrong of it, there's a very practical issue involved. You'll get extra allowances if you're married, and you would be able to provide for her better."

"Money isn't a problem. She's a businesswoman."

"Oh? What sort of business is she in?"

"It was foodstuffs, wines, and things of that nature when I first met her, but now she's involved in other affairs as well."

"She owns a grocery store?" Toby replied.

"Not exactly," Henry said wryly, but did not elaborate.

"Well, it's up to you what you do, Henry," Toby continued. "Do you feel like any dessert?"

Henry put his napkin down beside his plate. "No, I don't, Toby. I'm ready to leave anytime you are."

Outside, they stood and talked for a few minutes. Henry declined Toby's offer to see him off at the train station the following day, and their parting handshake was friendly but brief.

As Henry's carriage moved along the street, he reflected that the reaction from Toby had been more critical than he had expected, but not unreasonably severe. In the man's place, he mused, he probably would have taken the same attitude. After all, Toby was a Holt, and believed that his sister had been treated unfairly. Henry was thankful that at least the atmosphere between them had been civil.

Back at the hotel, the desk clerk took a telegram envelope from the key slot and handed it to Henry along with the key. Henry's spirits immediately lifted, and he tore open the envelope. The message was absurdly long, expressions of affection following one after another, and some of the words had been garbled by an operator unfamiliar with German. Then he found the key sentence, containing the news he had secretly hoped for since he had left Portland. Gisela would be at Fenton.

"I trust it's good news, sir," the desk clerk commented, smiling in response to Henry's wide grin.

"It certainly is," Henry replied, putting the telegram back into the envelope. "I'd like to see the train schedules and the schedule for ship departures from the East Coast ports, please."

The clerk bustled about and put them on the desk, and Henry scanned the ship departures first. On the list for Charleston, an entry seemed to leap out at him. A fast cargo steamer with available staterooms was departing for England. Its first port of call was Bristol, which was only about thirty miles from Fenton. Henry turned to the train schedules, looking to see if he could reach Charleston before the ship left.

The desk clerk hovered about helpfully. "Will you be able to get there in time, sir?" he asked.

"The train will arrive at Charleston six hours before the ship leaves," Henry replied. "But in order to make connections, I'll have to be on a train that leaves here in less than an hour."

The clerk turned away, slamming his hand down on the desk bell and jangling it loudly. "Front! Front!" he called. A bellboy approached hurriedly, and the clerk took the key from Henry and tossed it to the boy. "Get a maid and go pack Lieutenant Blake's belongings! Move!" As the bellboy rushed away, the clerk took out a telegram form and put it on the desk. "You'll want to send a telegram to reserve your cabin, sir. I'll have the doorman find a fast carriage for you, and we'll get you there in time for the train."

Less than twenty minutes later, Henry was in a carriage that lurched along the street, slowing abruptly where the traffic was congested, then careening through side streets that were clear of other vehicles. Arriving at the train station with only minutes to spare, Henry hurriedly checked his baggage, which was carted off without delay,

then bought a ticket. After running to the platform, he
hopped onto the steps at the end of a car and climbed to
the vestibule as the train began pulling out of the station.

Opening the door, he went into the car and looked
around for an empty seat. As he walked down the aisle, he
took a second glance at an attractive young woman sitting
by herself. The woman looked up at him with a smile.
Touching his cap, Henry walked past her to a vacant seat,
then sat down.

On the edge of his vision, he saw the young woman
looking over her shoulder at him, willing to converse and
make his acquaintance. But he looked out the window,
uninterested. The only reason he had glanced twice at her
was because she had vaguely Teutonic features that reminded him of Gisela.

He took out the telegram and read it again, with
happy anticipation. Although once more he would be leaving the country of his birth, he felt as if he were finally
returning home. And in a sense, he reflected, he was. He
was returning home to Gisela.

Toby Holt was deep in thought as he rode in a carriage to his lumberyard. Until he had talked with Henry
Blake over lunch, he had been unable to accept what he
had read in the brief, emotional letter from Cindy and the
more detailed if no less heated letters from Janessa. The
deep love between Henry and Cindy had seemed inde-
structible. For Henry to give her up had appeared so
strange that Toby had wanted to believe it was simply a
mistake, that an explanation would clear up everything.

But it was no mistake, and now Toby understood
why. The Henry Blake that he had known had changed.
Some twenty pounds of additional weight had transformed
his lanky, rawboned frame into the muscular body of a
large, well-built man. Inclined to overlook the fine details
of appearance in the past, Henry had been immaculately
neat and groomed in an expensively tailored uniform. But
other changes had been even more profound.

Outgoing, candid, and inclined to be impulsive before, now he had a watchful reserve about him and thought at length before speaking. Toby was pleased that Henry had in a surprisingly short time matured into an officer who commanded respect, but all in all he preferred the Henry Blake of before.

As the carriage approached the lumberyard entrance, Toby put the entire matter from his mind. What had happened between Cindy and Henry could not be changed, and he had more urgent business to occupy him. Two weeks before, he had gone to the rail yards to look at the ashes of what had been four carloads of lumber destined to be houses for farmers on the plains.

And there had been other incidents. Wagons left outside the lumberyard had been damaged, and the night watchman had driven away loiterers who could have been men intending to sabotage something in the lumberyard. But it appeared that the focus of the trouble was shifting to the logging camp. A week before, most of the draft animals had been incapacitated by a strong laxative oil that had been poured on their feed.

A more ominous worry had presented itself today. The steam launch had been scheduled to leave the logging camp the night before, and it should have been at the lumberyard at daybreak. But there had still been no sign of it when Toby had left to go to lunch with Henry Blake.

After paying the driver, Toby walked through the gate to the lumberyard. The busy, noisy atmosphere was unchanged by the threat of sabotage. Men moved about in the saw house as saws whined through wood, and Henshaw was talking with customers near the stacks of lumber at the side of the yard.

Walking to the office building, Toby looked at the log basin beside the breakwater and saw the same number of logs floating there as before, which meant the launch still had not arrived. The foreman left the customers and crossed the yard toward him.

"It still hasn't gotten here, Toby," Henshaw called as

he approached. "It might just have engine trouble or something, and it might not have even left the camp."

"No, it left the camp on time," Toby said, shaking his head. "If it hadn't, Frank Woods would have sent someone to Wedowee to send us a telegram and let us know about it. With the way things are right now, he knows that we'd be worried."

"Yes, you're right," Henshaw agreed. "Well, maybe it's broken down out on the lake somewhere. That would be bad, wouldn't it?"

"I can think of much worse things," Toby replied. "But if it doesn't get here within the next few hours, I'll hire a launch or a tug to take me out to look for it."

The foreman nodded and walked back toward the customers as Toby went into the office building. Harold Phinney looked up from his ledgers and murmured a sober, formal greeting as Toby entered.

Toby went straight to his desk and resumed the work he had been doing that morning. Leafing through papers and signing them, he thought about his last conversation with Ted Taylor. Ted was reasonably certain that the source of the sabotage was a man named Dieter Schumann, who owned two large lumber mills in Wisconsin, among other holdings.

Through a process of eliminating those mill owners whose property had been damaged in suspicious accidents during the past years, combined with checking into the background of others, Ted had identified Schumann as the likeliest of three possible suspects. Then, while watching them, Ted had seen Schumann surreptitiously meeting with another man in a park in Madison. The man he had met lived in comfortable circumstances, yet had no visible job or occupation. But there was no proof of wrongdoing by either man, nothing that Toby could use as a reason to confront Schumann.

An hour passed, Toby glancing at his watch occasionally. Contemplating the possibility that the launch was disabled out on the lake, he decided to go and hire a vessel as soon as he finished his paperwork. As he was leafing through a last folder of bills, Henshaw came into the outer office.

"The launch is just entering the harbor, Toby," he called through the door.

Toby got up and followed him outside. They crossed the yard and walked out onto the pier. The launch was in the outer harbor, gradually slowing so that the tons of logs it was towing would lose their forward momentum. Everything appeared normal.

As the launch drew closer, Toby noticed something odd. "That towing cable is shorter than it usually is," he said to Henshaw.

"Yes, it does look somewhat shorter," Henshaw agreed. "Maybe the captain pulled some of it in for one reason or another. I'll go get the men ready to winch those logs into the basin."

The foreman walked toward the saw house, shouting and beckoning to the men. By now Toby could see Captain Crowell through the windows in the wheelhouse of the launch. The man's beefy face was flushed, and he was scowling in anger.

The launch edged up to the pier, its engine cutting off. As the men ran along the pier to help the deckhand, Turner, unhook the towing cable, Toby stepped aboard and crossed the deck to the wheelhouse.

"What delayed you, Albert?" he asked. "We've been worried about you."

The captain picked up a length of cable from the deck. "This delayed me," he replied grimly, handing it to Toby. "It broke just after daylight this morning. Take a look at the end of it."

The wire cable had been sawn more than halfway through, and the remainder of the metal threads had frayed and snapped. Toby frowned. "This certainly wasn't an accident."

"No, anything but," the captain growled. "That was the end holding the logs together, and they began drifting all over the place as soon as it broke. Besides being valuable timber, they would be a hazard to shipping, so I had to gather them up."

"I'm sure that was easier said than done."

The captain grunted. "That's what took me so long because they were really spread out by the time I got around to all of them. It was dangerous work, too, climbing down on those logs and hooking them back together. That boy Turner is the only hand on the lake who could do that, and it was plenty hard for him. But we got all twelve of them."

Jimson, the thin, wiry engineer, had climbed out of the engine room. The gray stubble on his face was smudged with engine oil, and he munched his chew of tobacco as he glanced between Toby and the captain and listened to the conversation. "There was thirteen of them logs," he commented quietly.

"I told you to stop that foolishness!" the captain snapped, wheeling on him. "Now, I've heard all I'm going to listen to out of you, Jimson! There were twelve logs, and that's the end of it!"

Jimson shrugged placidly and looked away, unperturbed by the captain's anger. "I'll be quiet about it, but that ain't going to change the fact that there was thirteen of them logs. I'd sure hate to be in the boat that comes along and hits that log."

"We didn't leave any log to hit!" the captain barked. "We set out from the logging camp with twelve logs, and we have twelve logs right there! And how would you know the difference anyway? You can't count over ten unless you take off your boots, and you haven't had them off for a week!"

"I ain't had them off for two weeks, because you're working me to death," Jimson replied calmly, chewing his tobacco. "And I can still count to thirteen."

"There were twelve logs!" the captain roared, shaking his fist in Jimson's face. "And I wouldn't have hooked up to them if there had been thirteen! That's an unlucky number!"

Jimson nodded, then spit tobacco juice over the rail. "You're right, Captain," he said. "Thirteen is unlucky. If there had been either twelve or fourteen of them logs, that cable probably wouldn't have broke."

The captain's face turned crimson as he made a choked sound, speechless with rage for a second. Then he found his voice. "Get down in that engine room and see to the engine!" he bellowed. "If I hear another word out of you, I'll throttle you!"

Jimson walked serenely back toward the engine room hatch, and the captain drew in a deep breath to control his temper. "Toby, there were twelve logs," he said.

"All right, there were twelve, Albert," Toby chuckled. "I don't see that it makes much difference; logs are constantly floating out into the lakes from the rivers. It's enough that you got here with any of them. As it is, it looks like Frank will have to put a guard at the log basin, too."

"Maybe not," the captain said. "Toby, Ted Taylor is looking into something that Fred Guthrie told him about. He wasn't at the camp when I was there, but he left a message for you. He wants you to go there as soon as possible."

Toby held up the length of cable. "As soon as I saw this, I decided to go to the camp. When can you start back up the lake?"

"As soon as we can take on some more coal," the captain replied.

"Good," Toby said, stepping to the rail. "I'll hurry over to my boardinghouse and get packed." He paused a moment. "You say Ted got some information from Fred? I hope he didn't interrupt the honeymoon."

The captain laughed. Two weeks before, to everyone's surprise, Fred Guthrie and Ursula Oberg had gone off and got married by a justice of the peace in Milwaukee.

The shy tavern owner had told no one about it, and Frank Woods had only learned of it from Paddy Rafferty.

Still smiling as he thought about Fred and Ursula, Toby started down the pier. The captain called after him.

"One more thing, Toby—"

Toby paused. "What's that, Albert?"

"Frank told me that Ted said for you to bring your guns."

Toby's smile abruptly faded. He nodded once, then continued toward the stable to get his horse.

XIV

It was past midnight when the launch approached the lighted pier at the logging camp. To Toby's surprise, Ted Taylor and Frank Woods were waiting on the dock, both of them holding lanterns and still breathless from having hurried down the steep bluff.

"We were expecting you back hours ago," Frank said as Toby and the captain stepped ashore. "We were worried. What happened?"

"This did," the captain replied, holding out the length of cable.

As Ted and Frank inspected the cable, the captain called to Jimson to bank the firebox for the night. Then he, Toby, Ted, and Frank started up to the camp. As they climbed the steep path, the captain described the difficulty he had experienced in gathering the logs back together.

"It certainly sounds like a headache, Albert," Frank commented. "With what Ted has found out, though, it could be that all of our troubles are near an end."

Toby looked at Ted inquiringly.

"It's a long story," Ted said. "Let's go inside and have a cup of coffee while I tell you about it."

Bettina and Marjorie were still up, and they called out a greeting as the men approached. Toby immediately noticed a change in Marjorie's attitude toward him, her handshake and smile much warmer. As they all went into the house, he also noticed that she linked her arm through Ted's.

Frank lit the lamp hanging over the kitchen table, and the others sat down in its soft yellow light as Bettina brought cups and the coffeepot to the table. When the coffee was poured, Ted began telling Toby what he had found out.

The information, Ted said, had originated from a lumberjack who worked at another camp. The man had been with a party surveying new stands of timber, and he and the others had smelled woodsmoke in a remote area, far from where anyone would ordinarily be. The man had mentioned the incident to Fred, and Fred had thought it unusual enough to notify Ted.

"The smoke was from a small, hidden camp," Ted continued. "It's in the hills south of here, not far from the shore. I spent three days searching for it, but even before I found it I knew it was the hideout of the ones we've been looking for. That's when I asked Frank to send you a message to come here, Toby."

Albert frowned, puzzled. "How did you know it was their hideout before you found it?"

"By where it was located," Ted replied. "If it had been just a good place to camp, I would have found it on the first day. But instead it's a good place to hide, so I had trouble finding it."

Toby smiled. "And he knew that because he's a good lawman, Albert. He's tracked down enough outlaws to know all their tricks. What did you find at the camp, Ted?"

Ted sipped his coffee. "I took a good look early this morning, and no one was around. But there were three hobbled horses, three rolled-up packs, and a big bottle of croton oil among the things around the fire. I got out fast, which was probably a good idea, since they must have been on their way back from sabotaging that cable. Anyway, I knew it would get your dander up if I made a move before you got here, Toby."

"That's the kind of smart thinking I admire," Toby said, chuckling. "So there's three of them, it seems."

Frank Woods grunted. "And that croton oil is what they put on my stock feed. Some of my oxen still don't have their full strength back."

A momentary silence fell, until suddenly Captain Crowell slammed his fist down on the table. "Well, let's go get them!" he barked. "I'll go fetch my gun from the boat!"

Toby exchanged a glance with Ted, then shook his head. "All you would find is some heel dust hanging in the air, Albert," he said. "If they're smart enough to hide their camp so well that Ted has trouble finding it, you won't catch them by charging in there. Ordinarily, I'd get the sheriff to arrest them, but he might run in there with a herd of deputies and let them get away, and then we'd be right back where we started. No, the fewer of us, the better. Ted and I will go after them. How far away is that campsite, Ted?"

Ted took out his watch and looked at it. "We can have two or three more cups of coffee and still have plenty of time to get there by daybreak. That would be the best time to jump them."

"Yes, it would," Toby agreed. "All right, let's have some more coffee, then we'll go saddle up and set out."

There was a pause in the conversation as Bettina stood up to refill the coffee cups. Captain Crowell started to speak, apparently intending to refer to the fact that Toby and Ted would be outnumbered, but then he thought better of it and remained silent. Marjorie also seemed to be thinking the same thing, but she, too, remained silent.

Frank tactfully changed the subject. "Fred Guthrie talked to me the other day about buying some lumber, Toby. He told me he would be needing twenty twelve-by-sixteen beams about thirty feet long. I told him that I would talk to you about it."

Toby whistled softly. "Twelve-by-sixteens? Surely he couldn't mean that?"

"I asked him if he was certain about the size," Frank said. "He got annoyed and said he was."

"What's he making, a cathedral? There are four-story buildings in Chicago that don't have a beam in them larger than a six-by-twelve."

Frank shrugged. "He wouldn't say what he's planning to do, but I'll tell you what I think. From the way he was acting, I think it has to do with Maida. You know how he is about her. He has to deal with her like he's walking on eggs, because Ursula would take him apart at the seams if he said anything bad about Maida."

Toby laughed. "I hope Fred knows what he's got himself into. How many of those beams did you say he wants?"

"Twenty, to begin with," Frank replied. "But he won't need them until two or three weeks from now."

"That's good," Toby chuckled, "because it'll probably take us that long to cut them. I don't even know how much to charge for a beam that size. I'll give them the best price I can, but it will be expensive."

"That shouldn't be any problem," Frank said. "From what Fred told me, Ursula is making money hand over fist now. Most of the camps around here are buying beer from her, and some of the big camps up north are starting to buy it. Paddy is hauling it to Wedowee and sending it to them by rail."

Toby smiled in satisfaction. "There's proof that quality counts, wouldn't you say? I'm really pleased to hear that, because they're all fine people. I'm sure Fred and Ursula will be happy together." He smiled, looking pointedly at Ted and Marjorie. "I've been hoping that I'll hear about some plans between those two."

As a smiling blush spread over Marjorie's face and even the usually inscrutable Ted grinned, Toby realized that they had indeed discussed marriage plans. Ted looked at Marjorie, lifting his eyebrows, and she nodded.

"I've asked Marjorie to marry me," Ted announced. "She has agreed to."

There was an explosion of delight around the table, everyone congratulating the couple. Toby stepped around to kiss Marjorie and to shake hands with Ted. "This is certainly good news," he said. "When do you plan to be married?"

"We haven't set a date," Ted replied. "When all this is over and we return to Chicago, we'll get married then."

"But we don't intend to have a large wedding," Marjorie added hastily. "We intend to simply get married."

"No, you're not going to get away with that," Toby said as he sat back down. "You have friends here, you know. We won't put you through the mill with any huge splash, but we intend to take part in this."

Bettina smiled, reaching over to pat Marjorie's hand. "Yes, let us do this, Marjorie," she said. "Nothing elaborate, but a nice ceremony and a reception afterward. Frank and I can go down to Chicago and arrange everything."

Ted and Marjorie looked at each other, then smiled in resignation. Bettina patted Marjorie's hand again as she continued talking about plans for the wedding, and everyone laughed when Frank asked who would photograph the occasion.

"That's simple," Ted countered. "Claude Leggett. He's a photographist friend of Marjorie's in Chicago. He can earn his invitation."

Marjorie agreed with that, and everyone was in good spirits as the conversation continued. After a while, Ted looked at his watch and mentioned the time to Toby.

The atmosphere immediately changed, the imminent danger of gunfire and even death creating a somber silence as Toby and Ted went out to saddle their horses and check their weapons in the dim light of the porch lanterns. Then they made their farewells.

Marjorie clung to Ted and kissed him fiercely, then stepped back and brushed at tears in her eyes. "I'm sorry," she murmured. "I know you'll be all right, but it's new to me, so I'm being silly."

"Don't worry about it, Marjorie," Toby put in. "When

Ted lost track of you during the fire in Chicago last year, he was taking on just about the same way."

They all smiled, but no one was in a mood to laugh. Their farewells finished, Toby and Ted mounted their horses and rode off into the night.

During the first hours, they concentrated on covering distance. They rode at a rapid canter along a wide forest road leading south, the bright moon illuminating their way. Later, when they turned onto a narrower, shadowy road, they slowed their horses to a walk and talked. Ted mentioned that he and Marjorie would be apart most of the time, his work taking him to one part of the country while hers took her to another. It was, he said, a subject they had discussed at length. While both of them regretted the prospect of being parted, they had decided it was the only course open to them.

"Several new gold strikes have been made in Nevada and other places," he said. "When that happens, the mine owners always need someone to set up a system of guards and couriers to take the gold to the nearest Wells Fargo office. When I'm through here, I'll probably look into that."

"Where does Marjorie intend to go?" Toby asked.

"She has several things in mind," Ted replied. "One is to photograph the plantations along the Mississippi. Also, she's looking ahead to the centennial year in 1876. Several eastern cities are celebrating centennials next year, and slides on those should be popular."

"It does sound like you're going to be apart most of the time, Ted. But as long as you can deal with it, nothing else matters."

"I can deal with anything as long as Marjorie is my wife."

They fell silent, reaching a stretch of wider road where the visibility was somewhat better, and they urged their horses to a trot. An hour or so later, Ted slowed his horse and pointed to the trees. Speaking quietly, he said this was the closest they could get to the campsite by road, and from here on they would go by foot.

The surrounding terrain was rocky, wooded hills, and the darkness in the trees was almost impenetrable. After tethering their horses a safe distance from the road, Toby and Ted began moving slowly through the thick, dark forest. The trail they followed was little more than an animal path, and they felt their way along, making as little noise as possible. At a small clearing, Ted quietly told Toby that the campsite was in a ravine less than a mile away, and he suggested that they wait where they were until dawn.

Time passed slowly as the two of them sat under a tree and waited in silence. Near dawn, the freshening breeze began stirring the trees, making a rustling sound that would mask their approach. Pale light began spreading across the sky, and at length the surrounding trees and brush grew more visible.

Toby and Ted stood up and rechecked their guns, then holstered them. "That ravine is to the northeast," Ted said quietly. "We'll approach it from the downwind side so their horses won't scent us and warn them."

Toby nodded, and they began threading their way through the underbrush. As the light continued brightening, the forest came slowly alive around them, birds starting to sing and fly through the trees. At the approach to the narrow ravine, Ted signaled for absolute silence.

The breeze wafting their way carried the scent of horses and woodsmoke. The smoke became visible in the air as Toby crept forward beside Ted, silently moving from tree to tree. Over the rustle of the leaves in the breeze, Toby heard men laughing and talking.

The voices became louder, and then Toby spied a movement through the trees, the camp just ahead. Craning his neck, he paused to look. There was a single large tree, plus a few smaller trees and bushes between them and the camp. As he silently pointed to the large tree, Ted nodded in understanding.

Keeping low to the ground, Toby crept forward, Ted crouching and moving behind him. Toby could now clearly hear the men talking. Glimpsing around the tree, he saw that two were sitting and one was standing beside the campfire.

He reached the tree and stood up behind it. Ted remained in a crouch and waited for Toby to call out to the men to surrender, as the two of them had agreed. In the shadow of his wide hat brim, Ted's tanned face was completely devoid of expression. Toby cocked his pistol, then nodded. He stepped around his side of the tree as Ted went around the other side.

At the same instant, one of the horses hobbled nearby either scented or heard them. It whinnied loudly, causing the other two horses to snort and stamp. The man standing beside the campfire turned toward Toby and quickly pulled out a pistol. Toby, who had started to call out, was suddenly looking down the wrong end of a gun barrel.

Abruptly the peacefulness of the early morning forest dissolved into a blistering exchange of gunfire. The man fired, the bullet ripping into the tree and sending shreds of bark stinging into Toby's face as he took careful aim. He squeezed the trigger, and the pistol bounced. The man jerked convulsively and fell backward, shot through the heart.

Another of the men was rising to a crouch, taking out a pistol. But his companion was lifting a shotgun, the most lethal threat. Toby and Ted fired at him simultaneously, and the man spun and fell, both barrels of the shotgun discharging with a thunderous roar and the leafy forest floor erupting as the pellets tore into it.

The man with the pistol fired at Ted. Ted's hat flicked off his head and spun to one side. Unflinching, Ted stood with his nickel-plated Colt held at arm's length and aimed down the barrel. The pistol fired and belched smoke. The man beside the fire pitched backward and fell, a spreading spot of crimson on his throat.

It was over. The three men sprawled lifelessly beside

the campfire, as the echoes of the gunfire died away into the chatter of fleeing birds and the frightened plunging of the horses. A haze of gun smoke blended with the smoke from the fire and drifted up through the trees. Ted picked up his hat and looked at the hole in the crown.

"Better that than my head," he commented, putting on the hat as he and Toby stepped toward the campfire. He pointed to the man with the shotgun. "That's the one I saw talking with Dieter Schumann."

"At least we can be absolutely certain we have the right ones, then," Toby said. "I wish we could have made them surrender, but they made the choice. Let's see if they have identification on them."

They began searching the dead men, and in the pockets of the one Ted had seen talking with Schumann was a large amount of money, along with papers that identified him as Clarence Quigley. Another had letters and papers with the name Alfred Hopkins on them. The third one was named Earl Fredricks. Among the things in his pockets was a wanted poster from Ohio with his name on it, charging him with armed robbery.

"He must have been proud of it," Toby commented, glancing through the things around the campfire. He looked at the croton oil bottle, then picked up a hacksaw. "They must have used this on the cable."

"Yes, they must have," Ted agreed, gathering up the things they had taken from the dead men's pockets. "How do you want to handle the business with the sheriff, Toby?"

"Let's tell him exactly what happened, but nothing more. Then we'll go back to the logging camp and get a good night's sleep. Tomorrow I'll go see Schumann and deal with him myself."

Ted nodded, picking up a bag beside the fire and putting the identification into it. Then he and Toby went to saddle the three horses.

The sight of three men being brought in across their saddles created a sensation in the small town of Wedowee, the county seat and the nearest rail terminal to the logging camp. A crowd of onlookers began gathering and following behind as Toby and Ted rode along the main street, leading the three horses. By the time they reined up and dismounted in front of the sheriff's office, the crowd had become large and noisy.

The commotion drew the sheriff outside. A tall, lanky man of fifty named Johnson, he had already met Toby, and his eyes widened in surprise as he looked at the bodies on the horses. "What in the world happened here, Mr. Holt?" he exclaimed.

Toby stepped up onto the porch, Ted following him with the bag containing the men's identification. "I mentioned to you that we've had some incidents of sabotage, Sheriff Johnson," Toby said. "These are the ones who were causing the trouble."

The sheriff shook his head, bemused. "Well, they won't cause no more trouble, will they?" he commented. He turned to his deputy, who had just come out the door, and directed him to take the bodies around back and disperse the crowd. "Come on inside, gents," he said to Toby and Ted, "and let's talk about what happened."

Inside, Ted put the bag on the sheriff's desk. They all sat down, and Toby briefly described the gunfight and the events leading up to it.

When he had finished explaining, the sheriff went through the contents of the bag. He lifted his eyebrows over the large amount of money from Quigley's pockets, then unfolded the wanted poster on Earl Fredricks and studied it. The deputy came back in, obviously excited. "What is it, Jake?" the sheriff asked.

"One of those men was named Quigley," the deputy said.

The sheriff was looking at a bankbook with Quigley's name on it. "Yes, Clarence Quigley. What about him?"

"He used to be a policeman in Philadelphia when I worked there," the deputy said. "But every time he investigated a robbery, he took whatever the crooks had left behind. So they got rid of him."

"Is that right?" the sheriff said, then looked at Toby. "Mr. Holt, it's plumb clear to me that what happened here comes under the heading of good riddance. I'll get a statement from you and Mr. Taylor so I'll have something to give the coroner, then we'll have done with this. Does that suit you?"

"That's fine with me, Sheriff," Toby replied.

The sheriff opened a desk drawer and took out pens and paper. "Those three horses the bodies were on looked like good ones," he commented. "That's quite a bit of money there, and those guns and other things will be worth something unless relatives claim them, which I doubt will happen. You can put in a claim yourself if you want to, Mr. Holt."

"Give it to charity," Toby replied.

The sheriff nodded agreeably, then gathered up the papers and money and put them back into the bag. Toby and Ted wrote out statements, signed them, and went back outside. As they rode out of town, both of them were silent for a long time, until Ted asked the question that Toby knew was coming.

"How are you going to deal with Schumann, Toby?"

Toby's expression was determined. "That," he replied grimly, "is up to him."

XV

It was early afternoon when Toby's train arrived in Milwaukee. Leaving the depot, he turned onto a street that led to the central business district. A few minutes later he approached a large stone structure that dwarfed its neighbors. It was the Schumann Building. He went inside.

Marble staircases flanked the spacious lobby, and after pausing to read the building directory, Toby went up to the third floor and along a wide, gleaming hallway. At the end of the hall, he opened a large oak-and-glass door and went into a secretary's office. The floor was covered with a deep carpet, and the room was furnished in expensive hardwood.

The secretary looked up from the papers on his desk. "May I help you, sir?" he asked.

"I'm Toby Holt, and I want to see Dieter Schumann," Toby replied.

"You don't have an appointment with *Mr*. Schumann," the secretary said, frowning. "Under no circumstances does Mr. Schumann see anyone without an appointment."

"This is one time he will," Toby said, walking toward the door on the other side of the office. "He's going to see me."

"Just a moment, Mr. Holt!" the secretary exclaimed

n alarm, scrambling up and hurrying toward Toby "You can't go in there without—"

Toby opened the door of the private office and stepped inside. Scowling, Dieter Schumann looked up from the papers on his desk. His eyes narrowed as the secretary followed Toby inside, stuttering a lame introduction and trying to explain the intrusion. Schumann silenced and dismissed him with a flick of his hand. The secretary went back out, closing the door.

A long moment passed in silence as Toby and Schumann studied each other. Dieter's heavy shoulders were thrust forward, his chin set at a belligerent angle. When Toby glanced around the office, Dieter relaxed, leaned back in his chair, and picked up a cigar from the ashtray on the desk. He puffed on it, waving his hand in a gesture that indicated the office. "Well, give me your opinion," he said sarcastically. "What do you think of it?"

"I don't like it," Toby replied. "It was paid for with tainted money. But you're not interested in my opinions, and I didn't come here to give them. In the event you haven't heard, Clarence Quigley and the two men he had with him are dead."

Dieter's eyes betrayed shock for only an instant. Then he smiled sardonically and puffed on his cigar. "Clarence Quigley?" he said, shaking his head. "I've never heard of him."

"You're lying through your teeth, Schumann," Toby said flatly. "And there's no point in it, because you yourself know that I know what's been happening and the reasons behind it. The minute I walked in here, you knew I was wise to you."

"What are you talking about?" Dieter growled.

"You know what I'm talking about," Toby replied. "But I'll go through it, if that's what you want. I'm talking about the so-called accidents at the lumber mills in Wisconsin that have kept the charges high for years. You're the one behind that, Schumann, and Quigley was doing your dirty work."

"That's enough of that!" Dieter barked, his shoulders hunching forward as he stabbed a finger at Toby. "If I hear any more of that kind of talk out of you, I'll sue you for slander!"

Toby folded his arms, his expression unruffled. "Go ahead and sue me," he said quietly.

"My lawyers will ruin you!"

"They won't decide the case," Toby replied. "A jury will. And I'm ready to stand before a jury of my fellow citizens at any time. But are you?"

The question hung in the air, unease replacing Dieter's belligerent self-confidence as he studied Toby again. Tall and lean, with strong, candid features, the man had an air of integrity about him.

This was a man, Dieter reflected, whom strangers would turn to for advice. Women in distress would automatically expect him to come to their assistance. People would believe him, believe in him. A slander suit against him would backlash with devastating force.

His cigar suddenly had a sour taste as Dieter puffed on it. He put it in the ashtray on the desk, shrugging off his uneasy feeling. "There are other ways to take care of you," he muttered.

"No, you're out of ammunition, Schumann," Toby said. "Hirelings like Quigley and shyster lawyers are all you have, and now they won't do you any good." He pointed a finger, his voice becoming hard and cold. "I'm giving you fair warning to your face. If anything further happens at my business or at any of the lumber mills in Wisconsin, I'll come after you. It's all over, Schumann, and you're finished."

Anger boiled up within Dieter, an automatic reaction to a challenge; but this time anger was immediately overcome by fear. With a sinking sensation in the pit of his stomach, he realized that he had made a serious error. Years before, while pushing a produce cart along the streets of Chicago and fighting with others for the best corner, he had learned never to underestimate a determined opponent. But this time he had.

The careful arrangement through which the charges at the mills had been maintained at a high level would fall apart, he reflected, and there was nothing he could do about it. The arrangement would disintegrate because of the tall man standing in front of the desk.

Toby noted the apprehension in Schumann's face. Having warned the man, which was his only purpose, he started to leave. Then he hesitated. The man behind the desk was wealthy, but not all his wealth had been acquired through schemes involving violence, threats, and hirelings like Quigley.

Keen intelligence shone in Schumann's eyes, Toby saw, and his face reflected dogged determination. Those were the two main prerequisites for success and wealth, and there had been no need for the man to use illegal schemes. "Why did you go about things that way?" Toby asked, puzzled. "Why did you resort to a scheme like that?"

The questions startled Dieter. His first reaction was that they were absurd, coming from where they did. The tall man in front of him was one of that kind who had never had to struggle, who always seemed to receive everything they wanted without effort. Now, with a sense of defeat weighing heavily on him, Dieter laughed with bitterness. "It was for money, of course. What other reason could there be?"

"But it wasn't necessary," Toby said. "In this nation, no one has to resort to criminal means. Others are successful in business through honest methods, and you could do the same."

Dieter sighed wearily. "You're talking about people like yourself. I began by pushing a produce cart in Chicago. I know what life is, and you don't."

"What makes you certain you're so different?" Toby challenged. "Many wealthy people in this country began poor. And if you think you're the only one who knows how hard life can be, you're mistaken. This is the only nation on earth where people can climb just as high as their efforts will take them. But others also have their rights, which you've abused."

"Others have their rights?" Dieter sneered. "We all either walk on or get walked on. That's all there is to life."

"No, there's more to it than that," Toby said. "This is a free nation, not a jungle. The freedoms we enjoy are accompanied by responsibilities. As a businessman, you have responsibilities to your employees and to all the others who make it possible for you to exist and prosper. And as a wealthy man, you have great power to do either right or wrong. You have been doing wrong."

Silent for a long moment, Dieter thought about what Toby had said. He had never before met anyone like this man, never before had a conversation like this one. His initial reaction was that Toby was naive, his view of life too idealistic. At the same time, something told him that the man's words had touched upon a fundamental truth he had never before recognized.

Feeling too weary to think about it, Dieter shrugged and dismissed the subject. "You have your ways, and I have mine," he muttered.

"Yes, but all ways lead to an end," Toby said. "And to the same, final end—the grave. What legacy will you leave behind? Will it be worthy of a lifetime of effort? Will it be something that will enrich the lives of others and make them remember you with respect? Or will you leave behind nothing but a crowd of people who are cheering because you're gone?"

Stepping closer to the desk, Toby leaned over it and looked into Dieter's eyes. "Everyone," he said quietly, "has only a given span of life. That life should have some point to it, some purpose. So ask yourself: What point and purpose lie behind what I am doing with my life?"

Standing straight, Toby put on his hat, then crossed the room with his long, lithe strides and went out, closing the door behind him.

*   *   *

Hours passed unnoticed as Dieter Schumann sat and stared blankly at a wall. The collapse of the means by which the charges at the mills had been kept high had been a crushing defeat, the most severe blow he had ever suffered. Yet for some reason he did not regret what had happened. He did not regret it at all.

He thought about Toby Holt and what he had said. The simple but profound words that had ended their conversation had touched a hollow spot at the very core of his being, a gaping emptiness. It had been there all his life, but he had recognized it only when Toby Holt had pointed it out. He felt numb with shock, stupefied. There was no point or purpose in his life.

He had been seeking success, but that had long since been achieved. When his life ended, its point and purpose would be no more substantial than smoke in the wind. All of his life had been a battle, but he had been fighting himself.

There was a light tap on the door. It opened and the secretary looked in. "Shall I light your lamp, sir?" he asked.

Stirring from his reverie, Dieter realized that the business day had long since ended. Outside, it was growing dark. His overwhelming sense of futility pressed on him anew, and he started to tell the secretary to leave him alone. Then he changed his mind and pushed himself out of his chair. "No, I'll go home now," he said.

The secretary went to the closet, took out Dieter's hat and cane, and handed them to him. "Good night, sir," he said.

Dieter nodded, putting on his hat as he went out. The hallway and stairs were dim and quiet, the tapping of his cane and his footsteps making hollow echoes. His carriage was waiting outside, the street almost deserted during the early evening hours. The driver climbed down from the box and opened the door, and Dieter climbed in.

At other times, the stately, imposing appearance of

his house had given him a sense of satisfaction. But when
the carriage stopped and the driver opened the door, the
house was nothing more to Dieter than his destination. It
was where he went each day after finishing work, and he
felt an impersonal detachment toward it and all his
surroundings.

His wife, Abigail, met him at the door. Attractive,
personable, and much younger than he was, she had always been a symbol of his success for him to display in her
expensive clothes and jewelry. Her smile of greeting had
an overtone of worry. "You're very late, Dieter," she said,
taking his hat and cane. "You said that you wanted us to
go to the theater tonight, and it's almost time to leave."

With the lost, hopeless despair that was aching within
him, the prospect of going to the theater seemed extremely unappealing. He shook his head. "No, let's stay at
home tonight."

"Certainly, if you wish, dear. We'll have dinner in
about an hour. Will that give you time to read your mail
and newspaper?"

"Yes, it will."

As was usual on the nights they remained at home,
Abigail started back upstairs to stay in the nursery with
their two sons as he went to his study. She did not seem
disappointed about missing the play, and he recalled that
she had always indicated in subtle ways that she preferred
to remain at home. Thinking about it, he realized that
being with her sons gave her more pleasure than anything.

It was the first time in a long while that Dieter had
thought about her reactions and motivations. She managed the household with thrift and efficiency, which he
had absently noted from time to time. He thought about
the hours she spent on a myriad of tasks and details that
resulted in an orderly, comfortable routine when he came
home each night.

As he thought about her, in his mind she suddenly
became a person in her own right, rather than a symbol of
his success. He stopped at the door of his study and

looked at her as she climbed the stairs. Hesitating on the landing, Abigail glanced down at her dress and touched her hair, wondering what had drawn his attention. Then she smiled interrogatively.

He realized that instead of being merely pretty, she was an extremely competent and charming woman. It seemed to him that he should say something to her, but he could think of nothing. He nodded and went into his study. Abigail smiled in reply and continued briskly up the stairs.

His newspaper and mail were on the table beside his chair. He sat down and started to read the newspaper, but found that he was completely uninterested in it and the mail. And for the first time in his life, he was lonely. He had often been alone, but never lonely. It was a sensation like teetering on the brink of a bottomless abyss.

He went back out of his study and looked up the stairs. "Abigail?" he called.

A moment later, Abigail came along the upstairs hall and looked down at him from the landing. "Yes, Dieter?"

"Would you come down and talk with me?"

"Is something wrong with your mail or newspaper, dear?"

"No, nothing is wrong with anything. I only wondered if you would like to come down and talk with me."

Perplexed, Abigail looked down at him in silence. Then she smiled quickly and, after calling to the nurse to stay with the children, hurried down the stairs. As she and Dieter went into his study, she glanced around and chose a chair, never having sat with him in the room before. He sat down next to her by the fireplace. Abigail arranged the folds of her skirt, then looked at him expectantly.

He looked away, trying to think of something to say, then turned back to her. "What did you do today, Abigail?" he asked.

"What did I do?" she echoed, puzzled. "What did I do about what, dear? Oh, you mean what did I *do*, don't you? Well, I spent most of the day shopping for groceries and household supplies. Why do you ask?"

Dieter shifted in his chair. "I simply wondered what you did today, that's all."

"I see. Well, I went shopping. The icebox began leaking this morning, and the gardener repaired it. He said the entire bottom should be replaced, because it's rusting out. I told him to get the metal."

"Yes, there's no point in letting things go," Dieter said. "That's a pretty dress you have on. Is it a new one?"

"Yes, it is," Abigail replied, smoothing the folds of her skirt. "I finished it last week, and I'm pleased that you like it."

"You finished it? Do you mean that you made it?"

"Of course I made it!" she exclaimed, laughing. "If I spent good money on a ready-made dress for the house, my mother would disown me."

Dieter smiled. "The sewing and fitting look as good as any seamstress could do. Have you heard from your family recently?"

Her eyes again revealed perplexity, because he had always disliked discussing her family, who were small grocers in Grand Rapids. She began talking about them, watching his reaction. Dieter smiled and nodded as he listened. Then, her pleased smile making her eyes sparkle, she began talking more freely, telling him about her last letter from her mother.

A large measure of the lost, forlorn feeling slipped away from Dieter as he listened to Abigail and looked at her beautiful, animated face. Mentioning her family and inviting conversation about them had given her more pleasure than the last set of expensive jewelry he had given her. Moreover, in some strange way she had returned the pleasure to him manyfold.

"I'm happy to hear that they're doing well," he said when she finished. "Would you like to visit them?"

Abigail hesitated, frowning in concern. "Why do you ask, dear? Do you want to be alone for a few days?"

"No, no," he replied, shaking his head. "I meant that I'd go with you. Would you like to do that?"

"Of course I would," Abigail said, smiling radiantly. "We never have visited my family, Dieter, and I would enjoy that very much. Could we go soon?"

As Dieter started to reply, there was a tap on the door. It opened, and the nurse looked in. The two boys were outside, one of them complaining loudly about something. "Excuse me, sir," the nurse said to Dieter, then looked at Abigail. "It's time for the children to have their dinner, ma'am. Shall I attend to it?"

"Let them come in here first," Dieter said. "Let me see what that boy is so upset about."

The nurse glanced from Abigail to Dieter in surprise. Before, he had never liked noise around him in the house and had taken little interest in the children. Abigail stepped to the door, dismissed the nurse, and brought the children in. The one who was complaining had a small wagon that had lost one of its wheels, and he was holding up the broken toy as he wailed.

Looking at the two boys and at his wife, Dieter suddenly realized that he had more than simply a point and purpose in life. Through his family, his life had meaning that was monumental. Before, his business affairs and symbols of success had occupied his every waking moment. Yet all the time, a far more satisfying life had been waiting for him to notice it.

"No, no, it isn't ruined," Abigail laughed, patting the boy as he held up the wagon and the wheel. "The gardener will repair it tomorrow."

Dieter beckoned the boy. "Bring it here and let me see it," he said. "Perhaps I can put it back together."

Abigail nudged him encouragingly, and the boy timidly approached. As Dieter took the wagon and the wheel, the boy watched hopefully, and Abigail sat down with the other child on her lap. The cotter pin that retained the wheel had bent, allowing the wheel to slip off its axle. Dieter began straightening the pin to remove it.

"My parents haven't seen the boys since they were babies," Abigail said wistfully. "It's so difficult to leave the grocery store, of course, and it's a long way for them to travel."

Dieter pulled the cotter pin out and slid the wheel back on. "Well, they'll see the boys again very shortly," he said. "And from now on they'll see the boys all they want. I intend to dispose of the lumber mills and other things that keep me so busy and invest the money. That will take only a few days, and then we can do whatever we wish." He replaced the cotter pin and handed the repaired wagon back to the boy. "There, put it on the floor and see how it works, son."

As the boy began rolling the wagon along the floor, his brother climbed down from Abigail's lap and joined him. The two boys began whooping and laughing noisily as they pushed the wagon back and forth between them across the room. Smiling, Dieter watched them.

Abigail looked reflectively at her husband. "Did anything out of the ordinary happen at work today, dear?" she asked.

Dieter hesitated, then nodded. "I met a man who is not an ordinary man," he replied. "A man named Toby Holt."

Darkness had settled by the time Toby returned to the logging camp. With the immediate threat of sabotage gone, the atmosphere at the camp was more relaxed and cheerful, with the windows gleaming with light and the lumberjacks singing and laughing noisily in the dormitory. Toby unsaddled his horse and put it in the stock pens, then walked toward the Woods house. Voices carried through the open kitchen window; Ted and Marjorie were sitting at the table, talking with Captain Crowell, Frank, and Bettina.

The conversation broke off as Toby went inside, everyone greeting him and Bettina pouring him a cup of coffee. He briefly described his conversation with Dieter

Schumann, and Ted and Frank agreed that he had taken the best course.

"It appears he'll take the warning seriously, then," Captain Crowell said. "We shouldn't have any more trouble from him."

"I think not," Toby replied. "We can put that problem behind us and get on with business. And so can the other mills."

Frank frowned darkly. "The problem may be solved, but I wish there was some way of punishing the one responsible for it. He's getting off too easy, and I, for one, would like to see him in jail."

Toby shook his head. "No, I disagree in this case, Frank. The man broke the law and caused trouble for any number of people, but I don't think it would serve any purpose to take revenge on him."

There was a general attitude of doubt around the table, but no one wanted to dispute Toby.

Captain Crowell shrugged, then stood up. "Well, as long as our trouble with him is finished. Toby, I have steam up in my launch and a tow of logs hooked up, and I was just waiting to hear how your meeting with that man turned out. When do you think you'll want to return to Chicago?"

"Probably late tomorrow afternoon, if that fits in with your schedule," Toby replied. "I'm going to make an early start in the morning and go to Madison to talk with the governor, and I intend to come back by Colmer and talk with Fred Guthrie. I should be finished by four."

The captain nodded and stepped to the back door. "Good. If the weather holds, I'll be back well before dusk tomorrow. I'll see all of you then."

After everyone wished the captain a good trip, the conversation continued, Toby mentioning to Frank his intention to talk with Fred Guthrie about the size of the beams he wanted to buy. "I saw Paddy Rafferty in Wedowee," Toby said, "and from what he told me, Fred wants those beams for a cellar. He might want some thick support posts to hold up the ceiling, but he won't need beams of anywhere near that size."

"Don't be so sure," Frank replied, chuckling. "That cellar is probably for Maida, and I've learned not to be surprised by anything having to do with her. That young lady has her own way of going about things. I only hope Fred and Ursula can afford what she wants." He became thoughtful. "Now that you've dealt with Schumann, the charges at all the mills will drop, won't they?"

"Yes, without a doubt they will," Toby replied. "So we can expect some competition from them. That will be good for all of us, though."

"That's true," Frank agreed. "Otherwise we might be tempted to rest on our laurels. Besides, the market is more than large enough for everyone. Chicago will be rebuilding for a long time, and practically every city in the country is growing. And we've barely touched the huge market for lumber on the plains."

Toby hesitated, then said cautiously, "Yes, if things stay as they are, the market for lumber will continue expanding at a good rate. My concern is that things won't stay as they are, what with the economic situation in the country."

"Well, I don't know anything about that," Frank said. "Like I've told you before, I don't see what stock speculators in New York have to do with the lumber business in Chicago. If they all go broke, they can get jobs and start working for a living."

Toby smiled. "I'll agree with you on that, Frank, but what they do does affect us. When I talk with Governor Washburn, I'll ask him what he thinks."

Later, when Toby walked to his cabin with Ted and Marjorie, Ted mentioned a railroad agent he had met while in Iowa. The man had been an investor in the stock market and had recommended that Ted do the same with his money.

"Perhaps it was good advice, Ted," Toby said. "There's

no question that a lot of people would agree with him. As
for myself, though, I tend to be more cautious."

"So do I," Ted said. "Still, the stocks he recommended have risen in price. Clayton Hemmings gave you
similar advice, didn't he, Marjorie?"

Marjorie nodded. "And as you did, I disregarded it.
My money is in a bank."

"That's good," Toby commented, "as long as the bank
is in sound financial condition. If it doesn't keep a substantial cash reserve, however, there could be a run on it, and
you could lose much if not all of your money."

"The only way I could lose my money would be for
the earth to open and swallow the bank building," Marjorie countered confidently. "I don't have my money in an
account. It's in a safety deposit box, in gold coin. That's
one thing I don't have to worry about, thank goodness."

Toby laughed at her shrewdness and agreed that her
money was perfectly safe.

Not all of Marjorie's money was where she thought it
was. A substantial amount was in uncashed checks that
Clayton Hemmings was looking at reflectively as he sat at
his desk.

His children were in bed, and the house was quiet as
he thumbed through the checks. The funeral that Marjorie
had photographed had turned out to be far more lucrative
than expected, and several of the checks were in payment
for the albums. Two more were from magazines that had
made etchings from negatives. One, by far the largest, was
from the company that sold the stereopticon slides.

Usually, Clayton's wife took the checks to the bank as
soon as they were received. She would deposit half the
amount in his account and cash the other half in gold
coins, which she would then put in Marjorie's safety deposit box, for which she had a key. However, when he had
begun receiving the checks for the albums, Clayton had
decided to wait until he received all of them before he
gave them to his wife to take to the bank.

When all the checks had arrived, the total amount had been a pleasant surprise. And on the same day that the last two checks had arrived, he had also received in the mail a prospectus for a new offering of railroad stock. Temptation had set in.

At first the temptation had not been strong enough to lure him into action, but it had made him delay. Marjorie was his friend and had rescued his family from poverty, but the thought of the stacks of gold coins piled uselessly in her safety deposit box was galling. Then, while he had delayed, the other checks had arrived. The one from the company that sold stereopticon slides was by far the largest they had ever received.

Hearing footsteps in the hall, Clayton put the checks in his desk drawer and picked up a photographic supply catalog as he averted the left side of his face from the door. Clara came in with a glass of warm milk on a tray. "Drink this and come to bed soon, Clay," she said, putting the tray on the desk. "It's getting late."

"Very well, Clara."

On the edge of his vision, he saw her hesitate as she started to turn back toward the door. With a feeling approaching terror, he hoped she would not attempt to broach the subject that was unmentionable between them—his disfigurement. The subject had festered too long and become too painful. It had passed the point at which words were adequate to express feelings, even between those who loved each other.

"Good night, Clay," she said, her voice a sad, resigned sigh.

"Good night, Clara."

After the door closed behind her, he sat and stared blankly. He yearned for a way to reach past that unmentionable subject and regain the rapport they had once known, but it was impossible. As a boy he had been exceptionally handsome, his good looks a matter of constant comment. When he had reached manhood, the fact that he fitted in easily with others had helped him and made life more pleasant in innumerable ways.

He had always had many friends and been in demand for social occasions. Being handsome had given him confidence in dealing with others, and it had assisted him in his career in photography. And to at least some extent, it had helped him win over the woman he loved and make her his wife.

The change from that to being grotesquely disfigured had been so traumatic that he had been unable to adjust to it. In the process of trying to rebuild a life for himself that would enable him to avoid even thinking about his handicap, he had become unable to discuss it with his wife. It had become a barrier between them, blighting their love.

Sighing despondently, he turned back to his desk. While he had lost the precious closeness he had once enjoyed with his wife, at least, he reflected, he would soon be able to give her everything that wealth could buy. His stocks and bonds, in which he had invested all the money he could scrape together, were now selling for many times what he had paid for them.

And now he had an opportunity for another investment that would rapidly multiply in value, according to the prospectus. Opening his desk drawer, he took out the checks and the prospectus on the railroad stock. By using Marjorie's share of the money, he could buy twice as much of the stock and make twice as much profit. She would never know, because he would put the gold in her safety deposit box after he sold some of his other bonds that would mature just before she returned. She would have no way of knowing the exact date the gold was put there.

Of course it would be necessary for him to take the checks to the bank himself, because Clara must not know. He would have to face a gauntlet of people who would either stare at him or turn away, as always happened to him in public. But he would do it for Clara's sake. He was unable to express his love by reaching across the chasm that had opened between them, but soon he would be able to shower her with all the beautiful things that money could buy.

XVI

Toby completed his business with Governor Washburn by noon the following day. The governor had already read the newspaper accounts of the shootout involving Toby, Ted, Clarence Quigley, and the others, and had immediately reached the correct conclusion. Toby did not identify the mill owner who had been behind the scheme, however; and given the lack of hard evidence, the governor was content not to press him for the name. It was enough that the mill charges in Wisconsin would soon be coming down.

As for the economic outlook in the state and in the nation at large, the governor was no more optimistic than he had been at their first meeting. He agreed with Toby that it only remained to be seen whether the recent feverish speculation would die down gradually or end with a cataclysmic shock.

Arriving back at Wedowee during the early afternoon, Toby got his horse from the livery stable and rode to Colmer to talk with Fred Guthrie. At the tavern he was told that Fred had left about an hour before with a wagonload of supplies for Maida, so he rode on to catch up with him. Near the turnoff to the barn, he saw Fred's wagon ahead and called out.

As Fred waited with his wooden leg propped on the

splashboard of the wagon, Toby was reminded of the last time he had met the shy, burly tavernkeeper.

"Paddy told me how you took care of those three troublemakers, and I read about it in the newspaper this morning," Fred said as Toby reined up. "I wish I could have been along on that."

"You didn't miss much," Toby replied. "And I'm just glad it's over." He smiled broadly. "So, how is marriage agreeing with you, Fred?"

The tall, bearded man returned Toby's grin. "To be honest, I just *thought* I was alive before. That woman has made me the happiest man in the world, and I don't know how I ever got along without her."

"I'm pleased to hear that," Toby said, "and I wish you the best. Fred, Frank told me that you want some beams, but I believe there's a misunderstanding about the size. Frank got the idea that you want twelve-by-sixteens in thirty-foot lengths."

Fred's cheerful attitude quickly fading, he pursed his lips and looked grim. "Yes, that's the size I want."

Toby remained puzzled. "Those are extremely large beams. Paddy told me when I saw him that you're planning to make a cellar for Maida. Now, I don't want to try to tell you your business, but I can't understand why you would want beams that large to build a cellar."

"It's because that cellar will be a hundred feet long by fifty feet wide, with a thirty-foot ceiling," Fred replied glumly. "It'll be big enough to hold several thousand casks of beer."

Toby blinked in surprise, then quickly did some mental calculations. "Yes, the beams across a span that large would have to bear an enormous amount of weight. Twelve-by-sixteens sound about right. It appears that Maida wants a lot of storage space."

"That's just the beginning," Fred sighed. "She also wants a stone building for her brewery."

"Well, again it's none of my business, but that makes

good sense, Fred. The temperature inside it will be more constant."

"Yes, but she still intends to use the barn!" Fred exclaimed. "We're going to build a house, then have masons put stone all around the barn. Can you imagine how much stone that will be? It'll make the biggest stone building in Wedowee look like an outhouse!"

"That will be large," Toby agreed.

"Toby, the rest of us have been going at a dead run, trying to keep up with her. We're selling plenty of beer now, but she's still making more than we can sell. And do you know what I've found out? She ain't even wound up good yet!"

"What do you mean?"

"I mean she intends to have Paddy build more tuns in that barn when it's faced up with stone. She's going to make bock beer, ale, stout, and Lord knows what else. It takes her five minutes just to *name* all the brews she can make! Here we are out in the middle of the woods, and she'll be making more beer than any two or three breweries in Milwaukee!"

Toby stroked his chin. "Yes, that's something to be concerned about, Fred."

"Concerned?" Fred exclaimed. "Toby, I worry about it night and day. It's the only dark spot in my marriage with Ursula."

"You shouldn't let it affect you so much, Fred," Toby said. "When you first found out about the beer Maida was making, you were worried then, weren't you? And you had no reason to worry, because it turned out fine, didn't it?"

"Yes, I suppose so," Fred muttered. "Maybe you're right." He shook his head resignedly. "Anyway, it's going to happen regardless of what I think about it. Do you want to come up to the barn and see where we're putting that cellar?"

Toby took out his watch and looked at it. "Yes, I'd like to, if you don't mind. I'm meeting the launch at the logging camp this afternoon to return to Chicago, but I have a few extra minutes."

Fred snapped his reins, and Toby rode alongside the wagon. When they reached the barn, a wagon from one of the logging camps was just leaving with a full load of casks.

Paddy greeted Toby with his usual cheerful exuberance, and Colleen and Ursula came outside to see him. While Fred and Paddy began unloading the supplies in the wagon, Ursula showed Toby where the cellar would be dug. The wooded hill above the barn had already been cut back to a sheer face of bare soil at one edge of the clearing. Ursula described the giant cavern that would be excavated into the hill, its entrance surrounded by a stone facing.

They walked around the barn to where the new house would be built. "Paddy and his family will also live in the house, won't they?" Toby asked.

"Yes, we will need about ten rooms," Ursula replied. "Fred said that we would also need a dormitory for the workmen who dig the cellar and the masons who do the stonework."

"The dormitory can be made out of scrap lumber, so it won't cost you anything. As for the rest of it, I'll charge you what it costs me. But I feel compelled to tell you that some people think this is a time to be cautious about investing and expanding."

Ursula was undeterred. "It may be, but even at the worst of times there is more opportunity in this country than anywhere else at the best of times. In the few months that Maida and I have been here, we have made more progress than generations of our family were able to make. It may be a risk, but we must proceed with our plans."

"I admire your confidence and determination," Toby said. "And of course I thoroughly agree with you that the opportunities in this country are unlimited."

As they walked back toward the barn and went inside, Ursula pointed up at the rafters and explained that the roof would be lowered, thus disposing of the hayloft.

Then it would be reinforced and covered with thick layers of tar and gravel to insulate the interior from the heat and cold, and the remaining partitions would be removed. Pointing out other changes that would be made, Ursula led Toby into the brewery side of the barn.

While listening to the plans, Toby had wondered how Maida would do the additional work involved. His questions were at least partially answered when he saw that she was training the older Rafferty boy as a helper. The boy was busy filling tiny cups from the bags of dried malt Paddy and Fred had carried in and was placing them on a workbench for Maida to examine.

The only other time Toby had seen Maida, she had been extremely distraught, worried about a tun of beer. Now both of the tuns, Ursula explained, were days away from finishing their fermentation, and Maida was more her normal self. Ursula introduced Toby to her, and Maida, who spoke only a few words of English, replied to his greeting with a polite nod. Then she turned back to tasting and smelling the malt in one of the small cups.

Toby walked back out of the barn with Ursula and talked with the others for a few minutes before he left. As he rode away, he thought about Ursula's plans to expand the brewery. He sincerely hoped that the economic condition of the country would not deteriorate as he feared it would and destroy the thriving business she had begun.

The launch was loaded and ready to leave when Toby reached the logging camp. He went on board, and an hour later the Wisconsin shoreline was barely visible to the west, the vast, gently tossing surface of Lake Michigan reaching to the horizon in all other directions.

The weather made the trip down the lake enjoyable, a few fleecy clouds in the late afternoon sky and a fresh breeze keeping the sunny day from becoming too warm. The youthful Turner played a harmonica as he and Jimson lounged on the deck. In the wheelhouse, Captain Crowell hummed cheerfully along.

Darkness fell, and the moon rose higher in the sky. It was well past midnight when the launch approached Chicago, the city's sprawling mass of lights brightening ahead. Since the lake was calm, the logs would be left floating beside the pier for the workmen to winch into the holding basin the following morning.

As soon as the launch was tied up, Toby took his leave of the crew and walked along the dark pier. The night watchman, holding a lantern, was waiting for him. The man touched his cap and nodded. "It's good to see you back, Mr. Holt," he said. "There's someone waiting to talk to you."

"A customer?" Toby said in surprise. "In the middle of the night?"

"No, he ain't a customer," the night watchman replied. "At least I don't think he is. He looks like some kind of businessman. The foreman told him that you were due to get back tonight, and he's been waiting here for you since closing time."

The night watchman pointed to the man, who was sitting on a bench beside the saw house, in a pool of dim light cast by a lantern inside the building. Curious, Toby crossed the yard toward the visitor as the night watchman continued his rounds. The man stood up, silhouetted against the light, and Toby recognized his heavy, muscular build. It was Dieter Schumann.

His face was shadowed, revealing nothing, but Schumann mutely put out his hand. Toby hesitated, then shook hands with the man.

"I'm pleased that you'll shake hands with me," Dieter said quietly. "Most people wouldn't, after what happened."

"That's probably true, but I like to make peace with people when I can," Toby replied. "Come on, let's go into my office."

Dieter walked beside Toby across the yard and into the dark, quiet office building. In his office, Toby lit the lamp on his desk and pointed to a chair. Dieter took off his hat and sat down.

In the lamplight, Toby thought Schumann looked much the same as before, his square face and steady eyes reflecting an aggressively determined character. But he had also changed, and the harshly belligerent edge to his attitude was gone.

"Insofar as possible," Dieter said, "I intend to make amends. Some of the mills in Wisconsin suffered financial losses, and I will send their owners money through the mail. If you'll tell me what your losses were, I'll see that you get the money."

Toby shook his head as he took off his hat and sat down behind his desk. "No, I don't need it or want it," he said. "I've had some losses, true enough, but I've also been making a profit all the time. I'd rather make a fresh beginning with you, starting here and now."

"That's very generous of you," Dieter said. "Generous in spirit as well as generous in regard to the money. I accept your decision, but I would like to make amends with you more than anyone else."

"Why do you say that?"

"I'm deeply indebted to you," Dieter replied. "The conversation I had with you was the most important thing that ever happened to me. Now I feel like a blacksmith who suddenly finds that the anvil he had been using for years is made of gold. I was looking in the wrong place for what is truly valuable and going about everything in the wrong way."

Toby nodded, and Dieter went on.

"I intend to make an entirely new beginning in every respect. For now, I'm selling my lumber mills and other properties and investing the money in securities. I haven't completely decided what I'll eventually do, but it will be something of more direct benefit to the people of this country. For example, I'd like to improve the standard of housing for the working class of people. It isn't very good in some places."

"That would be a very worthwhile undertaking," Toby said. "And I'm sure someone of your abilities could come up with novel solutions to the problem. When do you intend to start on that?"

"Within a few weeks," Dieter replied. "I've never taken a vacation with my family, so I'm going to spend some time with them in Grand Rapids, where my wife's family lives. Then we'll return to this area, and I'll settle down to work. But I don't intend to allow it to rule me, as it once did." He stood up. "My wife is at a hotel a few blocks away, and I'd better go. I told her I'd be late, but she may be getting concerned."

"I'm sure she is," Toby said, stepping around his desk and walking to the door with his visitor. "I didn't know your wife was in Chicago, and you didn't have to wait this late to talk with me. I'll be here tomorrow, which would have been soon enough."

Dieter was silent until they were outside, standing under the lantern over the main gate. "For years I've been a very fortunate man and didn't know it," he said. "I had a good wife and two healthy sons, but I've only just realized how fortunate I am in having them. So I intend to take my wife wherever I go from now on. As far as waiting until tomorrow to talk with you is concerned, I was anxious about how our talk would turn out. But now I'm very pleased about it."

"I am as well, and I'd like for us to be friends."

"I'd like that very much myself," Dieter said.

"Good." Toby smiled and put out his hand. "I'll look forward to hearing from you when you return, then, Dieter."

Dieter shook hands with Toby, then turned and walked into the night. Watching him leave, Toby had the deep satisfaction of knowing that he had been correct in his assessment of Dieter Schumann and had chosen the right course of action in dealing with him. The man had undergone a fundamental change, and in the future he would do far more good than he had done bad in the past.

Toby went back into his office to check his mail before he returned to the boardinghouse. On top of the stack of envelopes was a letter from Janessa. Smiling in pleasure, he sat back in his chair and opened the letter to read it.

As her letters always were, it was chatty and informative. Brief mention was made of Toby's mother and stepfather and the fact that Janessa, Cindy, and Timmy had gone to the fort for dinner a few days previous.

There was a paragraph about Calvin Rogers. Toby had been pleased to learn that Cindy had taken the man in at the ranch, and Janessa's past letters had reported in detail on Calvin's slow recovery from his injuries. Now able to get about on crutches, the man was doing light chores, helping Timmy with his kites, and planning to escort the boy to and from school when classes began in the fall.

Near the end of the letter, Janessa mentioned that Cindy had begun inviting Reed Kerr to the ranch, and he had become a frequent visitor. Reed had also escorted Cindy to social occasions in Portland and at Fort Vancouver. In a final sentence on the subject, Janessa stated her approval of the development, which was also Toby's reaction. Getting out, he reflected as he glanced back over the last part of the letter, was exactly what Cindy needed to do.

Cindy was also glad she had allowed Reed Kerr to court her. During the years of her engagement to Henry Blake, she had refrained from going to social events where she would normally need an escort, which had been most of them. Only since she had been going out with Reed had she realized how much she missed the laughter, music, and excitement of the parties and dances. It had been keenly enjoyable.

In the short time he had been courting her, Reed had won a place in Cindy's heart, even if she didn't love him the same way she had loved Henry. But Henry was far from her mind as she stepped out onto the front porch one warm summer's night, with Reed at her side. The fields surrounding the ranch house were awash in silvery moonlight, and Reed put an arm around her, with a total lack of

the diffidence he had shown toward her at first. It gave
her a warm, comfortable feeling.

"You shouldn't have come all the way from the fort
just to talk for a few minutes, Reed," she said. "Wait until
the weekends, or until you have a free afternoon. It's such
a long ride for only a few minutes."

"I'd travel ten times as far just to glimpse you, and
you know it," he replied. "John Cummings told me that
Polly Matthews is having a party at her home on Saturday.
Have you heard about it?"

"Yes, I saw Polly in town yesterday, and she asked if
I'd like to come. I told her that I'd see if you'd be free."

"The duty schedule for the weekend hasn't been posted
yet, but I can trade with someone if—"

"No, Reed," she interrupted him. "When the duty
schedule is posted, then we'll know whether or not we can
go."

"Cindy, it wouldn't be any trouble for me to trade
with—"

"No, Reed," she said firmly. "If you're scheduled for
duty, then you perform your duty. There'll be other parties, and your duty comes first."

Reed laughed, then bent over and touched his lips to
her forehead. "Very well, Captain Cindy," he said. "It's
the other way around with most of the fellows, you know.
When they're scheduled for duty and it interferes with a
party or a dance, whoever they're keeping company with
gets into a huff about it. But if I'm scheduled for duty
Saturday, I'll come over and take you to church on Sunday."

"Very well, Reed."

"And while we're in town, perhaps we could walk
past the jewelry stores and see what kind of rings they
have in the windows."

Cindy shook her head, smiling but firm. "No, I don't
want to talk about that, Reed. You'd better go before you
miss the last ferry."

His smile faded, but he quickly recovered and bent
down to kiss her. She put her hands on his shoulders, and

his strong arms enfolded her as their lips met. A warm glow suffused her, created by the intimate contact and her genuine affection for the tall, handsome man. The kiss became passionate, then ended. Reed started to go down the steps.

At the bottom he turned back. "When will you be ready to talk about it?"

"That *is* talking about it."

He looked up at her, his expression unusually serious. "As long as I know there's no one else, I can wait forever."

"Who else could there be?"

He frowned slightly. "That isn't a direct answer, Cindy."

"Then be content with an indirect answer," she said lightly, laughing. "Never expect a woman to tell you her life depends upon you. Now go before you miss the last ferry, Reed."

He weighed her reply, looking into her eyes in the dim light. Then he broke into the boyish grin that Cindy liked best. "Good night, Cindy."

"Good night, Reed."

He mounted his horse and rode away, waving. Cindy waved, then went back into the house. She stopped in the hall and peeked into Timmy's room. The boy was snoring softly, having kicked his covers off. She went in and put the covers back on him, then went to Janessa's room.

The room reeked of tobacco, but it was meticulously neat. Janessa was still awake, and she lifted her arms as Cindy stepped into the room. Cindy went to the bed and bent over it, giving Janessa a hug and a kiss, then went back along the hall.

After extinguishing all the lamps in the house, Cindy went to her room and lit her lamp. She carried it to her desk and sat down, then opened a drawer and took out a two-page letter. She slowly read through the letter, the paper rustling in the quiet. She had read it several times before, and she searched for connotations she might have missed.

The writing was not easy to read. Penned in a bold, masculine scrawl, it had a curious backward slant. All of the nouns were capitalized, and the sentences betrayed a lack of knowledge of the finer points of English grammar. The letter was from Captain Richard Koehler.

The first page amounted to an extended expression of appreciation for her hospitality while he had visited the area. Then followed a statement that he would return to Portland if he ever had an opportunity and visit her if she invited him. At the end of the letter was his address in Germany.

When she had said good-bye to Richard, the act of giving him her handkerchief had seemed natural. But if it had been Reed in his place, the gesture would have been absurd. Richard was different. It was easy to believe that in his veins ran the blood of Teutonic knights who had ridden off on their chargers to do battle.

Wasting anything was extremely distasteful to Cindy, but she had wasted more than ten sheets of paper in trying to answer the letter. She had tried to clarify her confused thoughts by writing them down, but the effort had been futile. She remained uncertain of what she wanted to write.

However, she knew what she wanted him to do. She wanted him to return to Portland with all possible speed. The melting warmth she had felt from simply looking at his handsome, smiling face promised a soaring ecstasy of emotions if he ever held her and kissed her. But a risk of equal proportions was involved.

She had experienced that rapture with Henry Blake. And it had ended in a grueling torment of wounded pride, devastating loss, and rejection. Reed Kerr offered nothing more intense than deep affection, but he was safe.

Biting her lip in indecision, Cindy thought again about trying to write a reply. Then she dismissed that in favor of reading the letter once more.

*   *   *

The wind that was pushing low, dark clouds inland from Bristol Channel stirred Gisela's rain cape and Henry's coat as they walked along a narrow rural road. It was a cool, damp day, and their boots splashed through puddles from the morning's rainfall. Crop fields and sheep pastures stretched away across the hills on either side of the road, and the broad, tossing surface of Bristol Channel filled the horizon ahead.

Henry took Gisela's hand to guide her around a deeper puddle that blocked the road. "Wilkerson told me that it should turn fair tomorrow," he said. "We could have waited until then to walk to the cliff."

"No, one should go walking when one wishes to walk, Heinrich," Gisela replied. "If it is raining or cold, one can wear a coat."

Her comment, Henry reflected, was a succinct statement of her philosophy of life; circumstances never prevented her from doing what she wished. But the forcefully energetic side of her personality had been more subdued than ever since his return from the United States. The bond between them was now permanent, and Gisela was radiantly happy.

Even when he had told her that he might be returning to the United States within a few months to organize the weapons procurement office, she had remained serenely content. And her happiness, Henry had noticed, seemed to make her even more enchantingly beautiful. It added a touch of color to her lovely face, an extra sparkle to her blue eyes.

Noting his admiring expression as he gazed at her, Gisela squeezed his hand. "Do you want to make love again so soon, Heinrich?" she murmured. "It has been only a few hours since the last time. You will have to wait until we return to Fenton, because the ground here is damp."

"Since when would that stop you?" Henry quipped, and they both laughed. As they continued down the road,

Henry mentioned the large pouch of correspondence Gisela had received the day before from her agent in London. It had gradually become clear to him that at least part of the reason she had begun investing in England was the more favorable business climate there than in Germany. "It appears that your holding company here is taking more and more of your attention," he said. "Don't you ever miss Germany?"

"Not if you are with me," she replied. "Besides, the taxes are much lower here, and England treats her merchants the way Germany treats her armies."

"When I was in the United States, the newspapers had many articles about the widespread speculation there. Some believe it may lead to a crisis."

Gisela shrugged. "I have no direct knowledge about it, but it appears to me that the United States is like a child who has grown very rapidly to his youth. He is inclined to be awkward and to stumble over his feet."

"Then you foresee problems?"

"It seems possible. I've been contemplating establishing a branch of Blake Enterprises there, with an office and a small staff. You are listed as an officer of the firm, so I may ask you to sign a few papers and attend to other minor details while you are there."

Henry smiled. "If that youth who has grown too rapidly happens to stumble, do you intend to help him regain his footing by investing in businesses there?"

"Of course," Gisela replied. "You love your nation, so I love it as well. And if something falls out of that youth's pockets to repay me for my trouble, then we will be helping each other, won't we?"

They reached an elevation in the road, and Gisela stopped and glanced around, the wind tugging at the hood on her rain cape. "We own the hunting rights here, and there are many pheasant and quail. You and your friends will enjoy the hunting."

Henry took in the view. The cloudy day enhanced the bleak, austere beauty of the windswept hills bordering the vast bay. In the direction from which they had come he could see Fenton, its huge stone keep silhouetted against the cloudy sky.

Ahead, the road ended and a path led up a slope covered with thick clumps of gorse and scattered, ancient trees that were stunted and gnarled. The rumble of crashing surf and the smell of salt spray carried to them on the wind. Henry and Gisela started up the path. At the top, a copse of the hardy, wiry trees perched on the brink of a precipice. Below was Bristol Channel.

Henry peered down at the points of rock and the massive boulders that had tumbled from the cliffs. As he watched, towering gray-green waves struck the jagged rocks and exploded into spray. A dark mass of low clouds drifted past overhead, and out in the channel curtains of rain draped down, trailing along the heaving surface of the water.

The wind and spray brought with them the feel of the vast ocean depths beyond. A few gulls and terns braved the treacherous winds along the cliffs in search of food, swooping and skimming within inches of the rocks. Henry pointed to them. "It's very dangerous for them to fly near the cliffs today," he said.

"Yes, but they can find more food today," Gisela replied. "They are the brave ones, and the ones who can fly best. Those are the ones who always get the most food." She gazed out over the water. "I like this place very much, Heinrich."

Henry put an arm around her, and when she leaned against him, he turned his head and kissed her. Her lips were salty from the spray, and they were damp and soft as she opened her mouth to his.

The tips of her fingers caressed his face. She looked out over the water again for a long time before she spoke. "When do you think you will return to the United States, Heinrich?"

"I'm not certain. As I said, it depends upon what

happens in Washington. But it will probably be within the next two or three months."

"And how long do you think you will be gone?"

"Six months, perhaps. It may be somewhat less than that, but it won't be any longer."

Gisela was silent again for a long time. "I will write to you often while you're gone, loved one."

Henry knew that she would indeed write often, but the comment had been more a dismissal of the subject than a statement of intention. Thinking back over the times they had discussed the same subject during the past days, it occurred to him that she had accepted the forthcoming separation with surprising equanimity.

"You don't seem very regretful that I'll be gone," he said. "Would you rather be alone for a time?"

Gisela looked up at him, her eyes wide. "Have you gone insane?" she exclaimed. "Every moment we are apart is torment for me! You are my very life! No, your duties require that you go away for a time, and I do not wish to complain about it and spoil our time together. That is love, Heinrich, not lack of regret."

Henry smiled and bent down to kiss her again. She put her arms around him and pressed against him, eager to reassure him. As they kissed, a misty rain started falling.

At length Gisela looked up at him and caressed his face. "Let's go home, loved one. The cook is preparing a special dinner, and afterward we will go to our room and make love."

Henry put an arm around her as they walked back down the path. Soon the rain became heavier, pattering down on the road and the mossy fences bordering it. In the distance, Fenton looked like an inviting refuge.

As they walked along the road, Henry thought about Gisela's quick, emphatic reply when he had asked her if she wished to be alone. During the time they had been together, he had learned that she never lied; but she was adroit in avoiding what she did not want to discuss.

He knew that she did not look forward to their coming

separation, but her choice of words had been evasive.
Something else that she intended to keep private was
involved. She did not want them to be apart, yet she
wanted to be alone for a time. He wondered why.

A roar of cheers and whistles rose as Ted and Marjorie Taylor came out of the church, and suddenly the air
was full of rice. Laughing and ducking, the newlyweds
hurried down the steps and along the walk to the carriage.
The guests ran to waiting horsecars, scrambling and crowding into them. Tin cans clattered along the street behind
the carriage as it moved away from the curb, the horsecars
following.

The reception was being held in a pavilion in nearby
Lincoln Park, and since it was Friday afternoon—the only
day the church had been available—the streets were
crowded with weekday traffic. When the procession reached
the pavilion, the band inside it struck up the traditional
wedding march as Ted and Marjorie dismounted from the
carriage. The guests followed them into the open-sided
building, crowding around and congratulating the couple,
and then everyone stood back and cheered as Ted and
Marjorie took a turn around the dance floor.

Soon other couples joined in, and Toby danced with
Bettina, then with Colleen Rafferty. Harold Phinney, the
office manager at the mill, was married to a plump, pretty
woman named Tabitha, who was as vivacious as her husband was phlegmatic. Toby danced with her, then with
James Henshaw's wife. The music continued without letup,
but soon everyone was gathering at the buffet tables to eat
and drink.

The food had been prepared by Bettina, Lucy, and
some of the lumberjacks' wives, and the guests did it
ample justice. There was plenty of champagne and cider,
but much of it was left untouched in favor of the rich,
foaming beer from the casks Fred Guthrie had brought
along.

As Fred himself dispensed the beer, he talked about

it with a group of lumberjacks that had gathered around. "I knew from the beginning how it would turn out," he was telling the men as Toby approached. "When I first met her, Ursula told me that her daughter made good beer. Then I took a look at Maida, and I knew right away that she could." He poured a mug of beer and handed it to Toby. "There you are, Toby."

"How does somebody who can make good beer look?" one of the men asked skeptically, and the others chuckled.

"For one thing, they look smart," Fred replied. "And that leaves you out right off. If looks was books, you wouldn't have a piece of paper." He poured a mug for another man and handed it to him. "It's the water that makes good beer, gents. And the only good beer water in this part of the country is on the land that my brother left to me."

"What's so different about it?" one of the men asked. "Water is water, ain't it?"

Fred clucked, shaking his head. "That shows just how little you know about it. My stepdaughter can tell all about water just by tasting it, because she don't ever eat pepper. Pepper ruins a body's taster, you know. . . ."

Toby chuckled as he went to another table to get a ham sandwich. He carried his beer and sandwich to the front of the pavilion, where he found a seat next to Captain Crowell. The two of them talked as they watched the festivities, and Toby was pleased to see that everyone was having a good time. It was a worthy celebration to commemorate Ted and Marjorie's wedding.

Other circumstances contributed to Toby's satisfaction and peace of mind. During the past days, the orders arriving at the lumber mill had increased manyfold. And the activity at the stock exchanges had moderated, with prices beginning to ease. It appeared that the national economy would gradually stabilize, as he had hoped.

Even the weather was favorable. Across Lake Shore Drive from the park, the water sparkled in the sunshine, and a fresh breeze swept the grassy, shaded expanses

round the pavilion. Toby got up and refilled his mug,
then stood to one side of the pavilion and talked to passing
friends.

The dancing stopped and a roar of cheering rose as
the wedding cake was brought out, its four large tiers
elaborately decorated with frosting. It was placed on a
table in the center of the dance floor, and Claude Leggett
set up his camera to photograph Ted and Marjorie posed
to cut it.

The celebration went on for several more hours and
continued unabated even after Ted and Marjorie had left.
It was near sunset when Toby said his good-byes, intending to stop off at his office to check the mail. As he crossed
the shady lawns of the park toward Lake Shore Drive,
happiness glowed within him as warm and as bright as the
late afternoon sunshine. The wedding between his two
good friends had been a spectacular success.

At the wide boulevard along the edge of the lake,
Toby stepped into a carriage, telling the driver to take him
to the lumber mill. He sat back and relaxed, looking out
the window as the carriage moved off. The quiet atmosphere of the park was soon left behind, the streets crowded
and noisy.

Noticing a crowd in front of a bank, Toby took out his
watch and looked at it, puzzled. Banks had closed more
than two hours before. As the carriage passed through an
intersection, Toby looked down a cross street and saw a
crowd in front of another bank. Then he noticed that
newsboys were doing a brisk business. It was an extra
edition.

When the carriage halted in traffic at a corner, Toby
leaned out the window and called to a boy who was
hawking papers. "What's the headline?"

"Special edition, sir!" the boy shouted back. "Late
news from New York and across the country! Today's
Black Friday!"

"Let me have one," Toby said, reaching into his
pocket for change. "What's Black Friday?"

"Black Friday on Wall Street!" the boy shouted as h
ran to the carriage. "The stock market is bust! Read a
about it for three cents!"

Chilling apprehension abruptly replaced Toby's sens
of well-being. He handed the boy a five-cent piece an
took the newspaper, then sat back and scanned it as th
carriage began moving again. The sunny day suddenl
became bleak and drab to Toby as he quickly read ke
sentences. The situation was far worse than he had feared

The failure of the New York Warehouse and Securi
ties Company had been the first crack in the dam. Tradin
in its stocks had been suspended at the New York ex
change, but then the second massive blow had struck. Th
great banking house of Jay Cooke and Company, which
had helped finance the Union Army during the Civil Wa
and had underwritten the Northern Pacific Railroad, hac
failed.

Pandemonium had followed, with traders franticall
trying to sell other railroad stocks and prices falling rap
idly. The frenzy of selling had spread into other markets
and speculators had been stuck with immense holding
that they could not dispose of at any price. With price
plummeting, the stock exchange had taken the unprece
dented step of closing at midday, announcing that it woulc
remain closed for two weeks. President Grant was hurry
ing to New York.

The crowds that Toby had seen in front of the bank
were explained by another paragraph. Banks had financec
many stock speculators. All over the country, people were
lining up to wait through the weekend so they would be
among the first to withdraw their money on Monday morn
ing. A run on banks was beginning, and those who de
layed would lose their savings. Few banks had sufficien
capital to cover all their deposits.

In the back pages of the newspaper was an analysis o
the situation by an economist. It stated that a financia
panic had begun that would sweep the nation into a de

ression, bankrupting thousands of businesses and throw-
ng millions of people out of work.

Folding the newspaper, Toby thought about the immediate local effects of the situation and what would hap-
en to his friends and employees. The demand for lumber
would dwindle to nothing. His employees, as well as those
t other logging camps and lumber mills, would soon be
vithout jobs.

Ursula Guthrie had just begun a large expansion,
xcavating the huge cellar, building a house, and refur-
ishing the barn into a stone brewery. With no market for
eer, the business that she and her daughter had begun
would fold. Dieter Schumann had invested all his money
n stocks and bonds. The man had been wealthy, but now
e was penniless.

As for himself, Toby reflected, he had viewed the
ogging and lumber business as a means of financial secu-
ity for his children, so he had invested all of his available
ssets in it. He could lose everything.